When you follo...
it can lead to some dark places...

"A STORY OF MADOFF-LIKE FINANCIAL CORRUPTION, MURDER, AND REDEMPTION...Sears has a good feel for New York...for the world of finance (intelligently explained), for dialogue, and for the thriller genre."—*BOOKLIST*

"SEARS'S BRISK PLOT PACKS IN BELIEVABLE ACTION while also delivering a heartfelt character study of a man trying to rebuild his life."—*MYSTERY SCENE*

RAVES FOR *BLACK FRIDAYS*...

Winner of the Shamus Award for Best First P.I. Novel
Nominated for the Edgar®, Anthony, International Thriller Writers', and Barry Best First Novel Awards

"[An] exciting and compelling Wall Street thriller [with] an insider's jaded wit."—*THE WALL STREET JOURNAL*

"Sears clearly knows his way around the financial world. What makes his debut novel, *Black Fridays*, stand out from other financial thrillers is Stafford's devotion to his five-year-old son... **definitely worth the investment.**"—THE ASSOCIATED PRESS

"A nice tale of Wall Street intrigue . . . In the end, Stafford pulls off a stunt that would bring a smile to the face of Lisbeth Salander, the avenging angel of *The Girl with the Dragon Tattoo*. It left me anxiously waiting for Sears's next book."   —*The Dallas Morning News*

"A thoughtful, intricate cautionary tale about greed, mismanaged money, and the thrill that the unscrupulous get from cheating the unsuspecting. An excellent character study about a man coming to terms with his own limitations while trying to be a good father to a difficult, special-needs child."   —*South Florida Sun Sentinel*

"More than a gripping procedural, it's a moving, deeply human story."   —Joseph Finder

"Never has Wall Street been so interesting and so dangerous."   —Lisa Gardner

"The writing is fresh and vivid, and the scenes with the damaged boy go from touching to harrowing . . . thrilling and haunting at once."   —*Booklist*

"A compelling, beautifully written thriller . . . the real deal."   —Jonathan Kellerman

"A novel for people who like thought with their thrills . . . One of the best books I've read this year."   —John Sandford

continued . . .

MORTAL BONDS

MICHAEL SEARS

BERKLEY BOOKS | *New York*

THE BERKLEY PUBLISHING GROUP
Published by the Penguin Group
Penguin Group (USA) LLC
375 Hudson Street, New York, New York 10014

USA • Canada • UK • Ireland • Australia • New Zealand • India • South Africa • China

penguin.com

A Penguin Random House Company

MORTAL BONDS

A Berkley Book / published by arrangement with the author

For information, address: The Berkley Publishing Group,
a division of Penguin Group (USA) LLC,
375 Hudson Street, New York, New York 10014.

ISBN: 978-0-425-27090-5

PUBLISHING HISTORY
G. P. Putnam's Sons hardcover edition / October 2013
Berkley premium edition / October 2014

PRINTED IN THE UNITED STATES OF AMERICA

10 9 8 7 6 5 4 3 2 1

Cover design by Richard Hasselberger.

for the Muses

| 1 |

According to the police report, the victim, Serge Biondi, an eighty-year-old tax and estate attorney and partner with the firm Kuhn Lauber Biondi, made two phone calls after his secretary left the offices at 6:48 that Friday evening. The first call was to Frau Hilde Biondi, his seventy-four-year-old wife of nearly fifty years. He informed her that he was working late, a not-unusual occurrence, but planned on being home for dinner by 8:30. They briefly discussed plans for the weekend that included some early Christmas shopping for their two sons and their families.

The second call was to the Zurich Escort Center, where, police later learned, he was a steady, but not frequent, client, generally preferring discreet sessions in his office after hours with tall, large-breasted, Eastern European women. Herr Biondi was just over 1.7 meters, or five-foot-five.

The assignment was given to a twenty-seven-year-old airline stewardess with LOT by the name of Adrianna

Marchek who had met with Serge Biondi on two previous occasions. When interviewed the following day, Ms. Marchek said that she had been held up by an emergency with her dog and did not arrive at the offices of Kuhn Lauber Biondi until sometime after 7:45. There was no answer when she rang the intercom, so she called her office. The dispatcher attempted to reach Herr Biondi by phone, and when that failed, told Ms. Marchek that she was free to leave. Detectives who took Ms. Marchek's statement further reported that she fit Herr Biondi's request in every particular.

Zurich police were first called to the scene at 9:09 by a hysterical and nearly unintelligible cleaning woman, one Nkoyo Adeyemo, a citizen of Nigeria. Adeyemo had a valid work visa and was also employed at a commercial laundry establishment in Kloten. Her testimony was that she had arrived at the offices at 7:58, two minutes early for her evening cleaning shift. She'd worked her way up, floor by floor, and so did not find the body for more than an hour.

Closed-circuit television tapes of the lobby confirmed Adeyemo's timetable. They also showed two men arriving exactly at 7:00 and leaving twenty-eight minutes later. The men were both approximately two meters tall, one slighter of build than the other, and dressed in nearly identical long overcoats, gloves, and broad-brimmed hats. Neither one's face could be observed because of the hats and the location of the camera. They entered from the street, proceeded directly to the elevator just outside of camera view. One man carried a light leather satchel. Judging by the way he held it, the bag was empty, or almost so. When leaving, they walked in the same un-hurried but very direct manner.

It appears that during the twenty-eight minutes the two men were upstairs, they went directly to Herr Biondi's office, where they tied the lawyer to his chair with gray duct tape and began to beat him about the face, chest, and groin. If their ultimate goal was the death of Herr Biondi, they were almost immediately successful, though if they were attempting to extract information, they were no doubt frustrated, as the first heavy blow to the chest precipitated a massive heart attack that dis-patched their victim in seconds.

The room was searched thoroughly, with the file draw-ers and the small safe receiving the most attention. Herr Biondi kept few files in his office, his secretary reported, as the custom at the firm was to move all inactive case mate-rials to a basement storage room referred to by all as *der katakomben*. Neither the secretary nor Herr Kuhn could identify anything missing from the room (Herr Lauber was not available, as he had passed away in 2001). The door had been removed from the ancient safe, and a jew-eler's box containing an emerald brooch—possibly a Christmas present for Frau Biondi, who admitted to a particular fondness for emeralds—was left untouched.

Upon further questioning of Herr Kuhn, the three junior lawyers, and the clerical staff, there was unanimous consent that there was nothing that Herr Biondi could have been working on that would have warranted such an attack.

Six months later, the file was still open.

| 2 |

I found that if I kept my focus on the horizon, I could almost convince my stomach that I was not traveling at one hundred miles per hour in a loud, throbbing, whining machine, tilted, like some perverse carnival ride, at an angle, so that forward motion actually felt exactly like falling out of the sky. My stomach rumbled in protest, threatening to liquefy all matter currently in my lower intestines.

I hated helicopters.

I squelched the impulse to make idiotic conversation, such as "Isn't this where John Kennedy's plane went down?" or "I understand this chopper has the highest safety record of any light aircraft in the world." It was all mental static, anyway, obscuring the single screaming question that was threatening to shut down all of my cognitive functions—if I were to die in a helicopter accident, who would take care of my beautiful six-year-old son?

We were flying east down the middle of Long Island Sound on a cloudless day in late May. Another man might have enjoyed the view.

The invitation to join the Von Becker family for an afternoon at their estate in Newport had come at one of my low points. I was eight months out of prison and finding it hard to find work. The Wall Street fraud consulting I had been doing was drying up, as the big firms realized I wasn't above sharing my findings with the FBI and SEC regulators. Wall Street greatly prefers self-regulation—hyphenated shorthand for "sweeping things under the carpet." So, if the currently most notorious banking family in the world wanted to talk with me about a project that might take me a few weeks to complete—with hints of a substantial performance bonus—I was willing to meet with them. Even if it meant taking an hour-long helicopter ride to get there.

I had assets—five million in offshore funds, which I had moved into a Swiss annuity, untraceable, but untouchable for five years—and a turret apartment in the Ansonia—in my opinion, the most beautiful apartment building in New York. What I didn't have was ready cash. I was hungry. And, I was curious.

William Von Becker had run one of the largest privately held investment banks in North America, with branch offices on four continents—he had not yet extended his reach to Africa, the South Pacific, or Antarctica. He ran investment funds totaling in the hundreds of billions, universally recognized as safe, consistent earners. He was also a philanthropist, giving away millions each year, and, after the multiple-hurricane disaster in Haiti, running a $10,000 per-ticket annual fund-raising party for the Hurricane Relief Fund.

Then the bottom fell out. It came at the end of a bad week. The stock market hiccuped for three days, and then hemorrhaged on Thursday. Friday morning, a South American finance minister announced he was pulling all of his dollar accounts. It was a bit of hysteria from one source—but it was enough. When the money from the Von Becker funds didn't arrive on Monday, the world took notice. On Tuesday, there was a run on both his funds and the banks he owned throughout Central and South America. And by the week's end, the truth was out. The Von Becker empire was just another hollow shell—a multibillion-dollar hollow shell. Bigger than most, smaller than a few, it was just one more in an ever-lengthening list of failed Ponzi schemes.

The pilot nudged my arm and pointed down at the water. Even from that height, the sailboat looked huge. The mast must have been two hundred feet tall. The sail could have gift-wrapped a small house. There was a full platoon of men in bright red uniforms sitting out on the rail waving at us as the boat heeled in the strong winds off Point Judith.

My stomach lurched again as we tilted and veered down into the harbor. The bay seemed to be rushing up at me.

I gripped the door handle hard enough to hurt—I

don't know whether I was getting ready to throw it open or hold it closed. Then, as abruptly as changing a television channel, we were flying over land—a rocky beach, a flash of trees—and we circled suddenly and settled onto a concrete helipad, the landing struts neatly framed by a big yellow "*H*." Two men in gray business suits ran to open the door and help me out.

Solid ground felt only slightly better, with the rotors still swirling over my head. Though there had to have been a four- to six-foot clearance, it still felt right to duck. I noticed that the other two ducked as well.

"Jason, thank you for coming out on such short notice. The family will certainly appreciate this." The man projected over the continuing whine of the helicopter engine in a nasal whine of his own. It was the kind of voice that came from generations of careful breeding or well-practiced mimicry. I knew Everett. It was a bit of both.

Everett Payne had been a constant on my personal radar screen for most of my adult life, but I could easily say I barely knew him, although, if you had charted our respective résumés, you might have assumed we were bosom buddies. He had been a business major at Cornell two years ahead of me and in a different fraternity. We never met at that time. Later, at Wharton in the mid-eighties, we were in the same class, though we hung out with different crowds—I was with the quants and grinds, he with the "coast to a C because I'm going to work at my father's firm anyway" crowd. Only, in his case, that plan bit the dust during our last semester, when Payne the Elder ran a billion-dollar S&L into insolvency. Instead of stepping into a sinecure, young Everett started his career as a sales assistant at a Memphis bond shop. But over the intervening years, he had networked his way through a succession of ever-improving positions, until he landed as a senior portfolio manager at the Von Becker funds.

Everett's greatest achievement, however, had been his ability to stay out of jail—to not even be indicted—following the collapse of the Von Becker funds. Though he had been nominally in charge of overseeing a wide range of investments and executives, he was still able to deny—convincingly—any knowledge of the mega-sized con game his boss had been running in the next room.

The second man was from a very different milieu. Though he was dressed in a simple gray suit, white shirt, and blue striped tie, he looked as though he would have been more comfortable in combat fatigues and a Kevlar vest. As security, he was more mercenary than bodyguard. In prison I had learned that reading tats quickly and accurately was a key element of survival, but the mixed message on the backs of his hands was confusing. On his right was a professionally done design of a fist holding lightning bolts that I had learned was a U.S. Army accessory for Fisters—Fire Support Teams, the forward spotters for artillery. They called down the lightning. But the left hand had a blued prison blur of a shamrock and the letters *AB*—Aryan Brotherhood. I had met his brethren before.

Everett didn't introduce us. The man looked me over, judged me to be only a minor potential threat, and mentally photographed my face, coloring, and body type. He would remember me, and be able to pick me out of the crowd at Yankee Stadium if need be. I gave him my best imitation of a smile, just to see what effect it might have. He didn't flinch.

"Right this way, Jason. Everyone's down at the beach. I'll introduce you."

A house was barely visible through a screen of tall pines. It was a big house—probably a bit small for a castle, but very big for a house. Guests would probably need a floor plan to get from their bedroom suites down to the breakfast room. Maybe not. There were probably enough servants on hand to keep anyone from getting lost.

We followed a freshly raked gravel path through a well-manicured landscape of gentle slopes and sand traps—a series of elaborate putting greens, though it took me a few moments to realize it. We took a turn and looked out at a two-hundred-and-seventy-degree panorama of Newport and the bay. To the left was the town proper, Goat Island, and beyond it the soaring bridge that spanned the bay on both sides of the island. Directly in front of us stood Fort Adams and the lower headland. And to the right, a pink-and-white-striped tent big enough to house a full band of Bedouins—camels, goats, wives, and children—blocked the view of the lower bay.

Everett filled me in as we walked. "Livy, the matriarch, is the decider. If she likes you, you're in. But Virgil is the one you'll be dealing with. He's all about details." He thought for a moment before continuing. "You two might actually get along."

He passed through a canvas portal in the back of the tent, and I pushed through behind him. A blast of frigid air hit me. A pair of air conditioners—each the size of a compact car—were spewing arctic breezes onto a string of buffet tables loaded with iced shrimp, oysters, clams, and what must have been the last of the Florida stone-crab harvest for the year. In the center of this bounty was a bowl of black caviar. My bathroom sink was smaller than that bowl. Buckets held bottles of Gosset champagne and Chopin vodka.

The women wore pearls, sipped champagne, and smelled of Chanel. The men all had cigars and glasses of a heavily peated single-malt scotch. They smelled like a Highlands brush fire. The premium vodka was going untouched. No one was eating.

The far side of the tent was open, giving a wide view of the mouth of the harbor. Three of the men at the party—all in dark suits, as though just come from a funeral—were standing at telescopes mounted on tall tripods, staring out to sea. I followed their gaze. Two miles or so away, I could see the big yacht we had passed just a few minutes before. It was still heeled over and flying.

Everett took my elbow and guided me through the small crowd. "Come, Jason. I'll have you meet the mater while the boys are playing with their boat." He led me toward a wall of four thick-necked men in gray suits. They all frisked me with their eyes, checking for threats. I passed. The wall parted. I didn't see any more tattoos.

A small, round, cloth-covered table had been set up, surrounded by six wooden folding chairs. Three of the seats were taken—a horse-faced woman in her sixties, a much younger woman who could have been her daughter, and a man with the still-trim figure of a tennis player. He had the unfashionable good looks of a silent film star, a Valentino maybe, the features a bit too prominent, the eyes too moody. His hair was black, so black as to make me question its provenance, but the eyebrows matched, and though he had no mustache or trace of beard, his chin and jawline were very dark.

"I'm Kurt Blake," he said, stepping forward. His head was cocked at a slight angle, as though he were constantly appraising the world and finding it all slightly below his standards. "I run security for the family."

Everett stepped in. "Livy, may I introduce my old friend, Jason Stafford. Jason, Mrs. Olivia Von Becker."

Blake took being brushed aside much better than I would have. He sat back down and watched—carefully.

"Charmed," the older woman said, sounding anything but. I'd seen warmer eyes on blackjack dealers. "Stafford? There was a Stafford girl at Miss Porter's when Morgan was there. My daughter, Morgan, Mr. Stafford." She gestured to the twentysomething, round-faced young woman to her left. Morgan Von Becker wore no makeup or jewelry, and her hair was cropped close to her head. Not a flattering look.

She greeted me by deigning to look briefly in my general direction. I didn't take the snub personally. Morgan looked like she had decided at a very young age that she didn't like boys and had yet to find any reason to revisit the question.

"The father sold office supplies," Mrs. Von Becker continued. "He had a chain of stores, I believe. Help me,

Morgan. The girl. You remember. She was named for a car."

Morgan turned to her. "Mercedes, Mother." She looked at me. "Her father started Home Office."

The first of the big-box stationery stores. I remembered reading the *Journal* article after the founder sold out to Staples for a hundred and eighty-three million dollars.

"No relation, I'm afraid," I said. "My family is in beverage distribution." My father owned a bar in College Point, Queens, and still worked the closing shift six nights a week. He would have laughed himself into a case of hiccups if he'd heard my description.

Olivia Von Becker was no beauty. I could not imagine she had looked much better at twenty-three when she married. Her face was long and large-featured, her nose more Roman than patrician, her eyes slightly protuberant. Her strength was her strength. She radiated power, supreme self-confidence, and a zero tolerance for any dithering or wool-gathering—unless she was the one doing it.

"Everett tells me you are the man to help us, Mr. Stafford. I hope he is not exaggerating again." She took a sip of clear liquid from an ice-filled tumbler. I had discovered who was putting away the vodka.

Everett made a visible effort not to wince. "Livy, I promised nothing. When Binks and Virgil are ready, we'll all have a powwow and see if Jason can sort things out for us. Jason, can we get you a drink? Champagne? Something stronger?"

"A bit early for me," I said. "What are you drinking, Miss Von Becker?"

The daughter looked startled—she was probably not used to being addressed directly by "the help."

"I . . . I . . . Iced tea," she managed, finally looking directly at me. It was my turn to be startled. Her eyes were a smoky gray, both compelling and frightening—like wolves' eyes.

"Iced tea it is," I said to Everett.

He leaned back and waved for a waiter.

"It's quite beautiful here, Mrs. Von Becker. I didn't know any of these grand estates had survived into the twenty-first century."

She looked at me over the top of her glass for a moment. "I don't know if you are paying a compliment or prying for information. I imagine both. Thank you for the first. The house is mine, as is the money to maintain it. My late husband had no claim to it, and neither do his creditors. It's all in a trust designed to survive our barbaric inheritance taxes. Were you ever a Tea Partier, Mr. Stafford?"

A waiter set down a tall iced tea, with a translucent slice of lemon.

"Sugar, sir?"

I shook my head. "This is the only tea party I belong to, Mrs. Von Becker." I raised the glass to her.

She was an arrogant blowhard, and I liked her.

I looked over at her protector. "Are you political, Mr. Blake?" I let my eyes scan over the four suits still guarding the sector. They all had the oversized jaw muscles of the steroid-addicted.

He smiled as though it caused him pain. "Not at all. I provide a service and I use all available assets."

I turned back to the dowager. "And do you feel safer now?"

She drained her glass before speaking. "There have been death threats against my children because of their father's activities. I have taken steps to protect them." It sounded too rehearsed, as though she didn't quite believe it herself.

"Serious threats?" I aimed the question at Blake.

He nodded. "After Mr. Von Becker's death, people turned their anger on the family. Serious enough."

William Von Becker had saved the state and his family the trouble and expense of a trial by taking himself out of the picture. Late one night in his cell at the Manhattan Metropolitan Correctional Center, he had removed his jumpsuit, tied the sleeves into a noose, and hung himself from the bars. At the funeral, the press outnumbered the mourners by ten to one.

"The threats against Morgan came first," Blake continued.

"Why do you think you were chosen, Miss Von Becker?"

She was busy looking away again. "I couldn't say."

Blake jumped in as though to protect her. "Visibility. Morgan ran much of the family's charitable works."

I didn't see the immediate connection, but I didn't pursue it. I knew I wasn't there to provide any more security, but if someone was threatening violence, I wanted to know about it.

"How were the threats delivered? Are we talking nasty e-mails or letter bombs?"

There was a pause while Blake sought and received silent permission from the head of the family.

"The first time, they tried grabbing Morgan off the street as she was coming out of Il Mulino one night. It was dumb. There had to have been a dozen limo drivers hanging around out front, and they jumped in the minute she started screaming."

"You weren't hurt?" I asked.

Morgan shook her head.

"You were lucky. What did you do?"

Blake answered for her. "She contacted me. We've worked for the family before. They made another attempt at her apartment two days later."

"What happened?"

"Again, nothing. We were there. But since then, she stays here on the compound and we have a twenty-four-hour watch on."

"Sounds like more than disgruntled investors. Have they gone after anyone else?"

Olivia Von Becker had watched our exchange as carefully as any poker player looking for tells. "No one else," she announced. "As yet. Mr. Blake seems to be doing his job with his usual efficiency." She spoke with absolute authority. The subject was closed. A waiter cleared away her empty glass and immediately replaced it with a twin. Or triplet.

The moment was saved from being uncomfortable by the arrival of the "boys" and a cacophonous chorus.

"Christ, Wyatt. It's not a toy. It's an eighteen-million-dollar boat, with twenty human beings on board."

"Give it a rest, Binks. I'm just keeping them on their toes."

Morgan scowled at their approach.

"Don't scowl, Morgan," her mother commanded. "You could be such a pretty girl, if you just didn't scowl."

Morgan dutifully swept away the scowl, but I had the feeling that she was just saving it up for later.

"Hello, Mother. Morgie. Everett, is this your man?" James "Binks" Von Becker was first into view. Late thirties, blond, and handsome in a forgettable way, like a J. Crew model. If I ever ran into him outside that environment, I would have no idea who he was.

"Hello, Binks. This is Jason Stafford."

I stood to shake hands with Binks and a second black-suited man stepped between us.

"Pleased to meet you," he said in a cold and brittle voice. "I am Wyatt Von Becker. Why are you here?"

As everyone else ignored the question, I elected to do the same. Wyatt was ten years younger than his brother, and had the arrogant air of a precocious teenager, more endured than enjoyed. He did not extend a hand to shake, as they were both occupied manipulating a large laptop computer.

The third black-suited brother stood back and waited—he was being polite, not shy. Virgil Von Becker radiated his mother's solid strength. He had his younger brother's dark coloring, but none of his unfocused energy. Virgil was all about focus. And he had his mother's long face. It suited him a lot better.

"Virgil," he said, extending a hand. "Nice to meet you."

Mrs. Von Becker placed her empty glass back on the table—hard enough to command attention. "You have business to discuss and I will only be in the way." She gave Virgil a steady look. "I believe we can thank Everett for bringing us Mr. Stafford. He will do quite nicely." She graced me with a prim smile. "Morgan, you and I will take our guests up to the house," she said, standing. She may have weaved just a bit on the way up. "Then I may take my nap." She turned to me again. "My doctor tells me there is no such thing as a bad nap. What do you think, Mr. Stafford?"

"Sound advice. A pleasure meeting you." I nodded to the daughter, who responded with the kind of grin one plasters on in polite company after eating too many raw onions. But then she did something that surprised me. As she stepped back from the table, her eyes swept over Kurt Blake, and for a brief moment, a look flickered over her stony face. It was gone so quickly, I thought I might have imagined it, but the feeling lingered. A look of yearning, making her seem both older and younger, but also almost beautiful. Then she followed her mother out.

Blake missed it.

Maybe I had her wrong. Maybe she did like boys.

The other guests, like a flock of starlings, swept along in their wake, still chattering and laughing in too high a register to sound happy. I had a sudden insight—they were the hangers-on and poor relations, too marginal in their world of wealth and long bloodlines to turn down a lunchtime cocktail party with the most despised family in America. I was left with the three brothers, Everett, Kurt Blake, and half of his posse of muscle.

I turned to Everett. "So I guess I passed the audition."

He gave a nod so subtle it might have been a tic.

Wyatt placed his laptop on the table, screen still up, and began pecking at the keys.

"Put it away, Wyatt." Binks sounded bored, annoyed, and ineffectual.

"In a minute," his brother said, obviously having no intention of doing anything of the kind.

Virgil reached over and took the computer and gently closed it. "Later for this." There was no room for discussion. "Excuse my brother, Mr. Stafford. He likes to take the helm of our boat, but as he suffers from seasickness, the only thing he can do is run the boat from his computer."

I was stunned. I turned and looked out at the bay. The red-uniformed crew was scrambling over the deck as the big boat made a sail-flogging turn into the wind.

"I have kinetosis," Wyatt was saying. "Because of a malformed inner ear. It is not seasickness."

"Whatever," Binks said, in a tone that said he had heard the excuse a thousand times before.

The crew seemed to be finally getting the boat under control again. I was sure that even at that distance I saw one of them throw a middle finger in our general direction.

I spoke to Virgil. "So he taps out a command and sends orders to the crew? Isn't there a captain on board?"

"Not quite," he said. "He taps out a command and the onboard computer receives it and overrides the helm and the captain on board. Then, without any warning, the boat tacks—or jibes, turns upwind or down—and the crew has to respond as though they've been prepped well in advance."

"It makes them better—faster," Wyatt said, somewhere between a pout and a tantrum.

"They hate it," Virgil said to me.

"I can only imagine," I agreed.

"May I have my computer back?" Wyatt managed to make the polite request sound like a demand.

Virgil tried staring him down, but Wyatt kept his eyes averted.

"Wyatt, we're about to discuss business with Mr. Stafford. You have asked to be included when we talk about business. This is your chance."

"I just want to watch. I won't touch the controls. I promise. I can watch while you talk."

Virgil gave a weary look. "Binks, can I prevail upon you? Take Wyatt up to the house for lunch?" He handed the laptop to his older brother. "He can have this back when he gets there."

Binks took it without showing any response at all. Either he was quite used to taking orders from his younger brother or he was a zombie. Or both. "Come on, Wyatt. Virgil doesn't need us annoying him right now."

Kurt Blake turned to the remaining two bodyguards. "Follow them up. I'll stay here."

The air felt just a touch cleaner once they were gone.

The two dinner-jacketed waiters began packing up the seafood. I hoped it was going to be donated rather than tossed.

Virgil made a little steeple with his fingers and leaned toward me. "As my brother is an adult, I never apologize for him, but I do ask for your understanding. He is far more intelligent than he sometimes appears."

"Asperger's?" I said.

Virgil looked mildly surprised. "You are familiar with the symptoms?"

"I have a son. We're still waiting to see just where he fits on the autism scale. I take it the boat is one of your brother's enthusiasms?"

"Enthusiasms?" He rolled the word around in his mouth like a taste of expensive wine. "I like that."

"My son likes cars."

Virgil smiled. "And does he race them by remote?" He chuckled.

"Not yet," I said. "He's six."

Everett had been quietly watching us talk, but his impatience was starting to show. He cleared his throat. "Ahem."

Virgil looked at him with a touch of regret. Then his eyes blinked once and a mask of duty hid him. "Everett makes a point, Mr. Stafford. I should explain why you were asked to come up here today."

"No, no," Everett said. "Please, Virgil. Take your time. I would never think of rushing you."

Virgil and I ignored him.

"You are, I am quite sure, aware of the troubles visited upon my family. I worked for my father for ten years."

The whole world was aware. But when I had Googled the rest of the family, Virgil and Morgan were the only two ever mentioned. Morgan because of her work with the charities that her father supported, and Virgil as the prodigal son. After finishing first in his class at Williams, and before coming home and putting on the mantle, he spent two years in Colorado as a ski bum, supporting himself as a bartender at night. Sometime during that period, he had sired a son, whom he still supported, though he had a restraining order against the mother—she had tried to stab him twice, succeeding the second time in opening a six-inch scalp wound. Virgil got himself stitched up and came home to work in the family business. He appeared to have worked his way up more on merit than on nepotism. When his father got caught, he was running the equity research department in the investment bank.

"Up until ten months ago, I fully expected to be running the whole brokerage business before I turned forty."

"Not the whole firm? I thought the holdings also included a few offshore banks in addition to the money management business."

Virgil winced at the mention of the money management

business. It was there that his father had run the con, paying investors double-digit returns—with their own money. When it ran out, he simply found new "investors" to keep the game running.

"Also, two restaurants in lower Manhattan," Virgil continued. "A livery service, an airplane and helicopter charter outfit, and until a few years ago, a printing company, which we closed when the firm went paperless."

"Your father believed in integrated resources."

"My father was a secretive control freak. So, you see, when people ask me how could I *not* have known what he was doing, the answer is fairly simple. I knew about equity research. I was learning about the brokerage. But I knew as much about his international banking business as I knew about his investment funds. He owned a sushi bar. Was I supposed to know how to cut fish?"

It was a stretch, but I saw his point. Wall Street is a business of specialization. Managers rarely get a chance to peek over the cubicle wall to see what the next guy is up to, and when they do, they may not understand what they're looking at.

"I reported directly to him," Everett said. "I ran two of the bigger funds. And I had no idea what he was doing." It was a well-polished performance. The Feds had bought it, which was all that mattered.

"So, who did? Those two clerks who cut deals and pled out?"

So far, the only two people who had been indicted, other than Von Becker himself, were two junior clerks who worked directly for the man. According to the

Times, they were sacrificial lambs, serving six months each for being in the wrong place at the wrong time. According to the *Journal*, they were the true villains and had gotten off much too lightly.

Virgil shook his head. "I don't think anyone really knew. Each line of business was set up as a separate corporation, all reporting to him only. Some people knew little bits, but more often, they didn't even know they knew it. My father fooled some of the brightest people on the planet. I don't include myself in that description, by the way."

"What do you think I can do for you? The way I hear it, you've got the full resources of the federal government combing through the firm's books—everybody from the SEC and the FBI to Homeland Security. NASA and the EPA, too, for all I know. What are they going to miss that you want me to find?"

"I'll get to that. I wish to save what I can of the firm, and to do that, the firm needs to settle up with the Feds and move on. Quickly. The money management business is lost, and all of our overseas operations as well. But the core businesses of underwriting, research, and trading are healthy. Untainted. Implicated only because of some missing funds. Given the chance—meaning if we can get out from under—my brother and I can salvage something of the family name."

"Binks?"

"James is one of our foreign exchange traders. He's always said he would rather grow grapes than count bottles."

"No taste for management?"

"Nor any ability, I imagine. It's not for everyone."

It was hard to imagine the handsome but profoundly disinterested man I had just met going head-to-head with the FX market, but it was harder still thinking of him trying to manage a bunch of booty-hungry pirates on a trading desk.

"And Wyatt?"

"Wyatt lives at home."

I nodded. I might be saying the same of my son for decades to come.

"These missing funds? How much are we talking?"

"Three billion dollars," he said with somewhat forced casualness.

If it was meant to impress me, it worked.

"You know," I said, "I might just take a short glass of scotch if it's still on offer."

"Or so." Virgil smiled and signaled for a waiter. "The Feds believe they have accounted for all of my father's misappropriation of funds. The 'missing' forty billion you have read about in the paper isn't missing. It never existed."

I understood. Before becoming a guest of the federal prison system, I had pled guilty to a similar fraud, though on a considerably smaller scale. The trading losses I had covered up had been recouped many times over. It was the falsification of trading profits that had done me in.

"They have also followed the paper trail of another twelve billion, which is, I am afraid, quite gone. My father maintained both a lavish lifestyle and a generous philanthropic image. The cost of fuel for his private jet is no more recoverable than the forty million he spent building a hospital in Puerto Barrios in Guatemala."

"And they can't account for a measly three billion? Sounds like a rounding error."

Blake was following the conversation with a preoccupied smile—I imagined that he had heard it all before and he was more concerned with protecting us from the deranged lynch mobs that might appear out of the woods, intent on taking revenge for their depleted 401(k)s. Everett, on the other hand, was practically drooling on my shoulder at the smell of so much unattached money still out there.

"The firm executed hundreds of international wire transfers a day. It has taken the Feds months to sift through it all. I have looked at their numbers, and I'm convinced. Somehow, my father managed to squirrel away as much money as a third-world dictator."

The waiter set down the scotch. I didn't want it anymore.

"And you think I can find it? An army of lawyers and accountants have come up bust. You've got Blake here, and his musclemen, who can probably twist any arms that need twisting. What do I bring to the table?"

Virgil was unfazed. He had his answer all prepared. "Two things. First, you have a unique perspective—one that cannot be easily learned."

I was a crook. Had been. Past tense. I tried not to let the reference rankle. But Virgil surprised me.

"You have seen this kind of thing from both sides, and you have had some success in uncovering obscured monetary trails." He smiled as though assuring me it was a compliment. "And second," he continued, "people will talk to you. At your level in this business, there are not three degrees of separation between any two major players. And those who know something may not know that they know it. Neither threats nor torture will work. They may tell you things that they would never say to an SEC lawyer. Things that would be meaningless to their spouse. Bits and pieces that will only have meaning to a man with your background."

It was a long shot—a Hail Mary pass. The numbers were blinding. A one percent finder's fee would set me and the Kid up for life. But I needed a paycheck, not another "maybe, someday, down the road."

"I guarantee nothing and I get paid up front. I don't work weekends, because I spend that time with my kid."

"Not a problem."

"Five thousand a day plus a one percent finder's fee. I'll get started tomorrow, but I have a few things scheduled over the next week. You'll have me full-time by Wednesday."

Virgil gave a slight frown. "But you will begin immediately?"

I nodded. "You only pay me for when I'm working."

He shook his head. "Do not misunderstand. I am not questioning your professional behavior, but there is some urgency to this affair. I hope you understand that. If the Feds find the money first, we have no bargaining power."

"Which leads me to the big question. What do I do when I find it? It's hidden now; I don't know that it stays that way after I go poking around in all the back closets. It will be hard not to draw attention to myself."

"Again, not a problem. But we do need to get to the money first. Then we can make our bargain with the authorities, turn it over, and all go on with our lives."

The size of the deal had startled me, but this was a deeper shock. Right up until that moment I had assumed I was dealing with fellow crooks. It had never occurred to me that Von Becker's son was willing to hand over three billion dollars to the courts, for the chance of clearing his family name. I wasn't so sure I entirely believed it.

Virgil saw the look on my face.

"I am not a saint, Mr. Stafford. I know what three billion dollars can buy. But what it can't buy is freedom from looking over my shoulder for the rest of my life. If I can persuade the Feds—and the press—that I am serious about making amends for my father's actions, then I can go about my business. My children will have sleepovers at their friends' houses. My wife can go back to volunteering as a docent at the Met. My brother gets to play with his boat. My sister, who was the only one of us not to abandon our father—she visited him in jail almost every day—is now a virtual prisoner herself, unable to step outside the compound here. She gets her life back. Do you understand?"

I did. Maybe not one hundred percent, but I got it. I often felt just the same. Anything for a quiet life. And he had a point. Handing over three billion dollars of the money his father had stolen would win him kudos in the

press. He could negotiate a clean slate from the regulators. He would go from being the son of a pariah to
becoming a role model. From Page Six innuendos to front-
page applause. It was a smart move.

"And, of course, I get to run the whole firm before I
turn forty," he acknowledged with a sly smile.

Of course.

"As for the performance bonus," he continued. "The
money is not mine to grant. If I were to give you thirty
million dollars, the bankruptcy trustee would come after
you. With a federal judge behind him. You would not
want that."

"Are you looking to negotiate? Make a counteroffer."

"A counterproposal. If this works and the firm sur-
vives, I am prepared to offer you a permanent, lifelong
consultancy with the firm. One million dollars a year for
life. A retainer. There will be times when I will need an
objective point of view. Are you interested?"

"And if the firm doesn't make it?"

"I will add your name to the list of unsecured creditors. Are you a gambler, Mr. Stafford?"

"Only when I've got the edge."

He gave a deep belly laugh. "Spoken like a trader. Do
we have a deal?"

He was right. A lump-sum finder's fee would be an
anchor around my neck. Not only would the bankruptcy
trustee be after me, so would the judge from my trial,
demanding that I repay the firm I had defrauded—of
half a billion dollars. And the IRS would jump on it, too.
I might end up owing all three. One mil a year, however.

As we used to joke on the trading desk, "Yeah, I could get by on that."

"Make it nine hundred ninety thou. I want to stay out of that one percent bracket."

"Done."

"I'll want to see the Feds' case. Not the whole paper trail, just their conclusions. Next, I'll need a list of your father's friends. Anyone he might have talked to."

"A list of his friends will be very short, but if I include close business acquaintances, it will be far too long."

"Err on the inclusive side. I'll know a lot of the names, and if I think they're nonstarters, I'll cross them off. And, finally, a list of all the employees, salaried or consultants or even outside counsel, that he met with, spoke with, or even rode the elevator with on a regular basis."

Virgil looked over. "Everett?"

He nodded. "I'll have it all messengered over tomorrow morning."

"Anything else?" Virgil asked.

I gave a half-nod, half-shrug. "It'll come to me. I might need you to make a call for me to prod some of the more reluctant ones on the list."

"Give Everett the names. I'll take care of it. That it?"

Business was done.

"One more thing, though I really hate to ask. Can I get a ride back to the city?"

Back in the helicopter.

| 3 |

Later that evening, Roger and I were sharing a booth in the back of Hanrahan's, our new friendly neighborhood watering hole ever since the old P&G had been forced to relocate six blocks uptown, losing both its clientele and its juju, and blinked out of existence in a New York minute.

Roger was a semi-retired clown—thirty-five years with the circus, three shows every Saturday and as many as could be booked the rest of the week. He did the circuit—Miami, Florida, to Bismarck, North Dakota, San Diego to Boston, living on a bus eleven months of the year—until he'd had enough and one day he just ran away from the circus. For the past ten years, he'd supplemented his pension by performing once or twice a week for anything from birthday parties to sales meetings to bachelor parties—his stage name was Jacques-Emo. His act could be corny and cute or ragged and raunchy, depending on the audience and, I suspected, how much cognac he had consumed on the way there.

He was also my friend. We'd started as bar buddies— one drink's distance from being total strangers—but my life had taken some unexpected turns. Roger had helped me through one of the rougher patches. So, despite his lack of almost any social graces, I knew that I could depend on him. And, over the last few years, I had come to value much more highly the few people who had stuck by me.

"So, ya trust 'em?" he said when I had finished telling him about my day.

"No."

"That's good."

"But I can't see how I get hurt."

"Yeah, but they're creative. Don't forget."

Roger had his usual snifter of cognac; I was drinking club soda. My stomach thought we were still on the helicopter, and I was due to pick up my son from his sitter shortly.

"I'd love to come up with something the Feds missed. It would be sweet."

"Think you'll do it?"

I wanted to. I gave it a moment's thought. "No. The Feds have hundreds of people working on this."

"So, you're cheatin'. Takin' these people's money on false pretexts. No chance of getting them what they want."

"Pretenses."

"What?"

"False pretenses."

"So, you admit it."

"No." I laughed. "I will do what I do and make sure they get their money's worth. I just don't know if I'll find it."

"I don't trust 'em."

"I don't have to trust them," I said. "I don't even have to like them."

"Watch yourself."

"Will do."

Roger knocked back the last drops in the small snifter and waved the empty glass at Nick the bartender, who gave a serious nod in reply.

"You don't get a good pour here, you know?"

I had not noticed that. My usual was a bottle of light beer, and twelve ounces was twelve ounces. "Maybe you're drinking faster," I said.

He stared at the pressed-tin ceiling long enough that I was beginning to think he'd forgotten I was there.

"Roger?" I said.

"Yeah, yeah. Here's what I'm thinking. You say this whole thing—the bank thing, or whatever—was nothing but a Ponzi scheme, right?"

"Classic."

"Okay, so here's my question. Who the fuck was this guy Ponzi?"

"Long version or short?"

"I hope that's not a short-person joke. I'm very sensitive about my height." Jokes about his stature were a staple of his act.

"Then you get the long version."

"Nyah, just give me the broad strokes."

"When's the last time you had a broad stroke you?"

"Hey! I make the jokes here."

PaJohn came over carrying Roger's drink and his own scotch rocks. John was one half of a mature gay couple—PaJohn and MaJohn—both retired, who had been long-time regulars at the old place. PaJohn was drinking solo that week, as MaJohn was visiting his mother in Boca. They were rarely seen apart.

"Mind if I join you? It's a Mets crowd at the bar today, and I don't know if I can stand listening to any more tragic love stories."

"Come, sit," Roger said. "Jason's about to tell me all about Ponzi."

"When does John get back?" I said.

"He lands Friday at seven-thirty-two, and I am counting the hours." He turned to Roger. "Carlo aka Charles Ponzi? Why do you want to know about him?"

"I didn't say I wanted to know. What I said was, Jason's gonna tell us."

"Is this something you're working on?" John asked me.

"I will be discreet," I said. "I'm not breaking client confidentiality."

"Then I am all ears. Though I warn you, I once got Carlo Ponzi as a Trivial Pursuit question."

"Oh, yeah?" Roger challenged.

"Yes. And I got it right."

"I never doubted ya." Roger took a long swallow and shuddered. "That's better. Ponzi. Let's hear it."

"Carlo Ponzi," I began. "He was a small-time con

man, a grifter, a thief. He spent time in prison here and in Canada before he came up with his one big-time game. It wasn't original—he basically stole the idea. But, for that time, it was big. He stole fifteen million dollars, back in the day when that meant something."

"When was this?"

"After the First World War," PaJohn answered.

"That explains why I don't remember any of this."

"It's like two hundred million in today's money," I went on. "The con itself was really pretty simple. People gave him money to invest. He promised them, I don't know, twenty percent or something outrageous, for ninety days."

"How was he going to make 'em that kind of money? That's way too good to be kosher."

"Exactly. But he had a good story. Back then, when people overseas mailed a letter to the U.S., they could include a return stamp issued in their own country. It was way cheaper than buying the stamps here."

"Stamps? Postage stamps?" Roger said.

"Bear with me. The U.S. postal system had to honor these stamps, or, if the customer asked, redeem them— for the price that a U.S. stamp would go for."

"Wait. We're talking pennies here. Nickels, maybe. How's he supposed to make any real money with this?"

"Well, he's not. But all the immigrants he sold on this had pulled this off themselves, or knew someone who had. Mamma back in the old country sends a letter with the return prepaid—for a penny, let's say—and her daughter in America cashes it in for a nickel. That's a return of four hundred percent."

"Stop!" Roger squawked. "You're making me nuts. This is still all about pennies. How does this Carlo guy turn this into fifteen mil?"

PaJohn had been listening quietly, nodding occasionally, but here he cut in.

"I've got it. He never buys a stamp. Not one. What he does is, he sells the story. That's the con."

Roger looked to me for confirmation.

I nodded. "That's it. He managed to convince people that he could do this stamp arbitrage on a huge scale and make a fortune at it."

"Could he?"

PaJohn took a loud slurp of scotch.

"What?" Roger took offense.

"Not you," PaJohn said. "I had dental work done this morning, and the novocaine hasn't worn off yet."

Roger appeared mollified. "So, could he?"

"No," I said. "Not a chance. The post office made you fill out forms and only redeemed the stamps one at a time. It was okay for somebody trying to scam four cents—or even eight, or maybe twelve—but it would never have worked on a hundred bucks, much less a million."

"But people bought into the story."

"That's the con."

"So they gave him fifteen mil to hear a story." He had it.

"He played it well," I said in agreement. "The first guy in had ninety days to brag about it to all his friends. Of course, they had to get in on it, too. When the ninety days were up, the first guy got paid off. Full return of principal plus twenty percent profit. Of course, the profit was coming from the money his neighbors were putting in."

"Sounds like you want to be the first one in on a deal like this," PaJohn said.

"Maybe, but think for a minute. What does our guy do when he gets home? He brags to his wife about what an investment genius he is, right? 'Look at this,' he says, waving the money in her face. 'I'm another J. P. Morgan.'"

Roger burst out laughing. "Only she says, 'You putz! Why did you take the money out? A real J. P. Morgan would have left it there and let it ride! You're nothing but an ignorant greenhorn, like my mother always said.'"

"There you go. Who would take their money out when they're earning those kinds of returns? Of course, if somebody needed the money, Carlo would pay it out. Cash. Why not? He was sitting on a pile of it. And every time somebody took money out, it just made the whole con seem safer. Better.

"It stops working, though, the day everybody wants their money at once. Then he's screwed."

"That's what caught Madoff, wasn't it?" PaJohn asked. "The market dipped, dipped again, then dove. When the dust cleared, people asked for their money back. When they didn't get it, they panicked, and when people began to panic, they all panicked at the same time."

"So, how'd Carlo get caught?"

"Too successful," I said. "Some post office official read about him in the newspaper and knew the story just wasn't possible. He went to the cops, and that was all she wrote. And Carlo Ponzi became famous, if not rich."

"What a schmuck," Roger said.

"Amen to that." PaJohn raised his glass.

We all finished our drinks.

"Whose round?" Roger asked.

PaJohn and I both raised eyebrows. According to Roger, the last round had always been his and the next was always someone else's.

"I got our first round," I said.

"And I bought the one you just finished," PaJohn chimed in.

"So . . ." I said.

"Okay. Okay. Jeez, you guys act like I'm some kinda cheapskate." He handed PaJohn a twenty. "I'll buy, but you gotta get 'em."

PaJohn had the outside seat on the booth. "Be right back. What's yours, Jason?"

"Nothing. I'm out of here. Time to free my son from the clutches of his tough-love shadow."

PaJohn slipped out and headed to the bar. Roger put a hand on my forearm. He spoke softly and urgently.

"This guy Von Becker looked people in the eye, lied to them, and took their money. You think his kid there really wants to give it back? Three billion is not like finding some guy's wallet in the back of a cab and mailing him the ID and credit cards."

"What about the cash?"

"Expenses." He grinned. "Stamps and shit."

"Envelope."

He nodded in agreement and raised his empty glass. "And, I got overhead."

| 4 |

The Kid was finally asleep. There were nights when he shut down at eight o'clock with no more resistance than a halfhearted breathy moan, and there were nights when he exploded with fears, tantrums, and furious stimming. Remaining flexible, creative, and patient helped. A little. After eight months or so of single parenthood, I was becoming almost sympathetic of my ex-wife's failure to cope.

I had mummy-wrapped my son in a spare sheet—the pressure helped him relax—and read to him from the only nontechnical car book that he allowed, *The Elephant Who Liked to Smash Small Cars*. While he did not often laugh—in fact, he was usually startled and frightened by others' laughter—he did giggle. It sounded like squirrels fighting, but it was the free expression of pure delight, for him and for me. So, though I could repeat all the words of the book by memory—and after the initial reading, so could he—I would have read it every night, if he had let me.

Most nights it was car books. *The Illustrated Encyclopedia of Extraordinary Automobiles*; *The A to Z of Cars*; *The Car: A History of the Automobile*; *Muscle Cars, Detroit Rising*; *Ford: The Car and the Dynasty*; *How Cars Work*; *Classic Cars*; *Antique Cars*; *Detroit's 50 Biggest Losers*. Some nights I read to him; other nights he read. He didn't read, of course. He memorized. When he read aloud, he mimicked the delivery of whoever had first read the page to him. Not the exact voice, but a simulacrum, with identical pace, inflection, and tone. Sometimes it was the half-Cajun, half-southern-syrup drawl of his grandmother; other times the sound of his mother, his uncle, my father, his babysitter, or his teacher at school. And sometimes it sounded like me.

I wrote a to-do list for Carolina, our Costa Rican part-time housekeeper, mentioning for the umpteenth time that his SpongeBob sheets should not be bleached because that made the colors fade, and my son liked his colors always to be the same. Exactly the same. Her English, however, was no better than my Spanish—what little I had was mostly expletives, learned in prison, or references to food and drink, the only trophy from a deep-sea fishing trip out of Cabo before I was married.

My laptop was open, recharging on the table while softly playing the *Ladies and Gentlemen . . . the Grateful Dead* live album. The twenty-two-minute jam on "Lovelight" deserved to be blasted from my KEF speakers in the other room, but I had deferred that bit of self-indulgence until my son went away to college.

I swung the screen around and typed a quick search for the Spanish word for bleach. *Lejía.* The pronunciation guide was no help. *Quitar color. Blanquear.* I tried out *"No quitar color, por favor"* until it flowed as easily as my best Spanish sentence, *"Una cerveza más, por favor."*

Then I remembered—he would need T-shirts for camp. I felt like I was always remembering something I should never have forgotten. School was almost out, and the Kid was enrolled in a special-needs day camp, though I was sure he would have been much happier spending the summer at an automotive school, or working at a car wash. He would need shorts, too. And sweatpants for the cool days. And bathing suits for the pool. Did they make kids' bathing suits in flat black? Beige? My son had strict rules about what colors could be worn on which days. And none of the clothes could have writing on them. He hated clothes with writing. Did the camp have a uniform? Impossible. Well, if they did, let's hope that it was colorful, so that he could attend at least twice a week! And then it occurred to me that his favorite black pants were now short enough to show his ankles. Could he get through the whole summer without them, so I wouldn't have to deal with the tantrum of trying to get him to wear a different pair—at least until fall, by which time almost anything could happen? I put my head on the table for a moment and closed my eyes. It wasn't the tantrums that wore me down, it was the day-to-day minutiae filtered through my son's unique perspective. Nothing was simple.

The obvious conclusion was that I was a terrible parent. I wasn't bad as a father. I read to my son, I took him on fun outings, I made him "Dad" kind of food—scrambled eggs and grilled cheese sandwiches. I bought him ice cream. But without his entourage of shadow, housekeeper, teachers, doctors, and occasional volunteer duty from my father, the Kid and I would have been at each other's throats. And the smart money would be on him.

But I had chosen this challenge and never regretted it. My ex-wife, Angie, had done her alcoholic, narcissistic best, but by the time I got out of prison and found them, she had abandoned the boy to her mother, who kept him locked in a spare bedroom. She wasn't being deliberately cruel; she just couldn't cope with a child who communicated mostly in grunts, growls, and quotes from commercials. A child who bit whenever threatened; would not be held, hugged, or kissed; flew into violent rages or deep depressions when his clothes were the wrong color; banged into furniture until he bled; and regularly threw himself down sets of stairs in an attempt to fly. He had other quirks, too. Those were just the highlights.

It took a small army of specialists to get him there, but the Kid was talking, his balance and coordination were much improved, and he was learning how to control his rages and fears. He hadn't bitten anyone in weeks. But every night, after he was asleep, I sat staring down Broadway from my eighth-floor window, reminding myself of all I had not done for him that day. The list got longer every night.

My cell phone rang.

"Hey, how'd it go?"

"Ah, *mia batata*." It was Skeli, in my unbiased opinion the most completely perfect woman on the planet. When we first met she was working as the decorative foil in Roger's clown act and finishing her doctorate. She was powerful, beautiful, and intensely independent—I did mention that I was unbiased—and a New York survivor. Despite having been doused in ketchup and bitten during her first dinner with the Kid, she kept coming back. She liked him. I liked her. Sometimes, she even deigned to share my bed.

"What did I hear you say?"

I turned the music off. Skeli's only imperfection was her taste in music, which tended to run toward Faith Hill and Dwight Yoakam. "I'm practicing my Spanish, so I can tell Carolina not to bleach the Kid's sheets."

"And you need to call her your 'sweet potato' to get her to understand?"

"I'll do whatever it takes, Skeli," I said. Skeli—a Greek pun on "legs." My nickname for her.

"Martyr. So answer my question. How did it go?"

"I'm hired. It's a treasure hunt. The old man misplaced some of the money he stole, and the family wants me to find it."

"Will you?"

"For five grand a day and a performance bonus, I will try really, really hard."

"When do you start?"

"Tomorrow. As soon as they send over the documents I need."

"You have a date tomorrow." As in, you have a date tomorrow, and *don't forget*!

Skeli was graduating from a three-year doctoral program in physical therapy from Columbia University. I was not going to miss it.

"I will be there. They'd have to pay me at least ten grand before I'd skip that ceremony."

"You'd skip my graduation for ten thousand dollars?"

"Wouldn't you?" I said, still thinking we were both having fun.

"Actually, no." She let me squirm for a moment before continuing. "But if you get an offer up around fifty, take two and I'll go with you."

For once I let wisdom win out over exercising my sometimes lame sense of humor. "Forgive me for making a bad joke. I will be there without fail."

"And one request? I know you'd like to buy me flowers. Everybody there will be getting flowers. But just for me? No flowers. Okay? Promise?"

Skeli associated bouquets of flowers with her ex-husband's repeated infidelities. Someday, I vowed, I would cure her of this affliction and cover her in rose petals.

"How about a potted palm?"

She chuckled. "How about a buzzed begonia?"

"A looped lily?"

"Bad. A schnockered nasturtium?"

"Say that three times fast."

She did.

"You win. Are you coming over?"

She gave a sigh. "You know the Kid hates it when I'm there in the morning."

"No, he just never sees me smile in the morning, except when you're here. It confuses him."

"And if I leave before you get him up, it's like I'm sneaking out. That panties-in-the-pocket feeling. In case you haven't noticed, I'm a lady."

"I've noticed. That's why I want you to come over."

"See you tomorrow. Pick me up at two? We'll walk up together."

"Dulces sueños, mia batata," I said.

"Oh, god. Carolina's going to bust a gut. Have you ever heard yourself speak Spanish? You make it sound almost Russian. See you at two."

And she was gone. But so was the blue cloud of guilt that had been pressing me down into the chair. I got up and went to bed.

The phone rang again fifteen minutes later. I had just dropped off.

"Change your mind?" A man is essentially an optimist where his libido is concerned.

"Jason?"

It was Angie. My ex. All libidinous thoughts vanished.

"The Kid's asleep, Angie. As a matter of fact, so was I. What do you want?"

"It's nice to hear your voice, too," she said.

"Sorry." I pulled myself together and fought the impulse to check to see that my wallet was on the end table. My money tended to disappear around Angie. "How are you? How's your mother? Tino?" I could do polite when challenged.

"Thank you. All just fine, thank you. I am calling to talk to you, not my son."

"My son"—this was about territory, possession. I discovered that I had a headache. Five seconds earlier, I did not have a headache.

"Angie," I said with a resigned sigh. "It's late. Is this an emergency? Can't we do this during normal hours?"

"What are you talking about?"

"Tomorrow? Midday?"

She ignored me. "I am coming to New York. Mamma and Tino are coming, too." Her brother. "I will spend some time with my son. Reconnecting. And I want to see you. There are things that need to be said. Things that need to be set right. I need you to hear me out. You owe me that much."

When I went to prison, Angie and I had worked out a plan. We got a divorce, and I transferred half my assets over to her—the Feds and my lawyers took the rest. The second half of the plan was that we would reunite once I was out. Instead, Angie had taken off for home—Beauville, Louisiana—taking our boy and the money. When things got hard, she dumped the Kid and kept the money. Then it got worse. A lot worse. I really didn't think I owed her a damn thing.

"Great. You know where to find us. When are you planning this for? No one but German tourists comes to New York in summer, but don't wait for Thanksgiving. I won't be able to get your mother good theater tickets, and the Kid absolutely hated the parade last year. Total meltdown when the Captain America balloon crashed into the Ethical Culture building." I was babbling. If I kept talking long enough, maybe she would just hang up and never come to New York.

"I've sublet an apartment for next month on Central Park West. Tino will call you with our flights."

"Next month?"

"Well, next week, actually. They let us have the place a little early."

"Angie. Next week? I'm working. The Kid has school. We can't just drop everything and—"

"We will work around all that," she interrupted. "I do not need your permission to see my son or to come to New York."

Technically, this was true. She had signed over sole custody to me six months earlier, and we had verbally agreed that she should keep her distance until the Kid rebounded from the treatment he had received while in her care. But if I tried to keep her away, she might easily demand a court review. I did not trust the courts to judge what was best for my son.

It was late. My head was splitting. "This is not what we agreed." I had a headache. When I was trading I never got headaches. Then, when I began the fraud that eventually brought me down, I had them all the time. But from the time I heard my sentence in court, through two years of incarceration, followed by eight months of learning to live with and love a very difficult boy, I could count on one hand the number of times that I had suffered a headache. I had one now.

She heard my unspoken acquiescence. "Oh, now, don't go all *nerval* on me, Jason. I am a changed person. I have turned my life over to a higher authority. I think I will surprise you."

Angie was always full of surprises.

"The Kid does not do high drama well, Angie. I'm going to set some boundaries, and I expect you to respect them."

"You make it sound so warm and inviting."

"No joke, Angie."

"I'll have Tino call you."

I got up, swallowed three ibuprofen, and sank back into my chair, staring down at Broadway.

| 5 |

"Good morning, Kid," I called from the door to his room. I had once made the mistake of creeping in and giving my beautiful six-year-old son a soft kiss on the forehead as a way of waking him. It woke him. He sat up screaming, almost colliding with me in the process, and rubbing at the spot with his pajama sleeve so hard that he still had a bright red mark there when I dropped him off at school.

I waited the agreed-upon ten seconds and called again. "Good morning, Kid." It was a ritual—or a formula. A slow count to ten following the first and second greetings, and he would answer on the third. It had taken me three months of trial and error—which translates as fights and screaming fits—to come up with a way of getting him out of bed that was both gentle and effective.

"Good morning, Kid."

"Good morning, Jason." He sat up and checked the alignment of his cars on the shelf over the bed. None had moved overnight. He swung his legs over the side of the bed and bent forward to look down. The floor had not disintegrated while he slept. He hopped down and shuffled past me and out to the table.

It was Thursday. Cheerios and milk. A thimbleful of no-pulp orange juice, a large glass of water, and a chewable vitamin—artificial banana–flavored.

On the advice of his tutor/minder/shadow—the usually infallible Heather—we had spent a week that winter experimenting with a gluten-free, dairy-free, casein-free diet. As far as I could tell, the Kid had not actually swallowed anything other than water and his vitamin pills all week. He didn't rant, or cry, or spit things out. He just opened his mouth and let the soy milk, nondairy cheese, and wheatless bread spill out onto the table. Then he would take a second bite, chew a few times, and repeat the openmouthed drool. I don't know how either of us lasted the week.

While he finished the Cheerios, I laid out his clothes. Tuesday, Thursday, and Sunday were the easy days. Colors were allowed. They didn't even have to match. Blue pants and a red shirt. Or a yellow shirt. Or green. Monday was blue. Wednesday and Saturday were beige or khaki. Fridays were black—all black and only black.

"Do you know what I did yesterday?" I said, coming back into the room.

The Kid looked thoughtful for a minute. "No," he finally answered.

"Sorry," I mumbled, speaking more to myself than to him. Of course he didn't know what I had done yesterday. "I got to ride in a helicopter." Which had left me feeling nauseated, weak-kneed, and feverish. "It was cool."

The Kid had learned that this kind of vocalization from another person was called conversation and that some response was expected.

"Why?" he said after a long pause.

Heather had taught him a few stock phrases—"That's nice," "Sounds good," and others—but he was still uncomfortable with them. "Why?" was his old reliable.

"I had to go to Newport. On business. They picked me up in the helicopter."

He thought about this for another long time. "That's nice," he said.

Too bad it wasn't a twenty-year-old Ford Pinto or an old Gremlin, I thought. Then we'd have something to talk about. The Kid lit up only for cars.

"Okay, get yourself washed and dressed, my man. Then we'll do flash cards."

"Stupid," he said. But he padded off to the bathroom.

Despite his comment, the Kid was ready and back in record time. I got the flash cards, and we sat down across from each other.

The cards had photographs on one side—of people interacting, or of faces in differing emotional states. On the back was a one- or two-word description of each. The subtleties of emotional communication, which most children pick up almost osmotically, were a mystery to my son. His school recommended the cards—maybe they helped. Some days the Kid scored one hundred percent; other days he was lucky to get one out of three.

"Happy." The Kid was supporting his head with one hand on his cheek, the elbow on the table, and his whole body slumped at a thirty-degree angle. If there had been a picture for it, the word on the back would have been "Bored."

"Very good." I always gave him "Happy" first. He never got it wrong, and I thought it helped for him to get an easy one to start. I flipped up the next card—a snarling, red-haired little girl.

His eyes flicked to the card and then rolled up to the ceiling. "Angry."

"Very good. Why would she be angry? Can you think of any reason?"

He thought for a moment and then tapped his free hand to his cheek in imitation of a slap. The Kid had been slapped once by my ex-wife's second husband. Once.

"Okay. Maybe she got slapped. I guess that would make her angry."

He gave one emphatic nod. We were making great progress.

"Okay. Next." I held up the next card. It said "Worried" on the back.

The Kid blew air out through tight lips.

"Come on. You remember."

He mumbled.

"No fair. No mumbling." Mumbling led to humming, which led to stimming and thence to a trance and so on. The key was to keep him engaged.

"Jared."

"What?"

"Jared," he repeated, and pointed at the picture.

I flipped it around and looked at it. There was a Jared in his class, but he looked nothing like the picture. Jared was white, for one thing, and the picture showed a very concerned black boy.

"No, Kid. This is not Jared. Try again."

He rolled his eyes back to the ceiling again. "Stupid."

"What's stupid? The game?"

He pointed at me.

"I'm stupid. Maybe so, but this is not Jared. Come on, you can do it."

He blew air out again. He pointed to the picture. "Jared."

And it hit me. He was right. Jared was the most timid, anxious child in the class. He was near the top of the class in communication and was obviously very bright, but he wore a constant mask of worry. The Kid saw what I had missed in the picture. He was doing better than I was. I saw a black kid first and a frowning one second. The Kid saw it as a frowning kid, no matter the skin color.

"Kid, I'm sorry. I see what you're saying, and you're right. I'm stupid. You teach me something every day."

I put away the cards.

"Let's hit the road." His look of confusion stopped me. "Sorry. Let's get on our way to school. Shoes on." I pulled on my running shoes and tied the laces. He worked his Velcro straps. I noticed that his feet were out-growing his shoes. Again. One more thing for my to-do list. "I'll give you today's big news on the way."

He ran and stood by the door. If he'd had a tail, it would have wagged. While I locked up, he ran ahead and called for the elevator.

I waited until he had pressed the button for the lobby and we were on our way down. "I spoke to your Mamma last night."

The Kid's eyes stayed focused on the elevator doors.

"She wants to come visit us. You. She's coming to New York."

He may have grunted.

"Mamma and Tino are coming, too." Angie's mother was also "Mamma." The Kid refused to be called by his name, Jason, because, he insisted, *I* was Jason, so there couldn't be two. On the other hand, he had no trouble keeping track of which Mamma was being referred to at any given time. Tino was Angie's brother, Antoine. He ran Lafayette's most upscale beauty salon, with his own line of products—L'Affaire pour Elle. Angie had stayed with him after her accident and all through her rehab. The guy topped my list for Most Deserving of Sainthood.

The doors opened and the Kid jumped out onto a white tile. We walked on only the white tiles.

"Help me out here, son. How do you feel about your Mamma coming to visit?"

He made a face just like the angry girl in the cards.

"Great," I said. "That makes two of us."

I TOOK the long way home after dropping the Kid at school, cutting over and running through Central Park, once around the reservoir, then down the drive past Belvedere Castle and out on Seventy-seventh Street. Pounding along at an even eight-minute mile allowed me to work up a sweat and still think about the Kid.

The Kid hadn't said another word to me the whole twenty blocks up to school. I hadn't pressed the issue, even when he refused to sniff hands with me—the usual conclusion of our morning ritual when I dropped him off at school. I was a bit surprised that he was taking the news about his mother's visit this way. He had not seen her since December, and before that, October—and things had certainly been bad at those times—but they spoke on the phone every Sunday morning. He answered her in monosyllables, but that was a big step up from the grunts or growls he used on most of the human race. Something would break. Patience was my gold standard. Eventually, he would talk to Heather or Skeli, or my pop, when he was ready. Maybe he would even speak to me.

"Package fuh you at the desk, Mr. Staffud." Raoul, the day-shift doorman at the Ansonia, was never one to waste his breath on any unnecessary *r*'s.

The information from Everett Payne. Time to put away my concerns for the Kid and my fears about his mother coming to visit. Time to solve the puzzle that had confounded hundreds of trained financial forensic investigators over the past ten months. Then I'd think about getting lunch.

The plain cardboard box held various loose papers, and a six-inch-thick manuscript, bound in plastic, with a nondescript gray cover. Emblazoned on the front in bold font were the words REPORT OF THE JOINT TASK FORCE FBI/SEC TO SOUTHERN DISTRICT OF NEW YORK, U.S. AT-TORNEY PETERSON—ONGOING INVESTIGATION "HOUSE OF CARDS"—NOT FOR CIRCULATION. Below this was a line in much smaller type: *Document #6 of 12. Return to Document Library, Federal Bureau of Investigation, 26 Federal Plaza, New York, NY.* It was a nice touch of bureaucratic optimism.

I scanned the loose pages—lists of friends, employees, and contacts at other firms and the various subsidiary companies in the Von Becker empire. I put them aside and started on the government report.

In my experience, the federal Justice Department was plodding, verbose, and lacking in finesse or subtlety. But very thorough. If they had been landscapers, they'd have used steamrollers. The report had all of those attributes.

There was a twenty-three-page introduction, which held only three vital pieces of information. First, William Von Becker had been running a classic Ponzi scheme for at least the past ten years, and likely for many years before. This was not news, but the case was clearly laid out. Von Becker reported consistent paper profits to his investors without ever actually investing the money they entrusted to him. When a client asked for a payout, he got it. The payouts came from new investor money. Meanwhile, Von Becker used the funds on hand to maintain a lavish lifestyle and to provide philanthropy to a range of causes.

Carlo Ponzi had not bothered with the philanthropy.

Second, the number of transactions within the funds—money moving in and out, sometimes for as quickly as a day or two—was circumstantial evidence of money laundering. Millions, sometimes fifty or a hundred at a clip, would come in from one account. A day or so later, a similar amount, less a small haircut, would be wired out—to an entirely different account. Most of the transfers were for foreign clients, but they still fell under the reporting umbrella. Some official body should have taken notice—the Fed, the SEC, or Homeland Security. But no one had shown any interest until after the fact. The report, having been produced by the FBI and the SEC, blamed everyone else for this failure to oversee.

I scanned the pages detailing these transactions. It was the smallest evidentiary section, but the amounts involved dwarfed everything else by billions. And it was here that the third and final important point was revealed. As Virgil had said, when you crunched all the numbers, there was about three billion unaccounted for. It would take me days to run through it all on my own, but I saw the pattern right away.

There was someone I knew who could help. I dialed the number in Vermont.

"Spud, what are you up to?" Fred "Spud" Krebs had been a lowly trading assistant on Wall Street until he was laid off last year after helping me with an investigation. When it came to wading through mountains of trade reports, he was the go-to guy.

"Hello, Jason. I'm leaving the end of the month. Two months backpacking around Europe. Then it's back here to start law school in the fall. So what's up?"

"Do you have time for a small project before you go? Usual rates?" Last time I had paid him a thousand dollars and a bonus for what had turned out to be a few minutes' work.

"What have you got?" He was hooked.

I explained what I wanted and arranged to overnight the materials to him.

"You'll have it by ten. Call me with any questions."

I copied the pages I wanted him to see, boxed them up, and ran them down to the mailroom. I had just gotten back when my cell phone buzzed and began to hop around the table. The caller ID read "Pops." My father.

"Hey, what are you doing?" I said, enormously glad as ever to talk with him.

"I'm talking to my son, I think. What are you doing?"

"Looking for a missing three billion dollars."

"I'll check all my old suit pockets."

"Still taking the Kid on Sunday?"

"Yeah, I was thinking we take a ride out to River-head, out on the Island. They've got a nice aquarium. I think he'll love it."

"Do the fish drive cars?"

"They've got sharks. All kids love sharks."

"My boy is one in a million," I said. "But best of luck."

"I'll pick him up at nine."

"That's a long drive to go to an aquarium. Isn't there one in Brooklyn?"

"Well, I thought we could go to the outlet mall while we're out there."

"Pop. Why would you want to go to an outlet mall?" He worked behind a bar. He wore a white shirt and black pants six days a week.

"Not me. I'm bringing a friend."

"You have a friend who likes to hit the outlet malls?"

"A female friend."

My father had a girlfriend. Holy crap. I mean, why not? But still. Holy crap.

"Pop. Is this a serious friend?"

"Define 'serious.'"

"Meet-the-family serious. Go-shopping-at-the-mall-together serious. As in, how long has this been going on and you haven't told me until now? That kind of serious."

"Son, you're a grown-up. I don't have to report to you anymore."

"Spoken like a true rebel. That's great. I'm happy for you. What's this gold digger's name?"

"Estrella. And besides being good-looking, kind, and recently widowed, she is also loaded. Her husband was Paulie Ramirez. He owned half the Laundromats between here and Astoria. They were regulars at my place—Dewar's and soda and Bacardi and Diet Coke—until he got the cancer."

I remembered the couple. They'd been coming in to

my father's bar once a week for thirty years or more. "I'm sorry to hear that."

"Yeah, well, he was a good bit older, and he went quickly. In the end, that's what we all hope for."

"And for a first date, you're going to test how well my son behaves at a shopping mall. You are either a masochist or a sadist. I thought you liked this woman."

"It is not a first date, and my grandson is always perfectly behaved when he's with me. You make such a fuss. He's a good kid."

I thought the single grandparent's bands of what was considered acceptable behavior were considerably wider than mine. Or maybe he just kept the Kid well bribed. New toy cars and plenty of vanilla ice cream could work wonders in the right setting.

"He's a great kid. Just don't spoil him too much, okay?"

"Hah! Do you spoil him? If I don't, who will?"

I quietly ceded the point.

"Are you ready for a challenge?" I said.

He chuckled. "What do you need?"

"Not me. The Kid. Buy him some new sneakers while you're at the mall."

"With the flashing lights?"

I never knew what the Kid was going to like and what would send him into screaming fits. He might be so fascinated with the little light show, he would try to watch his own heels when he walked and trip over his own feet.

"White ones with Velcro. After that, take your lead from him."

"I can handle this one, big fella. Thanks for your confidence in your old man."

"Want to go for the grand prize?"

"Where did you learn pushy? I never taught you," he grumbled, half in jest. "All right, what else?"

"Bathing suits. Solid colors only, and at least one all black."

"They sell kids' bathing suits in black? For all the little Goth kids who like to swim, I guess."

"And no logos or writing."

"I'm taking notes. What else are you up to? Doing anything fun?"

"I heard from Angie last night."

"Oh, boy."

"Yeah. She's coming to visit. Wants to connect with the Kid."

"Oh, boy."

"Uh-huh. She also wants to talk with me. She says she has some things she wants to clear up."

"Wonderful. Can't she just e-mail you like a normal person?"

"I told the Kid this morning."

"Yeah? How'd he take it?"

"He's not speaking to me. I think he's scared."

"We should all be scared. She's a scary lady. What does your girlfriend say?"

"I haven't told her yet."

"Oh, boy."

"No, it's okay. I haven't seen her. I'm going to her

graduation this afternoon, though. I'll tell her later. I don't see it as a problem. She won't have to meet Angie."

"You don't see a problem?"

"No."

"God, forgive me. I raised an idiot."

"Pop, you don't know Skeli."

"Yeah, I do."

He rang off, leaving me with a slight buzz of anxiety. I shook it off and went back to work. This time I focused on the lists Everett had included.

I recognized scores of names of clients, many of the friends, and a few of the employees. But one name leaped off the page.

Michael Moskowitz. Individual Client. Total investment $1.2 million.

"Mickey the Mouse" had been in the markets for years when I was starting out, having traded foreign exchange for the old Franklin National Bank until they went under. He managed not to be indicted and resurfaced a few months later as a foreign exchange broker working for one of the shops that acted as intermediary between the big players. For a few months he had been my broker, while I was learning the ropes. We would chat every day, do some business when it suited, and he would buy me dinner every couple of weeks. Then he went away to rehab and we lost touch. I knew he drank—too often; it was practically part of his job description. I hadn't known about the cocaine. When he came back to work, they assigned him to a different desk to keep him from slipping back into old habits. It hadn't worked—the old habits had become new again. We hadn't spoken in almost twenty years.

But the thing that had made the Mouse special was his love of market gossip. Mickey had the skinny on everything. You could not scoop the man. If Goldman Sachs was hiring away Solomon's sterling trader, Mickey knew which wine they were drinking with dinner the night they agreed on the contract. If anyone had a handle on where Von Becker had stashed three billion dollars, my money was on Mickey.

I checked the online directory. He still lived out on Long Island. Rockville Centre.

"Hello?" he answered, sounding both sadder and frailer than I remembered.

"Mickey?"

"Who's this?"

"It's Jason Stafford, Mick."

There was a short pause. "Out of the past. You ever see that movie? Robert Mitchum. The best. You should rent it sometime."

"How ya been?"

"Truth? Not so good. Not where I thought I'd be, at any rate. How you making out?"

"I'm good, actually," I said. "As you say, not where I thought I'd be, but good."

"I thought I'd be hearing from you."

"How's that?"

"You're working for them." He said the word "them"

like it was something toxic. "I figured you'd find my name."

He still had his ear. It was what I needed.

"What have you been up to?" I asked.

"The last year? The last ten years? I've been out of the market for at least that long."

"I guess I knew that."

"Yeah. Third time back from rehab; I guess they got the message. They made me take a disability. Funny thing. It was the right thing to do. I've been clean ever since."

"How did you get wrapped up in this Von Becker mess?"

"That prick. It was Binks. The son. He introduced me. Binks partied a lot when he first started out. He and I had some times together. He's into other stuff these days, what I hear. Anyway, when I got laid up on the beach I talked to him about some ideas I had of trying to work from home. Desperate stuff. It was never going to work. Binks put me together with the old man."

"Helping you out?"

"I was fifty-six and getting four grand a month from disability. The wife was still teaching, but she had her thirty in and wanted to retire. The old man said we could make twelve percent and still have some upside of principal. I jumped at it. We emptied all our accounts. Seven hundred and fifty thou. He said we would earn ninety grand a year—minimum. It wasn't Wall Street money, but we were okay."

"You didn't think it was too good?"

"No. Remember, this was ten years ago. Stocks were still going up and he had a good line, how he used covered calls and hedged leverage and I don't know what else. What do I know about stocks, anyway? It sounded good. And then, after a while, you get used to those checks coming every month. You get those statements every quarter and you see the principal edging up. Not by a lot, but still, you feel good about it. Then the market started falling apart and you look at the statement and you think, this guy's really a genius—he's still making me money. You get comfortable and you'll believe anything."

"What do the lawyers say?"

"Oh, we're fucked. No doubt. Our account said we had a million two. Of course, that was just a piece of paper. But over the years we got paid out more than that. The Feds count back ten years. Whatever you put in minus whatever you took out. We'll get nothing. Zip. I don't think they'll come after us, though. I hear some people are being told they're going to have to pony up."

"There was a piece in the *Journal* a week or two ago about that."

"Yeah? I don't read the papers anymore." He laughed. "I never read the *Journal*. None of that shit. I look at *Newsday* once in a while. The wife gets it."

"You manage to stay well informed."

Mickey laughed. "My sources didn't tell me what you're supposed to be doing for the family. But I can guess. The middle kid, whose name escapes me right now, he's trying to hold the firm together. How am I doing?"

"Who's your source? Binks?"

"That junkie prick. I plan on being around to piss on his grave."

"Junkie?" I said. This was news.

"Last I heard. He went from coke to crank to heroin. China White. He thinks he's a fucking connoisseur."

The too-laid-back attitude of Virgil's older brother now made sense—he was stoned.

"A guy I met in prison said it one time. 'Notice how you never meet an old junkie?' I think you'll get your chance."

"Yeah, I knew you went away for a while," he said, almost apologetically. "You take one for the team?"

There had been a conspiracy. I just wasn't part of it. I had been both the patsy and the crook. "If I'd known the words, I would have sung them an aria or two. I had nothing to give. I did two of the five and now I report to my parole officer once a month for the next couple of years. I'm on my third in eight months. They pass me around. I'm like a tofu salad at Luger's. Nobody knows what to do with me."

"They better learn. It seems the Feds are finally going after people. I haven't seen them this tough since the early nineties. Another few years and there'll be lots of white-collar guys sitting where you are."

"Mid-level execs. The big guys will just have their firms pay a fine."

"It's the American way," he said.

"The great wheel grinds slowly," I said in my best Confucian impersonation.

"When it grinds at all," he said. "So, what do you want from me? Tell me a story."

"Well, I can't say what I'm working on. I'm taking the man's money; I probably owe him that at least. But I need to find out where to start. There's more than a thousand individual investors, almost three hundred institutions—central banks, hedge funds, pension funds, charities. Who had the inside on Von Becker? I need to understand his whole operation. I need to know it cold."

"Besides Binks?"

"I thought he was just a trader—and happy that way."

"He should've been indicted. Only he never signed a thing. No paper trail. But I'm sure he knew."

"Well, I doubt he will talk to me. He'll know it's going right back to Virgil."

"Virgil! That's his name. I must be getting old. They're all named for the Earps, you know. James, Virgil, Wyatt, and Morgan. The old man had a thing about the Earps. The O.K. Corral. All that crap. Guy had memorabilia all over his office."

"The great lawmen of the Old West on Von Becker's wall? That's funny."

"Read your history. The Earps were gamblers, land speculators. They were only lawmen when they couldn't make money doing anything else. Doc Holliday was probably a psychopath."

"So give me a name. Where do I start? I can't interview them all."

"Only if you're willing to trade."

I knew what he wanted. "I'm not going to tell you why I was hired."

"Then I'll guess and you tell me if I'm wrong."

"I'm promising nothing," I said.

"There's big money missing," he began, pausing briefly to see if I wanted to deny it. "The Feds know and they can't find it. Virgil thinks you can find it. Right so far?"

I let it sit there untouched for a minute. "I will not confirm that."

"But you would tell me if I was wrong."

I thought for a long time.

"I would."

"And?"

I didn't say anything.

"So, I got my answer."

I still said nothing.

"You were always buddy-buddy with Paddy Gallagher, weren't you?"

I rose to the bait. "I haven't seen Paddy since before I went away—more than three years now."

"This would be a good time to reacquaint yourself," Mickey said.

"The paper said they were best friends. I didn't believe it."

"Believe it," he replied.

"Thanks," I said.

"Keep me posted." He was telling me that I still owed me. I wasn't so sure, but it paid to keep him in my camp.

"I will."

"Good enough." He let it go. "How's family? You've got a kid, right? Living down South somewhere with his mother. Right?"

"My son lives with me now. Since I got out."

"I didn't know that."

"And here I thought you knew everything," I said with a grin.

"Yeah, well, now I do."

| 6 |

A late-May heat wave had the temperature on the Columbia quad up in the mid-eighties, and the graduate schools' commencement exercises dragged on. A soft breeze briefly cooled the sweat pooling inside my collar. Skeli had insisted upon a suit, button-down collar, and tie to honor her achievement. I had requested that she wear nothing but her skimpiest underwear under her robe. It kept my attention from wandering.

The various departments moved forward and back, sidestepping when necessary like eighteenth-century military formations, until finally called forth to descend the steps in front of Low Library, where they were handed facsimiles of their diplomas—the actual document to be mailed at a later date, when the bursar's office determined that all fees, including overdue library fines, had been paid. It was an assembly line that Henry Ford would have admired. It was the last quick stamp of approval on the products of an elite factory system.

Then it was over. An amplified voice droned out the names, but no one slowed the pace with handshakes and quick words of praise. ". . . Phyllicia Samms . . . Robert Semple . . . Wanda Tyler . . ." Skeli, known to the rest of the world as Wanda Tyler, walked across the short stage, took the proffered piece of cardboard, and became the university's latest Doctor of Physical Therapy. She flashed a smile in my direction, which I managed to catch on camera, just before she reached the exit ramp. I threaded my way out of the crowd and hustled off to meet her behind the library.

"Cover me in diamonds and I couldn't be happier," Skeli said, tossing me her cap and shaking out her long brown hair. "Where do we eat?"

"How can you be hungry in this heat? It's got to be pushing ninety."

"I've been too nervous to eat anything since breakfast, and now I'm starving. Where are you taking me?"

"I thought you might want to go back to your place and get rid of the robe before we go anywhere."

"I can take it off right here."

It was a humorous challenge with no basis in reality—therefore, it deserved a counter-challenge.

"Luckily, I have a camera," I said, pulling it from my pocket.

She twirled quickly, and with her back to me, undid the snaps on the front of her gown. Then with the grace of a veteran dancer, she turned again and let her academic robes fall to the ground—revealing a short black silk dress with spaghetti straps.

"Ta-da!"

It wasn't her skimpiest underwear, but I took the picture anyway.

"Disappointed?" she said.

"No. The illusion was there when I needed it."

She gave me a quick kiss on my cheek and handed me her robe. "Now, feed me!"

THE TOWN CAR wound up the hill and circled the drive surrounding the Cloisters, the medieval art museum at the northern end of Manhattan.

Skeli gave me a questioning look. "Would you believe I have never visited the Cloisters before? It's lovely here."

"Yup. A little bit of magic hidden away uptown." And built by a man who had spent the better part of his life atoning for the sins of his own inherited wealth. "But we're not stopping here. I'll bring you back someday."

The driver continued down the one-way drive and stopped when we reached Fort Tryon Park.

"Ready for a short walk?" I said.

"In these heels?"

They looked fairly normal to my eyes, but the sum total of what I knew about women's shoes had been learned from my ex and could have been most easily expressed by a positively sloped sine curve charting height versus price. Still, I could tell Skeli wasn't wearing hiking shoes.

"A very short walk. I am trying to surprise you with something wildly romantic."

She took my arm. "Wildly romantic is good. And if you find a way to combine it with good food, you'll be well rewarded."

I told the driver where to wait for us after dinner and led Skeli down the short hill.

The wooded park and its environs, situated on the tallest hill on Manhattan, with a breathtaking view of the raw, undeveloped Palisade cliffs across the Hudson, may be one of the most romantic places in the city for an early-evening stroll through the winding pathways and heather gardens. In late May, the range of flowers, shrubs, and trees in bloom was at its peak, with occasional explosions of brilliant yellows, reds, and purples against a subtle background of misty lavenders, muted pinks, creamy whites, and wisplike honey gold. And though I once correctly identified a calla lily, to the amazement of both Angie and her mother, I am normally hard-pressed to name any flower other than a rose or a tulip. I vowed that if I ever proposed to a woman again in this life, I would do it here. But not yet.

"I know you said no flowers, but I thought this might be okay."

We strolled slowly along the pathway, Skeli's head on my shoulder, her arm wrapped around mine.

"Thank you, Jason. I love it. How can I have lived in New York for this long and never come here before?" She stopped and kissed me. "Don't say anything—I don't want you to blow it." She kissed me again. It was a very good kiss.

I kissed back.

"Mmmm. Take me home," she said. "Now."

"Without feeding you first?"

She laughed. "Ah, you know me too well. Then please tell me there is some divine eatery just minutes from here."

There was—the New Leaf Restaurant, a stone-walled, lead-windowpaned anachronism, resembling an Old World country inn as envisioned by a WPA team from the 1930s. And it was just another few steps down the path.

We drank two rounds of Bellinis and shared a dozen raw bluepoints while watching the first pink rays of sunset spread across the western sky. Skeli insisted on dousing her oysters in the sweet red cocktail sauce, thereby killing any chance of actually tasting the stony, cold, fresh salt of the ocean. Otherwise, she was perfect.

"May I propose a toast to the world's sexiest new DPT?" I said, raising my glass.

We drank.

"You know, this is the first time in my life that I was actually on hand for the big ceremony. I skipped high school graduation to come to New York to audition. It would have been nice to have had at least one speech today. Okay, not Bill Clinton or Denzel Washington, but maybe Kathy Bates or—"

"Margo Martindale?"

"Okay. I was going to say Meryl Streep, but Margo Martindale would have been okay, too."

"Allow me to give a speech?"

"Hmm. You're no Meryl Streep."

"Thank you," I said. "May I?"

She bowed her head. "You may."

I waved for the waiter and indicated another round of Bellinis.

"Stalling?" she said.

"No. Refueling."

A moment later the fresh drinks arrived. I held mine up and began.

"You are the world to me. A loaf of bread, a jug of wine, you, and a grilled cheese sandwich for the Kid, and I am in heaven. Every morning I wake with your name upon my lips."

"Every morning?"

"Most mornings. Well, some mornings. This morning, at any rate. Because this morning marked the beginning of your special day. After three years of study at one of the most prestigious—and rigorous—educational institutions in the world, today you get the recognition you so much deserve. Today, you held in your hands a document that testifies to your soaring intelligence, your diligence, and the massive outlays of cash by your ex-husband."

"It was the least he could do, the bum."

"We will not drink to him."

"I should hope not. Are you finished?"

I shook my head. "Just getting started."

A busboy appeared, removed the ravaged oyster shells and offered more bread. Skeli took another piece and gave him a smile that would have melted the last glacier. I wasn't jealous. Sometimes she smiled at me that way.

"There," I said as he left. "A perfect example of your

bottomless well of kindness. Though you seek approval from no man—or woman—you are attentive to busboys, coat-check girls, taxi drivers, even the cashier at D'Agostino's, a woman who could have provoked Mother Teresa herself into using the f-word. You are a true democrat—small *d*. And yet you never let them forget that you are a queen. No, a goddess."

"You're doing pretty good, for not being Meryl Streep. Continue."

"Give me a minute."

"Running out of subject matter?"

"The contrary. Too many positive aspects to choose from."

"Aaahh. Flattery is cheating. But it just may get you laid tonight."

The waiter returned with my duck and Skeli's rack of lamb, and for a few minutes we all smiled and fussed over the cutlery and fresh pepper and a choice of red wine. We each opted for a single glass of pinot noir rather than a full bottle—there was an incentive for remaining relatively sober.

We ate in silence for a few minutes. I spoke first. "I'm not stalling. I'm enjoying my dinner."

"And I am eating a perfectly cooked New Zealand rack of lamb and basking in adulation. I could get used to it."

I took a long sip of water. "To return to that very subject. You. I love you for yourself—who you are. I love you for what you mean to me. And I love you because you love my child, which I have reason to believe is not always easy. What have I missed? Of course. Have I mentioned your legs? Your perfect legs?"

"Are you going to eat your carrots?"

"I never eat my carrots."

"Pass 'em over." She sipped the pinot noir. Her eyebrows shot up in surprise. "This is excellent. What is it?"

"I didn't pay attention. Pinot. From Oregon."

"Find out. I want this to be our house wine."

"Ah. Does this mean you will finally agree to move in with me?"

"No. I would have to give up my apartment, which is more than twice the size of yours."

There was another issue that neither of us wanted to address. Skeli had recently accepted an offer to be the staff physical therapist for the national tour of a Broadway show. A show that had already racked up more injuries per performer than *Spider-Man*. Except for the fact that she would be out of town for the next four months, the job was perfect for her. Whether it was perfect for us remained to be seen. She was due to leave in two weeks.

"Maybe it could be your house wine, and I'd come over and drink it." She gave a brave smile. We were having the same thoughts.

"Fair enough. Can I go back to talking about your legs now? I can be eloquent—or try, at least."

She smiled, mollified for the moment. "You may continue."

I froze. There was no other word for it. Handed the opening with which to salvage a beautiful night and a most agreeable ending, I stood at the helm and drove our ship directly onto the rocks. All hands lost.

I took a bite of duck. I couldn't taste it.

"Well," I began, and with no clear plan in mind, forged ahead. "You have a mercurial emotional spirit. Ever-changing. Unpredictable. Laughter, tears, passion— all at once. It can be terrifying, mesmerizing, and ma- jestic." It sounded nothing like Skeli.

She stared at me, head cocked to one side. "That sounds nothing like me," she finally said.

It sounded just like my ex-wife.

"From everything you've ever told me," she con- tinued, "it sounds exactly like Angie."

My tongue seemed to have grown to three times its normal size. Maybe I could choke on it and die. Any- thing was better than trying to explain a faux pas I did not understand myself.

"That is a very weird thing to say, Jason." She placed her knife and fork down on her plate.

"Let me take another shot at it. I can do better."

Not even another guy would have bought into that line.

"What's wrong?" she said. "I mean, I know what's wrong, but what else is wrong? Is there something else we should be talking about?" She sounded reasonable and straightforward, and I was dumb enough to fall for it.

"It's not really that big a deal."

She nodded as though she understood. It should have been a warning alarm.

"Angie called. She's coming to New York. She wants to visit with the Kid. Try to reconnect." Having the bad news out there where we could both look at it felt a lot better than holding it back.

But as my father had once said, "If you feel good giving somebody bad news, you fucked up."

"And you're going to let her?" Skeli said.

This was not an unreasonable question. Angie's care of our boy had been one step short of child abuse. But there was, in my opinion, one overriding opposing argument.

"She's his mother."

"Mother crocodiles just eat their young."

"Actually, they don't. It just looks that way." Now I was defending crocodile mothers. Skeli gave me the look that said "You're an idiot." She had a point. "I can't keep her away. She has visitation rights. If I tried, she'd have me in court in a heartbeat. I'm not going down that road again."

After kidnapping my son, Angie and her abusive co-dependent drinking buddy—aka her second husband— had been stopped by the police and the FBI in Virginia, where, the next day, Angie had convinced a draconian Family Court judge to turn over the Kid and grant her full custody. It had been the worst day of my life.

Skeli was nodding as I talked, but whether in sympathy, understanding, or impatience, I could not be sure. "When?"

"When did she call? Last night."

"No. When is she coming?"

"Tuesday. She's bringing her mother and brother. They're going to stay for two weeks and go back. She sublet a furnished apartment on Central Park West."

"Wait. You said *they're* going to stay. How long is *she* staying in town?"

That was the bigger news. I might have gotten away with calling a quick visit "no big deal," but Angie had rented the place for a month.

"A month."

"A month!"

"Or less."

"She wants you back."

Too terrifying to bear thinking about. "No."

"You're an idiot. Sorry, let me rephrase that. This kind of thing is not what you are good at. Better? Trust me, she wants you back."

"When she signed over sole custody to me, she was at one of her many low points. Maybe she's having some second thoughts. Nothing serious. She'll come take the Kid for a few playdates, spoil him rotten, upset his routine, and fly back to Lafayette, where she gets to be the big-city celebrity in a small town. End of story."

"Credulity does not become you. You are a professional cynic; why are you so gullible where she's concerned?"

I thought that was a one-sided view of the situation. But I couldn't immediately come up with any other.

"Come on, Skeli. We can deal with this."

"Don't call me that." We had officially gone from a discussion to a dispute, and I was not keeping up. "She *will* upset the Kid's schedule, and you just shrug it off?"

"I will keep it to a minimum."

"Jason. It's you she's after. She doesn't care about the Kid. At best, he's a means to an end—you. And much more likely, he's an annoyance that she will fob off on her mother again first chance she gets."

"No más. No más," I said, hands in the air.

"And what am I supposed to be doing when she's around? Are you telling me that my next role is going to be running competition with Miss Tits on a Stick? The Cajun Queen from Narcissus, Louisiana! Like hell, I will. Christ!" She threw up her hands in recognition of the one subject we had been content to avoid. "I won't even be here!"

"Please, you're making way too much of this. Her being here changes nothing with you and me."

She finally stopped fuming, and her eyes went soft. "That's nice. You're a nice man. But, godalmighty, you can be such a dope." I thought she was going to tear up. She didn't tear up easily. Or willingly. "Excuse me." She stood up. "I've got to find the ladies' room."

I was alone with a cold duck and a great view.

"She's taking it well, don't you think?" I said to the duck. Cold and dead like me, the duck didn't say anything.

I sat there thinking how I could have handled the conversation better. I could not imagine how I might have handled it worse. I blamed myself and Skeli and Angie. It felt comfortable blaming Angie. And myself. But Skeli was the one who had taken the beating.

Was she right? That was what had me scared about Angie's visit. I had no wish to become entrapped in the briar patch of our old lives. I had moved on. Happily. I didn't think I was weak enough to fall for her all over again. I knew myself—and her—too well for that. But I didn't want to be tested. If Angie wanted to play visiting mother for a few weeks, I was willing to allow it. With my personal supervision, whether she liked it or not, though that would put us in close proximity more often than I would have liked. Or than Skeli would like. But why would she want me back? She had my money and she had her freedom. The best of both worlds. So, why was Skeli so sure? Was she just feeling threatened herself? I had had at least one too many Bellinis to deal with all those questions.

The busboy reappeared. "Is everything all right?"

Nothing was right. "Yes, thanks."

"Would you like coffee? Or would you care to see the dessert menu?"

"Not right now," I said. "I'll wait for my date to get back."

He gave me a very uncomfortable look. "I'm sorry, sir. I don't think she's coming back."

"What?"

"I just saw her get into a Town Car a few minutes ago. She's gone."

SUNDAY EVENING, Pop appeared at my front door with the Kid fast asleep in his arms. I held the door open, and he went directly to the Kid's room and laid him on his bed. I held the door and stayed out of his way.

The Kid gave a grunt and a short, snorting snore and rolled over, dead to the world.

"Nice work, Pop. Did you drug him?"

"He's had a big day," he said, peeling off the boy's new shoes. White with Velcro straps and red and blue flashing lights in the heels.

"Cool," I said, shaking my head in wonder. I would never have predicted that the Kid would have chosen footwear so obviously distracting.

"He picked 'em out," Pop whispered.

"Then they're the right ones," I answered.

I tucked a sheet tightly around my son, and the two of us backed out of the room.

"Can I get you something? Coffee? Water? Wine? Something to eat?"

"No, thanks. I've got to go. I'm double-parked. Estrella's watching the car."

"Just tell me. How did the Kid like the sharks?"

He shook his head ruefully. "Fish don't move the boy—yet. I think I may bring him around. But they've got a pool with seals out front and he would have jumped right in with them, if we'd let him."

"Thank you for not letting him. And thanks for getting him his shoes."

He shrugged and headed for the door. "How was your day? Did you and Skeli do anything fun?" he said over his shoulder.

"Ah," I said.

He stopped and turned back to me.

"What?"

"As much as it hurts me to say this, you were right. Skeli is not happy about Angie coming to town— especially now that she'll be away."

"Ahuh."

"And I think I could have handled it better."

"Ahuh. Have you said that to her?"

"She's not answering her phone."

He looked as though he had something more to say, but he stopped himself. "I'm sorry, bud. And I think, for once, I will keep my good advice to myself."

"Thanks, Pop."

He was gone.

| 7 |

Patrick "Paddy" Gallagher had lunch at Joe Allen's six days a week. Sundays he took his mother to brunch at the Plaza.

He was sitting alone at a deuce against the wall with a good view of the front door. He waved me over the minute I walked in.

"Jason, howahya, howahya? Siddown, whacha drinking?"

"Nice to see you, Paddy. I'll have a Guinness." Paddy claimed not to trust people who didn't drink, so whether I wanted it or not, I was having a cocktail with lunch.

"And have a shot with it," he said.

Paddy turned and flashed a young waiter a million-dollar smile and gave the order. The waiter nodded and headed for the bar.

Then Paddy turned the smile back on me. He was not a large man, but he always seemed to take up more than his share of the available space. He had an actor's face, the features all a bit oversized, with Paul Newman eyes and a pair of thick, silver eyebrows that seemed to be in constant motion, signaling each minute change in thought or emotion. But the smile was what grabbed you. Teeth that large, bright, and perfectly formed had to be store-bought.

"So, whadaya know? What's the good word?"

Paddy had started three different Wall Street firms over his forty years in the securities business. He had sold each one in succession for ever greater numbers. Each time, he had signed a short-term noncompete clause, spent a year or so working on other projects, and then come back and started a new firm, hiring away all the best talent from his old firm. He had tried to hire me twice, and though I hadn't jumped, we had become friendly, if not friends.

"Doing odd jobs. Getting by. My son just turned six. Life is good."

He nodded. "Somebody told me you helped Stockman clean up a mess during the buyout last year."

"The Feds are taking their time following up on it."

The waiter arrived and placed my beer and two large glasses of amber liquid in front of us. There wasn't much ice.

"Could I get a water, too?" I asked.

He nodded and left.

"*Sláinte,*" Paddy said. We touched glasses and drank.

Paddy drank only top-shelf Irish whiskey. Midleton or Jameson's Gold at thirty dollars a shot. It tasted like firewater to me.

"Did you hear they're making Stockman move to Nashville?" he said.

I tried to imagine the little Napoleon having to sell his Park Avenue duplex and move his art-collecting-circle wife to mid-America.

"It won't last," I said.

"Ahdohno. They got him wrapped in golden chains. If he bails on them, he's gonna leave some serious money behind."

Stockman had paid me well and on time. Other than that, though, he was never going to be on my A-list. I wasn't going to waste tears on him.

"So how's showbiz, Paddy?"

Paddy had started investing in Broadway shows thirty years ago. It had been a sideline. Fun. But the first time he had to sit on the bench for a year—after he sold his first firm—he began devoting more time to it. By the time he took his final buyout—from a Dutch firm looking to expand in the U.S.—he was a full-time producer with three Tony Awards to his credit. He got involved in anything that grabbed his attention. He had done new musicals, revivals, dramas, and comedies on Broadway, Off-Broadway, and national touring companies. Never married, he had started appearing at restaurants, clubs, and openings, always with a carousel of famous female actors or entertainers on his arm. He was a regular on Page Six of the *Post*. He wore dark suits that looked almost black—they were actually deep purple, but you had to catch him in the right light to see it—with gold-colored socks. He was the only person I have ever known who wore an ascot—also gold. And he carried it off.

"I'm reading scripts. Talking to some people. Maybe something comes of it, we'll see. Meanwhile, I've still got two shows on the boards that made it through the winter. They're not making me rich, but . . ." He waved his hand in the so-so gesture.

The waiter returned with my water. "Did you want to order, Mr. Gallagher?" The waiter pronounced it correctly, with the silent *g* in the last syllable.

"Yeah, my usual, thanks."

"And you, sir?"

"I'll have what he's having," I said.

"No, don't do that," Paddy said. Then, to the waiter, "Bring him a burger. Make the fries well done. How do you like it? Medium rare?"

I nodded.

"Medium rare." His attention went to the door behind me. "Benny! Howahya?" He flashed Benny the smile and gave a small wave. He continued the big smile while whispering to me. "I hate that sonofabitch." Then, in normal tones again, "So, you doin' anything in the markets? I think maybe gold is toppy here."

Gold had made another all-time new high the day before.

"Only the sight of the Four Horsemen of the Apocalypse could justify these levels," I said.

"Yeah," he said. "So maybe I stick with the trade a

little longer." The smile flashed again as someone else came in the door.

When it came to trading, Paddy never showed his hand. Though officially retired, he still traded, mostly futures, every day from his desk in the production office.

"So, you want to hear about me and William Von Becker."

I had mentioned it when I set up the lunch.

"My 'old friend' William Von Becker. People think we met on Wall Street. Not so. We grew up together." He paused. "Kinda."

Paddy Gallagher let anyone and everyone know that he had grown up on one of New York's toughest streets in what was now called Clinton, but was known back then as Hell's Kitchen. Not many kids made it out of that neighborhood, unless it was on their way to Sing Sing or Attica—or the morgue.

"Little Billy Becker from Forty-seventh Street. That 'Von' stuff? Bullshit. It suddenly appeared when he went to Trinity. I don't mean to speak ill of the dead, but Becker was always a con. I just never knew how far he'd take it."

"How do you get from Forty-seventh Street to Trinity?" Trinity was in the top ranks of New York City private schools.

"Same way I did it. You bust your goddamn ass. It helps if you're also smart, but it still takes a lot of hard work. We both got scholarships in high school. I went to Regis, Billy to Trinity."

"And you were friends back then?"

"No. We knew who the other one was, but we grew up on different blocks. That was very important back then."

"But you met up again later."

"I came out of Fordham still talking like a Westie with the kind of polish you get from eight years with the Jesuits. Which is none. I landed a job as a runner at Merrill. When I met up with Becker he was fresh out of Williams and spoke, dressed, and acted like he grew up on Sutton Place. The kind of guy who you know doesn't ever fart, know what I mean? He was a trainee in private banking at Morgan. They already had him marked for big things."

"So, how did the friendship get started?"

"Let me set the record straight, all right? We were never friends. The press called me his best friend because his wife told them that. The guy never had a friend in his life. She also said I engineered the whole deal—which is also bullshit. We did a lot of business together over the years. He invested in every one of my firms, and a few of the shows. I let him manage some of my money over the years. And we played poker once a month with the same group of guys for eighteen years. But we were never 'friends.'"

"Your lunch, gentlemen." The waiter set our plates down. My burger was huge. The pile of fries was even bigger.

Paddy had a fillet of some white fish that appeared to have been poached in milk. "I got stomach issues," he said in response to my stare. He took another sip of whiskey.

"Paddy, I'm sorry I said that. I won't call him your friend again. Okay? I was just spouting off based on what I heard."

"That's all right," he said. "No harm, no foul. No, we kept running into each other over the years. We did some deals together. It was more like a habit than a friendship."

I bit into a french fry. I immediately wanted another. "You want to try some of these? I've got more than I'll ever eat."

"No, thanks. I'll just watch."

I ate in silence for a few minutes. Paddy broke up the fish with the side of his fork and moved the pieces around on his plate. Then he sipped his whiskey again.

"Paaaahhddy!" a mannered voice said from behind me. An attractive blonde in her late forties bent over and placed a kiss on his cheek. She gave me a quick look to be sure I wasn't someone important that she might be snubbing, and having obviously decided that I wasn't and it was okay to snub me, turned back to Paddy. I knew her from somewhere.

"You haven't been to see my show yet," she scolded.

Paddy flashed the big smile. "I got seats for Friday, doll. You know I wouldn't miss it."

"Come see me afterwards. Ethan is coming Friday. We'll all grab a drink. You know how much he likes you."

I was still struggling to place her. Did she live in my building? Go to the same dry cleaner? No. She was different. She looked older than I remembered. It was making me nuts.

"Kisses, Paddy, I've got to run." She waved and turned to me. "Nice meeting you," she said, finally giving me a full view of her face.

Law & Order! That was it. She'd had a recurring role as an annoying defense attorney for a season or two. All the defense attorneys on *Law & Order* were annoying. I'd seen her in late-night reruns years ago.

"Love your work," I said.

"Oh, thank you," she gushed, as though accepting a Tony Award. She completed her exit.

"So," I said. "Are you going to see her show?"

Paddy gave a look of pain. "It's a three-character drama about the Brontë sisters at their brother's wake. No intermission. I'm hoping it closes on Thursday."

I laughed, and he joined in, which set me off again.

Paddy finished his drink and waggled his finger for the waiter.

"I notice you've still got most of yours," he said.

"I was never very good at drinking during the day, and I think I've gotten worse over the years."

He sighed. "I should quit," he said. "At least my doctor thinks so."

I could as easily see him giving up his right arm.

"Back to Von Becker?" I said.

He shrugged in acquiescence.

"How much did he get you for? I've heard quite a range."

"Depends on whose numbers you use. This is my disagreement with the trustee. I put twenty-eight million into his funds over the course of thirty years. Not all at once. I took money out. I put it in again. All that time, I'm thinking I'm earning ten to twelve percent."

"You never suspected?"

"I didn't say that. But when Billy started out, I am convinced that he was doing it straight up. He used leverage carefully. He hedged when it made sense. He did a lot of covered call writing to boost returns. The markets liked him. And he was smart. Those returns were legit."

"And later?"

"After the tech bubble burst? Back in 2000. It got harder to play the same games he'd been playing. The money wasn't there anymore. But Becker kept posting the same returns. I didn't buy it, but at the same time, I couldn't be sure."

"What'd you do?"

"When they shut him down I had four mil still there. According to *my* calculations. Not a huge amount of money. Only, the way the Feds look at it, they count up all the money I took out as well and figure I made out on the upside to the tune of six million. They want me to give it back."

I whistled. "Or?"

"Or they indict me as a co-conspirator. That's why I don't like all this 'friend' talk."

"Are they going to get it?"

The eyebrows drooped. "In the end. They always do, don't they? Look, it's not like it's gonna hurt or anything. I'm good for it. I got lots of it, and no matter what I do, I can't spend it fast enough. It just really pisses me off."

The waiter brought Paddy's drink and cleared our plates.

"So what else can I tell ya? All this is stuff you can read on the Internet."

I still had half my beer and I'd barely touched the whiskey, but I felt a mild diffusion, a lack of focus. I picked up the water and drained it.

"All right, Paddy. Here's the drill. Somebody . . . people . . . are saying that there's money hidden. Lots of money. Von Becker socked it away. The Feds haven't found it yet, and they most likely won't."

"And this 'somebody' says I know where it is. That the story? Who is this asshole? And don't tell me it's whatzit Payne. The guy is both stupid and dishonest, which would be okay if he was also lazy, but he's not."

"Everett brought me in, but he's not directing me. Your name was on the list of investors."

"He's been trying to see me for three months. I keep telling him to get lost. So now he gets my old friends to come bother me."

"Don't shoot the messenger, Paddy. I had no idea he talked to you already."

"I didn't talk to him."

"Okay. He got me hired to look into this, but he never pointed me in your direction."

"If you're working for a cut, get it in writing."

"I'm on salary."

"Get it in advance."

I gave him a smile. "Why do I get the feeling you don't trust Everett Payne?"

"That guy lies just to stay in practice. He was one of Von Becker's top boys. He brought in billions. If anyone knows where the bodies are buried, it's him."

Paddy looked up to greet a trim-looking older couple who had just come in. "Howahya, Petey? Who's the arm candy?"

Pete and his wife cracked up.

"Howahya, Della?"

They both waved and headed for a table.

Paddy turned back to me. "Nice people. Where was I?"

"What do you know about Von Becker and offshore money?"

"Really, Jason, I have no idea. Becker ran a bank or two somewhere in the Bahamas or someplace like that. He was always flying to tax-shelter lands. But that's all I can tell you. We really weren't that close."

I gestured for the check.

"I got this," he said. "They run a tab for me. I'll tell you who you should talk to, though. You remember a salesman back at Case named Randolph?"

"Doug Randolph? The Boy Scout? The guy who wore Brooks Brothers and wingtips every day of his life. What was he doing tied up with Von Becker?"

"Long story. Get him to tell it. It ain't pretty." He signed the check and we got up to leave. "I gotta do a turn of the room here. Say my good-byes. You go on."

"It was great seeing you again, Paddy."

"Come here." He gave me a very showbiz hug and air-kissed my cheek. "You ever want to get back in the game, you let me know. I'll back ya. We'll have some laughs."

"I don't think the regulators will ever let me back. I should have taken you up on your first offer ten years ago. My life would be a lot simpler right now."

"Hey, you can't think of it that way. What happened is what was supposed to happen. You only get to choose what happens next. Good luck to you, Jason. Don't be a stranger."

I was almost out the door when I heard him call me.

"Jason! Wait. I almost forgot. Well, I did forget, but then I remembered." He reached into his inside jacket pocket and pulled out an envelope. "Here ya go. Vouchers for four house seats to my show. Take your son and some friends. Kids love the show."

He flashed me the smile again and waved before he turned back into the dining room. "Petey! Della! Howahya?"

| 8 |

No New Yorker in his right mind goes out to Kennedy Airport to greet arrivals. On a good day with minimal traffic, it's an hour from the Upper West Side. That never happens. It had taken the Town Car driver close to two. But the JetBlue flight had sat out on the tarmac waiting for an open gate for forty-five minutes, so I got to baggage claim well before the passengers.

Five Eastern European limo drivers, all wearing cheap black raincoats despite the grueling heat outside, were congregated around the base of the escalator, each armed with a baggage cart and white rectangular sign. My driver was Haitian and wore a beret over a lopsided Afro. We stood out.

Angie was in the first wave of passengers. She flowed down toward me looking every bit as beautiful and dangerous as I remembered. She wasn't looking for me; she was waiting to be seen. The pose held until every male in the baggage area had taken notice.

"Hey, *cher*. Thank you for coming out like this. You are lookin' good." She gave my prison-issue biceps a squeeze and I felt a zap of something halfway between lust and fear. She stepped back and, with a flourish as though unveiling a work of art, she took off her sunglasses. She stood waiting to be admired.

She had had her eyes done—making her look a little like one of the aliens in *Avatar*. It was probably a good job—I wouldn't know. She must have had the doctor do it when they were finishing the rest of the repair work. Most people wouldn't have noticed. I noticed.

"Hello, Angie," I managed. Her black widow's dress covered her from jawline to mid-calf, but still managed to reveal every dip and curve in the landscape. She would have stopped traffic in Vegas. Angie probably thought it was conservative. "Good to see you." It *was* good, I realized. The anger was long gone, replaced by an at-a-distance sympathy, and a touch of forgiveness. She'd been dealt a shitty hand, and it wasn't her fault that she hadn't been able to make a royal flush out of it. "Tino? And your Mamma?"

"Mamma wanted a wheelchair, so Tino waited with her. They'll be along."

"She all right?"

Angie made a face like she was thinking hard—maybe it helped. "She just likes to be made a fuss over. She's got the sugar now, but she can walk. Where's my *petit boug*?"

"The Kid's in school. You'll see him this afternoon."

She pursed her lips in a demonstration of disappointment. "A boy could miss one day of school to come greet his mamma, couldn't he?"

I failed to rise to the bait. "No, Angie. The Kid needs his school more than he needs either of us. They're doing miracles with him."

I saw the old flash of fire in her pale blue eyes, but she blinked and made it go away. "You're right. Of course." Agreeing with me must have been a unique experience, because she suddenly appeared flustered. Her hand came up and fluttered in front of her face. "I brought him a present," she said vaguely. She looked around as though surprised that whatever it was wasn't right there. "Oh, damn." She smiled in confusion. "Tino has it."

I felt the old urgings of wanting to reach out and help her. I squashed them. Instead I cleared my throat and tried to smile back.

She was still a startlingly beautiful woman, but her face no longer had that perfect symmetry that the camera had so loved when she was modeling. The repairs from the accident were good, just not that good. The last time I had looked at her was when my father and I had brought the Kid down to visit her over Christmas. Her face had been swathed in bandages and what skin showed had been puffy and discolored with bruising. The Kid hadn't seemed to notice, but Pop had been outraged.

"That's not right. Why in hell did she drag us all down here, whimpering about needing to see her baby? No child should have to see his mother like that."

"She needed an audience, Pop. She's now the Widow

*Martin and a survivor of the crash that killed her hus-
band. It's her greatest role yet."*

They'd been married three months. Long enough for
TeePaul to reveal himself as a bully and a drunk, although all the indications had been there from Day One.
He had beaten Angie on more than one occasion, and he
had hit my son. Once.

The day he died, he had been trying to punch Angie
with his right hand, while using his left both to steer
the monster pickup truck she had bought for him and
hold the half-empty bottle of Early Times. Angie was
crouched down away from him when the truck hit the
concrete divider and launched itself into the oncoming
lanes. The plastic casing on the air bag hit her in the face
rather than the chest. She was lucky. TeePaul was vaulted
over the steering wheel, and his head went through the
windshield. The trucker, deadheading in a Peterbilt on
his way back to Denton, Texas, for a faulty air condi-
tioner repair, had stood on his brakes the moment he saw
the big F-150 veering across the road. So, he was only
doing around fifty when the pickup—airborne, and
north of eighty—connected with his left front fender.
That was all for him. TeePaul had bled out through multiple head and neck wounds, screaming and cursing until
he choked on his own blood. I couldn't see why anyone
but his mother would have mourned him.

Angie felt me staring—examining her. For a moment,
she faltered. Her face reddened and she turned away, hiding
a look of fear. The doctors had implanted, grafted, stitched,
and smoothed, but the best they'd been able to do was to

produce a close copy of the woman who had once com-manded a high-four-figure day rate. If I could see the marks and imperfections at four feet, what would they look like to Angie in her magnifying makeup mirror?

"You're a beautiful woman, Angie," I said quietly. "Forgive me for staring. You're easy to stare at."

"It's cars. I brought cars. Those little cars he likes." She gave a short gasp and looked at me. "He does still like them, doesn't he?"

"He'll love them. Don't worry."

She turned away and looked back up the hall. "Where can Mamma be? I mean, how long could it take? They're not going to hold her up until the whole plane empties, are they?"

"You were in first?" Of course they were. Angie still had enough of my money to treat herself and her mother and brother to first-class airplane tickets. Also meals, hotels, shopping. Angie had been a sharp business-woman in a cutthroat environment who had watched every penny—even if she spent it on champagne—but she was also generous, especially with family. "They won't keep them."

They didn't. Down the hall came Mamma Oubre, being wheeled in state by a burly black woman, followed by her son, Tino, who was weighed down with three carry-on bags and a big Dillard's shopping bag. Tino saw us and waved first. I was glad to see him. Tino owned Lafayette's most exclusive salon, but at thirty-three had yet to come out to his mother. Still, he was the sanest member of the family. I liked him.

"Hey, y'all," he called. "Well, well. New York comes out to welcome the Boudreaux. I swear they were checkin' our bags for alligator skins. Oh my god, Jason, who are you letting cut your hair? I am going to do something about that while I'm here."

Tino was wearing white linen pants and a lavender guayabera shirt. No socks and woven loafers. While his sister was blond, blue-eyed, and fair-skinned, Tino looked almost Latin with his dark eyes and hair. He turned almost as many heads as his sister—from both sides of the aisle.

Mamma saw me and squealed. "Ooohhh, Jason! Come here, young man, and let me see you." She jumped up from the wheelchair like a cured penitent at a Pentecostal tent church, raising a few eyebrows from the otherwise jaded New Yorkers waiting for their bags. I let her hug me and gave a short squeeze in return.

The alarm sounded and the belt began to move. Tino and the driver went over to recover the bags. Angie had the Dillard's bag and was rifling through it, seeking the Kid's present, I imagined.

Mamma still had my elbow in her grip. She pulled me to her and whispered in my ear, "My little girl has been so excited to see you. I just know you two will find a way to patch things up now she's done with that *coullion*." She released me and patted my cheek fondly.

I got that cold, liquid feeling in my gut, the one you get just after swallowing a bad oyster. Things were going to get a lot worse before they got better. And there was nothing to be done about it.

HOW DO YOU TELL a mother not to hug her child?

We had left Mamma and Tino to settle in at the rented apartment. Three bedrooms, three baths, sunken living room, newly renovated kitchen, designer furnishings, and a tenth-floor view of the park. "Not too shabby," my father would have said. Angie and I took the Town Car up to Seventy-third Street to greet the Kid. On the way, I tried to describe some of the differences, or near-unique characteristics, of our child.

"The school is doing wonders, Angie. He knows his letters. He's good at numbers. He doesn't really read yet. He recognizes symbols, though, and they think he'll get it eventually."

"Mamma says I was a slow reader."

"For instance, he knows the letters *F, O, R,* and *D,* and when he sees the Ford logo he knows what it means. But show him the word 'ford,' like a ford in a stream, and he has no idea. He can't get it."

"Well, that's a hard word."

He could also "read" the words Chevrolet, Maserati, and Lamborghini, but he couldn't figure out "dog."

"But he is beginning to talk about things other than cars. He understands the concept of conversation, but he's still not good at it." And sometimes he simply refused to partake.

"He gets that from his father's side," she teased.

That was fair. I was in college before anyone suggested to me that constantly asking questions wasn't really conversation and that it could be annoying, or even rude. I barely spoke to anyone for a year after that.

"He still doesn't like to be touched. He's going through a bad patch right now. Not a big deal. Things get worse before they get better. That's what Heather says."

"Heather?" Angie managed to make the single word conjure up visions of vampires, serial killers, and afternoon talk-show hosts all in one. "Heather is a color."

"Heather is his shadow," I said.

"Your new fuckbuddy?"

There went the sympathy and forgiveness. I stared out the window, counting the things I would rather be doing than escorting my ex around town. When I was well into the double digits, I risked answering her. "Heather is more than a nanny, less than a doctor. Neither the Kid nor I could make it through the week without her. She is a pain in the ass sometimes. She can be tough. But I trust her. More important, I think the Kid trusts her." I spoke calmly, rationally, kindly. "She wears more facial jewelry than Marilyn Manson's whole fanbase, and she's got forearms the size of my calves. And I think she's a lesbian, though, honestly, I'd be afraid to ask."

It was her turn to stare out the window. Then she said something I never thought I would have heard from her again. "I'm sorry."

We both took a moment to take that in. I wanted to say I was sorry, too, but I couldn't think of anything to apologize for.

"I was reacting," she continued. "I meant to ask if you were seeing anyone."

A water moccasin slid through my lower intestine. I was all too conscious of her long bare legs, the gravity-defying lift of her million-dollar breasts (they'd been insured when we were first married), the faint scent of Bolt of Lightning, and the memory of a limo ride in Paris our first year together. I felt a rise in my pants.

"We had us some times, *cher*, didn't we?" She said it casually, as though she didn't know exactly what I had been thinking. "So, are you?"

"Am I?"

"Are you seeing anyone?"

When in doubt, tell the truth; it's easier to back down from the high ground. Another of my father's aphorisms.

"I am." My throat was tight, and I almost coughed it out.

Angie laughed. "*Mais,* boo, you sound like you swallowed a *tooloulou.*" She patted my thigh. "I'm happy you got youself *une bebelle foh de gogo.*" Angie the Cajun—one of her playful poses. Once I would have enjoyed it; now it sounded practiced, forced. I had a rare flash of insight about my ex-wife; Angie was as uncomfortable as I was.

THE ELEVATORS at the Ansonia were built to carry grand pianos. With just the two of us riding up together, the space felt impossibly small.

"Angie." I paused, not sure of quite how to proceed.

"Anh?" she said after five seconds of dead silence.

I jumped in. "When you take the Kid through the lobby, you can't walk on the black tiles. Only on the white ones. I should have said something before we came in, but I didn't want to sound like a nutcase."

"That is just what you sound like. What are you talkin' 'bout?"

"Holes. The Kid thinks the black tiles are holes. He gets scared. It's just a . . . a thing, but it's . . ." I couldn't think of what it was. It made sense as long as I didn't have to say it out loud.

"Foolish?" she snapped.

"Important," I said. "And don't be surprised if he's not talking. He goes through these periods."

She was one degree from boiling over. "You said he was getting better."

"He is. You'll see."

The elevator glided to a stop and the doors slid open. Angie seemed to bite back some reply and then stepped into the corridor. I did a quick hop-skip to walk with her rather than follow.

I wanted her to see the Kid was doing well. He god-damn was doing well. She'd left him locked in a room at her mother's when caring for him had become inconvenient. I took him to school every morning. Checked his scrambled eggs for spots. Made sure he had clean blue clothes to wear on Monday. I was the one who wrapped him up tightly in a sheet at night until he fell asleep. And sometimes two or three times more through the night when his terrors came on. And when I walked through the lobby I was careful to step on white tiles only—even when the Kid wasn't with me. And why in hell should I be worried about proving something to her? She was the one who'd stolen him away eight months earlier, only to abandon him back at her mother's. And if I hadn't gone and brought the Kid back, he might have been in the truck that day and . . .

I took a long breath and counted the beats as I released it.

"And if you think of it, say something nice about his shoes."

That stopped her. "His shoes?"

"They're new," I said. "He picked them out himself."

She absorbed that. "I will do that."

"I'm sure he'll be glad to see you," I said.

Angie softened at this unforeseen kindness. "Thank you, boo."

And as I looked back at her, it suddenly hit me what was different about her. It wasn't the doctor's work—that was minor. This was deeper than the brittle beauty of her face. It had been niggling at me from the moment I saw her coming down the escalator at the airport, but I had been too preoccupied with my own insecurities to see it.

Angie was sober.

| 9 |

Doug Randolph lived at the end of a quiet lane in Sands Point out on Long Island. I rented a car for the day, even though I hated driving on the expressway. I would rather drive cross-country nonstop than spend an hour getting through Queens.

Sands Point was a small community with two-acre zoning and narrow winding roads with tons of trees. It was not the most expensive place to live on Long Island. That was about two miles away. You could still get a starter home for under a million and a nice house with a view of Long Island Sound for under two. Or you could spend four or five times that. Most of the teenagers drove Beemers or Audis, except for the poorer kids, who got by with Lexuses. They all played lacrosse.

I passed through a break in the wall of twelve-foot-tall boxwood and pulled up the white gravel driveway.

Randolph's house was a yellow stucco, with red-tile roof. Sort of an ersatz Mission. Very California. Modest by Sands Point standards.

His wife let me in and walked me through the living room. It was not just clean, it was spotless. Immaculate.

"Your house is beautiful, Mrs. Randolph."

She was a small woman, short and impossibly thin. Once upon a time she might have been described as elfin and cute, but age and stress had cut deep lines around her eyes and mouth. She was struggling, as though she didn't know whether to thank me or burst into tears. "Thank you. We have an open house scheduled for this weekend."

The dining room and kitchen were so clean it looked like a boatload of Navy midshipmen had been through polishing the brightwork. It felt like no one lived there.

Doug was working on a laptop under an umbrella out on the rear patio. Books and a few legal pads were strewn across the top of the latticed-metal table. Steps led down to about an acre of perfect grass with a marble fountain right where a grade-school kickball team would have put second base. The grass ended at a rocky beach and the water. The view was to the north and west. The sunsets over Manhattan off in the distance must have been spectacular.

He shut down the program he had open—something like the Bloomberg trading platform, with graphs and flashing colors—and stood up to greet me.

"Jason, long time."

"How you doing, Doug?"

"I just got back from seeing my therapist. Does that answer the question?"

I nodded in commiseration. "Believe me, I understand."

I could see I offended him. I had been guilty of creating my own mess. He had just been swept up in someone else's. I held up a hand. "I just mean I understand the stress of what you're going through. I've been there."

He gave a tight smile. "Pull up a chair."

"Can I get you boys something?" his wife asked.

There was a brittle tension in the air between them—or around them—as though a raised voice or an unkind word would shatter their world like a glass figurine hitting a marble floor.

"I'm good," I said, shaking my head.

"No," Doug said. "I have a wine cellar downstairs. I'm no collector, I just bought what I liked, so it's not worth much to the auction houses. And I can only fit so much of it in the apartment we're moving into. So . . . ?" It was what the moment needed. It was a magnanimous gesture, wiping the slate between us clean, and announcing that despite all his troubles, he could still treat a guest to a nice glass of wine. It would have been rude to refuse.

"Red or white?" I answered.

"Merlot all right? Hon?" He continued without waiting for my response. "Bring us a bottle of the Duckhorn, would you? And three glasses."

She gave a more relaxed smile and left.

We made ourselves comfortable and gazed out at the Sound.

"How long has it been?" I asked.

"I left Case five years ago."

"Long before I blew up."

He nodded.

I gestured to the laptop. "And now you're day-trading?"

He nodded again.

"And how's that going?"

He smiled sheepishly. "I was never a trader. I can't seem to figure out when to take a loss and move on."

"It's the hardest thing to learn. Cut your losses and let your profits run."

He gave a self-deprecating laugh. "That's what all the books say."

"But you were a great salesman, Doug."

He shrugged. "They'll never let me back. The minimum I can expect is to be permanently barred. I will be very lucky to avoid a felony record."

"But can't a good salesman sell anything?"

"That's what we say when we're selling you something."

I laughed politely. He was making an effort to open up.

"So, how's Paddy?" he asked. "How does he look? I haven't seen him in two or three years."

"How does he look? Just the same. One of a kind."

"He's been feeling the heat on this mess, too."

"Can we talk about that? Working with Von Becker, I mean."

He developed an immediate tic below his right eye. He took a few seconds looking for something in my face. He must have found it.

"Sure. But we'll drink a little wine first."

I was going to have to get used to drinking during the day or find another way to make a buck.

The wife—"Mo," for Maureen, when we were finally introduced—arrived with the wine. Doug opened it. I asked her about their children.

"Two boys, if I remember," I said. There had always been a picture on Doug's desk.

"Bill just finished his sophomore year at Harvard. He's teaching sailing at Sewanhaka again this summer. Buddy starts Tulane in the fall."

That sounded like a hundred thousand dollars a year for the next two years and another fifty for each of the following two. Before grad school.

Doug saw me doing the math in my head. "Tulane was very generous. Buddy's in the honors program. As long as he lives in a dorm and maintains a three-five he only pays five thousand a year."

Which still left Harvard and fifty grand or so a year.

"Do you and your wife have children, Mr. Stafford?" Mo asked.

"Jason, please. Mr. Stafford is a really nice man who runs a bar over in College Point and takes care of my son every other Sunday."

She smiled. "Just the one son? How old?"

"The Kid just turned six. He's a handful. And there is no Mrs. Stafford at this point in my life."

The wine was very good. Mo stayed and helped to keep the conversation going until the bottle was more than half empty.

"I have some things I just have to take care of inside, Jason. Please excuse me." She made to pour the remaining wine into our glasses. I covered mine. She smiled and poured the balance into her husband's glass. "You two finish this up. It's much too good to go to waste."

There was another long silence after she left.

"Nice wine," I said.

He nodded.

"Nice view." I gestured with my glass. The lighthouse at Execution Rocks. City Island and Hart Island. The two bridges. The slanting roof of the Citicorp building sparkling with reflected sunlight. The only jarring note in the whole expanse, the ugly phallic monstrosity of the Trump building in New Rochelle.

Randolph was staring into his glass, building up steam for an eruption.

"Enough!" he said. He took a couple of deep breaths and spoke again. "I'm fifty-two fucking years old. I'm bankrupt and I don't want to go to jail. A year ago I was worth fifty million—on paper, but still. Fifty million. My old man gets by on a school superintendent's pension out in Johnson City, Pennsylvania, and he sleeps like a baby every night. I get two or three hours a night and wake up sweating, asking myself, How the hell did I get here?"

His hands were shaking, his eyes suddenly red and wet.

"I'm sorry. I'm dragging up a bunch of bad shit. You don't have to talk about this."

I suddenly found I wasn't capable of pushing him. If he wanted to talk, fine. But if he didn't . . .

But he did. He *had* to talk about it.

"Thirty years in the business and I never saw it coming."

There wasn't anything to say.

He took another sip of the Duckhorn and slurped it around in his mouth. "Yup. Good juice." He pulled himself together and sat straighter. "Okay. What do you want to hear about?"

"Anyone who knew you back at Case would have a hard time believing you did anything wrong."

"Yeah, well, thanks. I haven't heard from too many supporters. But that's where it started, actually. Back at Case. There was a guy I was friendly with in the mortgage research group. Eric Purliss?"

I shook my head. I hadn't known him.

"Good guy. He lives in Port Washington. We rode the train together. Got together with the families sometimes. Well, he and another guy there, David Hu, had a sideline business going, buying and selling buildings in Brooklyn and Queens. I never paid much attention because I never thought you could make any real money that way. I was making a good bit more than they were, so it looked like a lot of effort for not much return. Eventually, though, the two of them left the firm to work on that stuff full-time."

"Those were good years for commercial real estate."

A flock of small sailboats appeared in front of City Island, the boats too small to be seen with the naked eye, each one seeming to arise from off the water as the sails were raised. They fluttered into a tight group and began a swirling dance between two large orange markers.

We both sat watching the zigzagging jumble of boats suddenly break into a wedge of speeding sails, knifing through the light chop. The race had started.

"I was up in Newport last week. I saw some of the boats doing drills." A gross exaggeration, but it made Randolph more comfortable.

"Really?" he said. "My brother is doing the race again this year. He crews on a J-boat out of Stonington."

I nodded as though I was envious of someone crossing half the Atlantic Ocean on a bucking, heaving platform the size of a studio apartment, braving storms, wet clothes, lack of sleep, and bad food for four days.

"Where was I?" Randolph frowned as though undecided whether he really wanted to continue or not. He took a long swallow of the wine. He was long past the sipping stage. "Yes, Eric and David Hu. You're right, those were good times. Lots of low-hanging fruit. But those guys were both lucky and smart. Two years later, they were back. They had a partner and a business proposal. They'd opened a small office in the next village over—Plandome. They were buying up notes on private mortgages—at a nice discount—and were looking for investors so they could expand."

"Do I need to know what that means?"

He held up a single finger, asking for patience. "I listened to the pitch and asked them how much they wanted to raise. They said they weren't really sure, but maybe as much as ten mil. When I heard what they had going, I laughed. I wanted in. How about a hundred mil? I asked."

"Some pitch."

"Tell me about it. There's a whole field of private lending that goes on in the commercial real estate market that never makes headlines. Here's an example. Let's say you run a car wash in Staten Island and you want out. You're ready to retire. You figure the place is worth a million or so."

"For a car wash?" I turned to face him.

"Car washes are good businesses. When's the last time you saw one with a 'Going Out of Business' sign out front?"

"I'm from Manhattan. I don't think I've been to a car wash more than two or three times in my life."

"In Staten Island, people go every week. At twenty bucks a pop. And they wait in line for it."

"Gotcha."

"But it's hard to find a small-businessman with a million dollars in cash. If he's successful, his cash is already working for him. And it's almost impossible to get bank financing on a cash business with potential environmental issues."

"I can see that."

"So the seller agrees to take a chunk of money up front and the rest over time. A note. A private commercial mortgage. The buyer pays it off over five or ten years, usually with some kind of balloon payment at the end."

"Isn't that risky? Suppose he doesn't pay?"

"It's a mortgage. There's real property involved. Worst case, you foreclose. But with a big down payment up front, you're in a good position."

"I can see that." I could also see the potential problem. "But meanwhile, I'm down in Orlando with the wife, sitting by the condo pool, worrying about my cholesterol. I don't want to be chasing after some idiot back in New York who's getting divorced, or discovered horse racing, or snorting cocaine."

"Exactly. So you're going to be very happy to talk to our representative when he calls and offers to buy out your note. Ohhh!" He pointed out at the water. Three of the sailboats were in a tangle as they made the turn around one of the orange markers. "That's a two-turn penalty."

It looked like boat goulash to me. I thought about the business model. There were plenty of pitfalls in running something like that, but none that couldn't be fixed with good underwriting and frequent monitoring.

"I would guess that you offer to buy the notes at a discount. Right? Isn't that where the real money would be?"

He smiled. "Sure. But you're down in Orlando, sweating in the humidity and dreaming of a nice three-bedroom on the ocean, where the grandkids would come and stay more often, and here I am offering you a big lump sum of cash right now. All our clients were businessmen, re-member? They knew what they were getting and they knew what they were giving and nobody was making them sign. You can't hard-sell a guy who ran his own business for thirty or forty years."

"You're making it sound like a public service."

"Oh, it was a business, all right. Those three guys were making returns of fifteen to twenty percent. Their average foreclosure rate was under five percent. I waited until bonus time, cashed out, and became their fourth partner. My commute shrank to less than ten minutes. Over the next two years, I brought in almost a billion dollars of investor money. The other three partners focused on the underwriting and pricing side of the business. I focused on growth. We expanded into markets all along the East Coast. We ran ads on local cable. We bought billboard space in Florida and South Carolina. Big ads with my face under block letters announcing PLANDOME CAPITAL—WE BUY NOTES."

"You were famous."

"Getting there. Which became a problem in itself. We couldn't find deals fast enough to satisfy the hedge funds and other investors. All our investors were either large institutions or hedge funds. The four of us were the only private investors. We didn't want the regulatory head-aches of dealing with the mom-and-pops. No widows. No orphans. We raised the minimum investment from ten mil to fifty. We capped it at one hundred mil for any given client. It didn't matter. Money was still coming in like Niagara Falls.

"We talked about relaxing underwriting standards, taking a little more risk—and rejected the idea. Our worst nightmare was to wake up someday and find the foreclosure rate soaring and we were suddenly in the business of running a car wash in Staten Island or a dry cleaner in Philly. Or both."

He drained his glass. "I don't suppose you want to open another."

"I have to drive back to the city later, but you go ahead."

He thought about it. "The days get really long sometimes."

I understood that. "The nights are worse."

"I'm getting a glass of water. You want one?" He stood and headed for the patio doors.

"Sure."

The day was starting to heat up. I leaned forward and pulled my shirt away from my back. There appeared to be plenty of wind out on the water—the sailboats were all still moving quickly—but the Randolphs' yard was protected. Leaves in the tops of trees rustled. I could have used a bit of that breeze.

Randolph returned with the water.

"So, finish your story." I said. "I have yet to even hear Von Becker's name here."

He nodded and sat back down.

"We're getting there. The partners all agreed to just sit on our hands and keep milking it. We were each taking a million a year in salary and letting the retained earnings just build up at double-digit rates. We were having fun and getting rich. We closed the fund. No new money. We had invented the golden goose."

But, of course, someone always kills the golden goose.

"The first approach from Von Becker came from a financial advisor in their private banking group. He heard about us and had a client who wanted to invest. I told him the fund was closed, but thanks for the interest and so on. I forgot about him ten seconds after I hung up the phone. A week later, Von Becker himself calls. He wants to buy the firm."

A tugboat came around the point, towing a big barge, the cable invisible at this distance. It looked like a runaway barge chasing a tugboat. The sailboats veered away like a covey of quail running for cover.

"He saw all that cash."

"The sonofabitch worked us over nicely. It started with cases of wine, Cuban cigars, little presents. Then he turned it up a notch. Eric liked to shoot skeet. Von Becker bought him a shotgun. A Perazzi?"

I shrugged. It sounded like an expensive stereo system.

"It's Dick Cheney's gun. Retails for around twenty-five grand."

"It doesn't seem to have done Cheney much good."

"But it wasn't all just flowers and chocolates. Von Becker had ideas as well. He wanted us to go national. Instead of just the East Coast, he wanted offices in Atlanta, Memphis, Chicago, Dallas, and Los Angeles. He wanted us to do an infomercial and set up a website where note holders could get a quote in five minutes or less. He wanted the fund reopened. He said we could go from one billion to ten in two years."

"He must have been slavering over the possibility of that much new cash."

"When the offer came, it was way over the top. One hundred and fifty million. We would each get ten mil up front, the rest in a single balloon payment at the end of five years. During the five years, we would stay in our current positions and each take two million a year in salary. Even without performance bonuses, I figured it was twice what any reasonable party might pay. I thought it was a no-brainer."

"But not everybody agreed?"

"Three of us voted to take it. Eric said no. We tried to work it out. Instead we ended up in a screaming match. Everybody got a lawyer. Eventually we bought him out. Then I had to go back to Von Becker and convince him to stick with the deal without one of our top underwriters."

I was beginning to see where this train wreck was headed.

"Von Becker said no problem, but he had to cut back on the up-front-cash part of the deal, am I right?"

Doug let out a long breath. "Right. From forty mil up front down to thirty. How the hell I didn't catch on right then."

"So he ended up buying a seventy-five-million-dollar company for thirty mil down and a promise. And in the meantime got control of a massive stream of new money coming in."

He nodded. "And the three of us used all of our savings plus the up-front money to buy out Eric, who still isn't speaking to me. Buddy, our younger boy, is his godson, by the way."

"How long did the honeymoon last?"

"About six months. Then there were delays opening up in the other markets. Then Von Becker wanted us to lower underwriting standards. Take on riskier loans. Speed up the foreclosure process. No more workouts with slow payers. Every goddamn day there was another e-mail with some directive that had all of us foaming at the mouth. Gunther, the other partner—Gunther Pratt—started getting stress migraines. David and I were drinking a good bit more than usual. And the tap was still on. I had one month where three hundred million came in. We had nowhere to put it."

"And Von Becker offered to park it for you."

"Right. One of his funds. He offered us a decent rate of return, so our earnings still looked good to investors. The plan was to keep buying loans and take it back out of the Von Becker account as needed. Only, money was still coming in faster than we could find new deals."

"Did investors know what was happening? That their money was actually sitting in Von Becker's account?"

"They knew. Some questioned it. If they didn't like it, I offered them their money back."

"Did they take you up on it?"

"Not one. But when Von Becker heard about what I'd done he threw a fit. Reamed me out. That's when I started to think we had a problem."

"But no proof."

"I kept telling myself he must be clean, otherwise the regulators would be all over him. He had auditors. The SEC had been over his books. I assumed that those guys were actually doing their jobs. I can't believe how stupid that makes me sound right now."

"So it comes down to who knew what when."

"Well, that's what the lawsuits are all about. Every penny we took in—I took in—is in limbo. When Von Becker got caught, it all fell apart. On paper, it looked like I was fronting for him—bringing in money and immediately moving it into his scam. The Feds took me out in handcuffs. They still don't know whether they're going to charge me or not. Every client I ever worked with sued me personally. All my money was tied up in Von Becker funds and I may never get a cent back. David and Gunther are still in the office every day, working to unwind all the notes. They brought Eric back to help out. They're still collecting salary at least, but Eric is the only one with any real money, though he's under investigation, too. Meanwhile, the bankruptcy trustees are on their backs every day to sell off the loans and raise cash. Goddamn bloodsuckers at Goldman offered them twenty cents on the dollar for the whole portfolio. Eric told them to stick it."

"What will the final damage be? Any idea?"

He pursed his lips and squinted one eye. "About a third of our cash was tied up in Von Becker funds. Our investors will lose seventy to eighty percent of that. That's a guess, but probably a good one. My partners will hang tough. They know they've got good paper. I would think they eventually unload it all at cost or close to it."

"So your investors may end up down twenty-five percent or so. That's bad, but not a disaster. I mean, you could lose that in a blue-chip stock fund."

"It depends on how our case turns out. If we're found guilty of conspiracy with Von Becker, all the money goes into the same pool and gets divided up according to whatever the trustee thinks is fair. In which case, our people lose three-quarters of whatever they put up. Or more."

"Do you think they've found all the money?"

He took a moment to think about it. "Everybody who worked with Von Becker is under investigation—except for those who have already cut a deal. And the only way to cut a deal is to tell the Feds everything. It would be hard to keep something hidden. If you don't give up all you know, you run the risk that the next guy rats you out to make his deal sweeter."

"Do I hear a 'however'?"

He grinned. "You do. Von Becker had more moves than Kobe Bryant. There could be millions—tens of millions—out there somewhere. Maybe more."

"Who would know?"

"Paddy told me you were working this angle. I'll tell you what I told him. I don't really know. In many ways we were very much on the outside of Von Becker's operation. The family might know, but that doesn't help you."

"All that money moving around, and you have no clue where it ended up?"

"None."

"If it would help your memory, I'm sure I can negotiate a finder's fee. It could solve a lot of your problems."

He was insulted. I could see it flash across his face—but the cold reality of his depression came right back. "My wife is one martini away from a nervous breakdown. I've lost every penny I ever made and still might have to spend some time behind bars. If I had any information that could turn our lives around, don't you think I would have already given it up?"

I believed him. He was "the Boy Scout."

"Sorry," I said. "I should go."

He didn't disagree.

The wine was long gone, and I had gotten as much as I was going to get.

I backed the car out of the drive and pulled up to the stop sign at the head of the lane. The sign sat in a little island where the road split, surrounded by wildflowers of some kind. Lying in the midst of the flowers was an empty bottle, as though someone had tossed it from a car. Joyriding teenagers, most likely, I thought. Only, I was in Sands Point. The empty was a fifth of Rémy Martin.

EVERETT ANSWERED VIRGIL'S private line—not a surprise. Everett was doing what he did best—embedding himself in the power structure camouflaged with sycophancy, and mopping up as much of the trickle-down cash as possible.

"It's Jason. I'm in a car. I don't want to go into too much depth on an open line, but I thought it was time to check in."

"Excellent. Virgil asked me just half an hour ago if I had heard from you."

"I've got an expert working on the cash transfers. He's very good. I've worked with him before. If there's anything there to find, he's the one to dig it out."

"Padding the bill already?" he said and snickered.

My gut response was to sink to his level and tell him to "shut the hell up and just do your job, asshole," but I managed to hold back.

"I'm paying him, Everett. Not the family. Not the firm. Me."

"Certainly. Understood. Only making a small joke." Everett could retreat better than anyone.

"Thursday and Friday, I made calls. Monday and today, I'm out interviewing people. I had personal business to take care of yesterday, so Virgil owes me for four days so far. I'll e-mail him a bill when I get home."

"Any news for me to report?"

"Early days. But from what I see, I would be surprised *not* to find a stash somewhere. Can I run some names by you?"

"Clients?"

"Just tell me whatever you know. Paddy Gallagher."

"He was in the office from time to time. I didn't trust him."

"Oh? Why not?"

"Just a feeling. And that gold ascot."

"Next. Douglas Randolph."

"What did he tell you?"

"Sounds like he and his partners got royally screwed."

"I would bet he knows something. He was their rainmaker."

"Hmm. One more. Rose-Marie Welk. I'm going to see her tomorrow."

"She and the other one. Tucker? The two clerks. They sat at his feet."

"Thanks, Everett. You've been a great help."

"I have? Well, good."

There is a level of self-adoration that is immune to sarcasm. Everett was there.

| 10 |

The dreams always came in those last moments of sleep, the cusp of wakening, when the hard border between dream and reality is softest and you wake up seconds later, prepared to believe almost anything.

There were two dreams. Recurring dreams.

The cognitive areas of the brain attempt to interpret sensory signals, which in turn are mere neurological oscillations, easily ignored when one is fully awake. How and why, then, do dreams recur? And why are they often so painful?

The first dream arrived three months after my release from prison. Three men are standing around my bed—one of them is my father, who explains, sadly, that a mistake was made by the prison officials, and that these two men are there to take me back to finish the three remaining years of my sentence. He is more upset than I and it is hard for him to speak. The two men with him, anonymous prison guards, are stone-faced yet patient. I try to comfort my father, a strategy that I am fully aware serves mainly to keep me from screaming in terror and despair. Then I dress quickly, give him a last hug, and head for the door. When the door opens, I wake up. Usually bathed in sweat, my throat hoarse from not screaming.

As unpleasant as it was, this dream was relatively easy to put aside as I started my day. The message from my subconscious was clear. I didn't want to go back. And as long as I lived a life on the straight and narrow—and kept my P.O. happy—I would not go back. By the time I finished my shave and shower, the dream was behind me. At least until the next time it returned.

That morning, I had the other dream. The one that left me fearful, angry, and guilty all day.

The Kid and I are standing on a flat, gray plain beneath a solid gray sky. There is no horizon. Water—seawater, plain green and smelling of salt and marine life—begins to swirl around our feet. The Kid is, at first, thrilled, and kicks and splashes. I am concerned. The Kid senses my growing anxiety and looks up at me. The water is already higher, up to his knees. He begins to grunt, then tries to run. The water is higher, almost to his waist, and he staggers. I grab for him and lift him up. For once he doesn't fight it. He clings to me, his legs wrapped around my torso, his arms around my neck. I can feel his warmth and his heart beating against my chest. For a moment I can luxuriate in his closeness, but the water is now up to my waist and still rising. Without moving, I am able to see all around us—a full 360-degree view—and a dark line has appeared at the horizon. It is approaching and growing in size. It is a great circular wall, and as it gets closer, I realize that the water is rising because of the encroaching barrier. The water is now at chest level. Though I have never been much of a swimmer, I am not afraid of water. I can float. Eventually the wall will arrive and I will float to the top and escape. But I can't float while holding the Kid. He is small for a six-year-old, with his mother's lean genes, but he now feels like a bag of rocks. He is frightened, tense, heavy. He has identified our mutual problem and is clinging tenaciously to my neck. The water rises up over my mouth and I kick upward. We both gasp for breath— and sink back down. Panic sets in. I kick again and again, and each time the water is higher, our opportunity to grab for air less. The Kid can't swim, not even float. If I break his hold on my neck, he will die. If I don't, we will both die. I reach for his arms and pull, but whether to abandon him or not, I cannot say for certain.

I woke up with a sobbing gasp, feeling a rush of vomit burning at the back of my throat. The ambiguity was enough to eat me alive. My mind demanded to know whether I had left my child to drown, and, at the same time, recoiled in horror from the thought. That's how the dream always ended. That's how I started the day.

Skeli had been there the second time I had the dream, a pitch-black Friday morning in January. I sat up, kicked the blankets away, and swung my feet to the floor. My claustrophobia kicked in immediately, so I got up and went into the living room. I stared down at Broadway until my breathing began to quiet.

"Are you all right?" she whispered.

I had not heard her rise. I let her put her arms around me and hug me from behind—her breasts pressed into my back, her hair nestled against my neck.

"Thank you. I'm better. That feels good."

"Come back to bed. It's early."

I turned my head and gently kissed her cheek. "Not yet."

"I'm freezing."

So was I, now that she brought it to my attention.

"Come," she said, taking my hand.

We lay side by side, her arm roped around mine, and stared at the ceiling as I told her about the dream. She listened all the way through, then stroked my cheek with her finger.

"Close your eyes. Go back there. Into the water."

I did. It was too easy.

"Now imagine an ending where you both live. Relax and let your mind play it out. Watch it happen, like it's a movie."

I imagined the water warmer. It rose over us and we both relaxed into it. The Kid stopped fighting and let himself become the water. And as he relaxed, he became less heavy. I could no longer feel the sand beneath my feet; we rose up on one breath all the way to the top of the wall. And when we looked over, there was a world of color on the other side. I helped him over and we were free.

I took a long, shuddering breath. "Thank you." It had helped.

Skeli nuzzled my neck. "You're welcome."

I kissed her forehead.

"Mmm," she said. "Now go make the coffee."

The dream had returned three times since, and each time I swallowed my bile, lay down, and rewrote the ending. Then I started the day. I got up and reminded myself to talk to Carolina about bleaching the Kid's sheets again. I checked to see if we were running out of Cheerios. White bread. How could we always be low on ghastly white bread? I never ate it. Did Heather? The dream sank back into the unconscious. The fear and anger faded, but the shame remained. The guilt. It clung like a parasite, sapping my energy, feasting on my spirit. I could walk and talk and make the coffee and get the Kid his breakfast and take him to school and read to him and play games and wrap him in a sheet that night, but through it all I carried the knowledge that some part of me, some deep part of my psyche, some aspect that I never wanted to see again, was capable of something unforgivable.

| 11 |

here's no money. You're all dreaming."

Rose-Marie Welk had agreed to let me come interview her, but she made no bones about it—there was nothing to say.

She was one of two clerks who had worked directly for Von Becker—fabricating the customer documents that maintained the smoke screen of his scam. The other clerk, Ben Tucker, had refused to talk to me at all. "I know nothing," he had said before hanging up the phone. I couldn't blame him—either of them—as they'd each served six months in federal prison.

We were sitting in the screened-in back porch of Rose-Marie's house in East Rockaway, a block off Atlantic Avenue on a street of once-identical homes, now differentiated with fifty years of added colors, porches, stoops, dormers, and lawn statuary ranging from pink flamingos to the Blessed Mother. The devastation of Hurricane Sandy had not reached this far. Mr. Welk brought lemonade in a pitcher, making an awkward attempt at playing the good host. Then he sat in stony silence while his wife and I talked.

"The lawyers asked me this over and over. It's just not possible. For the love of Mike, the man only got caught because he ran out of money. If he'd had money stashed away, wouldn't he have used it? I mean, to keep the thing going?"

Mrs. Welk looked more than a few years older than her husband, but otherwise they could have been sister and brother in their early fifties, both a few pounds over-weight, with big hands and large features on small frames. The house showed no signs of ever having been inhabited by children, and I didn't ask.

"Maybe he saw the end coming," I said.

"Oh, he saw it all right. Benny and I heard him in his office talking to himself, crying, slamming things around. He knew for months."

"But he never said anything?"

"You're as bad as those SEC people. Benny and I weren't his friends. He didn't confide in us. He told us to prepare reports and we did it."

"But you also made wire transfers. Offshore. Couldn't there be some stash somewhere?"

She looked up to heaven for patience. "I've been home six days. And this is the third time I get to answer the same questions. Sure, it's possible. Any fantasy you want to come up with is possible. Mr. Von Becker was moody, paranoid, and very secretive. But is it likely? I don't think so. You're all wasting your time."

"Who else has been here?"

"That creepy guy from the SEC. I forget his name. He left his card."

She made a move to stand up and look for it, but I waved her back down.

"Please, please, don't go to any trouble. I'm sure I wouldn't know him anyway. I'm just curious. The other person?"

"Oh, well, he was very nice. Mr. Castillo, I think."

Mr. Welk nodded.

"He was Spanish," she said.

"Puerto Rican," her husband spoke.

She shrugged. "I guess. He said if I needed any help getting resettled, I should just give him a call." She looked to her husband. "Help," she said with a disgusted sigh. "I had all of my money in Mr. Von Becker's fund." Then she gave a sad laugh. "He offered matched contributions to me and Benny. Every dollar I put into his fund, the company matched it. Ha! We thought we were lucky. Walter spent all of his savings on my lawyer. We now have two mortgages, no pensions, not a dime in the bank, and I'm an ex-con with the kind of clerical skills that aren't worth much outside of Wall Street."

Walter took her hand. "But we don't need help," he said simply.

She looked him in the eyes and nodded firmly. "That's what we told him."

"Did he say what his connection was to Von Becker?"

"Oh, he was a client," she said. "Mr. Von Becker always took his calls, and if he was out and missed a call, he'd get right back. A very big client, I would guess. He was very polite."

This was intriguing. I didn't remember a Castillo on the lists I had received from Everett.

"Did he happen to leave a card?" I said.

Rose-Marie looked to her husband again, as though to jog her memory. He shook his head.

"No. I think I'd remember," she said.

No leads, merely a hint of mystery. A polite Puerto Rican. Or Spaniard.

"If you think of anything else . . ." I let the request hang in the air between us.

She shook her head vigorously, as though trying to clear the cobwebs once and for all. "I spent six months up in Danbury and it put ten years on me, Mr. Stafford. I don't know where Mr. Von Becker stashed anything, and I would have a hard time believing it if you stuck my nose in it."

Mr. Welk showed me out.

| **12** |

Saturday morning—yoga.

As with anything new, or out of the normal routine, the Kid had expressed extreme reluctance to try yoga. According to his very expensive Park Avenue doctor, he needed to develop core strength and improve his balance and coordination. Heather and I had then explained to the Kid why yoga would be good for him— a remarkably dumb waste of time on our part and a violation of my father's first rule of parenting—"It tastes like bacon" always beats "It's good for you." But his resistance evaporated at the first class. He was good at it, and he had fun. Two months later, he had graduated out of the special-needs class and was now the star pupil—in my unbiased opinion—of the fours-fives. Mainstream fours-fives.

Tino drew appraising sidelong stares from the group

of mothers gathered in the waiting room outside the small gym. Those women with more acute gaydar turned their attention from Tino to me—in questioning re-appraisal.

"I think a couple of the women over there are ready to volunteer to help you with your reparation therapy."

Tino looked over at them and smiled. "It's been tried before," he murmured. "It didn't take."

We were the only males present—Angie and her mother were having a lie-in before heading out to catch a matinee. Most of the mothers, upon releasing their children to the care of the yogi's assistants, had immediately broken into groups of two or three and begun exchanging information and opinions on schools, doctors, and after-school arts, sports, and music programs—D-day was planned with less information. It was all a world that the Kid would experience only on the periphery, like an aberrant comet that circles the same sun but rarely crosses the path of any other heavenly body. Nevertheless, I took mental notes—just in case. They managed to conduct these conversations while simultaneously text-messaging nonstop so that I wondered about the future crash of the medical insurance industry, done in, sometime in the next decade, by the tsunami of cases involving crippling tendinitis of the thumbs.

The instructor called the class to order, and everyone's attention shifted to the wide observation window. Cell phones disappeared, and conversations were cut short, or continued in a hushed, reverent whisper.

Sometime later, Tino leaned to me and said, "You

think anybody would notice if I went over and slapped that boy silly?"

The boy in question insisted on making fart noises every time the class went into Stretching Puppy.

"I like the redhead," I answered. A strawberry-haired girl in pink unitard meandered around the room, following some random route. She had a blissful smile on her face that transformed into evil-looking anger when one of the two assistants approached her. They each tried twice to get her to settle down and do the exercises, but she was obviously much happier when they left her alone.

"Too cute. And I've got a dozen clients back home who would name me in their wills if I could give them hair like that."

"I think that's her mother." I gestured with a flick of the eye to a silky-haired redhead across the room. She was wearing jeans just a tad too tight for what Skeli would have called her "Kardashian hips."

"Ooooh." Tino winced. "Brazilian. That is so bad for you. I won't do them."

Brazilian? "How can you tell?"

Tino looked at me questioningly for a moment, then burst into laughter. The women looked over briefly, then went back to adoring their progeny.

"Not a bikini wax. A blowout."

"Ah," I said, feeling proud of my deductive powers. "A hair treatment."

"You slap enough chemicals on a head of hair and you can just about make it do anything. Stand up, lay down, roll over, or sing Christmas carols in July." He gave the month the Deep South accent on the first syllable. "But that doesn't mean it's actually good for you."

"The price of fashion?"

"I have a friend in L.A. I visit sometimes. He's an orthopedic surgeon out there. Anyway, we were walking along Rodeo one afternoon, and as we're passing Jimmy Choo's, Laurence stops to stare at the shoes. Well, Laurence is not like that, if you know what I mean. So I teased him about it, saying wouldn't he rather be looking at the new line at Timberland."

I chuckled politely.

"Laurence just smiled and said, 'Tino, it's shoes like these that paid for the house in Provence and the first-class tickets to get me there and back every summer.' Shut my mouth."

The instructor, a children's nurse from Roosevelt Hospital with a ready smile, stopped next to the Kid, bent down and spoke to him quietly. He grinned. What could she have said?

Tino followed my eyes and looked out toward the Kid.

"He looks just like a cat, doing that."

The Kid's animal poses were his best—of course. "They call it Halloween Cat. I think he's proud of himself. If you're lucky, you might get to see his Cobra."

The class ended with the Fallen-Down Tree. The Kid lay flat on his back, totally relaxed—without having to be bound in a tightly wrapped sheet. I didn't have the words to explain to Tino how proud I felt.

"My yoga teacher tells us that's the hardest pose of all," Tino said.

"You have no idea how hard it is for him to relax—anytime. It's like his whole body is constantly on guard—waiting for something bad to happen."

Tino sighed. "Too bad Angie couldn't come."

Part of me—the part that suffered through cringe-worthy morning dreams—wanted to point out that Angie *could* very easily have come, but that she *chose* to sleep late instead. But another voice told me to listen to Tino and learn. It was too bad. For Angie. She was the loser for not having come. The Kid wouldn't have noticed or cared. My opinion didn't much matter to anyone but me. But Angie had missed the chance to see her son do something wonderful—and I found that I could spare a touch of sympathy for my ex.

| 13 |

The façade of the Merchants and Traders Club on Fifth Avenue was as shy and understated as the Metropolitan, two blocks south, was ornate and built to impress. There was a simple awning out front, facing the side street, covering an oak-paneled entryway leading to double-hung dark oak doors. Through the doors, there was a cloakroom to the left, a concierge post on the right, and a dark and comfortable bar beyond. It might have been the entrance of an older steak house.

I gave the concierge my name and the name of the member I was visiting, Tulio Castillo.

The invitation had been waiting for me at the desk at the Ansonia that morning. Just a handwritten note on club letterhead. I would finally get to meet the Welks' mystery man. Von Becker's "big client."

"May I ask if you are carrying a cell phone, sir?" The

concierge wore a starched wing collar and tails. "Cell phones and laptops are not allowed in the main rooms of the club."

"Thanks," I said. I turned it off and handed it to him. He displayed a white linen envelope and, taking out a black Montblanc fountain pen, wrote my name in perfect Catholic grade-school cursive. Then he carefully tucked the phone in and sealed the envelope.

"If you would care to have a drink while you wait," he gestured, "I will announce you."

I sat down at the bar and ordered a club soda. The bartender looked like he had never told a joke—and didn't want to hear one.

There were still one or two bubbles in my glass when an ancient waiter in a dark red jacket whispered my name and gestured for me to follow him. We passed through a curtained archway beside the bar and stepped into a marbled, two-storied hallway. Directly in front of us was a curving staircase that could have held the Mormon Tabernacle Choir with room left over for Scarlett O'Hara to sweep down and make her entrance to the ball. Golden light glowed from a pair of giant chandeliers.

"This way, Mr. Stafford," my guide whispered. Our steps echoed through the hall as he led me past the staircase to a small wooden door. He held the door for me, and I stepped into an elevator. He joined me, pushed a button, and the elevator slowly rose. Brass plaques on the panel listed the floors—Dining Hall, Conference Center, Library, Gymnasium, Dormitory A, Dormitory B, and Penthouse.

"Dormitory?" I whispered. Whispering seemed to be the preferred method of communication in those environs.

The old man smiled and gave an almost imperceptible shrug. "A euphemism. The rooms are all mini-suites. Quite nice."

"And the Penthouse?"

"The members' bar. It looks out over the park. Very popular at sunset."

We lurched to a stop and the door slid open.

The Library.

Bookshelves climbed three walls twenty feet or more into the air, where a narrow balcony ran around the room and a second set of shelves soared up another ten feet. The fourth wall had a row of windows facing Central Park, which were heavily draped in gauze. Forty watts or so of natural light made its way through. The rest of the room was lit only with low, green-shaded lamps that sat on the desks and small tables around the room or floor lamps that threw a cone of light on dark leather armchairs. Somewhere up in the dim stratosphere was a mural that, as near as I could tell, depicted the history of world trade from pre-Roman Silk Road travelers to the New York Stock Exchange. On the wall above the windows were portraits of prosperous-looking men in suits who all stared down on us with mildly disapproving looks.

A few of the armchairs were occupied by third-generation descendants of the men in the portraits. Gray-haired men in gray suits who examined us over their newspapers as the old man led me down the long room. The room was so big it probably had its own zip code.

The carpet, the drapes, the furniture, and probably the books as well, all sucked up sound. I thought that if I yelled at the top of my lungs I'd have a hard time hearing myself. Sets of eight-foot-tall bookshelves, strategically placed, created a warren of semi-private alcoves.

Tulio Botero Castillo was sitting in one of those alcoves.

The man was in his mid-thirties, impeccably dressed in a fawn-colored suit, white long-collared shirt and handkerchief, and a solid red tie, the color of fresh blood. You could have sliced sashimi with the crease in his pants. He was startlingly handsome, with dark, wavy hair, cheekbones like ax blades, black eyes with lashes so long they were almost feminine, and a nose too long to be pretty but large enough to give character.

"Mr. Stafford?" He rose with an actor's grace and shook my hand. "Please." He gestured to a neighboring armchair. "Eamon," he said to the waiter. "Can we get something for Mr. Stafford?" He addressed me again. "Coffee? A drink?"

"Water would be nice," I said. "Thank you, Eamon."

"And coffee for me, if you please," Castillo said.

Eamon smiled again and disappeared.

We sat, and he gave me a long appraising look. It wasn't rude; he wasn't judging. He was just gathering information.

"Does anyone ever come here to read a book?" I asked.

He laughed. "I don't think so. They probably bought them by the yard. Is this your first time here?" The voice was accentless, the result of much practice, I was willing to bet, but his rhythms and pitch betrayed his Latin roots.

I had been introduced to a senator at a black-tie affair at the Metropolitan Club, and been trounced at backgammon at the Harvard Club. But New York has more private clubs than elementary schools. Despite the name, Merchants and Traders, I had never known a trader who belonged.

"First time. Quite handsome. It's certainly well hidden."

"The club claims its roots are in Renaissance Florence. A bit of comic fiction, with a hint of truth. You see, the Church forbade lending at interest in those times, and it was only the Jews and other outcasts who were allowed to profit from what we think of as modern banking. They were the merchant bankers. The word 'bank' itself comes from the Old Italian word for 'bench.' The moneylenders would place a bench in the piazza and sit there conducting their business."

"And the traders?"

"Bankers need liquidity. If they become overextended, they may need to sell, or find partners to share the risk. The traders were the risk takers and the intermediaries, as necessary to the system as the letters of credit and futures contracts they traded. But they too were looked down upon. They were gamblers, living by their wits. Not fit company."

Seven hundred years and not much had changed.

"So the club dates to the 1400s?" I let a touch of incredulity show.

"No," he said and laughed politely, "1901. The first members were all the outcasts who were not allowed to join the clubs with the Vanderbilts, Carnegies, and Morgans. Jews and other olive-skinned men. Speculators, private lenders, merchant bankers."

I looked back up at the portraits on the nearby wall. I had missed it at first because the men were all dressed in period suits, no different in style or form from any group of early-twentieth-century men of business. But looking again, I could see the faces, the skin, the eyes, the hair. There wasn't a single Anglo-Saxon present.

"But times have changed, Mr. Castillo." I was enjoying myself. He was a bit in love with himself, and did like to hear himself talk, but he was interesting. Intelligent, cultured, and engaging.

"Maybe." He tilted his head to one side. "Maybe not so much."

"And so what are you? A merchant or a trader?"

Eamon reappeared at that moment and placed a silver tray on the end table. A bottle of Evian, a glass of ice, and a linen napkin for me. Then he poured the coffee.

"Will there be anything else, Mr. Castillo?" he murmured.

"Possibly some privacy, Eamon. Can you help us?"

"No one will bother you gentlemen." He backed out of the little alcove and took up position just out of earshot.

Castillo and I watched him take up his sentry role.

"Is this all part of the service here?"

"Many deals have been struck in this room. Many secrets shared. If anyone strays inadvertently to this end of the library, Eamon will gently encourage them to sit somewhere else. They will understand."

"So, is this a good time to ask . . . why the invitation?"

"You are impatient?"

"Eager."

"Touché." He smiled. "Then I begin. All this week I hear your name. Friends, business acquaintances, even some of my employees. They all think I should know about this Jason Stafford. I hear you are looking for something. Our interests there may coincide."

"I'm no longer making any secret of it—everyone I talk to seems to know my business. I've been hired to see if I can locate some of the missing assets from the Von Becker mess. So far, all I've got is a list of angry people."

"Yet you keep looking. You are here. You do not give up. You are persistent. That is an admirable trait."

I sipped the Evian. It tasted like water.

"Tulio Botero Castillo," I said. "Born January 8, 1975, in Bogotá, Colombia. Named for an archbishop. You're the second son. They shipped you off to the States when you were still in grade school. Dalton. Princeton. You started the MBA program at Harvard, but switched to economics. Finished a doctorate in three years. Your dissertation was on the effects of black markets on productivity as a drag on the multiplier effect."

"I prefer 'underground economy.' 'Black markets' has more negative connotations."

I continued. "The family was very big in coffee production and export. Now banking and politics. They've been investigated a dozen times or more for ties to the cocaine and heroin trade—in both Colombia and Honduras—and cleared, but the smell never seems to go away."

"Congratulations. You can Google."

I'd hoped to shake him just a little. Let him think I knew things. He wasn't even mildly annoyed.

He leaned forward and spoke in a low voice. I leaned in. We were close enough to kiss.

"I have read quite a bit of your history as well. I have done my research. I would not wish to hire you without a full background check."

I sat back. "I'm already employed."

"Your employer is unreliable."

I had to smile. Everybody was telling me that.

"I'm here. I'm listening."

"Good. Then we may begin. My family are bankers— facilitators. We do not produce commodities, though we often act as agent in their distribution. It is a simple business model. But some of these products have unique problems in distribution and payment."

"We're not talking about coffee now, are we?"

"You are offended?"

"I want nothing to do with the drug trade, Mr. Castillo. I'm surprised that your research led you to think I would."

"Mr. Stafford, do not take too much comfort from what you see as the moral high ground. For almost one hundred years, your government has tried to limit the amount of drugs entering this country. They have spent trillions of dollars. And the end result is that more drugs pass through your borders than ever before. Yet your politicians still expect a solution from the supply side. Stop the Afghani or Peruvian farmer from producing! Arrest the importer. The distributor. When will your countrymen accept that the problem is one of demand? Reduce demand and the market goes away. But somehow such a voice in your debate is considered to be 'soft' on drugs. What is 'soft' is the rigor of intellectual honesty."

"People aren't murdering each other over coffee."

"Do you mean the Mexicans? My Honduran clients? My own countrymen not that long ago? Who sells them their weapons, Mr. Stafford? Or do you mean your own Bloods and Crips? Why do you expect desperately poor men with no other hope of even a marginal existence to behave more ethically than your average American politician? That feeling of moral superiority is nothing more than arrogance and ignorance."

"Sounds like I've struck a nerve."

He stopped, took a deep breath, and forced a smile. "Perhaps so."

"I'm not equipped to debate these big issues. I just don't want anything to do with drugs. If that's what you want to talk to me about, then we're done."

"Give me a few minutes more of your time. What I have to say may yet intrigue you."

I nodded and forced myself to sit back.

"I mentioned unique problems. Obviously, delivery is

a problem. It is what gets all the press. But an even more vexing issue is simple cash management. It is a cash business at the retail level—which is appropriate for such an ephemeral product. But when you move up the supply chain, the dollar amounts become quite problematic. Do you know how much space ten million dollars takes up? How heavy it is? It can be burned, marked, stolen, or counterfeited. Any cash transaction as small as five thousand dollars must be reported to your government. If you attempted to deposit a million dollars in cash into your bank account, you would find yourself and every aspect of your life under a very unpleasant microscope. You see the problem?"

I nodded again.

He took a sip of his coffee and grimaced. "The richest country in the world, and yet you insist upon drinking hot brown water instead of coffee." He put the cup down and shifted position. "Tell me, are you familiar with bearer bonds, Mr. Stafford?"

Everyone on Wall Street is a specialist to some degree—the world of modern finance is too complex to survive otherwise. My expertise was in foreign exchange. But some knowledge of certain basics of other markets is necessary, if for no other reason than to pass the licensing exams. I knew what a bond was, and in my first investigative job out of prison, I had quickly relearned the basics when I was hired to investigate the book of a recently deceased young trader.

A bond is essentially a contract between the issuer—which could be a government or a government agency, or a corporation looking to borrow money through the sale of securities—and the buyer or investor, who might represent a mutual or pension fund, an insurance company, or even an individual. Bonds represent debt, as opposed to a stock, where ownership passes hands. The contract usually states that the issuer agrees to pay some rate of interest to the investor for a certain number of years, and then to return the principal. It gets more complicated quickly—with collateralized bonds, senior and subordinated debt, insured bonds, variable rates of interest or maturity, and so on. I did not pretend to understand much of that. It wasn't the math that gave me trouble, it was the overwhelming details of each particular bond. U.S. Treasury bonds are near commodities, but most of the millions of different bonds that are out there are closer to unique packages of cash flows. Each one has its own story.

Bearer bonds comprise a whole other subset, which lives by its own rules. The sum total of my knowledge of them had been learned in a single terminally boring lecture in B-school many years ago, by a professor so consumed with jealousy that in a few years we would all be earning in a year what it took him a decade to earn, that he managed not to notice that half the class was asleep.

Unlike other bonds, and most stocks these days, which are all registered and exist only as micro-bytes in a computer, bearer bonds exist only on paper, in physical form. They are printed on heavy paper in some official-appearing font like the document you get with a set of commemorative coins. Only, the document itself is worth a lot more than a bunch of silver coins from the 1980 Moscow Olympics. And they come in large denominations. Very large.

Once upon a time, in the ancient days of finance—the first half of the twentieth century—all bonds were bearer bonds. When it was time for an interim interest payment to be redeemed, the owner of the bearer bond clipped off a dated coupon and presented it at a bank for payment, similar to a check. The bank made sure that the coupon was legitimate—not a forgery, nor the obligation of some defunct entity, like the Confederate States of America—and paid out in cash. The wrinkle was that the bank had no obligation to determine that the holder of the coupon was the legitimate owner. Whoever had possession of the bond could redeem it for cash. This anonymity makes them particularly valuable for anyone who needs to move large amounts of money without leaving a trail for regulators, the IRS, or the police. Bearer bonds are not so much investments as they are a proxy for cash. The U.S. government stopped issuing them in the early 1980s and the IRS penalized U.S. corporations that issued them. They issued them anyway. The savings in interest payments were worth paying the penalty.

"Didn't the Treasury do away with bearer bonds? Thirty years ago?" I said.

"It is true that the U.S. Treasury no longer issues bearer bonds, but it is still possible to redeem one. It is legal to own them. But the paperwork involved removes the cloak of anonymity. Anyone who presents a bearer bond for payment in a United States bank must provide identification. The transaction is reported to various government bodies which are on the lookout for tax evasion, money laundering, organized crime, terrorism."

"But outside the U.S.?" I said.

"Exactly." He smiled at the good pupil. I was being schooled again. "In certain money centers around the world, bearer bonds are used for transactions daily wherever anonymity is of concern."

"The drug trade again," I said. "Not interested."

"And would it surprise you," he continued, ignoring my comment entirely, "to learn that many of the issuers of these bearer bonds are the foreign subsidiaries of A-rated American corporations?"

I wasn't surprised.

"They are also users of bearer bonds," he went right on. "How else could they pay for Iranian oil? Any other transaction would be traceable. It is not just the arms and drug trades that benefit. How better to convince a reluctant bureaucrat in a third-world country that your company's proposal is superior to any other? Cash is bulky and awkward."

I held up my hands. "Please. I am convinced. There is corruption in the world. What I would like to know is, where did Von Becker hide his billions? Bearer bonds? Is that what you're saying?"

Castillo made a steeple of his fingers and pursed his lips in thought. "I don't know," he finally said. "But I have an idea. I am being quite honest with you, Mr. Stafford, because I think our interests coincide. Von Becker was more than a little familiar with the product."

If Castillo was going to resort to telling the truth, I was sure he had something to hide.

"My family did a considerable amount of business with William Von Becker—business that benefited mutual clients."

Money laundering.

"From time to time, a client would need to purchase or divest of some bearer bonds. Mr. Von Becker was most helpful. Money would be wired into one of the Von Becker banks and a meeting would be arranged. Lawyers—or couriers—for both parties would meet in Zurich and make the exchange."

"Always in Zurich?"

"Mr. Von Becker insisted. The clients did not mind. They used couriers if they wanted the bonds moved elsewhere."

"Where did they meet? At a bank? I assume the certificates were kept in a safe-deposit box or a vault."

Castillo grinned. "A meeting in a bank would defeat the purpose of using bearer bonds. The meeting would no longer be anonymous. If both parties had to enter the vault, they would have to sign in, show identification. There would be a paper trail. Impossible. Therefore, the meeting would always take place at a café. Across the street from the bank. Away from the surveillance cameras."

In a world of computers, cell phones, and instant access to money, information, or communication, Von

Becker had relied on the anonymity of the sidewalk café to conduct his business.

"So only the lawyer would go into the bank vault," I said. "No one could ever connect him to the other courier."

"Exactly. There must be no trail—no connections. And the system worked well right up until last fall. On the day that William Von Becker surrendered to the Feds, one of my clients had initiated a purchase of one hundred million dollars of these bonds. The money was deposited and wired, but the authorization for the physical transfer was never made. No doubt, Mr. Von Becker was preoccupied that day with the details of his arrest and he never made the call to Switzerland."

"No one else could handle this?"

"Mr. Von Becker did not normally trust anyone else to make the arrangements."

That fit with what everyone else had told me about him.

"My clients," he went on, "tell me that they made some early attempts to contact other family members, but failed. They did not share the details with me."

"So your client was out a hundred million dollars? Was that a normal-sized trade? How bad was he going to miss it? Enough to have Von Becker executed in jail?"

"It was far from normal. But killing him would have been counterproductive. As long as he was alive, he would, at some point, be able to make the necessary arrangements. He was being held at the MCC downtown. It was easy to get messages in or out. It was only a matter of time."

"So you believe he killed himself."

"Out of shame? That's what the family is trying to spin. No. I think one of the sons had him killed."

"Why?"

"Because they found out what he was doing and wanted to keep the bonds for themselves."

Which meant I could be working for a murderer.

"That's an interesting theory. What about contacting the lawyer directly? They must have had some contingency plan."

"Approaches were made—and rejected. The lawyer—Herr Serge Biondi of the firm Kuhn Lauber Biondi in Zurich—was an old man and somewhat rigid in his ways. He insisted we wait until word came from his client."

"But Von Becker died."

"Well, actually, the old man died first."

"That is a very ugly coincidence."

"The newspapers said it was a heart attack." Castillo removed an invisible speck of dust from his sleeve and flicked it to the floor. "He was eighty and lived a sedentary life."

"And since then? It's been more than six months."

"The chain is broken. My clients grow impatient. So do yours, I imagine. That's why you were hired. Somewhere there is a key or a code. Somewhere those bonds are waiting to be found. Approaches to the bank have been made, but without that code—or key—there is little hope of recovery."

"And if I find them?"

"My clients want only what is rightfully theirs. And

they will be generous in rewarding the person who returns their goods."

"And if I don't find them? What then?"

"They are already impatient. They will find other means."

There was no doubt in my mind that Castillo knew much more than he had told me—but whether the information would have helped me or not, I had no idea. There were still people I had not yet interviewed and there was no guarantee that finding Castillo's money would lead me to Von Becker's, but he was right, our interests might yet coincide. His confidential manner suggested that he assumed that I was as big a crook as he. I didn't like that, but I was used to it. I thought I could handle it.

"What's the name of the bank?" I said.

He relaxed back into the chair and smiled. "Welcome on board, Mr. Stafford."

Schooling began in earnest.

| 14 |

FBI Agent Marcus Brady had lost some weight and gained some gravitas in the eight months since I had last seen him. He'd saved my life and I had given his career a boost. Thanks to his efforts, and my engineering, he had been instrumental in wrapping up a multiple murder case that covered three jurisdictions. The powers that be had rewarded him with a transfer out of forensic accounting.

"So there I was," he said, smiling coldly.

There's an old trader's joke—What's the difference between a fairy tale and a trader's story? A fairy tale begins "Once upon a time" and a trader's story starts "So there I was."

"There you were," I answered.

We were sitting in his office at the Federal Building downtown—a windowless walk-in closet holding a desk, two chairs, and some filing cabinets. It was worse than my old cell, which was bigger and at least had a window. Of course, Brady didn't have to share the space with a roommate with gang tats.

"And I'm scrolling through surveillance tapes of the entrance to the Merchants and Traders Club . . ."

"Our tax dollars at work," I said.

"And, whoa! Who do I see? An old friend . . ."

"Acquaintance."

". . . arriving for a meeting with one Tulio Castillo, the main subject of a major interagency investigation. And I think, there must be some very good reason that a guy with almost two and a half years to go on his parole would risk being seen with a bad guy like that."

"You'd think."

"So I figured I'll ask. It can't hurt."

The FBI seemed to know my schedule. The two agents had been waiting outside the Ansonia when I got back from dropping the Kid at school. They had been polite but firm, offering me a choice. I could come downtown with them with the handcuffs on or off.

"Mr. Castillo invited me to come down and talk with him. Same way you did. Only he did it classier. Do I tell him what you and I talk about?"

"Suppose I put a wire on you and send you back?"

"Not a chance."

"Why not?"

"Because I have a strong aversion to being dead."

Brady chuckled. "I understand."

"Thank you."

"Shall we start over?"

"Old friends?"

"Reluctant allies?"

It was my turn to laugh. "Done. Who goes first?"

"You do."

There was never any question on that. "Okay, I've been hired by a wealthy New England family to recover some money."

"Who's this?"

"Just let me finish."

"Come on. I know you're not working for the Kennedys. Are these people connected?"

"You're way off base."

"If Castillo is teamed up with the Patriarca people, I need to know about it."

"Who?"

"The New England mob."

"Stop. Stop. Let me tell it." How was it that everyone I talked to knew who I was working for—except for the FBI?

"Get to the point."

"Castillo invited me to his club. Politely. He sent a card. We had a long chat, and he wants to hire me, too— to find the same money, which he says belongs to his client."

"Client!" Brady snorted.

"Do I get to tell this or do I get to go home?"

"Start from the top."

Everett Payne. Newport. The Von Becker family. Paddy. Douglas Randolph. The clerk, Rose-Marie.

"She says there is no stash, right? Wouldn't she know?"

"Not necessarily. What I'm beginning to see about Von Becker is that he was brilliant at keeping everyone in the dark. No one got to see the whole picture, only their little part in it. Maybe the other clerk knows something— but he's not talking. At least not to me."

"How did Castillo find you?"

"I don't know, but it feels like everyone knows what I'm supposed to be doing."

I filled him in on the whole conversation with Castillo. The bearer bonds. The lawyer, Biondi. The Swiss bank.

"So you're working for him?"

"No. I told him that if I come up with something that looks like it belongs to him, I'll let him know. That's it. He's run out of ideas, though he gave me one lead. If anything comes of it, I'll let you know."

"You're in trouble. Way out of your depth."

"I promised him nothing. Zip."

"Did he say who this client is?"

"No."

"Did you ask?"

"I don't want to know."

"Well, I can guarantee they know who you are. And you don't want that. That is not a good thing. It is a bad thing."

"I've got nothing to do with any of that. I plan on staying squeaky clean and out of prison."

"There's scarier things than going back to jail. Let me tell you a little story. You need to know who you're dealing with. Then I'm going to bring some other agents in here. They'll want to hear your story—in triplicate—so get comfortable. And if you don't believe what I tell you, ask these guys. They've seen it all."

Brady's story was an eye-opener. When the U.S. and the Colombian government finally broke up the two big cocaine cartels, back in the late 1990s, they left a power gap at the top that still hadn't been filled. But they hadn't stopped the flow of drugs—there was just too much money involved. The remaining players—mostly the Mexicans, Guatemalans, and Hondurans—had rushed in to take over the distribution. And when the Taliban shut down the poppy growers in Afghanistan in 2000, the Central American gangs had seen a new growth opportunity—heroin. With considerably shorter distribution routes to the world's largest market, they were able to provide a product much closer to pure in a much shorter period of time. They captured market share. The profits they were raking in made the old Medellín and Cali cartels look like kids' lemonade stands in comparison.

But without centralization of the power structure, there was no way to maintain agreed-upon areas of influence. The drug war became a free-for-all. The violence ratcheted up. It wasn't just the Mexican border gangs that were out of control, killing one another, policemen, politicians, and innocent bystanders in a crazy bloodbath. Honduras had the highest per capita murder rate in the world. Guatemala was not much better. There no longer needed to be a reason to murder someone—terror was now the objective.

"Castillo is an aristocrat. His family has been at the

top of the food chain in Colombia since they arrived three or four hundred years ago. That makes him think he has some control over what these people do. He doesn't. They are very scary people and they now know your name. If you're not scared, you're an idiot."

"I'm not an idiot." Everyone was calling me an idiot.

"Good. Stay here."

He went out and returned a moment later with three members of the team—two from the DEA and Brady's senior agent. I started again from the beginning.

15

With Tino visiting friends out in Greenport for two days, I had been inveigled into escorting Angie and her mother to a Wednesday pre-matinee lunch at Sardi's. We were finishing our coffee, Mamma had just gone to "freshen up," and I was waiting for Angie to pick up the check.

We were "discussing" which show would be best for the Kid's first time in a Broadway theater the following weekend. It wasn't going well.

Angie had purchased four fifth-row orchestra tickets for Sunday afternoon to a show I considered to be wildly inappropriate for young children—and probably outright dangerous for my son. She had paid almost three times face for them—an extravagance made doubly painful by the fact that all of her money had once been mine.

I had Paddy's four vouchers for house seats to a

lighthearted 1920s musical revival with a book by P. G. Wodehouse and a plotline that could easily be followed by a golden retriever. It also featured an original Stutz Bearcat that rolled on stage at the end of the second act—a theatrical event guaranteed to put a rare smile on the Kid's lips.

The show Angie picked had been panned by every reviewer in the Northeast and was playing to sold-out crowds eight shows a week. Paddy's show had won raves and was covering costs, and if they made it through the summer, they had a good shot at keeping it running through the end of the year.

"Angie, I spend hours each week trying to keep him from biting people, and you want to take him to a fucking *vampire* show!"

The sound of the fricative *f* followed by the hard consonant caught the attention of the four matinee ladies at the next table. They did not look our way, but their antennae went up.

"It's a *love* story," Angie countered in an acid whisper that could easily have carried to the back of the house. "And I don't like that language."

Unless she was using it.

"Fine. I won't say 'vampire' again."

She actually smiled. It reminded me of how rare smiles had been when we were together.

"When did you turn into such a worrier?" she said in a more conciliatory voice. "All boys like vampires. He'll be fine."

I wasn't a worrier, I was a parent. The distinction was perfectly clear when you were a parent.

"The Kid doesn't like vampires—he doesn't know what they are. He knows about cars. If you don't want to see Paddy's show, that's fine. But can't you find something better for the Kid than this?"

"Mamma is dying to see it."

"So, take her! Tino and I will take the Kid to the zoo and meet up with you later. No problem." I thought I scored some points with the ladies across the aisle.

"Tino wants to see it, too."

Impossible. Tino had taste. "Challenge."

"Now, stop with this," she continued. "If the Kid doesn't like it, I'll bring him out at intermission and you can come pick him up."

My cell phone rang. I checked the screen. Skeli.

"I have to take this," I said.

Angie waved her hand in dismissal.

I had called Skeli three or four times every day since the disastrous graduation dinner, but I had not spoken to her. Her phone went straight to voice mail every time. After two days I stopped leaving messages, though I kept calling. I turned away from Angie and answered the phone.

"Please tell me this is not a butt-dial."

"How come you stopped leaving messages?"

"Nice to hear your voice," I said.

"Well?"

"Well?"

"How come you stopped leaving messages?"

Because I hated sounding so pitiful. "I'm not good at talking to machines."

"You're not alone, are you?"

I was not a natural dissembler, but having traded trillions over the phone in my time on Wall Street, I thought that my control over my telephone voice was one of my major strengths.

"I don't know why you would think that," I said.

Skeli burst out laughing. "Call me when you can. I want to take you to lunch tomorrow. Someplace special."

I hung up, feeling more than a touch better than I had a few minutes earlier. And possibly a touch more generous as well.

"Angie, I'm being a bear. Take the Kid to the show. I'll come, too, in case you need help."

"Thank you, boo," she said, looking up at me with a model's blank smile. "But it's sold out."

"I'm sure I can find one lousy scalper's ticket." For six or eight times face value.

"That will not be necessary. I can take him. This whole trip you have insisted upon watching over my shoulder whenever I am with the boy. I think I know my limitations, and don't need your constant reminding."

"It's not like that." It was exactly as she had called it. Good intentions—mine or hers—were not going to cut it. Try as I might, I was not prepared to trust her. And, I was sure, neither was the Kid.

"And I will have Mamma and Tino with me." Her voice ratcheted higher and louder. The four matinee ladies had given up all pretense and were watching us with an intensity usually reserved for *Real Housewives*.

"That's not the point." I let my voice top hers.

"No, Jason. The point is that you still don't trust me." She leaned forward, and I expected her to lower the volume. She didn't. "It was my intention to invite you to come to see me get my ninety-day chip. I thought you'd be pleased. Happy for me. Well, you can go fuck yourself, Jason."

I leaned across. We were almost touching. The two wolves were fighting in my head—the ones from the old Cherokee fable. The story where the wise old man tells about the good wolf and the bad wolf fighting inside all of us and the child asks which one will win and the old man says, "The one you feed." My angry wolf said, "You have got to be shitting me, Angie. Did you really expect me to fly halfway across the country to watch you pat yourself on the back? I've got a life! And you don't figure in it. And *that* is making me happy, thank you very much." But the wolf didn't say it out loud, and neither did I.

I tried feeding my good wolf. "Angie," I said out loud, "you have done a wondrous thing. I salute you. And I appreciate that you would ask me. But I can't do this. I'm not your pigeon. I'm not your buddy. We have a history and we have a son—and that's all it's ever going to be."

"You have never been there for me—when I needed you. Never." Her index finger threatened to pierce the table as she beat out the rhythm of her words.

To hell with the good wolf. "That is such BULL SHIT."

Whatever meager goodwill I had with the matinee

ladies was exploded. One of them began waving frantically for the check.

Further escalation would have required physical violence. We glared silently. Angie recovered first.

"You and I were finished years ago, but I didn't leave. You did." She was still angry but managed to sound calm and reasonable, as though this madness might actually make some sense—on her planet.

"Christ, Angie. I went to jail."

"Don't you hide behind that! You were gone long before then. As soon as I got pregnant, you were looking the other way. You were done with me. I was fat. Moody. I had hair growing in all kinds of new places, and you turned your back."

I was floored. It wasn't like that.

"No! I was afraid to touch you. You were growing like some perfect honeydew and I just knew if I did the wrong thing, it would be all twisted around backassed. I'd mess it up. How could you think it was you? Jesus, I'm sorry. I thought you were beautiful."

"Fat? Hairy?"

It was like dancing through a field of land mines.

"No! Glowing. With life. Twice over."

"You barely spoke to me."

I had been juggling a half-billion-dollar accounting fraud that required forty-eight-hour-a-day attention.

"Jesus Christ! I was a little preoccupied there. My goddamned career was swirling down the drain and I was looking at serious jail time and you were bent out of shape because I wasn't *chatting*! So I didn't have much to say when I came home and you ran on about the new nanny quitting. Again. So sue me. You want an apology? Fine. I am sorry. Shit. I can't tell you how many times I wished I had never started down that road. But, Christ, I spent two fucking years in federal prison for that shit. Isn't that enough? I thought that once I was out we could have found some way of putting everything back in place. Moving on. Together."

It was the longest, most heartfelt speech I had made to her—possibly in my life. And I wanted nothing in return but for her to release me from the guilt of making her unhappy. I got it. In spades.

Her face went rigid. "Thank you, Jason. Thank you very much."

An arctic blast swept through me.

"I came to New York to see my son, of course. But I also came here for my recovery. Step nine. Making amends. Whether you find it in your heart to forgive or not is not the point. The point is that I acknowledge my mistakes and apologize for them. Are you understanding me?"

Her voice was like toxic honey.

"Angie, please. None of this matters anymore. We both made mistakes. You don't owe me a thing." It was a feeble attempt to head off the inevitable. And it failed.

"No. I have to say this." She paused while the four women scraped back their chairs and filed out, all doing their best to ignore us—and failing.

I would gladly have traded the next ten minutes of my life for an hour in hell and called myself lucky.

"I told myself I was helping you," she continued. "That it was going to help us. Our marriage. That was a lie. I didn't know it was a lie, but I know it now. I did it to hurt you. That's the truth. Cheating never helps a marriage—it can only hurt. That's what I have to say. Oh, and, I'm sorry."

"Angie, I don't know anything about this. I'm not sure I want to know. When are we talking about? I hear the word 'cheating' and the brain starts shutting down."

"Oh, please. Are you saying you knew nothing about this? I cannot believe that."

I wanted it all to go away. And I wanted to hear it all. Who? How many? How often? Dates. Times. Concrete facts that I could look at and set into a logical, emotionless story line that would fit into a minor chapter of my life, so I could turn the page and make it go away and not hurt. I was wrong. It was all going to hurt.

"You had an affair. One?"

She was offended. "Of course one. What do you think I am?"

"I'm sorry. I don't mean to offend. I'm just trying to take this in. When was this?"

"Before we got divorced. I mean, of course; otherwise it wouldn't have been cheating, would it? While you were having your troubles. It only lasted a few months."

"Was this anyone I know?" Please say no. Please say no.

"That's why I was sure you knew. I thought it was all over your office. Jason, I didn't bring this up to go over all this old stuff, I just wanted to tell you that I was wrong in lying to myself about why I was doing it. That was wrong. I don't know what could have saved our marriage then, but my lies to myself certainly didn't help. So, I'm sorry."

The depth of Angie's faith in her pre-Copernican view of the universe always took me by surprise.

"Who?" There was no good reason for me to know. This was all ancient history. Three or four years in the past. I had thanked the gods of fortune a thousand times that Angie and I were through. On the other hand, once I knew the worst, there would be nothing left to hurt me.

"You really didn't know? David."

David who? I only knew one David. Impossible. "David Chisholm? My boss? You were screwing my boss? Are you kidding me? The guy had permanent halitosis from too much bad coffee." And she was right. The whole trading floor would have known.

I remembered a strange conversation with the head of the bank funding desk. It was strange because although we had always been friendly and gotten along, the story he related was a bit of gossip—almost salacious, but related in a tone of both confiding in me and comforting me. He told me that Dave, our mutual boss, had been approached by a young trader who was going through a hard time. In addition to losing money in the market, he was afraid that his wife was cheating on him. Dave patted him on the back, told him to take some time off to clear his head. Recommended a fishing camp in Belize where the guide had put him on to permit, snook, tarpon, and bonefish—all on the same day. Then, while the guy was away, Dave broke it off with the wife, because of course it was all true and Dave was the one doing the deed. He broke it off, but not until he got one last good ride. It was such an ugly story, I wasn't entirely sure why he had told it to me. Now I understood. He was telling me that Dave was a shithead and everybody knew it. If they also knew that I was one of his victims, it was no reflection on me. I silently thanked him. It was just what I needed.

"Angie. Here's my take on all this. Four years down the road and it hurts. No doubt. But what really gets me is how somebody as classy—as fucking *regal*—as you would be willing to spread 'em for a creep like that. I know for a fact that you weren't his first, and I would bet dollars to doughnuts you will not be his last. This asshole had the power to save my career—to stop me from digging the hole I buried myself in—and he sat back and watched and cashed the checks. He didn't *make* me run a fraud. I own up to my own goddamn mistakes. But he is about as low as they come, and you fell for his line, whatever it was. I hope it was all worth it. And if I never talk about this again, it will be way too soon."

"I never came with him." I thought she really believed she was offering me comfort.

"Are we still in step nine? Christ, put that on his tombstone. I don't want to hear it."

Mamma returned to the table and dropped into her chair.

"What a line to get in there! Y'all would not believe alla soaps an' lotions an' perfumes they have in the little girl's room. It's like the whole perfume counter from Abdalla's Department Store in one bitty room. Oh, listen to me talkin' 'bout Abdalla's. Showin' my age. How long has that store been gone? Years anyway." She beamed at us. "It is so nice seein' you two jawin' away together. Jes' like old times."

Yup. Just like old times.

| 16 |

The Caribbean Hurricane Relief Fund shared a renovated three-story brownstone in the East Forties, a bit too far from United Nations Plaza to be considered chic. There was a weathered brass plaque on the front of the building that listed the offices of the missions to the United Nations for three different countries, not one of which could I confidently place on a map. Beneath this plaque was a second, much newer, which read CARIBBEAN HURRICANE RELIEF FUND. A man in overalls and blue work shirt was in the process of removing it.

Pauline Sinha had once been a beautiful woman—she still had many of the requisite external components—blond hair, black eyes, full lips, a mocha complexion, and the right amount of curves in all the right places. But the heart and soul had been ripped out of her. I pegged her for a tired thirty-eight. She spoke perfect BBC English, with only an occasional *t* substituting for a *d*—a slip as cute as a lisp—but her tone was flat, as though she had just come to accept the news of a terminal diagnosis.

"Mr. Castillo has been a friend to the fund since the inception. If not for his introduction, I would not be speaking to you." She had been on my list for a week, but until I asked for Castillo's help, she had not returned any of my phone calls. So, despite the fact that I was still reeling from Angie's lunchtime revelations, I had to go through with the interview. "The fund's history with Von Becker has been covered extensively in the media. I don't know what I can addt."

There was that little slip at the end. If she had been able to summon up a smile to go with it, I might have fallen in love—if I weren't in a foul mood and ready to blame all women for the perfidy of one.

"I've been hired by the Von Becker family as an investigative consultant," whatever that was. "Mr. Castillo has shown an interest."

"Mr. Castillo has been a major supporter of the fund, since the beginning."

I didn't bother keeping the skepticism out of my voice. "I am sure he is very generous."

Why was I hurt? It had happened years ago. I was well rid of the woman in question. The man involved was already a known factor—his character lying somewhere on the scale between dogshit traitor and backstabbing worm. Sinha was talking again. I pulled my attention back to the business at hand.

"Because of his involvement, we have been investigated

by the U.S. Justice Department and the Secret Service no less than four times, Interpol and Europol twice each."

"And you were surprised at this? The man moves money around for drug cartels."

Pride. It was my pride that was hurt. When I stopped whining and just faced facts, that's all it was. What else was left, and not much of that? I felt stupid. Betrayed, yes, but mostly stupid. I'd had countless opportunities— the news that I was married, and to a model who had twice appeared in the *SI* swimsuit issue, had brought forth a deluge of explicit and implied invitations from colleagues' wives and girlfriends, casual acquaintances outside the firm, barmaids and perfume saleswomen, and the always hungry big-busted cougar saleswoman in money markets who reportedly was screwing her way through the firm's trading desks. In putting on a ring, I had achieved a level of magnetism that had eluded me my whole life. Why, I now asked myself, hadn't I taken what was being so freely offered? Honor? Some hitherto unknown sense of self-esteem? Stupid. Was I seriously regretting not having slept with the office slut? Stupid. Stupid squared. I had been faithful. She had not. End of goddamned story.

Sinha seemed to be unaware of my split focus. "And we were cleared of wrongdoing every time—an important distinction that the media consistently fails to mention when discussing our situation." She was starting to show some fire.

I fought to stay on point. "Why don't you just tell me about the Von Becker connection?"

She slumped back in her chair and exhaled in a long sigh. I caught a whiff of lavender.

"William Von Becker called me eight years ago and said he wanted to make a substantial donation. One million dollars. The fund was just two years old at the time, and we were struggling. Right after a storm we tend to get a rush of small contributions, but our only major sponsors at the time were the country of Venezuela and the Caribbean Coffee Growers Association. Together, they barely covered salaries for my two assistants. Von Becker's pledge was a godsend."

Gottsent.

"And all he wanted was to invest the funds for you, am I right?"

"No. He asked only if he could host fund-raisers for us. Which he did."

"No strings?"

She shook her head. "He was much too sly. The first party he threw was at the Guggenheim Museum. Seven hundred guests. I understand the evening cost over a million dollars. We never saw the bill, and we had pledges for over thirty million."

"He twisted a lot of arms."

She gave a shrug. "He invited the right people. Morgan, the daughter, made sure of that. She was invaluable. She handled all of it, from the guest list to hiring the caterers and vetting the security."

"And Castillo? Where was he in this?"

"I am from Suriname. We do not have the same view of the Castillo family that your country does. The Castillos are wealthy and aristocratic Colombian merchant bankers. They invest in our bauxite mines, lend money for infrastructure projects, help to negotiate more favorable trade agreements with larger, more powerful corporations. My family is in banking—on a much smaller scale, of course— but we have done business with the Castillos for over a hundred years."

She hadn't answered my question. "Without them, the drug cartels would be out of business."

"No. Without them, another group of bankers would come in. HSBC? Standard Chartered? And I could name a dozen U.S. banks that already do their business. Your Justice Department only intervenes when the fines they can extort are large enough to be worth the time and trouble."

I couldn't argue. Criminal fines against Wall Street were a source of revenue; policing and prosecuting were expenses.

"Von Becker was one of these? Already engaged in that business?"

She twisted a plain gold wedding band. "If you say so. I don't know."

She knew.

"So how did Von Becker get hold of the cash?"

She gave a rueful smile. "I gave it to him, of course. He had donated ten million of his own money by that time, and helped us to raise over half a billion dollars. In fact, you could say that the whole fund—which stood at close to two billion at one point—was due to his work, because we would never have had such visibility without him. It was quite natural for me to ask for his help. Managing the fund's portfolio was taking too much of my time. I could have chosen Case Securities or Goldman Sachs, but I chose Von Becker. He seemed reluctant. I insisted. He agreed. I can see now how well he played me."

"You never questioned how he produced those double-digit returns? Year after year? Nothing ever made you think, Hey, how does this guy do what nobody else can?"

"When I managed the investments, we earned six to eight percent. With Von Becker, it jumped to twice that. That meant we had a lot more money to spend on hurricane relief every year. Which is why we're here, after all. Americans remember Katrina and Sandy, but in the island countries, they remember Ivan and Dennis and Dean. In 2008, Haiti was hit by four major hurricanes. In a row. I needed the returns Von Becker offered." She had thrown off the lassitude and the cynicism. I had found her passion point. So, I pushed on it.

"To do what? Fly some celebrities around and show them the poor people. Get them a few good photo ops. Come on, this whole thing was rigged, and the fact that Von Becker gutted it is a minor subplot."

"No! This fund helped real people get back on their feet after the kind of devastation you couldn't imagine. Oh, you might watch it for a few minutes on CNN or Fox News, before flipping back to ESPN or the Playboy channel, and if you remember later you might write a check or send us five dollars from your PayPal account. But you don't *see* it. We hire people—local people—to dig latrines, build huts or lean-tos, deliver clean water and rice and flour. Who do you think sorts through all that used clothing that gets sent down? Good god! Thongs, for heaven's sake! Who sends thong underwear to hurricane survivors? Overcoats! People get a tax deduction for sending their old down coats. To Haiti! Canned food? How about pumpkin-pie filling? You would not believe how much pumpkin-pie filling is donated the week after Thanksgiving. And a container ship docks and a few politicians have their pictures taken in front of containers full of 'relief supplies' and then they disappear . . ."

She finally noticed I had my hands up in surrender.

"Sorry," I said. "I needed to know if you were for real."

"And what did you find out?" she sneered.

"I'm ready to shut up and listen. Now, will you finish telling me about Von Becker?"

She glared for a moment, and when I didn't melt, she sat back and took a deep breath. "William Von Becker was a very charming man. He seemed both very sure of himself and yet very humble. He was always giving credit to those around him—and it is only later that you realize that he was the one who did all the talking and he is the one who will be remembered. It is an ugly talent."

"He was managing the funds," I prompted. "All of them. Everything?"

She shook her head. "Almost all. I still managed the daily cash fund—a few million. There's enough left to pay expenses as we wind down. Whatever's left at the end will go to the Red Cross or Oxfam."

"But it can't all be gone, right? I'm hearing most of his investors will be getting back somewhere between forty and seventy percent. You can still do a lot of good with that kind of money."

"We will get nothing back. It is not yet public information, but we have been told this by the judge's clerk. There is, of course, some pressure from the DEA and the FBI and others at Justice, who think that even though we have been cleared time and again of any criminal dealings with the Castillo family, that somehow we 'got away with something.' Your justice system is not about discovering truth, or even catching bad guys. It is about winning."

"Believe me, I understand."

"So, I will close the fund and if I'm not indicted, I will rejoin my family in Geneva. And I will try to think like an American when I hear news of some disaster, and write out a little check."

I'd been thrown as badly. I thought about what had finally brought me through it.

"Do you have children?" I asked.

She smiled. "Yes, two. A boy and a girl. They live with their father in Geneva."

"Sorry," I said. "I saw the ring. I didn't realize you were separated."

She gave a sad laugh. "We are not separated. I visit often—three or four times a year. They are both in school there and I would not disrupt their lives. If Suriname ever fields an Olympic ski team, they will lead it. My husband is very busy, but he is a good father. He makes time for them."

And, I would bet, he did not cheat on her with her boss. If he did cheat it would be very European, discreet.

She didn't cheat, I was sure. I had found an honest woman. And now that my pride and stupidity were no longer vying for my attention, I realized that I knew others. Skeli, obviously. Would she cheat on me? Not unless I deserved it—and probably not then. She had been married to a serial philanderer; she took the issue seriously. Would I cheat on her? No. Unless? No. There was no *unless* about it. The answer was no.

"Thanks for your time, Ms. Sinha. I wish you luck." I stood up and we shook hands. She had long fingers and a strong grip. "Do you mind one more question?" I said. "A personal question." I had a hard time leaving the Kid at school each day. I could not imagine living the way she did. "How did you do it?" I said. "Your family, I mean. Didn't missing them just tear you apart every day?"

"Of course it did." She was mildly offended. "But I thought it was my duty to try to do something good for the world."

That was where she'd gone wrong. The world has per- verse ways of showing appreciation.

| **17** |

First Avenue was moving two miles an hour faster than a parking lot, so I walked up to Third to catch a cab back uptown. I had one foot on the curb, one in the street, arm in the air, and was trying to remember the last time I had eaten at Smith & Wollensky's—well before my incarceration, I was sure—when my cell phone buzzed.

"You son of a bitch!" the voice greeted me.

"Wrong number," I said and clicked off. Then I checked the call log. Douglas Randolph? What had I done to him? I could think of a great number of people who might initiate a conversation with me by calling me a son of a bitch, but Doug was not one of them. I waited a moment, giving him a chance to call again. It didn't take long.

"Stafford," I answered.

"You son of a bitch!" He was close to screaming—as frightened as he was angry.

"Whoa. Hold up. What is this about?"

"Those two goons you sent. Nice job. They scared the shit out of my wife."

"Doug, I don't know anything about this."

"You lying sack of shit. I get home and I find the house trashed and her locked in the bathroom, crying. They fucking *told* her you sent them. All right?"

"This is all wrong. I sent nobody. I don't know who these people are." Who would I send? Roger and PaJohn? My crew.

"Bullshit. You didn't have to do this, you know. She's goddamn terrorized. I shouldn't be surprised, though, coming from a class-A crook. Don't you fucking get it? I don't know anything. I'm not holding out on you. I just don't fucking know anything."

"Did she call the cops? What did they look like? What did they sound like? Give me something here!"

"The cops? And what makes you think they'd believe me?"

"I believe you." I did, and I had no idea what else to say.

"Know this, you fuck, if there's any way I can put your ass back in jail, I will find it."

I was on very good terms with my parole officer, but something like this could change that in a heart-beat.

"Doug, I'm sorry. I really had nothing to do with this. Let me help."

But he wasn't there. He had already hung up on me.

EVERETT WAS AGAIN standing guard over Virgil's inner sanctum when I called.

"Virgil will be in meetings all day. I will pass on any information you have."

"What I have are questions, Everett. I just got a very strange phone call from Doug Randolph. Someone threatened him—rather, someone threatened his wife."

"Who threatened him?"

"That's one of my questions."

"As I understand things, Randolph has a lot to answer for. He defrauded a lot of people. I would not be surprised if one or more of them retaliated."

"They used my name," I said.

Everett didn't respond.

"Did you get that, Everett?"

"I will pass that on to Virgil. Is there anything else?"

I promised myself that someday I would grant myself the luxury of venting a bucketful of frustration on Everett. Not today. "I spoke to Mrs. Welk. She swears there's nothing there."

"Welk? I'm taking notes."

"The clerk?" Was he playing games? "The old man's clerk. You said she 'sat at his feet,' if I remember correctly. Well, she just got out of prison, and I spoke to her.

I don't know that she was innocent, but I really don't think she knows anything that would help us."

"Any other messages?"

I had never trusted Everett, and so far I had heard nothing to make me change my mind.

"Yes. I need to speak to Virgil."

He sighed impatiently. "He'll just tell you to talk to me."

"Then he'll have to tell me that himself."

| 18 |

The next morning, Randolph's call still had me looking over my shoulder as I hurried out of the Ansonia lobby and headed for Central Park. I was seeing those goons everywhere—grabbing a hot dog at Gray's Papaya, using the ATM at Citibank, waiting to get served at the Red Velvet Bakery. There had been no call from Virgil.

Skeli was waiting at the Imagine plaque in Central Park, surrounded by a gaggle of middle-aged Chinese tourists, all vying for, and boldly nudging one another out of, position for a photo op. The women were the worst—all elbows and shoulders—while yelling orders to one another, the men, and anyone passing by who might be blocking a shot.

Skeli was watching and smiling as though it was a madhouse comedy being put on for her benefit alone. She was wearing a light paisley-print dress that I had not seen before and was carrying a plaid blanket and a brown paper bag. I held back and enjoyed a moment of just looking at her. As my pop would have said, she was easy on the eyes.

"Come here," she said. "You look like some weird stalker staring at me like that."

"I'm enjoying the view. New dress?"

She laughed—one of her big, openmouthed guffaws. "No. God, you are such a *guy*. You've seen me in this about a thousand times."

"You look nice," I managed.

She shook her head and took my arm. "Here. You carry this." She handed me the blanket. "Now repeat after me. Sisters look nice. Co-workers look nice. Maybe mothers look nice, I don't know. But girlfriends look *great*."

She had me smiling. "Got it. I will try to remember it. I appreciate all this remedial work you've been doing with me. I'm sure it will all pay off someday."

"Do you know the real tragedy of marriage?" We began to walk away from the Lennon memorial and up toward the lake. "A woman gets married thinking her man will change, and, of course, he doesn't. And the man gets married thinking his woman will never change, and, of course, she does."

"We're not going to talk about our exes, am I right?"

"Right. So, how is the psycho?"

I would rather have talked about prostate cancer.

She had led me up to the Bow Bridge. "Where are you taking me?" I said, looking ahead to the wooded area known as the Ramble—the perfect place for an ambush. I could imagine Randolph's goons hiding in the brush.

"Just up here. I want you to see something." She stepped off the manicured trail and into the woods. "Come on, I'll watch out for you. And I do want to hear. How is whatshername?"

I remembered my father once dispensing advice to one of the regulars at his bar—a man who had managed to stay unmarried while dating the same two women for more than twenty years. "Never talk to one woman about another woman. The deck is stacked against you. You've got three ways to get it wrong for every chance of getting it right. The best thing you can do is fold. But, if you absolutely have to, and there's no other way out, say something nice. It may not keep you out of trouble, but you'll feel better about it afterwards."

So the question that I had to face was: Could I get away with not talking about Angie?

"Look, you're acting like I'm going to bite your head off," Skeli said, while stretching out her stride and forging up the slight hill. "If you don't want to talk about her, then don't."

So that answered that question. I composed a response that would skirt all the truly aggravating bits.

"Evangeline Oubre is and always will be a handful. But she is trying hard not to be a royal pain in the ass right now. I may not be giving her enough credit. Or maybe my expectations are just so dreadfully low that she only *seems* halfway human."

"Uh-huh." With two soft grunts—not even syllables—Skeli managed to communicate a full rant on the subject.

"And she is sober," I manfully continued in the face

of her complete disdain. "Forty-something days. Even while she's up here, she's been making a meeting every day. She wants me to come to Lafayette to see her get her ninety-day chip."

"Uh-huh." She repeated the whole thing, all over again.

"Stop. I'm trying to give her the benefit of the doubt, but I have no interest in her romantically. She is here making amends."

Skeli gave me a skeptical look. "And how's that going?"

I applauded myself for conveying so much distanced reason. Maybe I really was free of her. "We are doing our best to get along for the sake of the Kid—and that's all. Okay?"

"So will you go to Lafayette?"

"No. If I'm going to make the Kid travel, it will be to come see you on the road somewhere."

She turned off the main path and headed up a narrow trail into the woods.

"You know where you're going?" I asked, trying to pierce through the leafy curtains around us. Whole platoons of armed thugs could have been hiding steps away from us.

Skeli stopped. "Are you all right? You seem awful skittish taking a walk in the woods—I mean, for a guy who survived cell block D or whatever."

I debated telling her about the phone call from Randolph the day before. As I stood there with Skeli under a cloudless sky in the quiet of the park, Randolph and his panic, fear, and threat were fading quickly, leaving a feeling of mild unease. I could shake it off.

"I'll be okay. Lead on."

I followed her up a winding stone pathway to a small clearing with a tiny pond and a great view of the Lake below. Around us was a dense wall of sprawling, big-leafed shrubs. The pond fed a tiny, inch-deep stream that led back down the hill. We were in the center of Manhattan, and could have been in the depths of some primeval forest. It was a warm, sunny day in June and the park was filled with people—and it felt like we were all alone. Miles from anyone or anything.

"Is that rhododendron?" I asked, rolling out the blanket.

She looked around. "No. Mountain laurel."

I nodded. "What's the difference?"

She rolled her eyes. "I'll tell you when you need to know."

She knelt on the blanket and patted it with her hand for me to join her. "This is what I wanted you to see." She bent forward with her face a foot above the water and looked down. "See. There they are."

I looked as well. At first all I saw were rocks and sand and iced-tea-colored water.

"I'm looking," I said.

"Look harder."

I tried looking harder.

"There. See? One just moved."

What was she seeing?

"Uh. No."

"Really? Look again."

I tried even harder. And I saw them.

"What the hell? They look like tiny lobster."

"Yeah," she said. "Exactly. They're crayfish."

Crayfish lived in the Mississippi River, and when they were served up in heaping mounds on beer trays they were called crawfish. I had eaten a beer tray's worth one night in Lafayette. Angie had not taken one bite. She was prepping for a shoot, which meant that she was living on cocaine, tissues, and vodka. The coke kept her going and the tissues filled her up. As for the vodka—at least she was getting some caloric intake.

"That's impossible," I said. "Crawfish don't live this far north."

"They're crayfish," she said, leaving no room for further discussion.

"They call them bugs down South."

She blew air through pursed lips in mock desperation. "You are such a pain sometimes. Here I bring you to see this wonderful freak of nature—this amazing miniature lobster, living wild in Central Park, right smack-dab in the middle of the greatest city on earth—and what do I get from you? 'Bugs.' Why do I bother?"

"Think I'll ever change?"

"Well, I'm planning on it." She opened the brown bag. "Virginia ham, Vermont cheddar on sourdough. An all-American. That or the veggie wrap."

"Veggie wrap?"

"Well, it's really grilled eggplant and buffalo mozzarella on semolina with a schmear of pesto, but if I think of it as a veggie wrap, I can ignore the calories."

"Half and half?"

"You'd let me have half your ham sandwich?" she said.

"I thought you were going to take the ham. I could hear you salivating as you described it."

We ate in silence. Food was practically a sacred rite with Skeli. Both sandwiches were mere memories when she spoke again.

"It's my last day in town. We have to be on the bus by six. If we leave late, they don't have to pay us the meal allowance. Goddamn cheapskate producers. It never changes."

My heart stopped. I knew it was coming, but I'd managed to place that very important piece of information in the mental file cabinet, labeled TO BE OPENED ONLY WHEN YOU NEED TO GET DEPRESSED. I'd been too busy to take the time to get depressed.

"So, I was thinking we might have this picnic," she continued. "A special picnic."

"We'll visit," I said. "The Kid and me. We'll visit."

She gave a sad single nod. "You have to promise me—you will never come here with anyone else."

I smiled. "Promise."

"Because I will know if you do," she said.

"How will you know?"

"Because I will look in your eyes and I will know."

I believed her. "I promise. Does this also mean you'll move in with me when you get back to New York?" I asked.

"You just want a live-in babysitter, maid, and call girl all in one."

"Well, there's that. But I like you, and that's important, too."

We lay down, her head resting on my shoulder.

"I was scared. The other day. Your ex scares me."

I brushed the hair from her face and kissed her temple. "I know. She scares everyone."

She propped herself up on one elbow and looked into my eyes. "Then how the hell did you two ever get together?"

I shrugged. "When I think about it, it's like I don't recognize myself. That guy didn't know who he was or why he was here."

She put her head back on my shoulder. "And now?"

"I'm here for the Kid. As soon as I saw that, everything became very simple."

"So you did change. Didn't she?"

I gave it some thought. "I don't know. I don't think I knew her very well when we were married. And I don't know that I know her any better now. I have a ton of very good reasons for hating her guts, only I find that I don't." I ran my hand down her back, gently massaging and prodding. "Can we not talk about my ex anymore?"

Skeli pulled the other half of the blanket over us and patted my chest with her palm. "You're a good dad."

"I wasn't. I was terrible. Not a monster, just not there. I'm working at it now. Getting better."

I felt warm under the blanket.

"Are you cold?" I asked.

"No."

"Then?" I made to move the blanket back.

Her hand slid down to my belt buckle. "You might want to leave it where it is."

My throat tightened up. She lifted her face to me and we kissed—a long, probing kiss. Her hand found my zipper.

"Remember," she said as her head disappeared under the blanket. "You promised."

"I'll remember," I managed to croak.

| 19 |

Skeli and I said our farewells on the sidewalk across from the Museum of Natural History. I bought her a soft pretzel and told her it was a forget-me-not. We both laughed, avoiding any tears. Then I put her in a cab and walked home, taking the longest, most winding route I could, killing time until I was sure Angie would have left the Kid with Heather and gone out with her mother.

In the past, a walk through the neighborhood, taking stock of the changes as businesses moved in or out, sold out or cashed out, took me out of my head. Mapping the changes in skyline is for tourists—save for the empty scar of the Twin Towers. You were a local, a member, almost family, when you could carry on a conversation at the dry cleaners that began, "Hey, did you see the shoe store going in where the Korean market used to be?"

But appreciation had given way to depression after my

favorite bar—on the same corner for more than sixty years—had been forced to move uptown to make way for a bank, which turned into the Blossom Nail and Wax Lounge when the bank went under halfway through renovation. Now I saw only the holes. The stores no longer there. The Royale Pastry Shop, the All State Café. I felt old. Not forty-five-old, Methuselah-old.

I stopped in front of the kosher butcher on Seventy-second Street and stared in at the late Thursday afternoon bustle, as shoppers who wanted to avoid the Sabbath crush on Friday stocked up for the weekend. Skeli loved their barbecued breast of veal. I wondered if they'd deliver to Washington.

Then I saw the man's reflection in the window before me. He was behind me, across Seventy-second, squinting into the sun, standing still in the middle of the sidewalk, creating a small eddy in the pedestrian traffic flow, and watching me. I didn't turn around.

He was big, too big to be an effective tail—he stood out. And he wasn't dressed for it. He had on a distinctive, if not quite unique, hat—a broad-brimmed Australian outback hat. Otherwise, he wore a rumpled gray suit, a wrinkled white shirt, and a dark tie, three decades too wide. I couldn't see his face under the hat, but I knew he was staring at me. I felt him.

I turned to my right and walked quickly down the block, then stopped abruptly and made a U-turn and headed back to the butcher's. The guy in the hat almost fell over himself. He had been hustling to follow me and had been caught flat-footed when I turned. He ducked behind an illegally parked delivery van. He couldn't be one of the goons who had terrified Doug Randolph's wife—he was big enough, but he seemed clumsy and stiff. Oafish rather than thuggish. I stopped and stared, waiting him out. A full minute passed before he dashed out, striding off, making a point of looking everywhere but at me. I lost sight of him as he approached Broadway.

My cell phone rang.

Unknown Caller.

"Stafford," I answered.

"Jason? Fred Krebs."

"Spud!"

He sighed. "Fred. Please. I'm going to Yale Law School in two months. I don't want to be Spud anymore."

"Sorry. I was just thinking about how nothing remains the same, and you call to say you don't want to be Spud anymore."

"Spud doesn't argue cases before the Supreme Court."

"Is that your dream these days?"

"So, what are you doing?"

"Out for a walk. I just scared off some guy who was following me. Crocodile Dundee in a cheap suit."

"Weird."

"Even for the Upper West Side," I agreed.

"How's your son?"

I had learned that most people, no matter how kind their intentions, did not want the long answer. "He's good. How's those files? Come up with anything?"

He gave a short laugh. "You got your money's worth out of me this time around."

"But you found something. Otherwise you wouldn't have called."

"Aaaa-yup."

"Let's hear it." I started walking toward the Ansonia.

"Okay. First, there's not three billion dollars missing. I see why they think so, but they're wrong—whether it's on purpose or not, I can't say. The trades and money movements don't always match, and if you add up all the anomalies you get a great big number."

"Like three bil?"

"Three bil, eighty-seven mil, two hundred twenty thousand, and then whatever."

"So?"

"But this guy moved money just to move it. No economic purpose. It's all camouflage."

"All of it?"

He paused. "No. There are two areas where money is not where it should be. The first is money that was being washed through this Hurricane Relief Fund, into and out of various Von Becker investment funds. It comes to just under a bil—nine hundred and change."

"All stolen from the Hurricane Relief?"

"No, dude. None of it. That's just where he parked it. It was like his rinse cycle. The money was siphoned off from all the investors. Everybody chipped in, whether they wanted to or not."

"Do I denote a touch of admiration in your voice?"

"It's a work of art. I cannot imagine how many hours the guy must have spent on this. And from what I can tell, it is all very gone. Poof."

"Spent?"

"No. I can see the transfers to his checking accounts. Those are friggin' huge. But, no, this is just gone. Vanished."

"A billion is still a lot of money."

"Oh, yeah."

"You said there were two areas."

"This is good. Money comes in from different banks all over Central and South America. The money then goes into one account. Then a few days later, the account is empty. No transfer, no record of an override, no nada. A month or so goes by and it happens again, or, even weirder, it happens in reverse."

"I know what that is."

"Do you?"

"Yeah, an interested party explained it to me the other day. Von Becker was washing cash at one end and paying off in bearer bonds at the other. This guy told me there was a good chunk missing somewhere. How much did you find?"

"You mean how much did I not find. Just north of one hundred mil."

"Ah, you have done well, grasshopper."

"Grasshopper?"

"Before your time," I said, feeling more like Methuselah than ever. "Are you ready for the bonus question?" I was sure I knew the answer.

"Do I get a bonus?"

"You've already earned a bonus. But before you rush off to practice your best Euro pickup lines on the women of the continent, answer me this. In all those lists of banks, does the name of one Swiss private bank keep recurring?"

"What's the name?"

"Doerflinger Freres and Company. Et Cie." Castillo had given it to me.

I heard Spud, as I still thought of him, furiously tapping at the keys of his laptop.

"Doerflinger?" he said.

Aha. "Yes. What have you got?"

"Nothing."

"Nothing?"

"As in nada. Zip."

Shit!

| 20 |

The *New York Post* had made William Von Becker's mistress sound like a combination of Greta Garbo and a sexual gymnast—a mysterious recluse, brought up in a commune in northern Nevada where children were encouraged to experiment with sex as soon as they could walk. Mistletoe Evans had been married at thirteen to a sixty-year-old man. When she ran away six months later, it was her testimony that put the commune leaders in jail. The rest of the clan—including her parents—had disappeared into the ghost towns and dust-blown trailer parks that cling to the edges of civilization in the western desert. Mistletoe had been adopted by an aunt and brought to live in New York City. The media moved on.

Until Mistletoe became famous again.

This time, however, she had refused to speak to any of the hordes of reporters, which didn't stop them from writing about her, though it did keep them from actually reporting anything. She opted to remain a mystery.

Mistletoe was still a mystery—the mystery being why a sixty-some-year-old man with access to more money than an African dictator would choose as his mistress a thirty-something beanpole with no discernible hips or breasts, and hair that would have embarrassed a scarecrow.

At my knock, she answered the door and meekly bowed backward, allowing, if not exactly inviting, me to enter. I stepped over the threshold and tried not to react to the strong odor of cat.

"Thanks for agreeing to see me, Ms. Evans." Once I had convinced her I was an investigator and not a reporter, she had been more than willing to meet with me. She did insist on two things: that we meet at her apartment—a rambling three-bedroom on Park Avenue with twelve-foot ceilings and a marble foyer—and that there be no tape recorders.

"They lie," she had said.

An orange-striped cat wound its way between my ankles; a gray looked up from its perch on the back of the couch, as though considering whether or not to get up and greet me as well. It decided not to and turned its head away.

"Umhm. Umhm." The woman was looking around her living room distractedly. "Can I get you something to drink? I have cold chai tea. Very calming. I tend to drink a lot of it. I guess that says something, doesn't it?" She gave a sharp laugh. "Or water. I have water. I have a purifier. A filter, really. But I change the filter. You have to change the filter, or the water stops tasting good. Do you have a filter, Mr. Scabbard?"

She looked up at me for the first time and I saw a remarkably open face. Not pretty, but arresting. Interested. A nice face. She wore no jewelry or makeup, just a black T-shirt, comfortable-looking jeans, and nothing on her feet. And a Mets cap on backward. Already I didn't like her.

"Stafford," I said, correcting her automatically. "Actually, Jason is fine. No. No, I don't have a filter. Maybe I should get one."

The living room furnishings were all older, comfortable antiques, and except for a fine dusting of cat hair, they all looked to be beautifully maintained. The giant flat-screen television that dominated one wall was the only modern anachronism.

"Stafford, yes, yes. I have a good visual memory, but sometimes things don't come out right when I say them. It's better when I write them down. Stafford. Stafford. Does that ever happen to you?" She was like an enthusiastic teenager: she had a very definite, direct way of speaking, but she changed lanes too often without signaling. "Your son would benefit from a water filter, I am sure."

"How do you know about my son?"

"Google."

Of course. Even Mets fans and weird Upper East Side cat ladies knew how to Google.

"Well, yes, you may be right. I'll look into getting a water filter."

She smiled happily, having accomplished a little

something in our brief acquaintance. "Autism is an environmental disease, like breast cancer and asthma, so you need to do all you can to control his environment. Does he speak? Does he communicate?"

He did communicate. Just not this week. I might have challenged her blithe acceptance of the environmental explanation for autism but I had found that those who believed in it had zero tolerance for those of us who had accepted the single overwhelming, undeniable fact in all autism research: nobody knows.

"Ms. Evans, could we talk a bit about William Von Becker?"

"I see. You don't want to talk about your son. I'm sorry. I sometimes lose my sense of boundaries. That's what my therapist says. She says it's because of the way I was brought up. I must practice my boundaries, but I so rarely go out and I don't get many visitors. So, when do I get to practice?"

"I don't know."

"Hmm. My therapist said it was okay to talk to you, but that you wouldn't answer any of my questions. I hope she's wrong. Now, sit down here." She gestured toward a sagging armchair. "I brushed the cat hairs away today, just for you."

I sat. She had missed a few.

She sat on the couch, facing me. A long-haired, caramel-colored cat immediately leapt up beside her and accepted a single long caress from ears to tail. It leapt down again, and left the room.

"My aunt kept cats," she said, as though carrying on

the tradition was both a duty and a pleasure. Then she made another of her conversational leaps. "Who do you think killed him? I think it was the family, but there were probably a lot of people who wanted him dead." She rattled this off as though discussing dinner.

When I had first heard that Von Becker was found dead in his cell, I had immediately assumed that he'd been murdered. That thought lasted as long as it took the Bloomberg news announcer to read the rest of the sentence ". . . an apparent suicide."

"You know, Ms. Evans, you're not at all what I expected."

"Call me Missy. People stumble over my real name, as though they don't believe it, so I tell them to call me Missy."

"I can call you Mistletoe, if you'd prefer. Mistletoe. See, no stumbling."

She smiled and became almost pretty for a moment. "You went to prison, too. I read about that. Was it really bad? I didn't like to think of Willie in prison, but it's better than being dead."

I did not want to talk about my time in prison. Ever.

"Can we talk about you and Mr. Von Becker?"

"Willie," she corrected. "You won't tell *her*, though, will you? I called her right away to say how sorry I was about him getting arrested and she was not very nice."

It took me a second to realize who she was talking about. "You called his wife?"

She shrugged. "That boundary thing, right? I thought it was a good thing to call, but . . ." She trailed off.

"But your shrink said no?"

She gave a sad smile. "Guess not."

"As long as we're crossing boundaries, can I ask you? How did you and Willie meet?"

"In my therapist's elevator. Every Tuesday and Thursday at five of four we would ride up together. I got off on twelve and he rode up to sixteen."

"I see. Was he going to see his shrink?"

She laughed delightedly. "Noooo. Willie wouldn't see a therapist. He said he had too many secrets. Therapists want your secrets. It's how they live."

"Okay, but he had a regular appointment in the building. Do you know who he was seeing?"

"Oh, yes. He told me. I mean, he told me much later, after we fucked. He didn't tell me then. It was still a secret."

"And who was it?" I prodded, as gently as I could.

"His mistress. She was a model, from Brazil, I think, but I never met her, so I don't know. Willie said she was very beautiful, but cold. That's why he liked me."

"You're not cold?"

"No," she answered, suddenly quite serious. "I'm not cold. Willie stopped giving her money and she went home. Or he gave her money and she went home. I'm not sure which."

I wondered whether it was worth trying to track the woman down. Livy Von Becker would probably not want me to spend a week in Rio looking for her dead husband's ex-mistress.

"Mistletoe, the whole world seems to be convinced

that Willie offed himself. Why do you think he was killed? He was alone, locked in a cell." He took off his jumpsuit, made a noose out of the sleeves, and hung himself from the window bars. "Seems like a straightforward suicide."

"She was right."

"Who?"

"My therapist. She said you'd answer me by asking questions."

Impasse. One of us was going to have to give or the trip would be wasted.

"Fine. I don't think he was killed. However, *if* he was murdered, I'd say it was someone who had lost a lot of money. And, as you say, there are a lot of people like that out there right now."

She shook her head emphatically. "You're looking at it upside down. Who has the most to gain? That's what you should be asking."

I'd been talking with her too long—she was starting to make sense.

"Did Von Becker ever talk about business?"

"Willie."

"Willie. Sorry."

"Willie talked about business all the time. I liked it. He had a nice voice. Does your son like to listen to you talk about business?"

"I don't think I've ever talked to him about business. I talk about other things."

"You should try it. I'll bet he likes it. It's nice to listen to someone talk about things that excite them."

"Did he talk about offshore money? A Swiss account, maybe?"

"I don't know. I liked to listen, but I didn't always know what he was talking about. I'm not very good about money. I asked him to take care of mine, you know—my aunt left me some money—but at first he said he wouldn't do it. I had to ask him again and again before he agreed."

There couldn't have been much there or Willie would have snapped it up. Only, now it was gone.

"What will you do now?"

Her eyes flicked away. "There's a little left. Not much. I don't need much, but . . . I don't know."

There wasn't anything to say to that. Her name wasn't even on the lists of clients. Willie had just made the money disappear. I didn't want to think about what would happen when the little that was left was gone.

"Did you ever meet any of his business associates?" And what would any of Willie's Wall Street cronies have thought of Mistletoe?

"You're cheating. It's my turn. Do you think I'm pretty?"

The strange thing was, the longer I was in her presence, the more attractive she became. She was still a pale stick, but I felt myself wanting to please her. She radiated a comforting feeling that, while anything was possible, everything was safe and protected in this room. There were no demands, nothing to stress over. I could see what had drawn in Von Becker and held him here.

"I suppose I do," I said.

"I thought so. It's too bad. You're ages too young for me, you know. Not my type at all, but we could fuck, if you want."

I had never been propositioned in quite that way before. Did this kind of thing happen to George Clooney all the time? What would he do?

"Uh, thank you, but I'm in a relationship." Though I had been spectacularly forgiven, I was sure that casual sex with Mistletoe Evans was not on the list of Ten Things You Should Be Doing to Maintain Your Long-Distance Relationship.

"Okay."

"My turn?" I said, raising my eyebrows.

She chuckled. "Sure. You go."

"His business associates? Friends? Did you ever meet any of them?"

"No. Well. Just Paddy."

"Paddy? Paddy Gallagher?"

She nodded.

"Where did you meet him?" So much for Paddy's claim that they were merely business acquaintances.

"Here. We never went anywhere else. Paddy would stop by sometimes and we'd all watch the game together or maybe a movie and order in Chinese. Paddy drinks too much, though. I worry about him."

I tried to imagine Paddy Gallagher sitting in the chair I now occupied, plucking cat hairs off his two-thousand-dollar suit, and pushing General Tso's chicken around his plate.

"Paddy's a Mets fan?"

"No. Willie was a Mets fan. He tried to buy them once, he said. Paddy's a Yankees fan. Me, too."

My opinion of her improved substantially.

"What do you think of Jeter this year? Do they move him to DH?"

"He's got to get his OPS up over eight hundred again."

"And his fielding percentage back up over ninety-eight," I said.

"He can do that. Fielding percentage is kind of bogus anyway. If a guy only goes after the ones that drop in his glove, he's a one-oh."

She was enjoying herself, relaxed and smiling. So was I.

"So what's with the enemy's hat?"

She twisted it around to the side so the brim stood out over one ear. "For Willie." She dropped her hand to her lap and stared down at it. Our connection was gone—she was mourning.

And I had questions that still needed answers. "Would they talk about business together? Willie and Paddy."

"Not during the game." She pointed to the big TV. "Willie wouldn't let anyone talk when the game was on."

"How about after?"

"I guess. Paddy got angry one time. We were watching *The Man Who Would Be King*. Do you know that movie? They both liked Michael Caine movies. He was in that other one, too. What was it?"

"Why was Paddy angry? What did he say?"

She gave a big Paddy grin. "'There's a lesson there',"

she said. It was an excellent impersonation. "That's what he said, and Willie didn't like it. He said Paddy worried too much. Then he told him that he'd always be taken care of, and Paddy left early. But the next time he came over, everything was okay."

Paddy was right in the middle of it all.

"Mistletoe, try to remember, please. I am sure Willie had lots of secrets. But did he ever tell you any about money? Where he might have hidden some?"

"Everybody asks me that. The FBI must have asked about a billion times. I don't remember. If he did, I wasn't paying attention, because it never mattered. Willie came over. We talked. We sat on the couch and held hands. We'd eat dinner and watch a movie and he'd put his arm around me. Sometimes then we'd screw. Then he'd go home. It wasn't like he was here making calls and doing deals. He was here to be with me. Like we were friends."

"I'm sorry," I said. "It's a surprising relationship. You seem to have known a side of Von Becker that no one else got to see."

"He was nice."

"Can I be an asshole and ask you something I have no right asking? Did you love Willie?"

She sighed and rolled her eyes. "Oh, god, now you sound just like my therapist. She's always asking me that. I don't know! Let me ask. Do you love your son?"

"Absolutely. Without any shadow of a doubt."

"Well, see! That's great. You know that. You're lucky. I've never known anything that definite in my life. Certainly not when I was little. I think maybe my aunt loved me like that. She was nice to me. Willie could be nice like that. I miss him all the time. But when I heard he was dead I didn't fall apart and cry all night or want to die myself. I cleaned the litter box and vacuumed. I didn't watch a movie that night. Does that mean I didn't love him or that I did?"

I didn't know the answer to that.

The Kid and I were sitting with Roger in a booth in the back of Hanrahan's. The Kid was taking occasional bites from his grilled cheese while keeping up his end of the conversation with Roger. His line of five Matchbox cars was in perfect order down the center of the table.

"But why?"

"I already told ya, Kid. I got no idear." Roger shuffled a well-used deck of cards.

"But why?" The Kid adjusted the blue Citroën a tenth of a millimeter. I couldn't have said why it made a difference, but I felt better.

"Yeah, well, I can see your point, but that's just how the game is played, sport. Aces can be ones or elevens. Them's the rules." He stopped shuffling and gave the boy a hard stare. "And don't ask me why."

Hard stares had no effect on my son, but his normal attention span is far too short to maintain an argument. He picked up his sandwich and began flying it around his plate.

Roger dealt two cards. "So, what've ya got there? Jack of clubs and nine of diamonds. What've ya got?"

The half-eaten airplane continued to circle the ketchup-covered landing zone, now with an audio track, supplied by my son, of vaguely piglike noises.

"Why are you trying to teach my son blackjack?"

"Because I don't know how to play bridge. Come on, young fella. A jack and a nine. What've ya got."

"Leave him alone. Children don't add double-digit numbers until second grade. You'll stress him out."

The Kid gave a quick glance at the cards. "Fifteen!" He took a bite of airplane. He may have been wrong, but he was not stressed.

"Well, he's no Rain Man," Roger said.

While I was pleased to see that the Kid was communicating with someone, there was an annoying voice in my head demanding to know why it wasn't me. "That whole Rain Man story was fiction, you know." I was mildly surprised at how angry I sounded. "My son is even more special. For one thing, he's real."

"Sorry. I tried a joke without figuring in what kind of audience I was working. Won't happen again." He turned back to the Kid. "Try again, midget. You got it right yesterday. Nine and what? What's a jack?"

The Kid dropped the remains of the sandwich on his plate and stared at the cards. Then he cooed, "The man with the feather."

"Jacks are tens, aren't they?" Roger continued. "So ya got a ten and a nine. You can do this."

"Tell Roger to leave you in peace," I said.

The Kid ignored me—as he had all week.

"Jason Stafford?"

I looked up. A big, slightly unkempt man in a gray suit was blocking the end of the booth. He looked like nine out of ten of the government bureaucrats I had ever dealt with.

"Father or son?" I said. Then I recognized him. "Where's the hat?"

He didn't smile. He nodded as though he recognized humor as a common human failing.

"Charles Gibbons." He flipped a leather ID holder. "SEC."

"Nice to meet you, Mr. Gibbons. Talk to my lawyer." I was clean. Legit. A model citizen ever since my release from federal prison. And what wasn't quite squeaky clean was untraceable. "Why were you following me?"

"I wasn't following you." He looked away. He was a terrible liar.

"Yes, you were. I saw you. Two days ago, just down the block."

He ignored me. I wanted to ignore him back.

"I have some questions about the people you have been associating with," he said. "A quick chat with me might clear up some misconceptions. The kind of misconceptions that could get you sent back upstate."

I had been aces with my parole officer ever since I had helped the FBI catch a killer eight months ago. But I had more than two years to go keeping him happy, and an unkind word from another law enforcement agency could easily end our honeymoon.

"Listen, I'm serious. I don't discuss the weather with you guys without a lawyer being present. Nothing personal. Leave me your card and I'll have him call you and set something up. Deal?"

"Nineteen!" the Kid suddenly cried out, bouncing the jack off Roger's nose.

"Very good, Kid," I said without thinking. Then it struck me. Where was I when he learned his teens? A few months back, he refused to acknowledge eleven, and here he was doing second-grade math. "Really, that was great. You are a math monster!" I held my hand up for a high five.

He ignored me.

Roger was rubbing his nose where he'd been hit. "I been assaulted," he said. He turned to the Fed. "You're not going to protect me?"

Mr. Gibbons ignored him. "I'm looking for some specific information and I think you can help me find it. Give me five minutes, that's all."

I liked the guy better when he was begging—but not enough to deliberately hang myself. "I think you're wrong. I can't imagine what we might have to talk about. For five minutes or five seconds. Please, let me enjoy this quality time of being ignored by my son." I gave him my most ingratiating smile, the one I used on Skeli when it was my turn to do the dishes.

"I could come back with a warrant," he said. The

smile hadn't worked. It never worked with Skeli either. "On Friday afternoon, so we'd have to keep you all weekend until your hotshot lawyer gets back from his beach house on Monday morning. But don't worry about your son. We'll park him with Child Services. He'll sleep on a cot in the office and eat Happy Meals. He'll love it."

Or be watched over by Angie. A situation guaranteed to terrorize them both. Either way, his routine would be shot. The Kid needed his routine. Depended on it. Without it, he would begin to regress again. Months of hard-won adjustments to life in the alien world he inhabited would be lost. I was straddling a line between exploding in anger and total capitulation.

Roger intervened.

"You know somethin', Cholly? There's another way to play this. If I wanted something from somebody and I saw him in a bar, first thing, I'd offer to buy a round. Maybe it softens 'em up. It shows some respect. You see what I'm saying?"

Charles Gibbons thought it over. He wasn't stupid, just very deliberate. He weighed his options and moved only when he'd thought it all through. "What'll it be?"

"Rémy," Roger said. Then, quickly seizing the opportunity, "Double."

"Bud Light," I said. "And a water for my son."

He gave a quick nod and turned for the bar. I heard him ask for a Maker's Mark on the rocks for himself—he wasn't on a government expense allowance.

"I'll take the Kid home," Roger said quietly.

"No, stay," I said. "I might like a witness. This is the guy with the hat I told you about. Across from Fischer Brothers."

Roger nodded, then pointed with his chin. Gibbons was back.

The Fed set the drinks down. "Maybe you and I could have our talk over there," he said, gesturing toward an empty booth. "We wouldn't have to bother your friend."

Roger slid over, making room for him. "Don't mind me and the Kid. He's just been showing off his math skills." He took a sip of cognac and began to shuffle the deck again.

We all sat and drank for a minute. The Kid belched—loud enough to turn heads at the bar. I ignored him. I had learned to pick my battles, and a loud belch in a noisy bar was not important. Holding hands while crossing Broadway was important. Not biting his teacher was important. Not screaming "stupid cunt" at the driver on the M104 when the bus lurched before we were sitting down was very important.

"Four minutes left," I finally said.

He sat down.

"You're in trouble," he said. "If you are not now, you soon will be."

"I'm listening."

The Kid made bubble sounds in the bottom of his glass with the straw.

"Me, too," Roger said.

Gibbons was not reassured by this.

"You are talking to the wrong people."

"A lot of people have been telling me this. Who are the right people?"

"I mean that these people could be trouble for you."

"You are here out of concern for my welfare? Why am I not feeling all warm and cuddly?"

"You are out of your depth. Tell me whatever you've come up with. I will share it with the authorities. Take your son and go home and whenever any of these people call, tell them you found nothing and want nothing more to do with this."

"You're trying to scare me." I looked at the Kid, who was again lining up his cars on the table in front of him—dinnertime. "It's not working."

Gibbons looked over at the Kid and back to me. "Murder means nothing to them. You. Or your family."

"I think we're done talking, Mr. Gibbons. Talk to my lawyer. Now, beat it."

He surprised me. He stood up.

Roger smiled up at him and toasted with his glass. "I'll get ya next time."

Gibbons ignored him.

"Ask Virgil about the lawyer."

"What lawyer?"

"Ask Virgil."

"Give me a hint, big guy."

"In Switzerland."

"Biondi? Virgil knows about him?" That might be worth exploring.

"You know? And you're still playing with these people? You're an idiot."

That made it unanimous.

I laughed. "Well, thanks, Mr. Gibbons. That's pretty straightforward."

Gibbons tossed back the rest of his twelve dollars' worth of bourbon and stomped out.

"That guy's not right," I said.

"Howzat?" Roger said.

"No Fed ever bought me a drink before."

DESPITE MY SCHOOLYARD BRAVADO, I was beginning to get spooked. Both Brady and Gibbons had given me straight-up warnings, and Douglas Randolph's freak-out was beginning to feel like part of a pattern, rather than a one-off bit of hysteria. I seemed to have set something in motion—I just didn't know what. I reminded myself that a million dollars a year for life was a goal that could support some temporary discomfort. I waited until Angie and her family came to pick up the Kid, and then I began retracing some of my steps.

The first stop was back where I had started. An old friend. But Paddy Gallagher hadn't been into Joe Allen's in a week, the bartender informed me. She wasn't exactly worried about him, but she did admit that it was unusual.

"His voice mail box is full," I said.

She gave a double-shoulder shrug—which caused some eye-catching undulation in the deep vee of her blouse. "Can't help you. If you leave your name, I'll tell him you were by." She leaned forward and hunched her shoulders just enough to test my resolve. "And your number."

I failed the test—I looked. She smiled. We are all who we were in high school—I was forty-five, a father, an ex-husband, and an ex-convict, but I still became tongue-tied when a woman vamped me.

"I'll be back," I said, retreating.

"Do that," she called as I headed for the door. "I work days on the weekends and Monday and Tuesday nights."

Paddy kept a cubbyhole office in the Palace Theatre building over on Broadway, so I walked in that direction while I made another call on my cell. I knew someone who might know where to find Paddy.

"Mouse. It's Jason Stafford."

"Oh, yeah. I hear you're a dangerous man to talk to these days."

"Me? Not a chance. What do you hear?"

"What do you got?"

"An SEC bean counter named Gibbons—who tells me that I'm in danger—and Doug Randolph, who says I threatened his wife."

"Yeah, that's what I hear. Randolph, I mean. I don't know this other guy."

"I'm sorry for his troubles, but I didn't send anyone there."

"I believe it, but it's got some of your other old friends spooked."

"Paddy."

"In one. Randolph talked to him and the old guy took the next flight to London. He said he was going to see some shows, but I hear he hasn't left the Grosvenor since he got there."

I stopped walking. Paddy was a friend—or so I'd thought.

Hints and threats I had—answers were in short supply. Maybe I had not retraced my steps far enough. I had to talk to Virgil Von Becker—without Everett.

| 22 |

If I stood up and leaned over the heads of the motherly chaperone and three teenage girls—all of whom were entirely caught up in the action on stage—I could just see the Kid down in row E, one seat off the aisle. When I sat down, however, I could see only the back of the stage. "Partially Obstructed View." Last row of the upper balcony. I had a great view of the stagehands attaching the flying harness to the back of the vampire's costume just before he flew up and scared off all the werewolves.

Ten minutes into Act I and I was lost—thoroughly. The audience must have all read the book—or the whole trilogy. There was no dialogue—the lyrics drove whatever story line existed. The music had been written—if that's the word—by a pair of aging rockers, one of whom had famously admitted years earlier that he knew only three chords when they started out. I was sure that his musical knowledge had doubled over the years.

But my confusion couldn't be blamed solely on the play—my mind was elsewhere. I sneaked my cell phone out of my pocket and checked for messages—it was set to vibrate. Still nothing from Virgil—three calls in, none returned. The light from the screen attracted a nasty look from the overweight, balding man to my right. I smiled at him and nodded companionably. I'd caught him nodding sleepily halfway through the overture.

The damn phone shook in my hand. Incoming. Virgil.

I jumped up, and no longer bothering to smile, wiggled my way out of the row. I took a quick look down at the Kid before I dashed for the exit—I could barely see him. About all I could tell was that he was there and not on fire. I would have seen the flames.

"Virgil. Thanks for finally getting back to me." I stopped just outside the doors, at the top of the stairs.

"I've been getting Everett's reports." In other words, "Why are you bothering me?"

"I need some answers. There're way too many players on the field. I'm getting worried that someone is going to get hurt."

"You are being both cryptic and alarmist. Is this about Mr. Castillo again? I have already said that I do not know the man to be a client of the firm. I know who he is and what he represents. I have asked Everett to go through my father's phone logs and calendars for any evidence that they did business together. As of yesterday afternoon, when I last spoke with Everett, he had no reason to think they even knew each other."

"He may have to dig deeper. Tell him to talk to Mrs. Welk."

The sound of muffled applause came through the doors and I went farther down the stairs.

"Welk? The clerk?"

"Yes."

"All right," he said, sounding like I had asked him to eat raw garlic. "Is there anything else?"

"Plenty. Some nasty guys have been threatening people I've talked to—and claiming that I sent them."

"And you didn't?"

I swallowed the profanities that were about to start rolling off my tongue. "No. I don't work that way."

"Could it be this Castillo person?" He made the name sound like a particularly noxious form of fungus.

"I don't know. Also, I'm being followed."

"By whom?"

"The SEC."

Virgil paused. Then he spoke carefully. "That is unlikely. Their investigators are accountants. They can be unpleasant, but they are not thugs or undercover men. Are you sure you're not projecting?"

He meant fantasizing. But he was right. The whole interview with Gibbons had been wrong for someone from the SEC.

"I caught him following me. Two days later, he approached me and showed ID. Then he tried to warn me off," I said.

"He gave you his name?"

"Charles Gibbons."

"I will have Everett look into it," he said.

"He also told me to ask you about Serge Biondi."

He paused again. "Who?"

"Biondi. A Swiss lawyer your father used. He's dead."

"There is some mistake. That's not how things work here. We have a New York firm that handles everything for us. If we need representation in another country, they handle it."

"Unless . . ." I left it dangling.

"Ah. Exactly," he purred. "You think you have found a clue to the missing funds."

"I'm not ready to make any projections, Virgil. My sources are unreliable, either lying or withholding or with such a stake in the game that I would be skeptical if they told me the sun was out. And I've had a lot of people tell me I'm an idiot."

"What is the lawyer's name again? I'll have Everett check."

"Hold up on that, would you?" I said. "I want to do a bit more research of my own first."

"You're not concerned about Everett, are you? He has my complete confidence."

I was concerned about everyone at that point. Everett was as high on my list of unreliables as anyone else I had spoken to. And that list also included Virgil.

"Not at all. Just give me a few days."

I walked down the stairs, rather than back up. The second-floor lounge had a bar, and given the choice of a cold beer or returning to listen to a chorus of howling werewolves rhyme "evisceration" with "permanent vacation," I bellied up.

"A light beer," I ordered. "Any light beer."

Tinny speakers over the bar ensured that even here I could not entirely escape the constant 4/4 rock beat. The writers may have discovered a fourth or fifth chord, but they still knew only one beat.

A sixty-something bartender in a black vest and white shirt poured me an eight-ounce glass of beer and made my ten-dollar bill disappear. He looked familiar.

"Are you an actor, by any chance? Could I have seen you on *Law and Order*?"

He laughed in a gleeful, high-pitched cackle. "Nah. I know you, though. From the old P-and-G. I was a runner for Vinny. I'd come by every afternoon to lay off my book. I saw you there sometimes. You and the little guy. Whatsisname?"

"Roger. I'm Jason."

We shook hands. "Antony. People who don't know me call me Tony."

"I'll remember that," I said. "I haven't seen Vinny since they moved the bar uptown. Six months? How's he doing?"

Vinny the Gambler. Vinny had occupied the last barstool against the wall at P&G for as long as I had been going there. He had been more Roger's friend than mine, but I thought I knew the man. He sat with his *Racing Form* and notebook and watched the overhead television screens all day. I had always pegged him for a well-dressed retiree. Then my FBI buddies, Brady and his old boss, informed me that Vinny ran one of the biggest sports books in the Northeast out of a second-floor office on Seventy-second Street.

He pursed his lips. "You didn't hear?"

"No one's heard. It's like he dropped through a trapdoor." PaJohn and Roger had gone by the betting parlor on Seventy-second Street, but hadn't learned a thing.

"Trapdoor is just about right. He's serving three years in a minimum-security lockup upstate. The Feds shut down his offshore casino. They let him take a lesser plea. He's got another two and a half to go. But they'll be watching, busting his chops. He's out of business, I think."

"That's rough," I said, but Vinny had been running a book for thirty years or more. The odds have to catch up with you at some point. "But he can do three years."

"Oh, sure. He can do three with his head in the toilet. It's a shame, though. He always played straight, made his payoffs, never got greedy. Then the Internet comes along and he's got a choice to make—go with it or go out of business, right? It sucks, 'cause now it's a federal rap and there's no one willing to take an envelope and look the other way."

"The Feds can't be bought?" I sounded more than a little skeptical.

"It's not the same. Senators you can buy. FBI agents? Ya gotta be careful."

"Where is he?"

"Otisville."

My hands felt instantly moist and my scalp felt tight.

"I know Otisville," I said. Otisville was where I had served my last six months in the system.

"Nice place, if ya gotta do time."

"I suppose I should take a run up there sometime," I said. "See how Vinny's doing." Though the very idea gave me a case of the creeps, it made some sense. Vinny might be just the person to give me some perspective on my investigation. He had done it before.

"Do that. Tell him Antony remembers." He cocked his head to the side. "What the hell is that?"

I heard it, too. One of the male leads had been moaning about not having the necessary mojo to defeat the forces of evil. As an aria, it was slow, doleful, and boring, and could be improved only by major surgery. But that wasn't what made it weird.

A second voice had joined. A sobbing, single-note drone in counterpoint to the hero. A voice filled with infinite sadness, yet young, and therefore eerie beyond words. I knew that voice.

"Oh, no."

I dashed out, down the stairs and through the double doors into the theater.

There was an ancient, wide-bottomed and slow-moving usher ahead of me, starting down the aisle, flashlight at the ready, prepared to deal with whatever rude patron was committing such a mortal sin in her theater. It was my son, and she was not prepared for him at all.

"'Scuse me," I whispered, executing a perfect three-step cutout. She had to stop or trip over me. I gained another two steps on her.

The song came to an end. A tall, handsome, shirtless man with six-pack abs that made me hate him on sight was center stage, holding a silver sword aloft and awaiting the expected thunderous applause. In that hyperstill, breathless split second following the last dying note and before the first exuberant clap, a young voice cried out—screamed—in excruciating, existential pain, "WHY DON'T THEY JUST TELL THE STORY?"

The applause never arrived. Instead, the audience took a collective breath of amazement and released it with a howl of laughter. The guy with the sword glared out through the lights, seeking the face of his tormentor, amazed to be so attacked from the really expensive seats. His massive chest writhed with contained anger, his hands clenched in frustration. In the wings, a werewolf howled—with laughter.

The Kid began grunting, thunderous sounds that could not in anyone's imagination be issuing forth from such a tiny body. "Unh! Unh! Unh!"

I almost made it. I was two rows away and closing fast, when Angie broke. She stood up, her sticklike arms flailing, her head making that forward-backward bob like a cottonmouth getting ready to strike.

"You MAY not behave in that way, young man. Do you hear me? You MAY not. Now get yourself up out of that seat. NOW! You will come with me. NOW!"

She reached down to grab him.

I touched her shoulder with my fingertips. "No. Don't."

She whirled on me. "Take your hands off me!"

"Let me do this, Angie. I've got him. Come on, Kid. Ice cream."

He stopped grunting, and for a moment looked my way. Then his eyes closed and he began to rock back and forth. The chance for a quick and effective intervention slipped away.

"He is out of control," she yelled at me, doing her best to demonstrate that while she, too, was out of control, it was all my fault that our son was wigging out.

"Let the lady be," a voice behind me said. I turned. A burly man in a Hawaiian shirt was close enough to violate any sense of personal space. His hands were down at his sides, and he was leading with his gut. It's a pose meant to intimidate, but between prison gangbangers and derivatives traders, I'd already been intimidated by experts.

"That's my son, sir."

He pushed forward, crowding me and closing in. "I'm telling you, fella. You leave the lady alone." Do all frail-looking, beautiful women attract misguided Sir Gala-hads? Was it a pheromone thing? Or was it just Angie?

I stepped into him. His eyes registered surprise, then shock. I had dropped my right hand down to his crotch and grabbed his balls through his Tommy Bahama, razor-creased, silk-blend dress pants.

"You're out of your fucking league, Cujo. Now, back the fuck up, or I take these home with me."

He backed up two steps and flopped down in his seat. I turned back to Angie. She was standing in the middle of the aisle, hands on hips, ready to take me on. The usher arrived and managed to shine her flashlight directly in Angie's eyes.

"Please return to your seat, Miss."

Angie swatted the light away. The flashlight dropped to the floor and went out.

"Stay out of this, Jason. I can discipline my child without your interference, thank you."

The orchestra had started up again, a duet of violins and cello meant to convey tension and menace. The he-man, with one last angry look our way, exited stage left. The lights dimmed and four coffins opened, revealing the green-lit vampire family. The audience, most of whom had lost interest in our little drama once the Kid stopped grunting, all ooohed as the vampires rose into the air and began to sing.

I ignored Angie. I leaned across the Kid and spoke to Tino. "I'm getting him out of here. Call me. Maybe we can still meet up later." He nodded. Mamma paid no attention; she was staring at the stage in wonder.

Angie looked like she was building up steam for a full-out verbal assault; I didn't give her time to explode.

"Let's talk about this out front," I said, swooping the Kid up into my arms. He wriggled in preparation for some animal defense, and I hugged him to me and ran.

The usher was shuffling along the aisle, trying to find the missing flashlight—her badge of office—with her feet. She saw us coming and hopped out of the way. I kept moving. Angie had stopped to collect her purse and Saks shopping bag, but I could feel she was gaining quickly.

The Kid twisted around in my arms when I stopped

to negotiate the double doors. For a moment, his head was free. A moment. That's all it took. He lunged and sank his teeth into my chest.

I did not scream, but I wanted to. It hurt. I pressed his head into my chest, so he wouldn't be able to shake it, an action he was capable of that most closely resembled what a dog does with a squeaky toy.

Once out onto the street, Angie allowed herself to explode.

"Put him down! I am going to talk some sense into that child. This is how you let him behave? Screaming at the top of his lungs like that? I suppose this is more of the 'therapy' that I wasn't getting him. You are a hypocrite, Jason. A sanctimonious hypocrite. Turn him around. Now! I want him to look me in the eye when I'm talking."

At any other time, she might have been causing a scene, but at three-thirty in the afternoon on a Sunday, Forty-fifth Street was almost deserted. I stepped back against the building and squatted down, still holding the Kid as tightly as I could.

He wriggled halfheartedly.

"Easy, Kid. You're okay. I have you. You are safe now. We'll get you some ice cream in a little bit and you'll feel better."

He began to relax. He took his teeth out of my left pec. My own little vampire. I felt a tickling stream of blood down my side.

Angie took a quick breath between rants, and I jumped in.

"Angie, shut the fuck up," I hissed, trying to keep my

voice from spiraling out of control. "Right now, I don't want to hear your shit. You're pissed because he was acting up. I'm worried because he was stressed out. We're not even the same species. It's like we come from different dimensions. We both observe the same phenomena, but our conclusions are light-years apart."

The Kid heard the anger in my voice and was instantly a squirming, ferocious wild animal. But he was spent. Done. The spasm lasted seconds and he went limp. He did not slowly melt, he simply transformed into a liquid gel and passed out.

"I need to get him home," I said. He would need to nap for an hour or so and then he'd be ravenously hungry.

Angie took a moment to decide that she didn't need to continue her tirade on the sidewalk. She strode to the curb and put a hand in the air for a cab. I thought of telling her that she was delusional. She wasn't going to find a cab on a cross street in the theater district until late afternoon when the shows let out. Every New Yorker knows that.

An empty, off-duty cab came through the green light at Broadway and continued down the block toward us. Angie waved. Off-duty. It was never going to stop. It stopped in front of Angie.

While the cab lurched up toward Amsterdam Avenue, I checked my wound. My shirt was stuck to my chest with dried blood, but when I pulled it away I could see the damage was minimal. I'd have a bruise, but no scar. I thought I might not have minded a scar. It would be something to show the grandchildren someday and tell them how I got it.

I brushed a few sweaty hairs from the Kid's face,

marveling for the thousandth time how much he resembled his mother. Maybe we'd both be lucky and he'd outgrow it.

"You know something, Angie? You're going to think this is screwed up, but I'm proud of this guy. He just put a big sentence together. He identified what it was that was bugging him, and before he let himself go nuts or catatonic or wet himself or start biting people, he asked a question. A seven-word sentence! That's not a record, but it's damn good. Against all his natural instincts, he tried communication to get relief. That's huge."

Angie didn't say anything for three long, tense seconds.

"I may have my failings, as a person, as a mother, but I am not a witch. I want to love my son and have him love me. But I look at you with him and I see a man drowning in self-delusion. You claim the boy is so much better, but I just saw him *bite* you. He has no sense of discipline, no self-control. And you seem to think that's just fine. What exactly are you doing for him? Do you think he'll ever be able to live around other people? He is one step from a wild animal. I believe he can be better than that, and if it takes some tough love to get him there, then so be it."

It was like that asinine game from Psychology 101—the one with the picture in black and white where half the class sees a chalice and the other half sees two mirror images of a face in silhouette. We both had the same information, but we interpreted the problem entirely differently. And I was right. I believed it with all my heart. So did she, most likely. And anything I said would only further convince her that she was in the right. So I said nothing. Call me a coward or call me passive-aggressive, but I did not want to fight with her. I just wanted to be left alone to raise my son.

We pulled up in front of the Ansonia. I got out, awkwardly exiting with the Kid in both arms. I let Angie pay the fare. She had plenty of my money, she could afford it.

Raoul, our trusty doorman, saw us and rushed over to help Angie out of the cab. I started across the sidewalk.

The Kid moaned.

There were four of them. Dark-skinned mestizos, all with the sloped, bony brow and chiseled noses of the Maya. They could have been the Hondurans Castillo had mentioned—or Guatemalans, or Mexicans, or they could have been born in the Bronx for all I knew. Two were in suits, white shirts, no ties. The other two wore dark hoodies in the early-summer heat, partially eclipsing their faces, each with hands thrust in the front pockets and holding something heavy. I didn't recognize any of them, but I knew who they were.

"You were supposed to be finding something of ours, Mr. Stafford. Is there a problem? You need to let us know if there is a problem." The man was noticeably shorter than his three companions. In any gang situation, always be careful of the short man. He's the one with something to prove.

They fanned out across the sidewalk, the two hoodies backing up the short man, the other suited man facing off in front of Raoul, who looked frightened. I was, too, but I hoped I didn't look it. Angie marched through and went straight for the door of the building, Saks bag swinging—still angry, determined, and oblivious. She disappeared inside.

I tried a brusque brush-off. "I told Mr. Castillo I would keep him informed. I didn't say I was working for him."

"Are you not taking this seriously? That would be a mistake. You see that. You are not a stupid man."

Great. Everyone else thought I was an idiot. I didn't have much to offer. The bonds were still missing, and I had only a vague idea of where they might be.

"Tell Mr. Castillo I'll give him a call Monday morning." I tried to push past, an impossibility while carrying my son.

One of the hoodies stretched out a hand and stopped me. The other hand remained in the big front pocket. I didn't need to see it to understand the threat.

"This is your son?" the short man continued. "Very nice. Beautiful boy. He goes to school uptown, doesn't he? Yes, and the fat girl picks him up and walks him home every day. *La gordita*. A long walk, and some of those blocks are not so good. By the projects, I mean. Bad things happen there sometimes. You should tell her to be careful."

His tone was conversational, but the message was clear. I flashed on all the possible ways that a determined man or woman could get to me or my son. We were wide open. My only defense was cooperation.

"Believe me, I'm working it. If he wants to meet with me, just set a time and place. I'll be there."

He hadn't bothered to deny that he was there on orders from Castillo—or one of his close acquaintances. His stare turned hard and he tried looking through me. I met the gaze. Some magic must have passed between us. I didn't faint from fright, and he softened.

"I think you are sincerely a man of honor. I will take that back with me."

Angie took that moment to stick her head out the door and call, "Jason! Are you coming? I know you wouldn't give a thought to keeping me waiting, but I would think you would be in a bigger hurry to get our child to bed."

The four Latinos all smiled smugly. In one of my many impromptu language lessons in prison, I had learned that the word *"esposas,"* the plural of "wife" in Spanish, was also the word for "handcuffs." Raoul didn't smile. He was still too scared to move even a face muscle.

"We're just finishing up," I said. "We're coming."

The short man and I shared a look again.

"Your wife is very pretty, too. I see where your son gets his looks." He grinned to let me know he was both complimenting me and insulting me. And threatening me. "You will hear from us. Please have some good news."

They melted away—one moment a concentration of evil, the next just four vague strangers dispersing through the crowds on Broadway.

"You all right, Raoul?" I said.

He didn't look so good, but he pulled himself together.

"You know those guys, Mr. Stafford?"

"Me? Never saw them before in my life." I followed Angie inside.

The adrenaline rush that had carried me out of the theater, all the way home, and through the confrontation with the four Latinos, was now an adrenaline jag. My arms ached, my knees were shaky, and I felt like I couldn't catch a full breath. Nevertheless, I managed to cross the lobby on white squares only. Angie made a point of standing solidly on a black tile as we waited for the elevator.

"What were you doing out there?" She was not making a scene, she was simply hissing at me loud enough to turn heads the length of the building.

The truth would have set off an explosion that I did not want to witness. I offered a half-truth. "They're some men who wanted to talk business with me."

"Well, I hope you set them straight. It's Sunday, for goodness' sake."

When I met Angie, she had not been inside of a church since her confirmation. She claimed to be allergic to incense. This newfound respect for the Sabbath must have had something to do with her twelve-step recovery.

"I pointed that out to them."

The elevator opened.

"And?" she said in an arch tone.

"Then I had to give them directions down to Saint Pat's."

We rode up in silence.

Angie held off until I got the Kid settled in his bed. I came back into the living room to find her commanding center stage—her face a stone carving depicting "Righteous Anger."

"I have just as much a right as you to discipline our

child. You will not correct me in front of him. You will not take his side. You will not try to undercut me. Those are not requests. We have had our differences, and have failed each other in any number of ways, but as the mother of a child, I will not be disrespected by you or anyone. Is there anything about what I just said that you don't understand?"

She didn't sound Cajun at all. She was angry but controlled, superior without lapsing into a pose of haughty and abused. It was an excellent performance. A lesser man might have applauded. I took three deep, cleansing breaths—a necessary first step in pain and anger management, according to Skeli—and sat down. Sitting lowers the offensive profile without ceding ground. It is nonconfrontational, nonviolent, and maddening.

"I can see you want a fight, Angie, but I am not going to give it to you. Not right now and never again. The Kid is sleeping and he really needs it. I think you should go now." And the showdown with the four men out front had caused a major shift in my priorities. Fighting with Angie wasn't important. I needed her gone, away, as soon as possible. Survival was more important than being right or wrong.

She struggled. She was ready to blast me, but she held it back. "I'm going back and find Mamma and Tino. They'll be worried sick."

I doubted it. Tino was too steady to waste energy on worrying about things he couldn't fix. And I didn't think Mamma had even noticed us leaving.

"That sounds like a fine idea," I said.

She almost made it out the door. It would have been a perfect exit. Silent, proud, controlled. She couldn't do it.

"You think about what I said. This is so not over." Then she left.

| 23 |

Fighting with Angie was like screwing with her—it blinded me to anything else that was going on. Once she was gone, the scary stuff came right back. I had stirred up a nest or two. A million a year wasn't going to be worth it, if the Kid was in danger. I was in danger, too, but that bothered me a lot less directly. If I were gunned down by Central American midgets, the Kid would go back to living locked up in his grandma's attic. But at least I wouldn't have to be there to see it. Either way, the threat was to the Kid. I called in the cavalry. My good buddy, Brady, at the FBI.

"Jason Stafford," he greeted me. "Whenever I see your name on my caller ID, I know my life is about to become much more interesting."

"If it weren't for me, Brady, you'd still be carrying a calculator in your holster. Instead of being part of a hotshot team on a multiagency antidrug task force, you'd be adding columns of numbers all day as a forensic accountant."

"Any number of people have helped me in my career, but you are the only one who reminds me of it every time we talk."

"Working on Sunday? No wonder crime is down."

"I am a Special Agent. One of the perks of reaching that exalted rank is covering the desk on weekends while more senior agents are otherwise occupied. Is this a social call?"

"I need your help."

"Excuse me for not feigning surprise."

I quickly rattled off the highlights of the confrontation with the four Latinos. He didn't interrupt.

"I need protection. Not for me. For my son. I can't protect him twenty-four-seven." Another thought occurred to me. "And I'm afraid that Angie's on their radar screen now, too."

"I seem to remember a conversation earlier this week—"

"I know. That's why I'm calling." I tried to cut him off.

"—right here in my office, in which you were warned that just such a scenario was in the cards unless you backed out of whatever nonsense you were up to with Castillo."

"What can you do for me?"

"The short answer? Nothing."

"Can't you pick them up? You must have them all on file, right?"

"Four Latinos? One of them is short. Are you joking? It sounds like a landscaper's crew."

"You have no idea who they are?"

He was polite enough not to answer. "And second, they committed no crime. I can't even put you in witness protection—which you would not want—because you haven't witnessed anything. So far, a man stopped you on the street and complimented you on your son."

"No, no, no."

"Hear me out. You know they were threatening you, and I believe you. But I can't sell that story. Your witness, the doorman. What's he going to contribute?"

Nothing. "I get it. Any suggestions?"

"Take your son and go to New Zealand for six months."

"Not possible."

"In six months this group of toughs will all be in prison or dead. There's a lot of turnover in their line of work."

"Not even funny."

"I wasn't being funny. The way I hear it, talking to your buddy Castillo won't help either. They don't take his orders."

"I could just find them their money and be done with it."

"If you do, let me know. We would be very interested."

"I still need someone watching my back for the next week or so."

"I hear the family you're working for has a full security

team these days. Maybe they'll lend you some muscle for a few days."

Great. The Kid could have his own pet mercenary.

"I'll think about it."

"Good luck. Call me if anyone commits a crime, will you?"

FBI stand-up humor. Did they teach it at the academy?

"Hey! You can do something for me. I just thought of it."

"Oh, good. Now I feel better."

I could see his snarky grin right through the phone.

"An SEC guy. Gibbons. Charles Gibbons. Is he for real? The guy has been following me. He is not like any SEC accountant I've ever met."

"Don't know him. But I'll ask. Give me a day."

I didn't like the idea of Blake's crew watching over my son—I didn't trust them or him—but safety was a bigger concern. I called Virgil. This time he answered right away. I filled him in.

"It's your investigation that put me here. I can't work for you if my son is in danger. Period. I'll need twenty-four-hour protection for him until this is over."

"For you and the boy?"

The only way to get these guys off my case was to find Castillo's missing bonds. And I wasn't going to be doing that with the dogs of war looking over my shoulder. "No. Just the boy. But it's got to be twenty-four-seven."

"Talk to Blake. Tell him I authorized rotating

two-man teams for the next ten days. He'll set it up." He gave me the number and hung up.

It was a start. I wanted castles with shark-filled moats and minefields and barbed wire and Navy SEALs with machine guns, and maybe a company of Marines—but two big tattooed mercenaries was a start.

"Blake here," he said, answering his cell on the second ring.

I gave him the bare bones—it wasn't enough.

"I'm interested in how this connects to your investigation for the family."

"I explained it to Virgil," I said. "Threats—quite legitimate threats, I would say—have been made against me and my family, directly as a result of my involvement. I think the people who made these threats are both capable and experienced in this kind of thing."

He knew he wasn't getting the whole story. He remained silent for a minute, on the chance that I would keep talking and tell him more. I didn't fall for it.

"What do you know that makes these people think this is a productive strategy?" he finally asked.

Interesting. Virgil hadn't asked that question. I thought I knew, but I wasn't quite ready. But I wasn't going to share anything with Blake. When in doubt, equivocate.

"I'm not sure. I might know something, but I don't know that I know it."

He sucked on that for a minute.

"I can have two men there in less than an hour."

A small piece of the granite boulder that was resting on my chest broke off and rolled away.

"I'm not sure how to say this, but the type of men you had up in Newport the other day are going to be a bit conspicuous hanging around the lobby of the Ansonia."

He chuckled. "You'd like the special Upper West Side package? I can send you a pair of out-of-work community organizers and a drum circle."

"I'm just saying, Blake, that there are people living in this building who won't like seeing guys with Odin tattoos riding the elevator with them."

"My men will be discreet. It is one of the truisms of this business that genuinely nice people, the kind you might invite to a dinner party, are less effective as bodyguards than large, unimaginative types who have never read much good fiction. And don't worry, we've worked the Ansonia before. I'll contact the security people there before my people arrive." He clicked off before I could respond.

I didn't know the Ansonia had "security people." What did they think of me? Ex-con. Marginally employed. I vowed to try smiling more when I walked through the lobby.

But even with two berserker mercenaries in attendance, the Kid was only partially protected. The only way I was going to ensure all our safety was to come up with some answers. Soon.

| 24 |

My father and I share a minor nonfatal obsessive-compulsive behavioral tic. When planning a trip, any trip, like him, I must review every possible approach to my goal, even if it's just across Amsterdam Avenue to the Häagen-Dazs store. And though I am much better than he at controlling these impulses, I had plotted this trip to the site of my last incarceration with infinite care.

The GW Bridge to Palisades Parkway to the New York State Thruway, all the way to Harriman, where I picked up 17 West to 211. It's both quick and the scenic route, and the Dead's *Nightfall of Diamonds* kept me company until my anxiety over where I was headed got the better of me and I turned the music off.

My last six months in the federal penal system, I was domiciled at the minimum-security satellite camp at Otisville in the middle of the Catskills. Vinny had been doing his stretch at the main, medium-security facility there, but had already been transferred to the camp. I don't know that visiting any other federal prison would have been easier on my psyche, but returning to Otisville was giving me a headache, sour stomach, nausea, and a dull-headed exhaustion. I felt like I had all the side effects they warn you about in those TV ads for prescription meds.

A few miles west of Middletown, the winding curves of 211 finally got to me. I pulled over, but not quite off the road—I hadn't seen another car in miles—and opened the window. It was hot and humid—it was hot and humid all over the Northeast—but the mountain air smelled of pine, and I took a minute to pull myself together. It was deliciously quiet. My breaths came slower and freer. The rope around my chest eased. Confidence returned. I could do this.

Movement in the rearview mirror caught my eye. A white SUV with dark tinted windows was slowing down behind me. I rolled down the window and waved him on around me. A GMC Denali. A compact for those who found the Hummer too ostentatious. He stopped twenty feet back and waited. I waved again—a bit more force-fully. A moment later the big engine raced and he sped by me, deeper into the woods. I watched the truck bounce as it hit a pothole a few hundred yards down the road, then it was around a bend and gone. The silence of the woods returned and, almost immediately, became oppressive.

My hands felt clammy and I felt an annoying buzz in my head, like too much bad coffee or the first shades of an oncoming cold. Or claustrophobia. I was eight months on the outside and capable of going days at a time without thinking of the two years I'd been a reluctant guest of the U.S. penal system, but it didn't take much more than the sight of a roll of razor wire over a chain-link fence to churn it all up again.

I started the car and finished the drive. I made the right in the middle of town and a few minutes later the sign for the prison appeared.

Ahead, there was a series of orange cones guiding any traffic down into a single narrow lane that led to a free-standing guardhouse. I pulled up to the booth. A perfectly pleasant young man in a blue guard uniform very politely asked me my business. He scared the shit out of me. I had to clear my throat twice to answer.

"I'm visiting."

"An inmate?"

I nodded.

"Have you been here before? You know where you're going?"

Yes, I had been there before. And no, I had no idea where I was going. The last time I hadn't come in the visitors' entrance. I shook my head.

"Okay. Pull through the gate here and park in the visitors' lot. Someone will show you where to go from there."

I cleared my throat again. "Thanks."

"You all right?"

I forced a smile. "Allergies."

He smiled back and gave a half-salute as I drove off.

The gate—a section of the chain-link fence on rollers—pulled back as I approached, and I continued inside. My ears started ringing. I shook my head and tried to ignore it. I drove down a corridor between two fences. I passed a guard carrying a black pump shotgun and walking a German shepherd that looked to be the size of a small horse. I reminded myself to breathe again.

VISITOR PARKING. I looked around. Antony had been right. If you had to do time in the federal prison system, this is where you wanted to be. The buildings were mostly Quonset huts and two-story barracks, surrounded by green grass, bushes, and even a ball field. It wasn't the Club Fed, of a bygone era—those had disappeared twenty years ago—but neither was it designed to break your spirit. And that is what the Federal Bureau of Prisons is all about. It is punishment, not rehabilitation. From the ADX or ADMAX facilities—the maximum-security penitentiaries where terrorists like the Unabomber are kept in permanent solitary confinement—and the infamous USPs—high-security penitentiaries—like Beaumont and Big Sandy, to the Federal Correctional Institutions like Ray Brook, where I spent the first eighteen months of my sentence, they all share a unified purpose: to grind away at each prisoner's last shreds of dignity and humanity.

FPCs—Federal Prison Camps—like Fort Dix and the camp at Otisville, are a little different. Each has its own style—rules, privileges, privations—but they are all essentially holding areas for short-timers. Usually the camps are attached to some other facility, so that the low-security prisoners can do all of the maintenance for both facilities. Cheap labor. Fights are few, escape attempts almost nonexistent—the calendar is your friend. Any forbidden activity that might prolong your stay by even a day is to be avoided.

But that doesn't mean it's pleasant. It's still prison.

Two COs, armed with Tasers and clipboards, took my name, wrote down the license-plate number on my rental car, and directed me into the main office, where another steely-eyed bureaucrat with a badge checked my ID against the computer and told me to take a seat in the next room.

"When you hear your name called, go to the window at the far end and they'll take you through."

Stepping through the door, I had to make a conscious effort not to flinch. I was inside the "facility."

The waiting room was almost empty. Three lawyers—two men and a woman, all in suits and carrying both briefcases and expandable file folders—were tapping away on laptops. No families. It was Monday—a workday, a school day, not a regular visiting day. Brady had made the call to get me in. Another reluctant favor I owed him.

I went to the treasurer's window and completed the necessary forms to put a hundred bucks in Vinny's commissary account—he could buy cigarettes, snacks, or newspapers. I doubted he'd be able to get his beloved *Racing Form*, but maybe they let in the *New York Post*.

Then I waited.

A speaker crackled to life and a name was called. One of the suits got up and went to the window, showed his ID—again—deposited all valuables in a manila envelope, had his picture taken, stepped through the body scanner and the puffer machine, and went into the next room. A moment later, a second name was called and the process repeated, until, last, I heard, "Jason Stafford."

There was no logical reason for my stomach to lurch, or for the back of my neck to suddenly go ice-cold. I was a free man. Clean. Almost squeaky clean, if you ignored the money I had hidden in Switzerland. I'd even cleared the trip with my parole officer—an ignominious exercise, somewhat akin to raising your hand to go to the bathroom in middle school—though I had somehow managed to leave him with the impression that I was visiting with the warden rather than a fellow felon. Unless I tried to slip Vinny some item of contraband—like a gun, or drugs, or a copy of *Penthouse*—no one could lay a hand on me. Logic is a cold comfort.

The CO minding the scanners had biceps that threatened to tear his short-sleeved uniform to shreds. He was bored but alert, efficiently doing his job without giving it—or me—any thought. He waved me through. I patted myself on the back for how well I was handling being this close to the enemy once again—on his own turf.

A moment later, I almost lost it.

We were sitting in a large room that might have doubled as a small cafeteria. One wall held snack, soda, and coffee machines, and long tables, built like Formica picnic benches, lined the room. There was enough space that all of the visitors were able to spread out and get some privacy. Then an oversized metal door at the end of the room opened and the prisoners came in.

It was the gray jumpsuits that did it. I couldn't see Vinny's face. All I saw were four shadows fanning out across the room and approaching. I rose and stumbled back over the bench, almost falling. Vinny grabbed my arm and held me upright.

"Easy there, sport. You all right?"

Past and present flickered in my head. I was in prison. I was gagging on the acrid smells of men locked down in too-close proximity. Sweat, urine, semen, and a blend of cleaning chemicals that never seemed to truly rid the air of those other scents. My eyes wouldn't focus. I was not all right.

My third day of incarceration, I wandered down to the dayroom, a twenty-by-twenty space that boasted a television mounted on one wall and plastic chairs arranged in rows. A soap opera was on, a pair of beautiful actors mumbling at each other in deadly earnest. There was no one in the room. I stood there, still feeling like I had landed in an episode of The Prisoner, *with no idea of the rules of this alien world. Could I sit down? Could I change the channel? Was I allowed to be there? These issues had not been covered in the handout when I first checked in.*

After a few minutes, the murmuring voices on the screen were starting to get to me. I looked for some way of changing the channel. No luck. I grabbed a chair and stood on it. The small black buttons on the set had long lost their markings. I tried pushing one. The volume increased. I pushed another. The screen went blank. Shit.

Then the chair flew out from beneath me and I hit the ground. I felt a heavy foot swing by my head. I rolled away, smashing through a cluster of chairs until I was clear. I rose up to see three gray jumpsuits coming at me. One of the men was screaming something about me and TV and who the fuck did I think I was and how he was now going to welcome me properly to Ray Brook. Then he called me "Punk."

One of the services offered by my crack legal defense team, after the production of my PSR—pre-sentencing report—and just before I surrendered myself directly at Ray Brook, was an afternoon session with their team of Survival Consultants. Two ex-convicts answered my questions about my upcoming experience and gave me advice on a range of subjects.

Never look directly into another man's cell—it's an invasion of privacy and you will pay for it.

When you're on the can, be polite. Flush halfway through. It cuts down on the aroma.

Never join a gang. The protection offered is an illusion and they will own you.

Looking a man in the eye is an act of intimacy, which can lead to sex, violence, or both.

No one is your friend. Least of all, the Correctional Officers.

Don't be a snitch.

Don't hog the phone. There's a line of angry, impatient convicts behind you.

And so on, down to the final:

And never—never—let a man call you Punk. Punks belong to anyone. Prey for anything. It is far better to take a beating than to be branded.

I backed away, letting the guy follow, let him back me into a corner of the room. It was a dead-end move, but it made it hard for all three of them to come at me at once. The two on the flanks held back and gave me my chance.

I grabbed a chair and swung it as hard as I could at his face. He ducked back, but not quite fast enough. I caught him across the bridge of the nose. Not hard enough to put him down, but hard enough to hurt. He roared and swiped at me clumsily, giving me enough time for a second shot. This time I connected cleanly with his temple. The light plastic chair did not make a formidable weapon, but I lucked out. He dropped like Mike Piazza getting beaned by Roger Clemens.

The other two rushed me. I held the chair in front of me like a shield. It held them up for about a nanosecond. There was plenty of room in the corner for two guys to beat on me, and the walls made it worse, holding me upright a lot longer than my legs did. I flailed a couple of times, but I'd never been a fighter. I had no idea how to throw a punch and make it hurt. They did.

Long before the COs arrived, the two guys had to make a decision whether to kill me or let me collapse to the floor. Luckily for me, they chose door number two.

I spent three days in the hospital ward, with my ribs taped, a concussion, and a fracture of the left eye socket that the doctor thought could give me eyesight problems later in life. When the guards asked me who had done it, I was able to identify them only as "three white guys in gray jumpsuits." They thought I was wising off, so I did two weeks in SHU—Special Housing Unit—what was called "solitary" in less Orwellian times and otherwise known as "the hole" or "the bucket."

My first day back in gen-pop I was terrified—if my attack-ers wanted to see that I returned to the hospital, they could take me just about anywhere. When two nights passed and I was still alive, I began to remember some of the other lessons of my survival class. My cellmate, a black man half my age but with twice my street smarts, confirmed my thoughts.

"Check this out. See, G, them Caspers thinking they found themselves a Gregory to put the hurt on, but you come down like a clown with some serious drama. You peeled that ding's wig!" He slapped my palm at that point. "And when the COs wanted you to snitch, turns out you solid. You do the bucket and come out stand-up. You got cred now, dog."

And after some patient explanations on his part, I understood that in defending myself and refusing to give up my attackers—who I couldn't have identified anyway—I had gained the respect of my colleagues and had no reason to fear retribution.

And I had only another seven hundred and ten days to go.

Vinny sat me down and brought me a Diet Coke.

"I thought I could do this," I said. "Now, I'm not so sure."

"Come on, don't embarrass me, okay? I gotta live here. I can't have my tough-guy visitors having fainting spells."

I managed a small smile. "Sorry, boss."

"Jeez, I got cred to maintain in here."

I took a few deep breaths. "It was the suits that did it."

"No shit. They are ugly, aren't they?" He laughed. Vinny was thin, gray, and ageless but had always looked good. My father would have called him a "natty" dresser. Always put together but never showy. The jumpsuit hung on him like a shopping bag.

I fought my way to some semblance of normalcy. "How you doing, Vinny? Nobody knew where you were. We asked around, but it was like you just disappeared after the old place closed. People just figured you were drinking someplace new."

"Yeah, well. They shut down my shop on account of this bullshit over the Internet business. I don't even want to talk about it. I told my lawyer to get me a deal, and I took it."

"How much longer will you be here?"

"I copped to three—two and a half to go. I'm hoping it gets crowded, though, and they send some of us home early."

"You've got somebody rooting for you?"

"I've got some friends—investors, I guess—who owe me, 'cause I neglected to mention their names when the Feds were asking. They got me a very good lawyer and they're working pulling in favors."

I never knew just how connected Vinny was, or with whom. He ran a betting shop over the OTB on Seventy-second Street for a bunch of years without any interference from the NYPD. Someone must have been watching his back. The place was ostensibly a private club, but that was pure fiction. They'd take anybody's money. There was fresh coffee all day long, comfortable couches and chairs, and when Madison Square Garden put their first flat-screen TV in one of the VIP booths, Vinny already had six of them in his shop.

"And how's things here?" I asked. "You getting by?"

"I got no problems. I'm bunked with a three-hundred-pound ex-boxer from Albania with a wife and a two-year-old kid up in Hartford. I've arranged for her to get a check every month. It's not a lot, but Vllasi appreciates the gesture. No one bothers us. It's a quiet kind of place, anyway, you know?"

I filled him in on the community news. Chitchat. Gossip. When my pop had come up to visit me, I had found myself hanging on his stories of bar denizens I didn't know, just to hear a kind voice talking about something almost normal. I stopped when I heard myself telling a story about MaJohn's mother's knee operation.

"Sorry," I said. "I don't know why you would care about that."

He smiled. "Nah, it's okay. Tell John, if she needs anything, she should call my cousin, Al." He rattled off a phone number. "He works in Boca. He'll take care of her."

"Is he in the same business as you?" I could not imagine why an eighty-five-year-old widow with bad pins would need a bookie.

Vinny laughed. "No. Al's legit. Well, quasi-legit. He's a medical supplies distributor. He can get her a walker, or whatever she needs. One of those go-cart things. Scooter? Whatever."

What could be more profitable than your own casino? A medical supply house in Florida.

"I'll pass that on," I said.

"So, give me something juicy. You working on anything? Something with lots of rich people getting screwed, that's what I want to hear." He gave a mad grin.

"I was hoping to pick your brain."

"I got the time."

"What I say goes no further."

"Come on, who you talking to? Tell me a story. A good one."

"I've got just the thing," I said.

I filled him in on the last three weeks of my life—from the helicopter ride to Newport through dropping the Kid at school and convincing the formidable Mrs. Carter, who guarded the front desk and logged in every student, teacher, and parent who passed in front of her, that the two guys in suits and Terminator sunglasses were okay and would be hanging around outside all day to see my son back home. I left out the debacle of the theater, because I didn't think Vinny would care. And I left out Skeli's good-bye picnic, because it was none of his business.

He interrupted with a few questions as I went along, but when I was done, he was quiet for a long time.

"So," he finally said. "What are you thinking?"

"Well, first, I take it as a given that no one is telling me everything they know."

"You include your buddy Paddy in that?"

"Unfortunately, yes."

"Right." He gave a slow blink of approval.

"The dead lawyer is important." I described the method of meeting in the café and returning to the bank to place the bonds back in the safe-deposit box. "But I don't see yet how to bust it open. He'd have a key, I guess."

Vinny was shaking his head. "But that leaves a trail, don't you see? The bank clocks in every visitor to a safe-deposit box. There'd be a paper trail. Video cameras. I don't buy it. These guys are too smart for this."

"They're passing tens of millions of dollars of bearer bonds at a time, Vinny. They'd want to keep them fairly secure, ya think?"

"When you went away, you probably stashed a little something for when you got out, am I right?"

I nodded. "And my good watch."

"And did you put all that in a safe-deposit box?"

"No," I said, ready to concede the point. For the two years I was away as a guest of the Federal Bureau of Prisons, my father had kept my briefcase "hidden" on a shelf in my old bedroom upstairs over his bar in College Point. The briefcase had held fifty thousand dollars in crisp fifties, still in the bank wrappers.

"Whyzat?"

I was being schooled again. "So there would be no record for the Feds. They'd be able to trace a box."

He smiled.

"Okay," I said, "but I wasn't dealing in billions. I had fifty grand in my old briefcase. I left it in my pop's apartment. He's lived there fifty years and never had a break-in. I think it's the safest place in the universe."

"So why would this lawyer do things any different?"

"Size matters. I would think they'd be a bit smarter about it than I was."

He shook his head. "You're thinking like an investor. These guys aren't collecting interest. They're *hiding* principal. Their greatest fear is what? Losing their shirt? No way. Their only concern is having some cop put together an evidentiary trail. They'd rather keep the money under a mattress. They can always get more money. What they won't be able to buy is their way out of prison."

"We're talking about one hundred million dollars. No one takes that kind of hit and brushes it off."

"Where do you hide sand?"

"What?"

"At the beach. You with me? When you're that big, your number-one problem is visibility, not security. Trust me."

"All right, I hear you. But I'm not a hundred percent. Yet. And I still have a half dozen other trails to chase down."

He shrugged. "Go back and talk to the girlfriend. She's the only one speaking the truth, the way I hear you tell it. She knows more than she said, but she may not know that it's important."

I dreaded going back there. "She's nucking futz."

"Nevertheless."

"Gotcha."

"First, you've got to eighty-six the muscle. They don't work for you, they work for this other guy who works for your client. When something bad happens, they're not gonna be there for you—or the Kid."

"Any suggestions?"

"You want me to take care of it? It's done. There's

MORTAL BONDS | 265

people who owe me favors. Let me talk to Vllasi. He's very creative this way."

THE BIG WHITE SUV with the dark tinted windows picked me up as I drove out of the forest. It came out of the driveway of an abandoned house, the roof sagging so badly it resembled a pagoda. The driver hung back three or four cars once we were up on the Thruway, but he was still there as I came across the GW Bridge and turned down the West Side Highway.

I lost him getting off the Highway at Seventy-ninth Street. Or he kept on going because he'd never been following me in the first place. Or it was a succession of similar-looking vehicles. Or a second vehicle picked up the tail. Or I was turning into a first-class paranoid. I left the rental in the Ansonia garage and stopped by Hanrahan's before heading home.

| 25 |

Angie and I waved to the Town Car as it pulled away from the curb, taking Mamma and Tino to the airport. The trunk held two suitcases more than when they had arrived—Angie had made sure to take Mamma shopping. Our smiles lasted until the car was halfway down the block.

"I don't think there is much for us to say right now," Angie said. "I don't know why, but I thought you would be more supportive."

Two more weeks, I reminded myself. Two weeks and she would be gone, back to Louisiana. I could do it. I could make it two weeks.

"I'm going to be busy wrapping up some work things the next few days. Have some fun with the Kid. I'll be out of your hair."

"You're not going to miss his graduation?!"

It wasn't really a question—more an expression of annoyance.

"It's not graduation. There's no ceremony. No awards. It's his last day of school."

"And you would miss it?!" She did it again.

There had been a send-off the night before. I should have enjoyed it. The Kid stayed home with Heather and the bodyguards, while Angie and I took her mother and Tino out to Brooklyn—to Peter Luger's for steak. Pop and his honey met us there. I immediately liked her. They were both a bit formal with each other, but also comfortable—as though they'd been together years instead of weeks. Mamma had had two martinis and declared the creamed spinach to be "sinful." Judging by how much of it she had put away, "sinful" was a supreme compliment. Tino and my father swapped funny horror stories about the demands of dealing with customers in a retail service business. Angie and I had sat at opposite ends of the table and did our best to pretend we weren't there. It was the kind of night I would have enjoyed if Skeli had been there. A bit loose, a bit liquid, surrounded by funny, interesting people that I liked. But Angie—by her presence alone—managed to suck every bit of pleasure out of it.

"I'll be there," I said. "And listen, I don't like those bodyguards any better than you do, but they are there to keep the Kid safe. Just let them do their jobs."

"This is some paranoid fantasy you've come up with to interfere with my time alone with my son. I will give this nonsense just two more days, and then I will put a stop to it."

She gave me a smug, victorious smile and walked back into her building.

I shook my head three or four times, took some deep breaths, unclenched my fists, and went home.

I had just walked in the door when the house phone rang—the front desk.

"There are two men here to see you, Mr. Stafford. I thought I should check before I sent them up." The concierge sounded nervous.

"Thank you, Richard. Did they give their names?"

"No, but they say they were sent by Vinny. Is this okay with you?"

"Keep them there, Richard. I'll be right down."

I saw immediately what had made Richard nervous. While Blake's thugs were big men, muscle-bound and angry-looking—like giant trolls—these two were slender, wiry, and dark. They were polite, a bit formal, and oozed menace. I could see the trolls beating someone to death in slow motion, taking their time. These two would just get it over with.

"Jason Stafford," I said, holding out a hand.

They nodded in unison. They both wore expensive-looking light leather jackets, despite the heat outside. The darker of the two stepped forward. His eyebrows met in a single straight line, further defining a face that was all planes and angles.

"You call me Tom," he said in a coarse Slavic-sounding accent. He smiled without warmth or charm or humor. "Is not my name, but is easy for you to say." He took my hand and shook. It felt like gripping a boa constrictor— all muscle.

"Vinny sent you?" I said.

"We have mutual friends." He enjoyed saying the words.

The other man hung back, his eyes occasionally flickering side to side, keeping the entire lobby in view from where he stood.

"Does he have a name?" I asked.

Tom shrugged. "Is not important." He spoke for a moment in a language that might have been Russian— or any of a half dozen other Eastern European languages. The other man smiled.

"You call me Ivan," he said.

They both laughed quietly. I joined in. It seemed the politic thing to do.

"Follow me," I said.

We talked as we walked up Amsterdam. Other pedestrians tended to move out of our way, but when we overtook and briefly startled a twentysomething couple, strolling and holding hands, Tom and Ivan apologized in an almost courtly manner.

"What do I pay you two?" I said.

"No pay," Tom said.

I stopped. So did they. "That doesn't work," I said. "I need to know you're working for me. If I'm not paying the bills, how do I know you're going to be there when I need you?"

Tom looked bored. "No worries."

"But I am worried. You guys are going to be guarding my son. That tops anything else. I'm no Donald Trump, but I'm ready to pay. Name your price."

Tom thought while Ivan kept scanning the street and sidewalk. "Okay, Mr. Trump. You pay."

"Fine," I said. "Now, how much?"

"One dollar."

I had the good sense to see that I had been out-maneuvered. This was a gift from Vinny, and I should have the grace to accept it.

"For the two of you?" I said.

Tom almost smiled. "Each." Then he did smile.

"Are there any more of you at home? I want twenty-four-seven on my son. And I may want someone else guarded."

Tom rattled off a cell-phone number. "You call. One hour."

"Same rate?"

He shrugged. Of course.

I explained about seeing the Kid to school, watching out front, seeing him home, and keeping watch in the building. "Maybe one in the hall. One in the apartment. It's not easy to get by the front desk, but it's happened. How many shifts do I need?"

"No shifts. You have us. Is enough."

I believed him.

THE CHANGING of the guard was awkward—Blake's men initially refused to leave and I had to call Virgil to order some firm instructions. It was further proof, if I needed it, that Blake's people didn't work for me and getting Vinny's associates to act in their stead was the right move.

| 26 |

There was one other person whom I had talked to who might still be in danger. The next morning I walked over to Central Park West and Ninety-sixth Street and took the subway downtown. If someone was following me, I planned on making his life difficult.

The subway stations and connecting tunnels underneath Rockefeller Center were where I headed. There are more exits and entrances than in one of those meerkat villages on Animal Planet. I came up to street level twice, and ducked back into the next entrance I came to before making my way back to track level, where I rode the express downtown for one stop, crossed the platform and came back uptown, exiting at Lexington and Sixty-third. By that time, I was sure I had either lost anyone trying to tail me or convinced them that I was thoroughly lost myself.

It was a short walk from there to my destination.

The cats all welcomed me back—each in its own way. Orange stripe caressed my ankles, gray thought about it, and the light brown stalked in front of his mistress, warning me off. Mistletoe must have cleaned the kitty litter box because the apartment smelled less like cat and more like chai tea.

"I knew you'd be back, you know." Mistletoe had changed out of her black T-shirt into a white one. I sat in the same armchair. She folded her legs into a yoga pose and perched on the couch.

"I guess that's because you didn't tell me everything last time I was here, Missy."

She smiled. "Paddy called me Missy."

That was not a good start for what I had to say. "Mistletoe, I am worried about you."

"You shouldn't be. Willie told me not to be afraid."

"He had a plan for you?"

"He said I shouldn't worry."

"Right. That's what I need to talk to you about."

"No. Willie said not to talk to anybody about the plan."

"He must have said it was okay to talk to somebody. Did he say Paddy was going to help you?"

"No." Her eyes were blinking rapidly and she was looking everywhere but at me.

"Because Paddy's not coming, Mistletoe. Paddy's hiding from some bad people. Very bad. There's something they're looking for, but Paddy doesn't have it, does he?"

"I don't know." She wrapped her arms around herself and tucked her head down. She really couldn't lie.

"Who is it, Mistletoe? Who did Willie say was coming?"

"I don't think Paddy liked me." The change was abrupt—jarring. She had switched to a coy, flirtatious child. "I can tell you like me. You said I was pretty."

"Yes, I like you. And I want to help you. Who is supposed to help you?"

"But he didn't come," she wailed, now the hysteric again. "Willie's been gone for months and months and he didn't come!"

"Mistletoe, you are not a good liar. You are a sweet person, and you're not very good at lying."

"I can keep a secret."

"Yeah, well, three can keep a secret . . ." I stopped there.

She shook her head in incomprehension.

". . . if two of them are dead," I finished. "There was a lawyer. In Zurich. Is that who is supposed to come? Please, Mistletoe, help me out."

"Stop it! Stop it! Willie said not to tell. Can't you understand? It's a seeeecret!" She stretched the last word out in another wail of frustration.

"I'm so sorry your Willie is dead. But things are getting a lot scarier out there. We need to make some other plans for you."

She rose up and threw herself at me, kissing me hard, her tongue thrusting into my mouth, her hands groping at my crotch. It was an assault—ugly, pathetic, nearly psychotic, and, I was ashamed to realize, a turn-on. Syn-apses were firing up, directing blood flow into the appro-priate vessels.

She gave a moan in my ear and a soft laugh. "See. This is what you want, isn't it?"

"No, it's not. I . . ."

She covered my mouth with hers again, stopping the words.

I tried pushing her away—gently. I did not want to hurt her. But she was stronger than I could have imag-ined. And fiercer. She grabbed my hand and pulled it to her crotch, grinding herself into my palm. She moaned again, louder and deeper.

There was nothing else for it. I was either going to get raped in that cat-fur-covered easy chair or I was going to have to risk hurting her. I pushed her away—hard.

She tumbled back against the couch and lay still for a moment.

"I'm sorry," I said. My voice was harsh with fear, anger, and a mix of powerful hormones. "Are you all right?"

She mumbled something into the floor.

I leaned forward, careful to keep my distance in case she attacked again. "I missed that, Mistletoe. What did you say?"

"I thought you liked me."

"I do like you."

"And I could tell—you liked it."

I bent down and took her in my arms. "I like you. Just not like that. Okay?"

She shook her head slowly—either in confusion or denial. Then she began to cry. Soundlessly.

"I miss Willie so much," she said.

I pulled her to me, her face against my chest, and let her cry. Slowly, in the tiniest increments, I felt her body soften and melt into mine. Her crying stopped and she was asleep.

My body was twisted and strained, but I let her rest. I shifted slightly until my back rested against the front of the sofa. It wasn't a comfortable position exactly, but it was an improvement.

There was no doubt in my mind—if the "goons" that scared Randolph's wife showed up at Mistletoe's door, she would fall to pieces. Of all the fragile people I had met, she was the star. She made soft mewling noises, like a kitten, while she slept. They may have been tiny cries of grief. Or maybe I was projecting. Maybe it was just her way of snoring.

There were about a thousand things I should have been doing right then, but letting Mistletoe Evans sleep on my chest seemed important—and I wasn't going anywhere without waking her. And across the room beckoned the giant television.

I felt around the couch cushions. The remote was there. I hit power and followed it with mute immediately. The system woke up quickly. Channel 53. A YES Classic was showing. The Yankees–Red Sox opener from 2005. Boomer Wells throwing for the bad guys, wearing Babe Ruth's number 3, thumbing his nose at Steinbrenner and Cashman for trading him away. Randy

Johnson's debut in pinstripes. Matsui went three for five. Great game. A good time in my life. Angie and I had watched it together—she still watched baseball with me then. I moved the volume up just enough to hear the crowd's roar as a whisper. All three cats snuggled up against me and I could feel them purr through my clothes. A cold beer would have been nice. When Matsui hit his two-run homer in the eighth, Mistletoe whispered a soft "Yes!" and gently pumped her fist.

"How long have you been awake?" I said.

"Not long." She tapped my chest gently with her fingertips and stood up, unfolding with the odd grace of a heron. The cats followed her into the back of the apartment.

My back only hurt when I tried to move. I took my time getting up and stretching out. The game was winding down. 9 to 2 final. I heard a toilet flush farther back in the apartment and the sounds of opening and closing doors and the soft slap of bare feet on polished floors. I heard the refrigerator door opening and the cats began an insistent chorus, which ended abruptly as Mistletoe placed their bowls on the floor. A moment later, she entered the room with a tray of tea things.

"I'm having some green tea. Will you join me?" She was gracious and in control.

I hit the power button and the screen went black. "Thank you. No. I should go. But I need to know that you are going to be safe."

"Sit down, please." She had changed to an ankle-length Indian-print hippie dress. I hadn't seen anything like it since the last time I went to a Grateful Dead concert.

I perched on the arm of the easy chair, not quite trusting her—or myself—to sink back into it.

"Can I persuade you to go away for a few days? I'm worried for you. Someone is following me—and people I talk to are being threatened. It could get worse."

"I have not stepped foot outside of this apartment in months," she said, while pouring herself some of the pale green liquid. Her movements were both languid and elegant—like someone practicing tai chi underwater. "Everything I need is delivered. My therapist gives me a forty-five-minute telephone session every day at four. I have no need to go out. I do not want to go out. I don't do well in crowds. I will go out again someday, but not today. Or tomorrow."

Again, I was talking to an entirely different human being. This version of Mistletoe was calm, in control of herself, direct and firm. But still as nutty as a protein bar.

My mild post-prison claustrophobia gave a discomforting twinge at the idea of being cooped up in that space. The room seemed much smaller. Weren't we a matched set of neuroses?

"I understand. Then I want to have some people come here and keep an eye out for any trouble. Just for a few days. I hope I can make some arrangements by then that will take care of all this."

She sipped her tea, and her gaze went inward. Had she taken a pill? Or was this serenity the aftermath of a good cry and a nap?

"I'm not good at making friends."

I could believe that.

"I doubt that will be a problem. I don't think these guys are very good at it either. I don't even know if they'll speak English. But they will make sure you stay safe."

She looked up, and her eyes were quite clear. "Why do I need them? I don't really understand."

"I know. I'm doing a lot of guessing right now, but if I can figure this out, so can someone else."

She put down the cup and saucer. "Stay here." She glided down the hall, the sack of a dress billowing, accenting her thin, curveless frame. She was back in seconds.

"You'll need this," she said, holding out a black-enameled socket key. Short, stumpy, with a sturdy-looking flange. The type of key that might operate one of those U-shaped bicycle locks. Or a safe-deposit box?

"Did Willie leave you this?"

"He said if anything ever happened to him that a man would come, and if I showed him this, he would take care of me."

"I don't think he meant me."

"No. An old man, he said. A lawyer."

"Did he give you a name?"

"No. Only he never did come. I don't think he's going to anymore."

"No. You're right. The lawyer isn't coming."

"Did she kill him, too?"

I was confused for just a moment. "Mrs. Von Becker? The wife?"

"She killed Willie. I know it."

"I don't think so. I still think Willie killed himself."

She gave a pitying smile. She expected people to lack faith in her judgment.

I took the key. "I'll let you know. And I'll try to help, if I can. No promises."

"That's good. No promises."

I called Tom and told him what I needed. Twenty minutes later the doorman called up to announce two visitors. They could have been clones of Tom and Ivan. No one bothered with names.

"The lady never goes out. You guys just have to make sure no one else comes in."

"Ya." He examined the room and took note of the huge television. Then he turned to Mistletoe. "You like movie. Is okay. We watch. No one come in."

"I'll make some popcorn," she said.

I let myself out.

| 27 |

The cab pulled up in front of the Ansonia. I handed the driver a ten on a six-fifty fare.

"Give me two dollars back," I said.

"My last fare took all my singles."

My phone started ringing.

"I can give you quarters," he continued. "Is that all right?"

"Keep it," I said, feeling I had been mugged again by New York. I hit the talk button. "Stafford here."

"Tell me about this guy Gibbons again." It was Brady.

I slammed the taxi door just a bit harder than necessary. "I told you. He says he's with the SEC. He also warned me that I might get hurt, which I am starting to believe."

"He didn't mention that he is no longer working for the government, did he?"

"No."

"He was the lead accountant on two—repeat, two—government audits of the Von Becker funds. He cleared them. Twice."

Raoul began to swing open the front door for me. I waved him off and walked down toward Broadway. "Once might have been an accident."

"Exactly. Three would have meant he was crooked. Two is on the cusp. He could be a crook or he could just be a monumental fuckup."

"Either way, I think I don't want to talk to him anymore."

"That might be a good strategy, but he wasn't wrong about watching your ass."

"I've hired backup. They're covering the Kid twenty-four-seven. And I thought you weren't interested in threats against me." I scanned the people on the street, looking for short people, tall people, people in hoodies, people wearing Australian outback hats, Latinos, nannies pushing strollers, or men wearing suits. Everyone and no one looked threatening.

"What I said is that I can't do anything about it. I still think you're on the radar for some very bad people."

"Castillo."

"Two weeks ago, our people followed him out to a house in East Rockaway. You know the town?"

"I've been there." I crossed Broadway and plunked myself down on a bench in the park.

"It's a blue-collar town. What was a guy like Castillo doing visiting somebody out there? So we ran the address. The house belonged to a couple named Welk. Walter and Rose-Marie Welk. Her name pops out of the computer like hitting five sevens on the slot machine. Bells, sirens, lights flashing. She was one of Von Becker's assistants. Helped him keep the books cooked. She did six months, which was a gift, in my humble opinion. Castillo spent forty-three minutes inside, then came out and went straight back to the city." He stopped, but in a way that let me know he was far from done.

"You're awful quiet there, Jason. Did you know this lady?"

"Finish the story, Brady."

"Four o'clock this morning, the fire department gets called out for a gas explosion. It blew out windows three houses away. Someone had turned on the gas on the stove and left a candle burning in the living room."

"Ah, shit," I said.

"When they finally get the fire out and go in there, they find two bodies. The husband is in the bedroom, on the floor. One shot to the head. The guy actually slept with a little twenty-gauge shotgun under the bed, but he never had time for it." He paused for a moment. "You're still not saying much."

I cleared my throat. "And the lady?"

"Down in the basement. Also one to the head, but they worked her over first. And someone used a bolt cutter on her, clipping her fingers and toes."

I remembered her hands. Big hands for a woman. Long, strong fingers.

Brady was still talking. "She probably lasted awhile.

When they were done, they stuffed her in the freezer. The fire took care of any prints or other evidence, but someone wanted us to find her. They're sending a message."

I got the message. Loud and clear. "She didn't know anything."

"So you did know her."

"I spoke to her. A week ago."

"Confession is good for the soul, isn't it?"

"I have nothing to confess. I met her. She had nothing to tell me. I forgot about her the minute I walked out the door."

"But someone is out there, willing to torture, maim, and kill, and you just might be next."

I knew that. "I want him."

"Who? Castillo? Take a number."

"I'm going to help you get him, then."

"Think about your son. Despite the fact that he once bit me in the face, I hold nothing against him and I would feel very bad if his father got himself killed playing Junior G-man. Stay away from this one. Take your kid to Florida for a week. Let him swim with dolphins. Meet Mickey. But just get out of town. Not forever. Just for the next week or so—maybe two."

Angie would throw a fit—with lawyers attached. And we wouldn't be any safer anyway. The only thing that was going to get Castillo's hit men off my back was one hundred million dollars in bearer bonds.

"In a perfect world," I said.

"What's that?"

"I can't do that, Brady." I got up from the bench and

began to pace. People gave me room. "And I doubt that it would work. I can get shot in Orlando just as easily as I can in Manhattan."

"So what will you do?"

"I have a plan. If it works, you get Castillo and I get these people out of my life. And maybe my client wins, too."

"I don't like this."

I ignored him and plowed on. "I need you to talk to my P.O. I have to go out of the country. Just for a day. I could do it and he'd never know, but I'm trying to be a good boy."

"The P.O. is going to want to know where you're going. And don't tell me Switzerland or Brazil."

"Okay."

"Okay what?"

I flopped down on the bench again. Brady was beginning to get on my nerves. I needed him gung ho, ready to fight. "Okay, I won't tell you."

"You're not making this easy."

"If I wanted easy, I wouldn't be asking you."

"Am I supposed to be flattered?"

"I'm going to make you famous. Keep that in mind."

"Now I'm nervous."

"I'm going to need help there. I need to get into a dead man's safe-deposit box. How are your Interpol contacts?"

"You better tell me the whole story."

"A lot is still conjecture." I filled him in on what I was thinking. It took a while.

"It's not evidence."

"It will be."

"Suppose you don't come back? It's my ass on the line."

"I'm doing this for my son, Brady. I'm coming back."

"I hear you. But suppose you can't come back?"

"Then everything's fucked, isn't it?"

| 28 |

Thanks to something or other to do with air density off Nova Scotia, the flight landed in Zurich twenty minutes early. I went straight to the Swiss First lounge for a shower and to change into spare underwear and a fresh shirt. Other than those items, my five-thousand-dollar Valextra briefcase—a bit of self-indulgence from my previous incarnation—held only a well-thumbed paperback copy of Temple Grandin's *The Way I See It*, the Dr. Spock for the autistic crowd—representative of a very different Jason Stafford.

The concierge provided me a fresh amenities kit, complete with razor, toothbrush, comb, and enough gels, liquids, and scented semisolids to clean, freshen, and invigorate a baseball team, including the designated hitter—I took a pass on the complimentary champagne. The towel was on the small side, but it was clean, and by the time I finished shaving I felt ready for anything. Almost anything.

They were waiting for me just after passport control.

"Ah, Mr. Stafford," a short man with a sparse comb-over and a bristly salt-and-pepper mustache addressed me. "We had almost given up on you." His English was flawless and so neutrally accented, he might have been born in Omaha. "Would you step this way, please?" He held up an ID holder.

I focused on the light blue writing. Interpol. Police.

Police had never caused me any anxiety—before I went to prison. I felt my chest tighten.

"I thought we were to meet up at the bank." I checked my watch. "Not for another hour or so."

He smiled briefly—grimly. "There are some things to go over before we get there. We will escort you." There were two men in uniform with him. "Shall we?" He gestured for me to follow him. It was not a request—but it was polite.

The Interpol policeman handed me his card once we were seated in the smallish backseat of the BMW 1 Series hatchback; the two uniforms were up front. It was good I had no more luggage than the briefcase—it wouldn't have fit.

Michel Guelli, Zurich.

That's all it said. I guess if you needed to know more, you should already know it. The car pulled out into traffic with a single polite but insistent blast of the siren.

"I looked over your file, Mr. Stafford. You are an unlikely candidate to have friends in the FBI."

Friend. Singular.

"How nice to hear that Interpol has a file on me. Should I feel special? Or does everyone have one these days?"

There had been a trader in my group, when I was running the foreign exchange desk at Case, who would, when he was deep in his cups, transform from a pleasant, dry-humored father of three blond young girls into a muttering, conspiracy-imagining, delusional paranoid. He would quote Glenn Beck—without irony; whisper intensely about the New World Order and black helicopters; and decry that teachers were destroying our society. It was all relatively harmless, until one night in Basel at a client dinner, three vodkas ahead of the rest of the pack, he let it all come pouring out in purple vitriolic prose, horrifying the three proper bureaucrats from the International Monetary Fund. I wrestled him into a cab and told the driver to keep circling the hotel until he slept it off.

But there was one thing the guy got right—the part about the International Police. Interpol answers to no centralized body, only a consortium of its 190 member countries. In the U.S. they're embedded in the Justice Department, but they're outside the chain of command. They have all the investigative powers of the FBI and the CIA combined and none of the responsibility. Their methods, personnel, and files are exempt from any interference from any domestic agency. They cannot be subpoenaed, arrested, or sued. And they're hiring.

"What I found to be intriguing is the reference to your assistance in various ongoing investigations for both the FBI and the SEC. Have you switched sides, Mr. Stafford? Or have you become a professional snitch?"

Switzerland is a beautiful country, but you don't see much of it on the ride in from Zurich airport—I was having a hard time pretending to be interested in the view.

"I work for anyone who will pay my going rate, but I try to stay on the good side of people who have the power to put me in jail. Been there."

Michel Guelli smoothed his few overlong hairs into place. "I am curious, though. Your interest here in Zurich, and with the private bankers Doerflinger Freres et Cie, has to do with an investigation for the Von Becker family. The FBI has already made requests for any and all information relating to bank accounts here—and the Swiss have complied. But now you arrive. What do you expect to find that we seem to have missed?"

"A safe-deposit box."

He gave a sideways tic of his head. "Hmm. You don't think we would have checked already?"

"Let's see."

He gave that quick, unamused smile again. "And indulge me, please, as long as we are being so frank with each other. Why does an FBI agent assigned to a multi-agency task force on *drugs* show an interest in Mr. Von Becker and his Ponzi scheme—an investigation being conducted by an entirely different department?"

Why? Because there was only one FBI agent in the world who might take my phone call.

"I'm afraid you'll have to ask the FBI. I'm working

for members of the Von Becker family in cooperation with federal authorities."

We rode in silence for a few minutes. I could see the flash of sunlight reflecting off the lake in the distance.

"Tell me," he said in a less aggressive tone, as though we were acquaintances who might one day be friends. "Do you enjoy your work?"

I gave the question some thought. When I got out of prison, there had been few opportunities open to me. The fact that I had become very good at what I did in a short period of time was of less consequence.

"I didn't choose it," I finally said.

"I enjoy my work," he admitted. "I help to maintain order in a chaotic world. And I am good at it."

"Then you are in the über-class, Inspector. The one-percenters. The rest of humanity no longer has such luxuries as enjoying their work."

"You are a cynic."

"Do you know that there is a school of thought that in ancient hunter-gatherer societies, people spent no more than twenty hours a week hunting and gathering? Everyone did it, of course, making the culture very egalitarian by our standards for both men and women. It wasn't until mankind began farming that the concept of wealth—ownership—became part of our makeup. Then you developed strata—castes. Rulers owned the wealth—and if they were capable rulers they worked at it; those who didn't invented the leisure class. Full-time warriors were needed to protect the wealth. Serfs or slaves to work the fields and create the wealth. Traders—tradesmen—took the place of the hunter-gatherers, swapping one commodity for another, and living on the margins that the wealthy allowed. Those who couldn't make the transition became outlaws or pirates."

"And every cynic is a disappointed idealist," he said.

"You're the idealist. I just want to work twenty hours a week and spend the rest of my time caring for my son, loving a woman, and learning how to use some new apps on my iPhone."

"Not a very Swiss outlook. Not very New York, either, I would think."

"I'm still trying it on."

The car pulled off the highway at the river, down Wasserwerkstrasse and across the bridge into a warren of one-way streets. If I had been forced to retrace our path, I would have been lost before the second turn. Finally we turned onto Bahnhofstrasse. Traffic was slow and orderly. Very Swiss. Zurich never seems to change. As many times as I have been there, for foreign exchange meetings, monetary conferences, and client dog-and-pony shows, it always looks like the most understated financial center on the planet. You will see more Rolls-Royces in Hong Kong, but in Zurich the police drive BMWs. Hong Kong doubles in height almost annually; in London, the City continues to sprawl, gobbling whole blocks at a time; and New York—New York will always be unique. There is new construction—all cities sprawl or die, it seems to be an immutable rule—but Zurich manages to maintain the look of a medieval town holding back the barbaric hordes of modernism. In Hong Kong and Singapore, everyone's a capitalist, whether a coolie or a communist. In New York and London, you can almost feel money changing hands in electronic bursts at the speed of light. In Zurich, you get the feeling that money has been there for a thousand years and is very content to remain right there until the next millennium.

"Two blocks up on the right," Guelli said to the driver. "Don't make the turn. We'll walk. Wait for us there."

Guelli led me down the block. The near corner building was a gray stone structure with no windows on the ground floor. The door was polished brass, and a tiny plaque next to it read DOERFLINGER FRERES ET CIE. I stopped and turned around. Directly across the intersection was a café with twenty or so outdoor tables. Most of the tables were empty—it was late for breakfast, even for tourists, and too early for lunch. I could picture Castillo's agent and Von Becker's lawyer meeting there in near anonymity.

We must have been on CCTV because the door swung open mere seconds after Guelli touched the buzzer. A man with the size and build of a New York nightclub bouncer, but without the shaved head and black turtleneck, waved us in. We were immediately greeted by an elegant and attractive woman in her late fifties. With typical Swiss good manners, she welcomed us in four languages, pausing briefly after each in case we wanted to respond. Guelli, in deference to me, I imagined, held out through French, German, and Italian before responding in English.

"Thank you. Mssr. Guelli and Stafford. We have an appointment with Herr Gassner."

She was delighted to take us to him.

We were buzzed through another metal door, passing a room where a smiling young man at a handsome mahogany desk nodded at us. If the setup here was similar to other Swiss private banks I had been to, he was the sole teller—there on the remote chance that a client needed change of a tenner, or wanted to deposit a suitcase full of gold. Then we passed down a hallway, the solid gray walls broken only by solid-looking heavy wooden doors. There were no paintings, no adornments, not even name plaques on the doors. The space spoke of security and efficiency. And anonymity.

The woman ushered us into a windowless room with an oblong black granite table, surrounded by leather chairs.

"Herr Gassner will be with you momentarily. May I get you coffee? Tea? Something else?"

"Water," I said. "I'm still a bit dried out from the flight."

"Certainly, Mr. Stafford. Still or sparkling?"

"Still is fine. Thank you."

She ducked out and returned almost immediately with a small silver tray. A tall glass of water sat on a solid white doily, inscribed along the circumference with a fine gold circle and the words *Doerflinger Freres et Cie, bella gerant alii.*

Let others make war.

I preferred a T-shirt I once saw on Nantucket. *Omnes in mare.* Everyone into the water.

"Gentlemen."

Herr Gassner was a trim, athletic-looking man in his

forties. He wore rimless glasses held together with a sil-ver thread of titanium, and exuded the faintest scent of a spicy, expensive cologne. He carried an iPad, which he set on the table with the reluctance of an alcoholic relin-quishing his grip on the bottle.

He and Guelli exchanged cards, and I smiled in rueful apology—I didn't carry any. Any of my own, at any rate. I could have dug out one of Roger's old cards for his clown business. *Jacques-Emo and Wanda the Wandaful.*

"I am sorry that you have come so far on your errand, Mr. Stafford. As I explained on the telephone, Mr. Von Becker did not have an account with the firm. I don't know what I can do for you."

"Is it possible that he had an account, and you simply don't know about it?"

Gassner exchanged a quick look with the policeman. "You are speaking of numbered accounts, I think? Swiss secrecy laws have changed over the years. Numbered accounts still exist and ownership is secret, but only to the public and lower-level employees. Any senior officer has access to such information. We must. And we must provide that information upon the request of a wide var-iety of governmental bodies." He chuckled. "When Mr. Von Becker was arrested, every private banker in Swit-zerland received notice to turn over information on any accounts of his, his companies, and for members of his family. As we had nothing to provide, this made the firm quite suspect in the eyes of some of your regulators. They became disruptive."

I could imagine. I'd seen the Feds in action when they thought they were being stonewalled.

"We call it a shit show."

"How poetic. Both a metaphor and alliterative. I will remember it."

"Do you provide safe-deposit boxes for clients?"

"We do, but the same issues would apply. I wouldn't know what was in the box, but I would know who owned it, and there would be a record of every visit anyone made to it, and that record would be made available to the police upon request."

They both looked at me pityingly—I was an idiot, and while they felt bad for me, they also sincerely hoped it wasn't communicable.

"We came in the door facing the café—is there another entrance?"

Now they shared another quick look. Did they have an idiot on their hands or a madman?

"There are two other entrances—on the side streets. Employees tend to use them more than clients," Gassner answered with the politeness one employs when conversing with the insane.

I nodded. "But clients use them as well. You have the same security arrangements there?"

Guelli cleared his throat as though to interrupt. I shot him a quick glance. Stick with me for just a minute more.

"Yes," Gassner replied, turning it into a question.

"How long do you keep the CCTV images? I'm assuming they're digital."

"I wouldn't know. The cameras are only active when someone pushes the button for entry, so it could be months. I really don't know." He had given up and was shaking his head in bewilderment as he spoke.

I turned to Guelli. "You need to get someone on those," I said. "Herr Gassner, would anyone be allowed in those doors? Could we have come in that way today?"

He was on firmer ground now and looked relieved. "No. Only employees and regular clients. Frequent visitors. All others would have to come through the main door."

I nodded. It was what I had expected. "Last question, and then I'm out of your hair. One of your clients died some six months ago. A lawyer by the name of Serge Biondi. He had offices here in this neighborhood." I took my apartment keys out of my jacket pocket and removed Mistletoe's key from the ring—what better place to hide a single key? "My question for you is this. Is this the key to his safe-deposit box?"

Gassner was floored. For a moment he stared at me, then at Guelli. His mouth wasn't exactly hanging open, but his lips were parted.

I took my time, holding it up to the light for display. I was loving it. Beneath their smug superiority, these two were caught flat-footed. The evidence of money laundering and the uncovering of Von Becker's stolen billions wouldn't sink the bank. They'd survive. But not without considerable embarrassment. And some heads would roll. And I wouldn't be at all surprised if one of them belonged to the smug Herr Gassner.

He reached over and took the key in his hand,

examining it with the thoroughness of an entomologist with a new species of butterfly. Then he gave a sad chuckle.

"Excellent! Excellent, Mr. Stafford. Maigret could not have done better. Wonderful."

Guelli wasn't laughing at all. He looked like he was trying to bore a hole in my head with his eyes.

I plowed on. "You haven't answered the question."

"As the inspector can explain," Gassner began, "the death of Serge Biondi was a minor news event in our country. Speculation went on for weeks. The police froze his account here until the investigation is done. We are allowed to make payments to his widow for expenses, but nothing more." He looked at Guelli. "At least for now."

"And it might be quite some time," Guelli interjected. "Despite the cooperation of everyone who knew him, his partners, staff, family, clients, even"—he and Gassner shared a manly look of understanding—"even the escort service he employed for evening trysts in his office, the case is at a standstill. Herr Biondi died of a heart attack in his office after closing hours. He was discovered by the sole cleaning person. The only information that was initially withheld from the press was the cause of the heart attack."

I felt a change in the weather—a little dark cloud was coming over the horizon.

"He was murdered, you see. Two men came into his office, tied him to his chair with duct tape and began to beat him, either to torture or to terrorize. If they meant to question him, they failed. He died almost immediately."

The votes were in—I was an idiot. Castillo hadn't exactly lied to me, but he had held back the most important information. Information that I could have checked for myself. Should have checked. He hadn't blindsided me; I'd done it to myself. From Maigret to Clouseau.

"Forgive me for my initial response," Gassner was saying. "Your presentation was somewhat melodramatic. This is all very old news—much discussed many months ago. Once the details leaked out, there was a flurry of speculation in the press. It came to nothing."

"All we can say with certainty is that the men were looking for something. They searched his office and all of his current files, leaving at least one extremely valuable item behind. It is a puzzle."

"And the key?" I made one last attempt at salvaging my point of view.

"I'm sorry. We have done business with the Biondi family for three generations, but none of them have ever had a safe-deposit box here. If they had, the contents would have been already in the hands of the police."

"I see. Thank you."

"And," he said, taking enjoyment from his news as he handed me the key, "that is not a key we would ever have used. We did away with mechanical locks almost ten years ago. We use electronic cards and randomly generated digital passwords. What you have there looks like the key to a bicycle lock." He chuckled. "Or possibly an elevator key."

There was a connection—I was sure of it. The laws of probability were stretched too far for coincidence. But I couldn't quite make all the pieces fit. Yet.

Guelli rose. "I believe we are done here, Herr Gassner. Thank you for your time and your cooperation. Mr. Stafford?"

I wasn't done, and I looked up at Guelli to tell him so. Something in his eyes made me change my mind. I still gave him a hard look back, just to let him know there was unfinished business, but I stood up also.

Our guide was waiting for us back in the gray hallway. She showed us to the main door, thanked us for considering Doerflinger for our investment needs, and tried not to give the impression that we were one step shy of being ejected from the building.

"Would you care to join me for lunch, Mr. Stafford?" Guelli said as the door closed behind us. "I assume you are not in too much of a hurry to get back to the airport. Your flight is not for another five hours."

"Why did you let him off the hook? He may have had me on the ropes, but I wasn't done with him by a long shot."

Guelli shook his head. "Either he knows nothing or he is confident that no one can prove that he does know something. Either way, he was going to prevail. You and I, however, have much to talk about. I believe that you know a lot more that you haven't told me."

I thought about it for a minute. Guelli still might be able to open doors for me. He was never going to be my ally, but I didn't need to treat him like an enemy.

I pointed across the street. "I think that café right there would be an excellent place to sit and talk and have a meal."

| 29 |

I chose a table that faced directly across at the bank. We ordered and made polite small talk until the waiter ceased hovering. The background noise of the street and the café gave us a small cone of privacy.

I took a long drink of water and began. "Some of this I have been told and some of it is surmise and some of it is straight fiction. But the tale is true. You with me?"

Guelli gave a very European shrug that could have meant anything. It didn't matter; he was listening.

"Serge Biondi sat right here once a month or so, usually in mid-afternoon when the New York markets had just opened. He had to wait for confirmation that funds had been posted to the appropriate accounts. He met with another man—I have no idea who, or even if it was a man. It could have been a woman. It could have been someone different every time. I don't know. Sometimes he would have a file with him, which he would leave on the table as he left. Other times he would collect one."

Guelli just nodded. He had questions, but he let me get the story out my own way.

"When he left, he would walk across the street and through the main door of Doerflinger Freres et Cie. But as we have just learned, that was not his destination. It was a blind. He could not be followed inside, but he could leave by either of two other exits. It would have been very difficult to set up a tail."

"Only once a month?"

"That's a guess. But not a bad one, based on my guy's take on the money trail. You and the FBI can match up the money transfers and see. More often wasn't needed. They could afford to let smaller transactions accumulate, then execute a big trade only when they had a large amount of money to move."

Lunch arrived. Schnitzel with roesti for me, a spinach salad for Guelli.

"You are lucky," Guelli commented, looking longingly at my plate. "I still carry the weight of every plate of roesti I have ever eaten."

"If I lived here, I would eat roesti every day and the hell with my cholesterol. Life is short, and one of the few things in life that you can't find better in New York is real roesti."

Roesti is an elegantly simple dish—grated potato, fried in butter. But it is to hash browns what risotto is to rice cakes. You can tell both had the same origins, but their paths diverged dramatically. I vowed to bring Skeli to Zurich sometime—if only for the roesti.

"You are not going to share with me who told you this story, are you?"

Castillo would have me gutted, grilled, and served up churrasco for speaking his name aloud. "That would not be in my best interest," I said.

"Or what was in the file folders?"

"Oh, that I can give you." Castillo had been open, almost dismissive, about the financial details. "Honduran government bonds. Mostly. Dollar-denominated. There's probably some triple- and double-A corporate bonds mixed in as well. All in bearer form. No other sovereign debt—there's too little of it still in circulation. Too easy to trace ownership when the coupons are tendered."

"Herr Biondi was a highly respected lawyer. His client list included both some of our oldest and most powerful families. He was on the board of directors of one of Switzerland's largest banks. Why would such a man be involved in something like this?"

I shrugged. "I don't know. He worked for Von Becker."

Guelli bristled. "So that makes him dirty as well? You are too smart for that."

"In the last two weeks I've talked to some very smart people who got sucked in by Von Becker. He was a con man. An evil, manipulative son of a bitch, who deserved to suffer a lot longer than he did. But there's one thing every con knows—the mark cons himself. The pitch can be perfect, flawless, ripe, and easy, but if the mark doesn't want to buy in, there's no sale."

"But you are speaking of drug money, are you not? Biondi would have to have known. Why would he take such a risk?"

"Maybe he didn't know at first. I don't know. You're asking me to speculate."

"Isn't everything you have said speculation?"

"No. It may not be evidence, but I believe it all to be true. I'm still fitting it all together."

"Still."

"All right. Like I say, maybe he didn't know. Maybe he knew and didn't care." A thought occurred to me. "Or maybe he thought he had his own scam running. Look, Von Becker could have spun a very convincing line. The guy was a master. Look at all the supposedly very smart people all over the world who fell for his spiel. You think Biondi was different because he was Swiss?"

Guelli had the grace to chuckle. "Yes?"

"By the time Biondi figured out the real game, he was locked in. He couldn't back out. The kind of people we're talking about do not take no for an answer."

My roesti was already more than half gone. I drank more water to slow myself down.

"Von Becker laundered money for anyone who asked," I continued. "I don't know how the cash side worked. They could run it all through the Feast of San Gennaro for all I know. But once the cash was in the system—anywhere in the world—he would move it. He and his partners—the FBI knows who I'm talking about—would settle up once a month or so. They'd wire a large block of money—upwards of fifty mil at a clip—to one of Von Becker's banks. As soon as the funds cleared, he would get word to Biondi and a meet would be set up. Biondi would deliver the securities, or pick them up, if that's the direction the deal was going that time around."

"These other messengers—carriers—they would be lawyers as well, correct?"

"Lawyers, bank employees—they'd have the access. But it could have been government regulators, or even policemen. You live in a society that rarely questions authority, as long as all the fees are paid up. Though they'd have to be fairly senior. You'd want respectable burghers who weren't going to take your bearer bonds and do a runner."

"Biondi wasn't running."

"No. I think in his case it was just bad timing. Von Becker surrendered to the good guys late in the afternoon when Europe was already shut down for the day. He had no choice. If he'd tried to wait until the next day, they'd have been out looking for him, and he would have lost any leverage he might have had." I signaled to the waiter for more water. "But the money was already in the system, waiting to clear. The bad guys couldn't get it back. By the next day, all accounts were frozen and Von Becker was in custody. The Feds paraded him out in front of his office, his perp walk—or in his case, maybe a victory lap. But Von Becker was never out of sight of federal agents from the time he came in. He never got to make the call to Biondi."

"Von Becker couldn't get a message out?"

I was sure that Castillo knew more about that than he

had been willing to share, but I wasn't prepared to make a guess at that point.

"That's the thing with the guy. He never trusted anybody, so he had no backup. But as long as he was alive, nobody was in a panic. Eventually he would get word out and Biondi would make his meet. The bonds would change hands and everybody would go home happy."

"But someone did panic. Biondi was murdered—beaten—before Von Becker died."

"Two days before. And someone is in a panic again now. Two more people were killed this week. Others were threatened. I was threatened."

"But why? Why not just wait?"

"I don't know. The interested party who pointed me in this direction had no reason to rush things, but I don't think he's in control. The people he represents have their own agenda. And for all I know, there are other players involved."

Guelli pushed the remains of his salad away.

"And why wouldn't Biondi just pay them? Hand over the bonds and be done with it. The man was beaten to death."

"According to you, he didn't last long enough to tell anybody anything."

"I still don't see why he would have involved himself in this."

I savored the last bite of roesti before answering. "Are you inviting me to speculate again?" I shrugged. "Money, love, sex, fear, and guilt. Pick one. I think that covers your choices. And why did Von Becker kill himself?"

Guelli nodded. "Just two days after his money man dies."

"*If* he killed himself. He was being held at Manhattan Metropolitan Correctional Center on remand. At MCC they lump everybody in together. Bad guys and really bad guys. I spent one horrific night there waiting to be arraigned. It's a zoo. I'd say just about anything could have happened there. So I don't know what I believe about Von Becker dying. I've been told a lot of things."

"Have your friends at the FBI heard all this?"

"No. I had to come here to see these connections. And remember, my interest here is limited. I'm not hunting down a murderer. I'm just trying to track down the money."

"But you still don't know where the bonds are."

"Well, one last try on that score. What do you say?" I checked my watch. "I've still got time. Hours. Care to bring me by Biondi's offices? Let's see what shakes out when a senior Interpol officer stops by."

Guelli's eyes lit up. "Get the check."

| **30** |

The offices of Kuhn Lauber Biondi were less than a block away—a few steps down from the side entrance to the bank. The building was an unremarkable four-story redbrick structure built sometime between the Reformation and the First World War. The street-level entrance was a simple glass-paned white wooden door. I followed Guelli into a comfortable sitting room. The door chimed behind us, announcing our presence, but there was no one to greet us. Guelli seemed to take this as quite normal. He sat, shuffled through a pile of Swiss newspapers, and began to read. I set my briefcase on the floor and paced. We waited.

There was a single door on the far wall—locked from this side, I found—and a small elevator built into the adjoining wall, a comparatively new feature, probably added to the building no more than thirty or forty years earlier. The fireplace and a bare mantel occupied the fourth wall. A couch, two high-backed armchairs, a pair of matching end tables. No paintings or other artwork. The only windows were the glass panes in the door we had entered. A space to wait in, but not comfortably. The room was a sensory-deprivation chamber. The only sound was the crackle of the newspaper as Guelli turned pages. After ten minutes there, conversation with a lawyer would feel stimulating. I could feel my claustrophobia beginning to play tricks on me. Much longer and the walls would start moving.

I sat down. "How long do we wait?"

Guelli gave a small sigh at my impatience. "The receptionist is behind that door and is able to see us through that camera." He looked pointedly at a tiny hole in the crown molding. "Though she will have been alerted by the door chime, she may be involved in some other work-related activity. She will eventually check her monitor and then come and check up on us. Such an arrangement is not uncommon here."

The door in the rear wall opened.

"Et voilà." Guelli smiled.

A small gray-haired woman came in. Her face was all angles, but her body was all curves—like a snowman. Thick ankles peeked out from beneath a long gray skirt. Her shoes were black and sensible.

She looked me over. "Welcome. Good afternoon." She turned to Guelli and made another appraisal. *"Buona-sera, dottore. Come posso aiutarla?"*

Guelli rose from the chair and introduced himself in English. "We wish to speak with one of Herr Biondi's colleagues. A senior partner." He handed her one of his cards. "This is Mr. Stafford, an American who is assisting in our investigations."

If she was surprised or flustered, she hid it well. I couldn't imagine that a visit from Interpol was an everyday occurrence.

"One moment, gentlemen." She turned and went back out the same door.

"You've been here before," I said to Guelli.

"Not at all. This was never my case."

"Then how did you know?" I nodded toward the camera.

"I am a trained investigator," he said. "And I did some speculation."

This time we waited less than a minute before she was back.

"Herr Kuhn will see you now," she said. She walked to the elevator and removed a small black key from a pocket and inserted it into the plate next to the door. I slid my hand into my pocket and rubbed a finger over my key. If they weren't identical, I would be mightily surprised. I had to devise some strategy for checking it out.

Moments later she ushered us into a large, heavily furnished corner office. Dark wood, possibly mahogany, prevailed in the desk, chairs, and the glass-fronted bookcases. Leather cushioned the chairs and the couch. The blue-and-maroon Persian carpet felt like it was ankle deep. There was a faint aroma of expensive cigars. It was a space where decisions were made and secrets were revealed—though they never left the room.

I put Herr Kuhn in his early seventies, though he could have been younger. The crutches and leg braces added years. But despite the ravages of what I assumed was some degenerative disease such as multiple sclerosis, the man radiated power. He made a point of rising to greet us, then let us see the mechanical effort the act had required by releasing the braces on his leg, one at a time, as he lowered himself back into an intricate, motorized wheelchair.

Guelli took the lead and I sat back and watched. He explained that there were no new direct developments on the case of his murdered partner, but some new questions had arisen. Nothing that would challenge the firm or the other partners, of course. He was smooth, but Kuhn was impossible to read. Even his pupils were under control. He gave me a polite smile when Guelli introduced me as a "private investigator from the U.S. who is assisting police on both continents."

"He brings a new point of view to the case. Would you mind answering a few questions about your colleague?"

"As long as it does not interfere with client confidentiality, I am prepared to give you complete cooperation." He gave the same neutral smile.

If I opened with polite, he would be able to twist me in circles and tell me nothing. There was nothing to lose if I played the rude American.

"MS?" I said. "I had an aunt with MS," I lied. "When did yours start up?"

He blinked before answering. I had gotten to him. "This is relevant?" he asked Guelli.

I jumped in before the cop could answer. "No, not really. I was guessing that the elevator is for you, so I was wondering when it went in."

"You are correct. My father had it installed more than forty years ago, soon after my first series of bouts."

"You seem to be holding up pretty well. You're what? Seventy-something?"

He looked to Guelli for help with the madman in the room. "I cannot imagine how this bears on Serge's death."

"You're right. Sorry. Who has keys to the elevator? Everyone who works here? Do you ever inventory them? Who would know if one disappeared?"

Kuhn nodded. "You are thinking how did his killers get in? But the police have already been through that, Mr. Stafford. Unfortunately, the camera downstairs is focused on the door, not the elevator. But it is possible that there is no mystery about it. You see, there is an override switch on this floor. For me. In case I misplace my key. Serge must have let in the men who killed him. Obviously, he was expecting someone else."

"Everyone else has a key?"

"This is a law office, not a bank. Active case files are kept secure, but anyone can ride the elevator. There are probably hundreds of keys that fit that elevator. When someone leaves the firm, we do not check to see that they have turned in their key. If someone loses a key, they simply request another. Our office manager probably orders them ten at a time to get the discount."

"So, did you know that Biondi was doing business with the Von Beckers?"

He blinked twice—I had him on the ropes. "William Von Becker?"

"The same. The one and only."

"Your question presupposes that he was, in fact, working for the Von Beckers, a notion that I would challenge. Where does your information come from?"

Rude Americans don't have to answer questions, no matter how polite the questioner. "How would you know whether he was or not?"

Kuhn let some of his annoyance with me begin to show. "Because I personally reassigned all of his active files. There were not many. Most of his time was devoted to managing or mentoring our junior lawyers. I can tell you unequivocally that there was nothing to indicate that this firm has done any business for William Von Becker or for any of his companies, either directly or through their New York law firm."

"And if there was a cache of bearer bonds hiding in Biondi's files, you would know about it."

"Bearer bonds?" He looked to Guelli again, but the cop gave him nothing. "This is absurd."

"So if Biondi was doing something, he was hiding it. From you and the rest of the firm. Why would he do that?"

"I have answered that question. He was not working for the Von Beckers."

"Actually, Mr. Kuhn, you haven't answered me. The question is why. Why would he do it? It's actually a pretty interesting question when you think about it. Here's this senior partner at an exclusive firm, too experienced to get involved in something truly stupid, and yet he's helping a crooked banker launder money for Central American drug gangs. So, excuse my directness, but why would this guy be doing that?"

"And I maintain that he was not doing any such thing. This is fantasy. What evidence do you have for any of these allegations?"

"You said that you had been through all of his active files. What about old files? Are they warehoused somewhere nearby?"

"There are over a hundred years' worth of files in the basement."

"And have you checked all of those?"

Kuhn's eyes were threatening to leap out of their sockets. "To what purpose? To prove a negative?" He slammed both hands on the desk in frustration. "This is nonsense. Serge Biondi was murdered here, and in six months the best the police can come up with is this fantasy? What is next? Knights Templar? UFOs? An ancient curse?"

I nodded distractedly. "Is there a bathroom up here I could use?"

Guelli looked at me as though I *had* just started ranting about UFOs.

I patted my stomach and made a scrunched-up face, indicating intestinal discomfort. "That roesti seems to be going right through me. I guess I'm not used to your rich foods."

Herr Kuhn tried not to look disgusted, and almost succeeded. "Across the landing. The door to the left of the elevator."

Perfect.

I walked out of Kuhn's office, took the black key out of my pocket, and headed straight for the elevator. Was I nuts? Delusional? Or was the germ of an idea taking root? What Vinny had said about hiding sand at the beach—was that possible?

The key slid in like magic. I turned it. There was a click and a hum. The elevator car rose up and the door slid open.

The next step would not be looked on kindly. Once in the elevator, I was a snoop and a potential threat. I stepped in and inserted the key and hit the button for the basement. The door seemed to close very slowly.

The car sank, emitting soft chimes as we passed each floor. In case anyone stopped the elevator and found me, I put on my best dumb smile, imagining myself as a goofy tourist, out joyriding on the elevator. It was weak, but the best I could come up with. But I didn't need it. The car stopped, the doors slid open, and I was facing a wall of metal shelves loaded with identical cardboard boxes. The aisle stretched in both directions for forty feet. I flipped a mental coin and jogged down the aisle to the right, passing a giant shredding machine—industrial-sized. Rows of shelving extended to the far wall, fifty feet away. Four thousand square feet of shelves—I looked up and estimated—ten feet high. Forty thousand cubic feet. A team of forensic accountants and lawyers might be able to search through it in a week or two. If they knew what they were looking for. If someone pointed them in this direction.

I checked my watch. I'd been gone for three and a half minutes. Time to head back—almost. The elevator was still waiting, door ajar. I braced my foot to hold it while I examined the nearest boxes. Each had a handwritten label. At the top, a feminine hand had written the name Kuhn. Below, there was a series of numbers. Case numbers? The first four digits were definitely years—the section immediately in front of me was all in the last decade. Then there was a dash, followed by another four-digit number. Case numbers. Each box label showed anywhere from one to twenty case numbers. The boxes were all about a foot and a half wide. Eighty linear feet per aisle—fifty-three boxes, stacked eight high, each containing, on average, say ten cases. If each row took up five feet, there were forty-five thousand case files here. I revised my one- or two-week estimate upward. A month. But with luck, I wouldn't need a month. A plan was percolating in my head.

I stepped back into the elevator, inserted my key again, and pushed the button for the fourth floor. The door closed and the hum began. The car chimed once, twice, and stopped. Second floor. The door slid open. I was busted. What possible, legitimate reason could I give for being on my own traveling in the elevator? I tried to give myself a friendly aura. I stopped breathing.

The little gray lady pushed in with a small wire basket cart filled with sorted mail. She gave me a vague smile. She inserted her key and pushed for the third floor. We rode up. She exited. I started breathing again.

They needed to work a little harder on their security arrangements.

I stopped in the bathroom to wash my hands. The man looking at me from the mirror had a crazy look in his eyes, as though he was planning something that had the potential to put me in a Swiss prison for a number of years. I ignored him.

There was a thick cloud of silence hanging in the air between the cop and the lawyer when I reentered. Kuhn was too polished to seethe, but I could see he wanted to.

"Mr. Kuhn, I'm sorry to cut this short, but I have a plane to catch. If you have nothing more to add . . ."

Guelli stood up. "I have just finished telling Herr Kuhn that we will be seeking a subpoena to examine the firm's files."

Guelli was no fool. He saw the potential of the situation as well as I did.

Kuhn drove the wheelchair out from behind his desk. "And I will file an injunction to stop it."

I had to hand it to him—he was a fighter. He must have asked himself what his dead partner might have been involved in that got him tortured and killed, but he wasn't going to let us see his doubts. I'd done my best to shake something out of him, but he had nothing to tell. You can't bluff an honest man.

We saw ourselves out.

Guelli checked his watch as we walked out onto the cobblestone pavement. "This way." He pointed back up toward Bahnhofstrasse. "I'll take you to the airport. We can finish our talk on the way."

The car was still on the same corner. The two uni-
formed cops saw us coming and leaped out to open the
rear doors for us. Guelli gave them orders, and we were off.

"It will take me a day to make the arrangements.
Kuhn will eventually cooperate—there is no reason for
him not to. He is a proud man, and he was angry. Give
him a day or two and he will be reasonable."

"What will you ask for?"

"How good is your information? About the bonds
themselves?"

"The Honduran bonds? I think very good. My source
knows."

"Then I will request that they turn over all such
bonds and any records they have regarding the beneficial
owners. That way if I have to go back, I will have specific
account names."

I nodded as though it made a difference.

"Judges are more amenable to these kinds of fishing
expeditions if I cast with a fly rod than if I approach with
a trawling net."

My mind was elsewhere. I had my own arrangements
to make.

"You are unconvinced?" he continued. "Or are you
concerned for your client? If the bonds are there, they will
be delivered to the American authorities. That is where
they belong. Your client—and you—will be given all due
credit. There will be enough accolades to go around."

"You're coming at it ass end first. It won't work. Or,
rather, it might work, but it will take months."

"What do you mean?"

The police car pulled out onto the highway. The traffic was heavy. The driver put on the flashing lights and the cars in front of us immediately gave way.

"The bonds could be buried anywhere. I guarantee you they are not sitting in a file marked 'Von Becker's Bonds.'" Nor in a file marked "Honduran Drug Cartel's Bonds." "You'll be filing separate subpoenas for each and every business subsidiary and every charity that had any connection to Von Becker. And you may still not hit on the right file. If I were Biondi, I'd keep them in a file with my son's name on it. Technically, anything in that file legally belongs to my son. It might take you years to get your hands on it. And there's a very good chance that you'd lose in court in the end anyway."

Guelli stared out the window. He knew I was right.

"I'll fax you a list of all the subs, but I doubt it will do you much good. You're looking at a mountain of work, based on speculation, which may have a zero payoff. Best of luck."

I thought I could hear his teeth grinding. It didn't matter. I had my own thoughts and my own plans to make.

We pulled up to the curb at the airport. I shook Guelli's hand and hopped out of the car.

I turned to give him a final wave—and to watch him actually leave—when he rolled down the window.

"Just one question, Mr. Stafford. Did your key work?"

"Uh, what's that?"

"Your key. It fit the elevator in Biondi's offices, did it not?"

The stupid grin wasn't going to work with Guelli.

"It did," I said.

"Interesting," he said. "If I need to speak with you again, I am sure our mutual friends at the FBI will know where to find you."

"Yes."

"Then have a good flight." He rolled up the window and they pulled away.

I watched long enough to see that they really were gone, then I went inside—straight to the Swiss First lounge.

"What's the earliest flight you have to New York tomorrow morning? I may have to change my flight."

"Nine-fifty-five," the petite blonde behind the counter purred. "It gets in at one p.m. Would you like me to make that change for you?"

"I need to make some calls first."

| 31 |

The first call was to Tom.

"How's my son?"

"Is good. No problem."

Impossible. "Really?"

"Is good boy."

"Everything went okay getting him to school?"

"No problem."

"Where are you now?"

"In school lobby."

"No problem with Mrs. Carter?" The six-foot, three-hundred-pound dragon that guarded the gates of my son's school.

"I tell her we are on same side. Both want boy to be safe. Is good."

Tom got along with both my son and Mrs. Carter. His next assignment—peace in the Middle East.

"Any problems with my ex-wife?"

"Ah."

That spoke volumes. "What'd she do?"

"She tell us to leave. She get angry."

"What'd you do?"

"Ivan talk to her. She leave."

"I didn't know Ivan spoke English."

"He not speak English."

"I see. Give him my thanks. Listen, I won't be back tonight. Something's come up, so you guys are on for another twenty-four hours. Is that a problem?"

"No problem."

"I'm going to try and meet you at school tomorrow at the end of the day. With luck, I'll be there by two."

"Is good."

I wouldn't have minded having Tom watch my back for what I had to do that night.

HEATHER WAS NEXT. She was missing her Weight Watchers meeting, but that was okay because she was up two pounds and felt like ordering a pizza.

"How's my guy?"

"Great. He had a quiet night. Except for your ex. Excuse me."

"No, it's okay. I heard. She went off on the bodyguards."

"Autistic children make scenes, but they don't like to witness them." She had mentioned this before—at least a dozen times.

"What's her issue with those guys?"

"They are a little creepy. They don't talk much."

"Did the Kid eat anything green last night?"

"A few peas."

"He swallowed them?" He was quite capable of keeping them tucked in his cheek until they disintegrated; then he'd spit them out in the bathroom.

"He did," she said proudly. "We made a deal. I let him draw at the table. If he eats one pea, he gets to draw one car."

Drawing was something new for my son. All year at school he had refused to become involved in any organized art projects. Then one day he had suddenly begun drawing. Of course, all he wanted to draw were cars.

"Oh, and Carolina said she needs more of that all-natural cleaner. If you want her to keep using it."

Our housekeeper maintained a deep distrust of all household products that she considered to be "new" in any way, and that included anything "green." She would use them if I insisted, but she would not buy them. And I couldn't ask Heather to get it, because shopping was not in her job description. Managing a group of prima-donna foreign exchange traders had been a walk in the park compared to running a household—even one the size of mine.

"Listen, I need you to stay on for one more night."

"I thought this might happen."

"Is it a problem?" I could still make the afternoon flight.

"Nope. I can use the money."

"I'm on the early flight. I'll be there when he gets out of school."

"HMMPF?" SKELI ANSWERED her phone on the fourth ring.

"Did I wake you?"

"No." She paused. "I'm eating breakfast. Dancers are called for ten, so I have to be there. How's my boys?"

"The Kid's great. Heather told me he ate three peas last night."

"Woohoo! Wait. So where are you?"

"Zurich."

"Zurich? What are you doing in Zurich?"

"Breaking and entering. Grand theft, if I'm lucky."

"Very funny. All right, don't tell me."

"When do I get to see you?"

"We have tech-in tonight, dress tomorrow, and we open on Saturday. But by about six p.m. Sunday I am free, and don't have to be anywhere until Tuesday night."

It might work. It would make for a busy weekend tying up loose ends, but the Kid had no school and no camp the next week.

"We'll come down to D.C. for two days. We can see the cherry blossoms."

She laughed. I loved her laugh. "You are about two months too late for cherry blossoms. But did you know the Smithsonian has a Tucker 48?"

"Didn't he paint all those smoggy sunsets?"

"Oh, god. That's Turner. This is a Tucker. Ask the Kid."

"It's a car, then."

"Call me this weekend."

"Will do," I said.

"And bring me some Swiss chocolate."

"Come on. You can get Swiss chocolate anywhere."

"Fine. Then bring me a watch."

"What kind of chocolate? Dark, white, or milk? I think the Swiss invented milk chocolate."

"Or just some gold. They make gold there, don't they?"

"I'll see you Monday. If I don't show, it's because I'm back in jail."

We signed off.

That took care of the calls I wanted to make. Next were the calls I had to make.

"AGENT BRADY'S LINE."

"He's not there?"

"Who's calling?"

"Tell him it's Jason Stafford. He'll want to talk to me."

"He's not in, but he left instructions."

"What did he say?"

"Let me get the note." Papers rustled. "Here. He said to tell you to come home. Today. Not tomorrow. That he just spoke to someone named Guelli. This is interesting. He says Guelli knows exactly what you're thinking. Any of this making any sense?"

Too much. Guelli had figured out what I had planned

and told Brady. If I went ahead anyway, I could be sticking my head in a noose.

"Yes. I've got to run to catch the plane."

I OWED my employer a call.

"Virgil's line." A woman answered.

"I'm looking for Virgil."

"He's in a meeting. May I take a message?" The words were polite, but the tone said she didn't care whether I left a message or hung myself.

Only Virgil or Everett had ever answered on this line before. I did not want to risk leaving a message with a secretary.

"It's sensitive," I said. "And important. Can you break in on him for just a minute?"

"This is his sister," she said, her voice now as commanding as the Red Queen's. "You may leave a message with me or not."

"Morgan? My apologies." Was Blake really boffing this White Anglo-Saxon Princess? I'd known derivatives traders with more humanity. "It's Jason Stafford. How are you?"

"Is there a message?"

"I've enjoyed talking with you, too. Yes, please tell Virgil—or Everett if you can't get him—that I will be another day in Switzerland. I'm booked on the first Swiss International flight tomorrow morning. I'll talk to him tomorrow or over the weekend."

"Does that mean you have been successful?"

I had nothing but a plan at that point and had no intention of discussing it with her or anyone else. "Sorry. You're breaking up. Must be all the mountains here. My regards to your mother." I hit the disconnect button.

I WENT OUT to the duty-free and bought forty Swiss francs' worth of the same chocolate I could have found at Fairway for twenty dollars, half a block from my apartment. Then I agonized for a few minutes over the handsome miniature Swiss police car, finally deciding against it because it wasn't Matchbox and the scale was too large. It had doors that opened and closed, front wheels that turned, a bouncy suspension, and a spring-powered motor that loaded by pressing down and pulling the car backward. When you let go, it could scoot the length of a room. I loved it, but the Kid would look right through it. Too big. Then I picked up a zippered canvas tote bag and a mini-flashlight, both with the Swiss International logo. Then I went back and bought the police car anyway. It was cool. The chocolate and car went into my briefcase, which I left with the concierge back in the lounge. The little blonde changed my ticket. I tucked the tote bag under my arm and headed out to the taxi line.

"Bahnhofstrasse, please."

| 32 |

I circled the surrounding blocks, looking for any sign that Guelli and the police were waiting to trap me and also to give myself time to get rid of my jitters. The first part worked just fine. There were no SWAT teams hiding down any of the winding lanes. The jitters weren't going anywhere anytime soon, so I resolved to keep them under control. I used a mantra: "I'm doing this to protect my son." It helped a little. It was long enough—and emotional enough—to keep me from thinking too much about what I was about to do.

I swung the door open and stepped into the waiting room. As before, it was empty. I took a deep breath, made myself ignore the mini-camera in the molding, and walked to the elevator, trying with body language and attitude to give the impression that I belonged there.

I reminded myself to exhale.

The elevator clicked and hummed. I waited. The door slid open. I was halfway there. I stepped in, put in the key, and pushed the bottom button. Click. Hum. When the door opened, I stepped into darkness.

I waited for the elevator to close again before turning on the flashlight. The light switch was set to a timer by the door. If I turned it on, I wouldn't be able to turn it off again in a hurry if I heard the elevator coming. I went to work with the flashlight.

It took me ten minutes to realize that searching through those mountains of files with nothing but a Victorinox 4.8-watt flashlight just wasn't going to make it, even if it was an LED with a pretty white cross on the handle.

The elevator still lurched, banged, and hummed at times—it was early for junior lawyers in the middle of the week. The possibility that someone might need to visit the dead files still loomed and threatened. There was no way to explain my presence. On the other hand, the probability that anyone would have to research some forgotten case after six p.m. on a Thursday night in the first week of summer was not great. Easily far out on the tail end of the bell curve. In trading you don't hedge against the unlikely, no matter how disastrous. There is always the "end of the world as we know it" trade out there, which has the potential to blow up your whole portfolio, but the standard preparation for the end of the world is to ignore it. When the end of the world shows up, as it does from time to time, everyone takes their lumps equally. A trader manages risk, he does not insulate himself from it. He calculates probabilities and takes his chances.

If I continued to work with the lights off, I stood to have an extremely low chance at finding anything—if in fact anything was there to be found. If I turned on the damn lights and got to work, I might have a small chance of getting caught, but a much greater chance of success.

I turned the lights on.

Herr Kuhn's files seemed to take up all of the first two rows, until I realized that more than a third of them must have belonged to his father. His were the oldest files, and for forty years he had been remarkably productive, if the mark of a lawyer is how much paper he creates. Then, thirty years ago or so, he had begun to slow. The last file box was from 1988.

I edged around the huge shredding machine and looked around the corner. Most of the following row was devoted to the files of the long dead partner, Lauber, and to other lawyers whose names I did not recognize. Various junior members of the firm, I imagined.

And along the back wall, and running nearly the full length of the room, were Herr Biondi's files. Hundreds of boxes. Thousands of files.

My nose itched. Dust and the smell of decades-old paper were beginning to get to me. I realized I had neglected to bring food or water. I could be here all night.

There was nothing for it but to begin.

An hour later, I was frustrated. I had been through the most recent file boxes and found nothing. I mentally kicked myself. Those were the files that were least likely to have something hidden away in them. Someone might need to research a case from the last few years. It was much more likely that if the bonds were there at all, they were hidden in a box from longer ago. There were plenty to choose from. The labels all the way in the back on the bottom shelf were from the late 1950s. I got down on my haunches and looked them over. The dust hadn't been touched in decades, and the cardboard itself appeared ready to disintegrate. Not a chance.

I stood up, stretched, and walked back to the end of the aisle. Searching each box by hand wasn't going to cut it. There was no time for that. I needed to think like Biondi. Where would he have hidden them?

The elevator started up again. Click. Hum. I froze. I realized that the sporadic noises from the elevator had almost ceased in the last half-hour. The building must be near empty. But now the elevator was moving again. The elevator stopped. I exhaled. I ran to the light switch. There was no way to override the timer. If someone came down, they would have to find the lights on.

Click. Hum.

It was going up, the sound fading slightly.

I went back to work with my heart hammering against my sternum. At that rate, I was going to age a decade in one night. I worked on my mantra. "I'm doing this to protect my son."

Somewhere, I was sure, there was a list of the cases with corresponding file numbers, but even if I had it, I would still be in the same situation that I had described to Guelli. The bonds could be hidden under any name at all.

An idea occurred to me. One billion dollars, or so, in bearer bonds would make for a thick file, even in denominations of one million. So unless Biondi had spread them out, which would have made it more likely that someone else might at some point stumble over them, the box I was looking for would have fewer case file numbers on the label.

It was a Hail Mary pass, but that's what I was down to.

I began pulling out the boxes with the least number of file numbers listed.

The files in each box were individually contained in covered, expanding file folders, so that searching through a box entailed taking each folder out, unsnapping the elastic, examining the enclosed documents, and reversing the process. Each folder had a small label with the file number and the case name printed in large black letters.

A sneezing fit doubled me over, and I sat for a few minutes waiting for the stars to disappear from my vision. Dust, in varying degrees, covered the top of every box. And the faster I tried to work, the worse it got.

But I found them. It was just as Vinny had said—you hide sand at the beach.

There was no great genius to it. Anyone might have found them—if they were looking. But Castillo's people— and anyone else who might have been sent to find them—would have focused on the obvious. The bank. A safe-deposit box, or something similar. A lockbox. Security.

But security was not what Castillo's clients valued. They needed anonymity, and here it was. Buried among thousands of numbered, faceless brown file folders, all nearly identical save for thickness or age, were three thick expanding files, all with the same label. They may have been a decade or so less ancient than the rest of the folders in the box, but maybe not. The box may have had a lighter patina of dust than others on the shelf. Or not. But I knew as soon as I opened the box what it held.

The folders were all labeled Evans, Mistletoe.

I opened the first folder and removed the stack of documents inside. The bonds were printed on thick paper, and they were bound together in a block.

I pulled out a box from the bottom shelf, sat down on it, and began examining the bonds. The Honduran bonds were batched by series and denomination. Some had redemption dates three years out, others longer. Within each series, the bonds were clipped together by denomination. Quarter-million, half-million, and one million. All in U.S. dollars.

The other two folders held bonds by other issuers as well. Other Central American countries. U.S. corporations. All of these had their physical coupons still attached—perforated bits of thick paper, like the markers you might get for rides at an amusement park. Only these markers were promises of payment for thousands, or tens of thousands, of dollars apiece. In some cases there were two or three or even four coupons that should already have been redeemed. Someone, and I could only presume it had been Biondi himself, had carefully harvested the Honduran bond coupons, but had left the others intact. Not every bank in the world would redeem coupons off bearer bonds, but many would, and there were plenty of offshore banks that would be less careful about keeping records about who proffered them for payment. And to a few banks that catered to certain clients, they were as good as cash.

Click. Hum. This time, almost literally sitting on a billion dollars, my heart stopped. I waited, listening to the elevator rise up another floor and halt. My heart thudded painfully against the inside of my chest. I had to finish and get out. I did not have the constitution to be a burglar.

The three folders made a heavy load in the tote bag, but I grabbed a few other smaller files without examining them and put them on top for camouflage. Then I put the boxes back in place. Someone else might come along behind me and be able to determine that something was missing, but there was no way they could ever know for sure what had been there.

Click. Hum.

I ignored it. Mentally, I was already halfway out the door. Job completed and one million a year for life almost in my pocket. If there was still someone in the building, then the alarm would not have yet been set on the front door. I'd be gone with only a single chime before the door closed behind me. A taxi to the airport and I'd treat myself to a vodka martini in the Swiss First lounge. Maybe two.

A traders' rule—never calculate the profit on a trade before you've booked it. Shit happens.

The lights clicked off. I had forgotten the timer. I turned on the flashlight and made my way down the aisle to the elevator door. I waited until I could hear it stop before I inserted my key in the lock.

The elevator door opened.

I don't know who was more frightened—me or the African man with the tribal facial scars. I registered that he was wearing a khaki uniform and was carrying two clear bags of paper trash—cleaning staff. He began speaking quickly in broken bits and phrases. It wasn't in any of the Swiss languages, as far as I could tell. He laughed in relief and pointed to his heart and laughed again—his meaning obvious. I did the same, though my laughter had a more sickly tone to my ears. He gestured with one of the bags. I stepped back out of his way and flipped the light switch for him. He smiled and nodded in appreciation, then held up one index finger and made a pleading look. I looked at my watch and gave him one raised index finger in reply. He took the two bags of trash and hurriedly loaded them into the big shredder. I waited, holding the elevator door. He was finished in less than the one minute requested.

As he came back to the elevator, now carrying a single bag of compacted, shredded paperwork, he nodded repeatedly in thanks. He thought I belonged there. I was a lawyer working late. It was unusual to find a lawyer working in the basement after hours, but it wasn't outside the realm of normal possibility. I was using up a lifetime's worth of luck.

We rode up to the first floor together, me with my tote bag full of loot, he with his bag of trash. I gave a short wave and headed directly for the front door. I was about to touch the doorknob when he called out in concern. He was shaking his head. I stopped. He came over, stepped between me and the door. What now? How had I blown it?

There was a small plastic box halfway up the wall behind the door. The man flipped it up to reveal a small numerical keypad. He touched a series of numbers and the box gave a small beep. I had been an inch, a tenth of a second, from setting off the alarm.

I gave a big grin in thanks. He grinned back. Two unlikely conspirators, both working after hours. He would remember me. He might remember the bag. There was nothing I could do about it. On the other hand, who would he tell? Why would he? I waved again and left.

They really did need to upgrade their security.

| *33* |

The first-class passengers streamed off the plane and out of the gate, as though there was a prize for beating everyone else through customs. I hung back just a step or two on the off-chance that there was an inspector who wanted to take down the rich folks. By the time I had my passport stamped and was heading for customs, they were waving everyone through. What contraband were they going to find coming in first class from Switzerland?

But I must have had some scent of guilt around me.

"Passport."

I stopped and handed the officer my customs form and passport. During my ten years running the trading desk, I had traveled to fifty different countries on six continents. Never once had I been stopped by customs on my return. And it had never mattered before.

"Carrying anything of interest there?" he said.

"Just documents."

"Documents?"

"Yes. Legal files." My lips had gone so dry they almost smacked when I opened my mouth.

"Open the bag, please."

The file folders looked up at him, trying to look innocuous. They looked guilty as hell to me.

He moved the top folder aside and took the one directly beneath it. I couldn't read the label; I had no idea what was in it.

The officer opened the folder and pulled out a file of densely worded, very official-looking papers.

"Do you know what these are?" He held them out to me.

I did know what they were. I scanned the first page. I couldn't read it—it was all in German—but I knew exactly what it was. I had five million dollars' worth of them myself.

"It's an annuity," I said. "A Swiss insurance company annuity. They are all cut from the same template. Standard Swiss boilerplate."

Worthless to anyone but the beneficiary, whose name was prominently displayed numerous times on the first page.

"Then I doubt they fall under the definition of subversive materials, eh?"

He was making a joke. A customs joke.

I smiled. It felt like my cheeks cracked.

He dropped the folder back in the bag and reached in

again. This time he pulled out the box with the toy police car.

"This yours?" he said, smiling.

One of us was having a good time.

"It's for my son. The Kid loves cars."

"How old?"

"Six."

"Nice." He looked at the car again. "Nice car, too." He put it back in the bag and zippered it up. "He'll love it."

"I hope so."

He nodded and handed me my passport. "Welcome home."

I was through, having smuggled more than a billion dollars' worth of various bearer bonds into the country. And a slim folder of Swiss annuities made out to Mistletoe Evans.

THE CROWD OF LIMO chauffeurs, most looking like hearse drivers in black suits, white shirts, and black ties, were pairing off with their rides as I came out. I spied the one with the sign for JASON STAFFORD, a tired-looking, bandy-legged, very short older man who looked like a retired jockey.

"I'm your fare. Can you get me to the Upper West Side in an hour?"

He tipped his head to the side, a tic I sometimes employed when about to deliver bad news.

"The Van Wyck is not looking good. I can do an hour and a half maybe."

That still left me a half-hour of cushion before the Kid's school got out—it was tight. I had wanted to shower and shave and change into clean clothes—and stash the bonds in my apartment—but that could all wait.

"I'll follow you." I gestured to the outer doors.

"May I?" He reached out to take the tote bag. He had a luggage cart waiting. I hesitated for just a second. There was no sane reason not to relinquish the bag, but about a billion paranoid ones. If he tried to run away with it, I was sure I could overtake him—unless he had his horse out front. I reluctantly handed over the canvas tote, and in a spirit of "all or nothing," let him place my briefcase on the cart, too. He led the way.

When he reached the revolving door, I hustled in behind him, earning an exasperated look from the little man. We shuffled our way around and out onto the street.

The cars, SUVs, and limos were three deep at the curb, all with engines running so the drivers could argue with the attendants that they were not actually "parked," producing a carbon-rich heat haze that just about pummeled my jet-lagged brain into a state of semiconsciousness. I kept my focus on the cart and my bags.

The driver stopped at the curb and paused. It occurred to me that the light was with us. Why didn't he go? I looked at him questioningly and he turned his head away. Then he lurched forward—just as the light turned.

An oversized white SUV jumped forward and clipped the front of the cart, spilling both bags and tossing my driver to the ground. I leaped over him and ran for the tote bag.

I grabbed it and turned around. The driver had picked himself up and was screaming, making sure the world knew that, despite his fall, there had been no damage to his lungs or vocal cords. He invoked saints and demons as he described the succession of animals that were most likely responsible for siring the driver of the vehicle—and which orifices had been penetrated at his conception.

Out of the corner of my eye, I saw the SUV screech to a stop, and the little man jumped in sudden fright, covering his mouth in a burlesque parody of contrition. I almost laughed. Instead I turned just in time to see a hand reach down from the SUV's passenger door and grab my briefcase from off the ground. Then the big vehicle sped off.

People were yelling and one of the traffic wardens blew a whistle. I almost yelled myself, but the words died in my throat. I was stunned, not by the assault or the theft as much as by the intricacy of the play. Someone wanted my briefcase. But they could have had it any number of ways. Simpler, less aggressive, less dramatic. It was a feint. I thought of the driver waiting at the curb, not stepping out until after the traffic began to move. Someone had just stolen forty dollars' worth of chocolate and a five-thousand-dollar memento of my years on Wall Street, and when they discovered that they did not have a hundred million—or a billion—in bearer bonds, they would be back.

"You all right, there?" the driver yelled at me. "Got your bag? That's good." The cart was wrecked and he hauled it back onto the curb. "Here, let me take that for you," he said advancing on me. "Crazy son of a bitch, eh?"

They would want me where they could easily find me again. They would want me under surveillance. I remembered the commotion the driver had made—the screaming and cursing—distracting me at just the moment that they had grabbed my briefcase. That may have been a paranoid's deduction, but it fit all the known facts.

I grabbed him by the shirtfront and shook him hard. "Who were they?"

"Christ! I don't know!" He brushed feebly at my hand and I shook him again.

"Who are you working for? Those fucking Latinos? The Hondurans? Tell me!"

"Whaddayou, nuts? Let me go."

He sounded sincere, but I thought I could see just the flicker of something else in his eyes. "Who, goddamnit?"

But he had already recovered and began to play to the audience around us. "Get your hands off me, ya nutter."

The crowd was beginning to make noises that they were taking his side—he was the one who had been knocked to the ground.

"They took my goddamn briefcase!" I yelled into his face.

"So, whaddya want me to do? I didn't take it."

The traffic warden was headed our way. With a billion dollars in my hand, I could not afford to attract the attention of any official authority, no matter how far down the totem pole. I released the limo driver with a small push, swung the tote bag handles over my shoulder, and marched into the crowd. No one tried to stop me.

I dodged back into the terminal, wove through the milling crowds, and came out another revolving door next to the cab stand. There was no line—if there had I would have been forced to jump it.

"Ninety-sixth and Columbus," I said, settling in and hugging the canvas bag to my side. "Or anywhere around there. Whatever is quickest."

| 34 |

The afternoon pickup traffic jam had already cleared by the time I paid off the cabbie and ran up the block. I checked in with Mrs. Carter anyway.

"No, you missed them, Mr. Stafford," she said as though there was no greater sin she could imagine. "They waited. Mrs. Stafford seemed to think you were picking them up in a limousine." There was no such person as Mrs. Stafford. Hadn't been in forty years. Even when we were married, Angie had insisted on being introduced by her modeling name, Evangeline, usually followed by "But you can call me Angie. I'm retired now."

"How long?"

"Five minutes." She gave me a touch of the evil eye.

"In a cab?"

"No, they were walking down toward Amsterdam."

If I ran I'd catch up in a few blocks.

"Have a great summer, Mrs. Carter." I loved being polite to her. It always left her speechless.

THREE BLOCKS SOUTH, I finally saw them a half-block in front of me. I slowed my pace to a brisk walk and watched the Kid and his posse sidewind their way down Amsterdam. Heather was the center, to which the Kid returned and bounced away as he skipped, ran, and darted his erratic way along. Any pigeon he came upon had to be examined until it flew off—perhaps less frightened than unnerved by the Kid's eyeball-to-eyeball approach. Ivan matched the Kid move for move—a feat much more difficult than it sounds. If the Kid was the receiver, running downfield before breaking to one side or the other frantically, Ivan was the cornerback, matching his movements, anticipating his moves. Angie was the halftime show, perched on heels that should have been covered by the Geneva Convention; alternately strutting and lurching, she made frequent attempts to keep up with the Kid, but had neither the stamina nor the footwear for it. Too often, that left her walking at Heather's side, a situation that, judging by body language, was extremely uncomfortable for both of them.

Tom hung back. The safety. He was the only one not watching the Kid. He watched everything else. His movements were all about economy. He didn't walk so much as he glided.

Then the Kid fell.

Heather was used to seeing him fall—he fell often. She

turned toward him, but without breaking stride. She could see that this wasn't a serious fall. Angie didn't notice at first, her attention having been briefly stolen by a disturbance in the traffic. Ivan and Tom were still becoming acclimated to the Kid. They were bodyguards and their charge was in trouble. Ivan dashed to him, a move that saved the Kid's life. Tom, for a few short seconds, dropped the ball and took his eyes off the field and focused instead on the Kid.

The white van veered across two lanes of traffic, slowing as it came. The side door slid open. Angie saw it first. I saw her face register surprise and fear.

Phwat. Phwat. Phwat. It could have been the sound of someone slapping a folded newspaper into the palm of their hand. It wasn't.

The bullets caught Ivan just as he reached the Kid. His body took all three of them, stitching down his right side and throwing him down over the Kid. Angie screamed, flailing her arms and stumbling forward, offering herself as a target in front of the downed Ivan and the boy. Heather was pawing at Ivan, trying to get him off the Kid. Then there was the sound of three more slaps of the newspaper. Angie staggered, her scream cut off mid-note.

Tom had already swung around, a black automatic handgun having appeared in his right hand. He returned fire, emptying the magazine in a blaze of sharp cracking blasts. I couldn't move. I wanted to run to the Kid or to Angie, but anywhere I moved would put me in the crossfire, so I stood there, feeling less than useless, hugging the bag of bonds that was the root cause of this disaster.

Someone inside the van attempted to swing the side

door closed and a line of nine-millimeter-sized holes appeared immediately as Tom continued to fire. The door slid back and I could see two men in the rear, one down, the other scrambling to retrieve a gun from the floor of the van. All I could see was a long silencer on a short rifle. The guy didn't make it. Tom swapped magazines, pulling a fresh one from a back pocket as he calmly walked toward the van. Then he began firing again, slowly, more measured, taking the time to aim. Two men down.

The passenger door flew open and a hooded figure jumped out brandishing a handgun. He never got off a shot. Three down.

The driver must have had enough. The van had never completely stopped moving, and now it careened away from the curb, back across three lanes of traffic. Brakes squealed and horns sounded. The van raced across the avenue, diagonally aimed for the next side street. Tom followed, walking out into the street and emptying the second magazine into the retreating vehicle. It slowed, veered to the left, and plowed into a parked Nissan Maxima, setting off the alarm. A short, dark-haired man in a gray suit leapt from the driver's seat and ran down toward Broadway. Tom had no clear shot. He turned and walked back calmly.

For the next few seconds there was silence—stillness. It was as though I had lost not only all sense of hearing but all sense of being connected to the tableau in front of me. In defiance of science, logic, and proportion, my world had slid into stasis. Nothing moved; no sounds or smells could be sensed. Then a woman began screaming, and the universe started up again.

Sometimes seconds take forever. I ran toward the Kid. He was already up, on his feet, more troubled by having been touched by another person than by any of the shooting. Heather was with him, but not doing much more than blocking the Kid's view of the scene. Judging by her dazed expression, she was far outside of her comfort zone. I looked around wildly for Angie. I saw a red-soled high-heel shoe on the sidewalk. No sign of her. Tom passed me and crouched down by Ivan, helping him up to a sitting position. Where in hell was Angie? Then I saw her, lying between two parked cars, half in the street. There could be no doubt, she was dead.

She was facedown, lying on one arm, the other extended toward the street. There were two exit wounds in her back, each the size of her fist. Considering the size and violence of the wounds, there was surprisingly little blood. Her heart must have stopped immediately. Her head was tilted at an odd angle, as though she had died looking down at herself, but she had been dead before she hit the ground. Her platinum hair fluttered in the breeze of passing cars.

I walked to the next break between parked cars, bent over, and was sick. I vomited until I dry-retched. And then I kept retching, as though there were some stickle-backed creature caught in my throat gagging me. I couldn't breathe, and for a moment I felt as though I might pass out.

Then Tom took my arm. "I am not here. I take boy."

"What? You can't leave," I said. Where was the Kid? "The police will be here any minute." The woman was still screaming, but other voices, shouting, angry, afraid, and accusatory, were adding a chorus to her single-note aria.

"*Ja*. I go."

The Kid was back down sitting on the sidewalk, rocking back and forth and grunting furiously. There was a small smear of Ivan's blood on his black pants.

"Oh, shit. Heather!" I yelled. "Get him home and changed. Now." I looked around. Heather was standing in the middle of the sidewalk with a faraway glaze. She looked like the poster child for PTSD. "Heather!" Shit.

I made sure the Kid was not choking himself with his tongue, a recent addition to his arsenal of self-assault. His eyes were open slightly and I saw his fingers flying in their peculiar rhythmic manner. He was stimming, trying to gain control.

"Good man," I whispered. "You're doing fine."

I looked back. There was no way he could have seen his mother's body, though what he would have made of it was a question I wasn't ready to face.

"Come on, Kid. I love you. I need you to pull it together here. Please, son. Let's get you home."

Tom bent down and spoke to Ivan. Ivan handed Tom his gun and gave him that brave, stoic stare that the wounded guy in the movie always gives when the hero has to leave him behind in order to save the rest of the team. He wasn't dying, but he wasn't going anywhere in a hurry unless it was in an ambulance.

The other pedestrians were still hanging back. No one was running away, but no one was approaching to offer help. I suddenly saw them as Tom did. Witnesses.

I grabbed his arm. "Go. I'll do what I can. But go. Now."

Tom stood up and pointed to Heather. "Bring boy. We go."

Heather looked to me. For direction? Consolation? Reassurance? I didn't have any.

"Do what he says." I turned back to my son. "Go with Heather, Kid. She'll get you cleaned up."

I could see the flashing lights far down Amsterdam. The cops would be there in seconds. What the hell was I going to tell them? The whoop-whoop of the sirens punctuated my question. They were coming from all directions.

The truth. Or something like it.

I looked at the body lying half in the street. Angie looked tiny. She had never looked small to me before. Slight sometimes, or thin—my thumb and first finger could encircle her wrist with room to spare. But in death, she was shrunken.

I held my hand out to the Kid, palm down. After a moment, he stopped rocking and sniffed it. Then he stood up and held out his own to me. I bent over and sniffed it. Our private ritual.

"You go with Heather, bud. I'll be home in a little while." The sirens were getting closer.

"Now is good." Tom looked like he was finally starting to fray at the edges a bit.

I kept my body turned to block the Kid's view of Angie. He looked down at Ivan, who was leaking blood all over the sidewalk but otherwise seemed clear-eyed and aware.

"Bath," he growled. "Bath."

"Yes, I hear you," I said. "You're angry, right? That man touched you."

"Bath."

"Yes, Heather will get you a bath. But don't be angry. That man saved your life, Kid. He's a good man."

He thought about that for a moment. It didn't compute, so he shook it off. "Bye," the Kid said. He turned and looked for Heather.

She started walking. The Kid followed.

I had a decision to make and no time to agonize over the details. "Tom," I called. He stopped. If I stayed for the cops, they'd take the tote bag from me and I'd be screwed. If I ran with Tom, they'd find me and I'd be screwed. "Take this," I said, handing over the bag. I had to trust him—I had no choice. "Don't let it out of your sight."

He nodded, took the bag, and ran to catch up with Heather and the Kid.

I went to see if there was anything I could do for Ivan. Angie was past needing help.

| 35 |

Lawyers are like parachutes—when you're shopping for one, price should not be your main concern. I had a very good criminal attorney—he had negotiated two years of jail time for me when I should have served a full nickel. Still, it took him three hours to extricate me from the clutches of the NYPD.

The cops took me to the 24th Precinct on 100th Street, and almost immediately two detectives turned me around and gave me the ride of my life downtown to police headquarters, squad cars ahead and behind, lights flashing, sirens screaming.

Homicide and Major Crimes haggled over me. Major Crimes won the coin toss. The lawyer told me later that Anti-Terrorism and Organized Crime had put in bids, but had to settle for "advisory" status. It wasn't every day that five people were shot on Manhattan's "Yuppie" West

Side with one wounded, four dead, one a minor celebrity, another a known Albanian gunman from Pelham Gardens, and the other three all familiar to the Narcotics Division. It was a career-making three-ring circus.

The lawyer let me tell my story twice and then insisted we were done. There were some holes in the story, I had to admit—I kept Vinny's assistance to myself—but I gave up Castillo's name in the first thirty seconds. Gladly.

The cops wanted a paraffin test. Had I fired a gun? Had I hired these mercenaries to kill my ex-wife? I had just returned from Europe—had I transported any controlled substances?

We agreed to the paraffin test—no gunpowder residue was found on my hands—and then the lawyer drew the line. Five minutes later, we shook hands on the street and I jumped into a cab back uptown.

Immediately the flat-screen television came alive. I leaned forward to hit the off button but held up when I saw the breaking news. Angie's face—a much younger Angie—filled the screen, and a series of talking heads opined on her connection to European and Central American drug cartels. A paucity of facts shouldn't hold up a good news story.

I dug out my cell phone and turned it back on. There were people who would need to hear my voice—to know that I was okay, the Kid safe. And I needed to call Angie's mother.

The phone came alive in my hand and immediately informed me that I had twenty-three messages. I deleted

all the ones that looked like they came from the media
and started dialing.

Skeli answered on the first ring. "Oh my god. Jason,
are you all right? It's all over the news here. How's the
Kid?"

"Hey," I said. Call-waiting started beeping. I tried to
ignore it. "I'm okay. Christ, Angie and I fought every
time we were in the same space for more than three minutes, but I'm gutted. The only reason I'm not sitting in
a lump and sobbing is that I just don't have the time."

"And the Kid?"

"I don't know. I'm not sure he understands what happened. But he's safe. Not hurt. I've been with the police
for the last few hours, but I'll be home in a few minutes.
Heather's with him, but she took it hard. I don't know if
she's going to hold up."

"Oh my god! Her mother. Oh, Jason, it's all over
every station. She'll be crushed."

"The police got hold of Tino at his store before it hit
the cable news stations. I'll call when I get a chance."

The beeping would not let up. I checked the screen.
My father.

"Skeli, I've got to go. It's Pop on the other line. I love
you. Try not to worry. I'll get you back."

"Go. Go. I love you, too."

I hit the flash button.

"Pop? We're both okay."

"I just spoke to Heather."

"What'd she say?" I asked.

"She sounded shaky."

"But the Kid's all right, isn't he?"

The call-waiting began to flash again. Blocked this time.

"He was taking a bath—his second." I could hear my father smiling.

"That's my water baby," I said. "Pop. Let me go. We'll talk later."

"I love you, son."

"Thanks. I love you, too."

It could have been a reporter on the other line. I debated just hanging up and making my next call. Screw it; I chanced it and answered.

"Who is this?" I said in as neutral a voice as I could manage.

"Jason?" It was the first time FBI Agent Marcus Brady had called me by my given name.

"Agent Brady," I replied, keeping a professional distance.

"I think it's time to bring you in—get you into witness protection."

"You're late." And Angie was dead. And if I hadn't been playing superhero, it wouldn't have happened. The same loop kept grinding through my brain—over and over.

"There was nothing I could do," he said. "Now I can. Let us help you."

"You want to help me now? Great. My terms."

There were probably some very good reasons for taking Brady's offer. But a lot more against. I would never see Skeli again. Nor my father. The Kid would lose his whole support system and who knows if I would be able to re-create anything like it. But, mostly, I didn't believe the FBI could keep us safe. Only I could do that.

He chuckled. "We both know that's not going to work. Come on. This is something we do well."

"Let's see. I come in, bring the Kid. We live on take-out in some god-awful motel in Jersey while you spend eighteen months building a case. When the trial is over, the Kid and I get to move to Prescott, Arizona, and pretend we're some other people and everything is fine—unless, of course, they find us again. It'll be just like prison, but the bad guys will have guns instead of home-made knives."

"You'll have immunity."

"From what? I haven't done anything."

"I heard from Interpol."

"And? There was nothing there and no proof that there ever was anything there, and so you've got squat. Nada! Nihil! Zip! Or for those who speak Esperanto— *Nenio!* You know, Brady, you never could bluff."

I had pissed him off. "I don't need a charge to bring you in."

"Brilliant. Can I quote you on that when I call my lawyer?"

"Jason," his tone softened again. "Are you in a cab?"

"What?"

"Tell your driver he's better off staying on Eighth Avenue than trying to fight the traffic over by the Javits Center."

"You're tracking my phone!"

"Just making a point."

"Isn't that already violating my rights?"

"As a matter of fact, no."

"It should be."

"Get over it. It's an *app*! Anyone can do this. You are not safe."

"Okay," I said. "But I have to make some arrangements. It'll take me an hour or two. Then I'll come in."

"I can have our people there in ten minutes."

"No. One hour. Meet us in the lobby. And you have to be there. I'm not going to trust a couple of guys in suits flashing toy badges. I want you there."

"Fine. I can do that. You're doing the right thing."

"I see it now," I said. "You're right. One hour."

"One hour."

I hung up and called to the cabbie, "There's a twenty-dollar tip if you get me home in under ten minutes." I had a one-hour head start.

| 36 |

Raoul swung the door open as he saw me approach.
"Lots of excitement heah today, Mr. Staffud."

Lots more where I came from.

"What's that?" I said.

"The police just left. They asked a lot of questions about those guys you had watching your boy."

I'll bet they did. "What'd you tell them?"

He shrugged. "What do I know?"

"Exactly. Listen, I need you to cover my butt for the next half-hour."

"No problem."

"If anyone asks, I'm not home yet."

"That's it?"

"No matter who asks. I don't care if it's the cops, the mob, or the Pope. No one knows I'm here."

He looked a bit uncomfortable at my inclusion of the Pope. "For half an hour?"

"That's it."

He nodded. I rushed inside.

I STEPPED INTO my apartment, and for a moment froze at the utter normality of the scene in front of me. The Kid was clean, his hair still damp from the bath, and he was dressed in his favorite ninja pajamas and sitting on the couch. Heather had been straightening up in the kitchen—the aroma of grilled cheese hung in the air—but she turned when I entered. It was the same picture that greeted me every day at this time.

But everything was different. Tears were streaming down Heather's face.

"I can't do this, Mr. Stafford," she said. "I don't want to be around guns and bodyguards and people being killed." Her face was flushed in irate splotches, and even from across the room I could smell her fear.

The Kid was flipping pages in one of his car books. Flipping with a vengeance. He wasn't looking at the pages, just flipping them. I thought about attempting an intervention before the book ripped—which would definitely set off a meltdown—but realized that the intervention was as likely to lead to a meltdown.

"Heather, I am going to fix this." I needed her. So did the Kid. It was hard to say who needed her more. "And the first thing is safety. I want to get the Kid—and you—away. No one is coming after you, but they could easily make another try for him. Stick with me. He needs you."

"I'm a . . . fraid." Her voice cracked mid-word, but she forced out the last syllable.

I didn't have the time to reassure her; I didn't know if it was possible. "I know. So am I. Soon this will be over. Believe me, please. But for right now, I have to move. Very quickly. Can I count on you?"

She wiped her face. "What do you want me to do?"

"Where's Tom?" I asked.

"He left when the front desk called and said the police were on their way up."

I looked around. The canvas tote bag was leaning against the side of the couch, hidden in plain sight.

I gestured toward the Kid. "I'm taking him to the safest place I know. Help me get him packed."

She got out beige shorts and shirt for Saturday. Red shorts, white shirt for Sunday.

"Take a blue outfit for Monday, just in case," I said. Everything went into a pillowcase—the Kid didn't own matched luggage. "What cars should we take?" They covered two shelves.

"These." She quickly picked through, choosing ten or twelve. "Books," she said.

Books. Car books. Storybooks. Into the pillowcase.

"Damn it!" Where was the elephant book? I dashed back into the living room. It was on top of the empty television stand. Exactly where I had left it. "Toothbrush!" What else could the Kid not do without?

Wham! The book he had been playing with went

flying across the room, hit the childproof railing on the window with a solid crash, and fell to the floor.

The Kid may have had trouble reading emotional signs in others, but he had no problem picking up on my anxiety.

"Sorry, Kid," I called. "I'm in a hurry, but I'm going to be okay. We're going on a trip."

He threw himself back onto the couch, wrapped his arms around his elbows and squeezed.

"Very good, little soldier. Maintain. Maintain." Heather handed me one of the Kid's smooth towels—he said nappy felt like fire—and a plastic bag filled with his favorite toothpaste, soap, shampoo, and his toothbrush. "Thank you."

She nodded distractedly.

"Heather? Five minutes."

She had a sad faraway look in her eyes. "I'm sorry," she whispered. "I just keep seeing her lying in the street like that."

"Believe me, I understand. If this is all too much, just say so. But right now I really don't have time to stop and talk about it."

"Fruit Roll-Ups," she said.

"Thank you." I dashed to the refrigerator. I had never seen the Kid actually eat a Fruit Roll-Up, but if Heather or I left one by him while he was listening to music or arranging his cars, it would disappear, the only evidence of its erstwhile existence the wrapper and the Kid's pink lips.

"Kid!" I called. "We're out of here. Get your shoes on."

"Bedtime," he said.

"Yeah, but not today. Today is special. Shoes on."

I was still wearing the same underwear, socks, and shirt I had put on when I landed in Zurich. Forty hours and counting. There was no time for a shower. I changed into a pair of khakis and stuffed some other clean clothes into the pillowcase.

"Heather?" She was gaping again, her eyes slightly unfocused. "Help him with his shoes? I've got to make another couple of calls."

She nodded. I dialed.

"Roger, what are you doing?"

"What do you think I'm doing?"

I could hear the bar crowd in the background. "I need you. Can you be at the corner of West End and Seventy-second in ten minutes? I'll pick you up."

"I heard about your ex—" he began in a sympathetic voice.

"Can you be there?" I broke in.

He heard my frustration—desperation. "On my way."

Now for the long shot. I dialed Tom.

"Are you okay?" I started.

"Ja."

"Thanks for your help." There was no answer. "You need a place to lay low. I need your help. Let's trade."

He quickly agreed. "I have friend with me."

"The more the merrier," I said. "Can you get to the number 1 train?"

"Ja."

"I'll be at the corner of Broadway and Two-hundred-thirtieth Street in twenty minutes. Maybe twenty-five. If I'm not there in half an hour, make other plans." I hung up. "Folks? We're out of here."

Minutes later we were riding down in the elevator—the Kid rocking back and forth on his heels to set the little blue and red lights flickering. Heather was staring at nothing again. I needed her, but I could see she needed something else.

"You're not going with us, are you?"

She looked up at me as though about to say something, then shook her head and looked away.

"Thank you for getting us this far." I reached into my pocket and pulled out my clip full of bills—not many, and most of them Swiss francs—did a quick count, and peeled off two fifties and a twenty.

"Take this," I said. "There's a twenty to get home and enough for pizza and diet soda to get you through the weekend. I'll be in touch."

She gave a brave grin. "I think I may switch to a big bottle of Yellow Tail."

"Red or white?"

"Red. I won't have to waste time chilling it."

"Have Raoul put you in the cab."

"I'm so sorry."

"There is nothing to be sorry about, Heather. These are not normal times. I'll call you on Monday. See where things stand."

The doors opened on the lobby, and she stepped out.

"Wait," I said. "One more thing." I dug out my cell phone. If I turned it off, the Feds would pounce immediately. They might already be waiting outside. "Take my phone. Leave it in the cab when you get out. Drop it on the floor or tuck it down behind the seat."

Heather gave a conspiratorial smile. "Good luck."

"Bedtime," the Kid said as the elevator doors slid closed.

"Not yet," I said, hitting the button for the basement garage.

Mr. Samuels, the garage attendant, loaded the trunk of the rental car with our baggage—a stuffed pillowcase and the Swiss International tote bag. He and the Kid were old friends—they both liked cars.

"Just a minute, Mr. Stafford," Samuels said. "There's no seat for the boy."

The Kid hated car seats, but that wasn't why it had slipped my mind. I was stretched a bit thin at that point—with too many thoughts vying for center stage. I was a lot more concerned about machine guns than car seats.

"Uhhh, well, uh . . ." The adrenaline that was keeping me going didn't allow for side trips. "This is an emergency."

"Should have said so," Mr. Samuels said. "I keep one in the office for emergencies."

Samuels and I managed the Kid and the seat. The Kid was too exhausted to fight me. I checked my remaining cash. A ten-dollar bill and a handful of Swiss francs. I offered Samuels the ten.

"No, thank you, Mr. Stafford. The boy's a friend."

I was learning to take the time to recognize kindness—it's too rare to be ignored. "So are you, Mr. Samuels. Thank you." I hopped in and began to pull out. "Mr. Samuels?" I called.

"Mr. Stafford?"

"We were never here."

He gave a big grin and waved. "So be it." I pulled out and headed for West End Avenue.

Roger was waiting at the next corner. He jumped into the front seat and wrestled with the seat belt.

"So, ya gonna tell me where we're going?"

I smelled cognac, but by his standards he was cold sober.

"Sure. My pop's place out in Queens."

"How nice. I finally get to meet him. If you'd invited me a little earlier, I coulda brought a house gift. Or some pastries."

I turned onto the West Side Highway heading north.

Roger raised an eyebrow. "Have they moved Queens to Riverdale?"

Even in my befogged condition, I could compute half a dozen routes to College Point. The one I had chosen wasn't the most direct. I just hoped it was the best for shaking off anyone following us.

"We're picking up a friend," I said.

He looked in the backseat. "Hey, Kid."

The Kid was asleep.

"You better fill me in," Roger continued. "All I know is what's been on the news."

I gave him the highlights of the preceding forty-eight hours.

"So, you're telling me," he said when I finished, "we've got a billion dollars or so in the trunk and we might have some crazed Honduran gunmen following us, and there's also maybe some other scary people involved, but not to worry because Interpol and the FBI are ready to pounce on us as well. The only part I don't get is why you invited me along. I thought we were friends."

"The first thing you can do is watch for cars following us."

The West Side Highway traffic was rolling along at a sedate twenty-five miles per hour—typical for early evening on a Friday night the first week of the summer, slowing still further as we passed the volleyball courts, where lean, muscular women in bikini tops were in serious competition.

"This is a nice place for a drive," Roger said.

"Watch behind us," I said.

I could see an unbroken line of flashing brake lights extending up toward the GW Bridge. While no one was going to come up on us fast, anyone following us would have no problem keeping up.

Roger looked out the rear window. "Everybody's following us. Where else are they gonna go?"

To our right, the windows on Riverside Drive began to glow red with the reflected sunset over the Palisades.

"Look at that," I said. "Beautiful."

"Yeah," Roger said. "I love getting out in nature."

I saw a break in the left-hand lane as a church van with large Korean lettering failed to keep up with a momentary surge in the traffic—I took it.

"Watch. See if anyone tries the same maneuver."

The grille of the van filled my rearview mirror. Jerk.

"Nobody yet. So far you're the only one cutting people off."

Traffic slowed again. The van backed off. We were coming up on Riverbank Park. Only another mile to the bridge. I checked my watch. We were running a little behind.

"What are you going to do when you get to your pop's place?"

"I'm working on a plan."

"That's comforting."

"A plan that keeps the Kid safe. And me. And you."

"It's nice to be included."

"Keep an eye out back there. We're going to be through this in just a minute." All lanes were merging onto the ramp for I-95 on the right. Very little of the traffic was continuing north. "If anyone's following us, we'll see them here."

The highway opened in front of me. I punched it. The car gave a surprising leap forward. We raced under the bridge and up toward upper Manhattan and Riverdale. I checked the rearview mirror.

"Who's coming?"

Roger shook his head. "Nothing obvious. No one exactly racing to catch us."

Because they knew there were only two exits before

the toll bridge at the Spuyten Duyvil. "I want to see if I can shake them out."

Roger looked at me skeptically. "Who are you? Steve McQueen?"

I floored it, ripped past the Cloisters exit, then hit the brakes and pulled all the way to the right at the Dyck-man Street ramp.

"Shit," Roger said. "There he fucking is."

I checked the mirror. A big white SUV was switching lanes precariously, trying to mimic my move. I hit the gas again and bypassed the exit.

"Talk to me, Roger. What's he doing?"

"He's hanging back. He knows he blew it, but he's hoping we're as dumb as he is."

"Let's hope we're not."

The tollbooth appeared ahead at the top of a rise. I slowed and eased into the first E-ZPass lane. Three cars back, the SUV did the same. Halfway through the toll, the light flashed red. E-ZPASS NOT ACCEPTED. The rental had no device. Just what I had planned. I hit the brake and stopped, blocking the lane. An alarm was sounding. An MTA cop in a blaze orange vest came walking toward us. Behind me a black Porsche gave an angry blare on the horn. The cop waved him on to the next lane. I looked in the mirror and saw a hand with a raised middle finger. I waved back.

"Where are they, Roger?"

"Two back. Behind the church van. Who is it?"

The Porsche and the minivan were angling slowly into the next lane.

"I don't want to find out, but I'm pretty sure they stole my briefcase."

The cop came up to my window.

"License and registration."

"Oh, please. This is a rental. It was just a dumb mistake. Can't I just pay cash and go?" I checked the mirror again. The white SUV was sitting back thirty feet, waiting for the resolution.

The cop gave a dramatic sigh. "It better be exact change. Four bucks."

Shit! I had nothing but the ten and the francs. "Can you keep the change from a ten?"

He didn't bother to answer. "Pull over to the side there while I write you up."

"Wait. One sec. Roger, do you have four singles?" We didn't have time for this. Tom would be waiting for us for another four minutes.

Roger looked like I had just asked for one of his kidneys. "Why can't he make change? What's his problem?"

The cop had finally noticed the SUV and was waving him around us. The vehicle didn't move. The cop pointed directly at the driver, then pointed at the next lane, leaving no room for doubt about what he wanted.

"Roger, see if you've got four singles."

"Jeez, you don't have to shout," he said, reaching into his pants pocket with the expression of a man about to undergo a colonoscopy.

"You have the shortest arms of anyone I know," I said. "Here, take a ten. Just give me four singles."

The cop was angry. The SUV still hadn't moved. He

held up his ticket book and waved it. It worked. The big vehicle slowly edged into the next lane and through the booth. The setting sun backlit the deeply tinted windows as it rolled past the tollbooth. All I could tell was that there were two big shapes in the front seats.

"Here's the singles. Keep your ten," Roger groused. "But ya owe me."

"Roger, I owe you a lot more than four bucks. Thank you." I handed the money to the red-faced cop. He waved us through.

I moved out slowly. The SUV was fifty yards in front of us, playing the same game, crossing the bridge just fast enough to not hold up traffic. It was time to play my last card. I sped up.

"What are you doing?" Roger cried.

"I saw some guy do something like this last year."

"How'd it work out for him?"

"Ask me some other time."

The SUV must have seen me approaching. It sped up as well and raced past the Kappock Street exit.

"Fuckin' A!" I yelled, and took the exit ramp at fifty miles per hour. The car swayed as I raced through the tight turn, just catching the light at Arlington Avenue. The road in front of us was clear. I two-footed it, braking through the dogleg onto Johnson Avenue, and raced down the long hill. "Steve goddamn McQueen, Roger! You are riding with the KING!"

Roger had one hand on the door handle; the other was braced against the dash. "Don't wake the Kid."

I took the right onto 230th Street and headed for

Broadway. "The next place for them to get off the highway is four blocks up, and they'll be stuck on back streets with a ton of lights. By the time they get turned around, we could be on our way to New Jersey, or Boston, or Long Island, or who the hell knows. We're in the clear."

I pulled over in front of the bus stop and checked my watch. Twenty-eight minutes. "He should still be here."

Roger was still getting his breathing back to normal. "Who?"

The rear doors opened on both sides and two men slid in on either side of the Kid. Roger jumped and uttered a frightened squeak. The Kid didn't wake. It was Tom and another flat-eyed man with a bad haircut.

"It's okay, Roger. These guys are on our side." I made introductions as I sped across Broadway, under the elevated subway tracks and up the hill on the far side.

"Tom, this is my good friend, Roger. I'm glad you could make it. Who's your friend?"

Tom thought for a moment. "Ivan."

"Okay," I said. "Ivan it is." They could all be Ivan if they wanted, as long as they were willing to keep working to keep my son safe.

I made the right onto the entrance ramp to the Deegan, heading south, back toward the city—and Queens.

| 37 |

It's just about impossible to get lost and end up in College Point. The only way to get there is to go there. You don't just come upon it while looking for someplace else. It's hidden behind the *Times* printing plant and surrounded by the Whitestone Expressway on two sides. The other two sides face water—Flushing Bay, where shorefront property is under the incoming flight path for LaGuardia Airport and has views of the jail on Rikers Island—and the east end of the East River, which is not a river but a tidal strait, and has a current that regularly clocks five knots, so a quick dip on a hot summer day down at Chisholm Park is taking your life in your hands.

And once you find it, the first question a stranger might ask is "Why did I bother?" Even the college for which it was named closed down in 1850. I grew up in College Point, and like most of my friends, all I ever wanted was to get out. But pulling in on Twentieth Avenue and turning up College Point Boulevard, I felt safe. I knew my way around there. There would be no more surprises.

"Roger, go in and let my pop know we're here. I'll take these guys and the Kid upstairs and get everyone settled in." Roger was looking a little the worse for wear. I had asked a lot of him and there was a lot more to go. "And tell him I said you can run a tab on me." He brightened up just a tad.

My home was a three-story brick-faced, wooden-framed relic on a corner lot. The ground floor was my father's business. It had been a bar ever since the building went up, surviving through the disastrous experiment of Prohibition with an expanded kitchen and menu. A man named Sweeney bought it when he got home from the Second World War, and spent the next twenty years drinking up all of his profits, then his inventory, and finally all of his capital. My father bought the place—business and building—with not much more than a promise. The widow Sweeney just wanted out. The restaurant-bar became The Top Hat, then, possibly in honor of College Point's German heritage, The Rathskeller, and finally, in the late seventies, The Bistro. Everybody in the neighborhood called it Sweeney's. In spite of the name changes, my father kept the place packed. He worked the stick himself six nights a week—and for the first two years, spent his days renovating the two upper floors.

We lived on the second floor in a rambling three-bedroom apartment—the aroma of stale beer and a deep-fat fryer still smells like home. The two smaller apartments upstairs—furnished with whatever became available at the Goodwill in Astoria—were occupied by a succession of tenants who were willing to trade the hardship of a third-floor walk-up for the benefits of cheap rent and a lenient landlord. My father was never cut out to be a landlord, and once I was out of college and he could afford it, he retired from that business. The apartments had been empty for years—the mailboxes still read VINH and HERNANDEZ. I sent Tom and Ivan upstairs to the vacant apartments and carried the Kid into my childhood home. Eventually someone would figure out we might be hiding there, but I was betting that we had at least a day. I didn't plan on needing more.

The Kid—having slept through my Bullitt-like escapade racing through Riverdale—woke as soon as I laid him down on the bed. He woke up angry.

"Ennnnggggg." He kicked, aiming as he always did, by accident or design, for my crotch. I felt the attack coming and rotated my hip, taking the force on the outside of my thigh. I might have a charley horse later, but for the moment, I could stand upright.

"No, no, no," I repeated quietly, calmly. Then I moved quickly, wrapping him in the sheet.

He fought it, but without his usual vigor. He was tired. I pulled the sheet tighter, and threw a second and a third fold around him. He pushed against the restraint, and for a moment before his eyes closed and he fell back to sleep, I saw the light of pure pleasure on his face.

I sat with him in the dark room, listening to the muted evening sounds of the restaurant downstairs and the occasional passing car outside.

My father and I had worked together to redecorate and remove the most obvious signs of a nerdy childhood—at forty-five I regretted the loss of the signed Tina Weymouth photo that had caused me to cringe with embarrassment in my post-grad-school twenties—but there were still signs. The bookshelf held three math textbooks, one book of IQ puzzles and another on solving codes, a copy of *The International Mathematical Olympiad, Problems and Solutions*—not one of my great successes, but I made a respectable showing—and at the other end of the shelf the three volumes of the Sprawl trilogy. No wonder I was always the last one picked for the baseball team.

The Kid began to snore, a comforting sound, as he sometimes woke himself up by not breathing. His occasional apnea was not anatomical, the doctors said, and therefore not readily correctable. "Let's keep an eye on it," they said, which succeeded only in terrorizing me into repeated fretful checking up on him for the next month, until I finally accepted that this was just another one of the many things in his life that I could not control.

I dug his cars out of the pillowcase and spent the next ten minutes lining them up on the top of the bookcase, where he would see them when he woke. He had napped in this room, from time to time, when visiting my father, but this would be his first full night. His routine was broken, and the sight of the cars might help.

The linen closet door still squeaked loudly enough to qualify as a shriek, but the Kid was past disturbing. I set out a pillow, blanket, and fresh towel for Roger—he would still be up for hours and would be happy to sack out on the couch when he finally came up. Then I headed down the hall to what was called "the guest room," a bit of fiction on my father's part, as I could count on one hand the number of times we had entertained overnight visitors.

The baby furniture had been disposed of in a single day forty years ago—my crib, the folding playpen, the pink chest of drawers—and the room had been repainted once or twice, but the shadows and outlines of the rain forest–themed mural that my mother had designed and executed still showed through on the walls when the light was right. There was a butterfly—or a moth, I couldn't remember which or whether I had ever really known—near where the headboard now stood. I couldn't see it, but when I passed my fingers over the area, I could still feel the outline.

I tossed the tote bag on the bed and sank down beside it. The Kid and I were safe—for the moment—but I needed a foolproof plan to make the situation permanent. I opened the bag. The Swiss police car, still in the wrapper, sat on top. Only, sometime in the frenzy of the last few hours, at my hands or at Tom's, the package had been crushed. The car was broken.

One of the Kid's many phobias, which I had only discovered after a tantrum led to a wheel coming off his Camaro Z28, was a strong antipathy for broken toys. The Camaro could not be fixed, nor could it be merely dropped in the trash and ignored. I had to take the offending toy out to the incinerator chute and dispose of it immediately. Now I held a car he wouldn't have wanted in the first place, which I had carried a third of the way around the globe, and which was now destined to go directly to the trash.

The front door of the apartment opened and closed again, and I heard my father's tired steps as he approached down the hall. He stopped at my old room, and I could picture him checking in on the Kid, just the way he had checked in on me every night after he had closed up downstairs. It was too early for closing tonight, however. Many hours too early.

His steps came closer. He was tired. Or old. Was my father getting old? I realized that I had never framed that question before. He was who he was. Immutable. Then he was standing at the door.

"Hey, bud."

"Hey, Pop."

We were silent for a minute.

"Whatcha up to?" He gestured to the car.

"I picked this up for the Kid in Zurich. But it's broken." I showed him the bent roof, the misaligned door, the cracked plastic windshield.

He examined it and nodded. "It's too big anyway."

I took the tote bag off the bed and set it on the floor. "Come join me."

He sat. "Your friend Roger is a funny man."

"I hope so."

"Oh? Why's that?"

"He's a clown. I mean a real clown. Jacques-Emo. He was in the big time. Now he's semiretired. He does parties and whatnot. Be careful, he'll drink your top shelf dry."

"Oh, well. I left him in charge."

"Roger's tending bar?"

"I had to see that you two were all right."

I nodded. "We're okay."

"And"—he cleared his throat—"Roger thought you and I might want to talk. About today. About Angie."

That must have cost him a lot to say, because it was much too close to what we never talked about.

I don't remember my mother. What I remember is the tone of her voice when she sang me to sleep at night. That Beatles song. "Now it's time to say good night . . ." And I remember the first time I heard their version on the radio and I was shocked that anyone else in the universe knew that song. It was hers. Mine. Ours. I remember twirling her hair in my fingers when she let me sit in her lap while we watched *The Electric Company*. I remember listening to her belly and giggling with her over the sounds the baby was making. But I don't really remember what she looked like. When I thought of her, I saw only a gray blur, or I saw the face of the woman in the photographs that my father still kept on the shelf in the living room. I was only six. The same age as the Kid.

The baby was due to arrive in February, and it was November and we were walking to school—PS 29—when my mother fell down on the sidewalk. She didn't trip, she just sank slowly, her knees giving way. She moaned loudly. I must have been terrified, but I don't remember that part. Neighbors saw us and ran to help. Someone called my father. After the ambulance left, he took me to school.

My mother never came home. Just before Christmas, they let me come visit her. Not in the ward, though.

They wheeled her on her bed through big double doors and Pop and I were sitting on a hard bench against the wall and I just remember seeing tubes and machines with blinking lights and this little woman with lank hair who held my hand.

By then we knew that the baby had been a girl and that she wasn't coming home. I wasn't going to have a sister. Just as well; I'm sure I would have blamed her. Hated her.

I don't remember my father telling me that my mother wasn't coming home. I don't remember a funeral. I'm sure he did and that there was one and I was there, but I don't remember.

Pop and I sat together on the bed and stared out at the half-moon setting over the Bronx.

"She wasn't much of a wife or a mother, but I don't think she was a bad person. A sad person, maybe."

I stifled my shocked reaction, realizing in the moment that he was still talking about Angie, not his wife, my mother.

"Yeah," I finally forced out around the sob caught in my throat.

"You deserved better."

"I made my choice. It wasn't her fault. It's not like I didn't know what I was getting into." Talking about Angie, or not talking about my mother, the words came easier. "Well, maybe I didn't know. She was many things."

"Your son deserved better."

"He needed better, that's for sure."

Pop didn't say anything for a long time.

"Did you talk to Skeli?"

I nodded. "She called."

He nodded. "I like her."

I nodded some more. "Me, too. So does the Kid."

"You were six. Like him, I mean. Just six."

My throat started tightening up again. "Uh-huh." I cleared it. "He'll recover. Right now I don't think he knows. And if he knew, I don't know that he would care."

"Hmm." He meant he wasn't buying that, but he wasn't going to dispute it, either.

"If anything happened to me . . ." I stopped, choked by a rush of conflicting emotions, not least of which was fear.

Pop didn't say anything for a long time. Then he cleared his throat roughly and just said, "Shhh. Shhh."

So, we sat in what was supposed to have been my sister's room until the moon was down and we grieved, together and alone, for wives and mothers, and daughters and sisters, we had never known. I didn't cry. Pop did. Silent tears. Just a few. After a while he squeezed my hand and said, "You know something, son. You're not an idiot."

"Thanks." I gave him the smile he wanted.

"I need to go back downstairs and close up. And see if your buddy is protecting my interests."

"He's cheap, rude, and an almost constant whiner. But I trust him."

"Then so do I." He smiled. "And something else. You're a good dad."

"I learned from the best, Pop."

| 38 |

I knew exactly what I had to do to ensure the Kid's safety—and mine. There would be some risk, and I would have to bend the truth into Möbius-strip shapes at times, but if everyone, including me, played our parts correctly, it would all be wrapped up by Sunday night.

The first player I needed to coax into cooperation was Castillo. If he didn't buy into my plan, nothing else mattered and I might as well accept Brady's offer and sign myself and the Kid into witness protection. Also, I needed Castillo to hold the cartel's gunmen at bay for another twenty-four hours.

We had the library at the Merchants and Traders Club to ourselves at 8:30 on Saturday morning. I could smell the coffee brewing somewhere nearby, and the newspapers were all laid out and waiting, but the chairs were empty. The same retainer took our beverage requests again—coffee for me, and water for Castillo, this time. Neither Castillo nor I spoke to each other until the entire ritual was complete.

"I am very sorry to hear of your loss," Castillo finally began. "Violence and intimidation are no part of my business. Some of my business contacts, however, are not so disciplined. I regret that. But I must insist, I had no part in the death of your wife."

"Cut the shit," I said. I waved away his protestations. "Ex-wife. And we both know she wasn't the target. Your fucking friends tried to kill my son."

"They were not my friends, nor do I control these people. I am a banker, not a gangster."

"I'm not wired, so save the not-guilty crap for someone who cares. I have something you want. Something you need. If those assholes had been patient for another few hours, they'd still be alive and so would the mother of my son. And everybody would be happy."

"You have the bonds?" Relief. Perfect, it would help blind him.

I nodded. "Yes, I have the bonds. One hundred million in Honduran government bearer bonds. The coupons are intact back to last fall. Prior to that, I think Biondi was skimming them for himself. At seven percent, he was taking three and a half mil to the bank every six months. Money your people would probably not even miss. Am I right?"

He couldn't deny it, so he blinked.

"I would guess that's why he was stalling," I continued. "With Von Becker in jail, he had a good excuse for not handing over your bonds. If he'd been able to hold out for another six weeks, he would have been able to skim another three and a half mil. Not bad."

"Where is that money now?" His clients might not miss the interest on one hundred million dollars, but he and I worked for a living. We'd gladly pick it up and put it in our pocket if we thought we could get away with it.

I shrugged. "The question doesn't interest me."

He nodded. He was sure I had it.

I sipped my coffee. It was good—strong and acid. My body needed it—it had been a short night.

"So, where do we stand?" he finally said. Ready to negotiate already. Once the pieces are in place, the mark has to take the initiative or the play just won't work.

"This is what I want. And, please don't bother to make a counteroffer. I'd just as soon burn the damn paper and tell my story to the Feds."

"I don't think that would be wise." He was right, he was a banker, not a gangster. Even his threats sounded like a banker's.

"Don't threaten, Castillo. Your drug friends have pushed and it has not worked. Right now they're down three and no closer to getting what they want. It's time to try things my way for a change."

"I'll do what I can."

"Need an incentive? Think what happens to you if you fail to get them their money." He would be dead or in hiding for the rest of his life.

"I'm listening."

"Good. First, my finder's fee. One million in cash. I want a suitcase full of used twenties."

"That is a big suitcase," he said.

"Buy two."

"Is this the price you put on your ex-wife? One million dollars."

"My ex was a pain in the ass, but she died protecting our son, so shut up and listen." The library sucked up sound like a vacuum. All of those thousands and thousands of unread books sucking up secrets for the last hundred years and no one would ever know. We weren't loud, but if anyone had been trying to listen from more than ten feet away, he wouldn't have heard a thing. "My second demand, and it is no more negotiable than the first, is that I want ten kilos of prime, uncut China White."

Castillo laughed and threw up his hands. "Impossible. For I don't know how many reasons. Again, Mr. Stafford, I must remind you—I am a banker. I don't transport heroin."

"You can get it."

"What do you want with it? It will be harder to convert to cash than your bearer bonds."

"No, it won't. With a million dollars' worth of that shit hidden away, I get to control Binks. I can undersell you and anyone else who might try to buy him. The power shifts to me." I needed him to buy into this, even more than the first demand.

Castillo looked, for the first time, just a bit uncomfortable, but he tried for a bluff. "Binks? The Von Becker son?"

I almost laughed, the bluff was so bad. "Binks is your conduit. He does the trades through his foreign exchange book. They look like legit trades, but they're really just money laundering for you and your clients. The only reason the Feds haven't discovered the pattern yet is that the drug enforcement guys are working separately from the financial fraud guys. The minute I tell them where to look, Binks is toast. You, too. He's also your ears. He's the one who told you I was working for the family, and he's kept you posted on my progress ever since."

"So, I am paying for revenge for your ex-wife, a finder's fee for the bonds, and a bribe for your silence. Anything else?"

"We haven't covered the revenge part yet."

"There are three young men dead already. What more do you want?"

"I want their captain. The little guy. I want him delivered, hands tied, with a hood over his head. Alive. I plan on being there when he dies."

I had surprised him. He assumed that I was as crooked as he, while nowhere near as smart, but he was not vicious and did not expect to find it in me. "You don't know what you are asking. I don't control the situation."

"They'll go for it. You just have to sell it right. *Uno más mestizo muerte*. Why would they give a shit?"

"I don't like it."

"Why do you keep acting like we're negotiating? What part of this message are you not getting? This is how it will be or fuck yaz all. Do you think I give a rat's ass about your management problems at this point? You tried to KILL MY SON!"

The portraits on the far wall all gave me disapproving stares for raising my voice, but then that was what they always looked like. There was no one else to hear me. Castillo heard me, and that was what mattered.

"One million dollars, ten kilos of heroin, and the life of one more minor Honduran drug dealer. Are we done?"

"No," I said. "I want my briefcase back."

"What are you saying?"

"I want my briefcase. The one your people stole at the airport."

"Now you have lost me."

He was telling the truth. I could feel it. That sent me thinking again about the other possibilities.

"Fine," I said. "Then the briefcase is negotiable. You see, I'm not entirely unreasonable."

"When do I get back to you on your demands?"

"You don't. You show up tomorrow morning. Six a.m. If you're not there by six-thirty, I call the FBI and start lighting matches."

"Tomorrow?"

"Don't start!" I handed him a prepaid cell phone. "At exactly five a.m., I will text you an address. You will have plenty of time to get there by six. Bring the little guy all gift-wrapped, the two suitcases, and no more than two other guys to help carry the load. I can't expect you to do it all by yourself."

"And what guarantees do I have?"

"What guarantees do any of us have, *señor*? Life is like that sometimes, and if you move quickly and decisively, sometimes you get what you want. You have my word, I will have no more than two people of my own there."

"Will one of them be the shooter from yesterday? There are people who will want to stand up to him. It could make for problems."

"Play things straight and you won't even see my people. Fuck it up and take the consequences. Things didn't work out so good for your guys last time. You don't want to be in the middle of a firefight any more than I do, so just take care of it."

I got up and walked out. There was something truly delicious about being the bad guy, the heavy. I could see how some people got used to it.

| 39 |

Four-thirty on a Sunday morning is an awkward time in the city that never sleeps. A lot of people are sleeping. Who's up? Bakers and ravers, after-hours bartenders and newspaper delivery drivers. Long-legged girls in heels and short dresses, finally heading home. The first cabs of the day are gassing up on the West Side. In late June in New York, the sun is not yet rising, but the sky has gone from black to gray. Out in College Point, the hum from the Whitestone Expressway is about as quiet as it will ever get. The Boulevard won't start waking up until the bells at Saint Fidelis start ringing for early Mass.

I woke up on neither New York time nor Zurich time, stuck somewhere in between, hungover from jet lag and anxiety. A dull headache cowered at the edge of my awareness, not quite ready to announce itself. I shuffled to the bathroom and swallowed two ibuprofen and a palmful of tap water. I wanted to go back to bed and sleep until Monday. Or Tuesday. Any day but Sunday.

Ivan the Second, as I had come to think of him, was sitting in a straight-backed chair, propping open the front door with his foot, where he would be able to hear any sound from the outside door downstairs. A large black automatic pistol was in his lap. He looked up from his iPad, nodded, and went back to his Angry Birds game.

"Coffee?" I asked—some words are universal.

He looked up and nodded again.

I found the can of Chock full o'Nuts behind the bottle of grapefruit juice—my father's chosen medium for his daily dosages of Metamucil—and started a pot, adding an extra dollop of ground beans to the mix. A little jump start to the day.

I went down the hall and stuck my head in the door of my old bedroom. Roger was curled up across the foot of the bed, the Kid stretched out up at the head. There was plenty of room for both of them. Seeing the two of them laid out so near, I realized that the Kid was growing. He was so slight it was easy not to notice unless I had to buy him clothes.

Roger would be down for hours yet—he had helped my father close the bar again. The Kid might sleep for another hour or two.

Tom was pouring himself a cup of coffee when I got back to the kitchen. We nodded a silent greeting. I brought Ivan a cup, took one for myself, and settled down across the table from Tom. We drank coffee and stared past each other until the cups were empty.

I checked my watch. "Time."

Tom nodded.

I took out another prepaid cell phone, texted the cross streets in Willets Point, and shut it down.

We had been over it often enough the night before. We both knew what was next. Ivan got up and went out onto the landing. Tom took up position by the door. From those points, they commanded the narrow staircase down to the street. It was as close to an impregnable position as you could ask for. Anyone coming up the stairs would have to face crossfire from protected positions. With enough ammunition, those two would be able to hold off a small army—maybe even a medium-sized one. I was putting my head in the lion's mouth, but I knew the Kid and my father would be safe. And Roger, though I was sure he was too nasty to get hurt.

I wanted someone to wish me luck. I wanted to wish them luck. But if everyone stuck to the plan, we wouldn't need luck. But it never hurts. "I'll be back," I said and walked down the stairs.

Willets Point should have been redeveloped decades ago, but the area has resisted the threats of real estate tycoons, sports magnates, and multiple mayors. It was a ten-minute drive away, but I planned on being in position early.

In the center of Queens there is a series of parks bounded by, and bisected at times, by highways, from Jackie Robinson Parkway at the southern end to the Whitestone Expressway and Northern Boulevard to the north. There are lakes, museums, the Pavilion—a monument to the 1964 World's Fair—two tennis stadiums, and the new Mets stadium, Citi Field.

And across 126th Street from the brand-new baseball stadium, tucked up into one quiet corner of this expanse of beauty dedicated to the leisure activities of working/middle-class Queens, is a triangle of streets called Willets Point, ten or so square blocks of barely standing one-story enclosures—to call them buildings would greatly inflate their nature—and hundreds of businesses all dedicated solely to deeply discounted automobile repair.

The streets had not been repaired or resurfaced in at least fifty years and the potholes were a challenge to negotiate in anything smaller than a full-sized tow truck. In one sense, the whole area was a testament to the American entrepreneurial spirit, and also to our immigrant heritage, as nowhere else in the five boroughs of New York City looks so much like the mini-industrial blight of a third-world country. This was not where you would come to get your Ferrari tuned.

Sunday morning at 5:30 it was close to a ghost town, the doors and gates all padlocked, the nearly non-navigable streets empty. It had rained briefly in the night and many of the potholes held brown ponds of iridescent water, shimmering with the slick of petroleum products.

I positioned the rental car in the middle of the intersection, turned off the engine, and got out. A guard dog nearby heard the door slam and began a frenzied mad barking, warning me off the treasure he protected—a yard full of retread tires, used hubcaps, and rusting wheel rims. Another dog answered farther up the block, then another and another, and for a brief minute Willets Point sounded almost alive. Then, one by one, the dogs grew bored and settled back into sullen silence. The only sound was the occasional hum of traffic on the Whitestone.

Quarter to six. I could not see another human being, but there were scores of doorways, alleys, and walls that could have hidden an army. The fact that I couldn't see them didn't mean they weren't there.

Twelve minutes later, an SUV slowly made the turn off 126th Street and approached, bumping and lurching over the cracked asphalt. It stopped twenty feet away. A black SUV today. The midsized Ford. The Escape. I chuckled. Not today.

The front passenger door opened and Castillo got out. He looked both ways before crossing the street, as though we were standing at a busy Midtown intersection.

"You are alone?"

He was nervous. So was I.

"We're being watched," I said. "You won't see them if you don't screw up."

He stared into my eyes—it felt like he was fitting me for a coffin. "How shall we do this? Do you want to check your merchandise first?"

"No. You come over and check the bonds. They're in the trunk."

He scanned the street again.

"No worries," I said. "If I wanted you dead, it would already have happened."

He nodded once, then strode with me over to the car, head up. An aristocrat and unafraid.

I popped the trunk and stood back to let him look. The bonds were stacked in short piles, bound with wide rubber bands. Two hundred odd certificates in amounts ranging from two hundred and fifty thousand to one million. One hundred million dollars. Almost all of them were legit. A few were not. I knew that because I was the one who had made the fakes. All it took was a few packages of parchment paper and the color copier at Staples. I had spent a couple of hours there the day before. The fake bonds wouldn't pass a bank inspection, but I strongly doubted that they would ever have to.

"You need more light?"

The pale gray sunlight cast more shadows than illumination across the documents, and the trunk light was not much more than a glow.

Castillo bent over the pile and examined the top document. Then he looked up at me. "Do you have a flashlight?"

"No problemo, señor." I withdrew a heavy flashlight from a paper bag, turned it on, and handed it to him. The bag made a heavy thunk when I put it back down.

Castillo looked at the bag and then at me, questioning.

"It's not a gun," I said.

He nodded and went back to examining the documents. I tried burying my anxiety under thoughts of one million dollars a year for life. It wasn't perfect, but it was working. I felt calm. Castillo raised his head, turned to me and smiled. He looked relieved.

"Excellent, Mr. Stafford. My clients should have no complaints." He gathered up the bonds.

My artwork had not been discovered. "I hope not."

"*No problemo,*" he mocked. "What will you do with Hector?"

"Is that his name?"

"Hector Sanchez."

"Do you care? He's just another foot soldier. There are probably ten poor, ignorant, desperate, angry men ready to take his place."

"Hector will be missed. He is a captain. A leader. Trusted. It is a big price my clients have paid."

"Fuck that. They tried to kill my son."

"Return the man unharmed and these people will be forever in your debt."

I reached into the paper bag and pulled out the hammer.

"This is a framing hammer. Thirty-two-ounce head. But it's not the weight that does the damage. A thirty-two-ounce head delivers only twice as much punch as a sixteen-ounce. It's the speed that matters. You see this long handle? Fifty percent longer than a standard hammer. That increases the arc of the swing and therefore the speed. Are you following this? I can diagram it, or give you the formulas."

"That is not necessary. I understand."

"Speed of delivery produces a geometric increase in energy. A twelve-inch handle travels over a ninety-degree arc of six times pi, but an eighteen-inch handle travels nine times pi in the same amount of time. Energy equals mass times velocity *squared* over two. You see? Holding mass constant, your eighteen-inch handle is going to land with two hundred and twenty-five percent greater force. You don't look so good."

Castillo looked almost green. Despite the business he was in, he was a man of delicate sensibilities.

"Sorry. I get carried away. You get the idea. Combined, it's a fucking killer. You don't have to stay to watch. Just have your soldiers bring him here and put him in the trunk. I'll take it from there."

"Shouldn't you inspect your suitcases first?"

"Shucks," I said. "I plumb near forgot you were bringing me a million dollars, too."

"And ten kilos of finest-grade uncut Colombian heroin."

"Let's go see," I said.

This was the moment, I thought. If Castillo planned a double cross, this was when it would happen. Both of us in the street. The bonds in his hands. The prisoner and the two suitcases still in the truck. It would not change the outcome, but I might not survive the play.

"Wait." He stopped me halfway to the SUV. "You don't want this. Let him go. Let me take him back. If you kill him, his people will have to come after you. You will never be safe. Take the money, take the damn drugs if you have to, but let me take Sanchez."

I looked him in the eye. The argument was close enough to the truth to be tempting, but we both knew he was lying. They would come after me whether I killed Sanchez or not. My way was the only choice I had.

"No deal," I said.

His eyes flicked away.

Was I wrong? Had he been trying to save me, not the gangster? But they weren't going to let me have him. There was going to be a switch. I smiled. It was the right move. But it didn't matter.

"Let's finish this up," I said. Castillo was playing a role that he didn't want any part of. I almost felt sorry for him.

The driver was an older man, mid-thirties, with a heavy black mustache. Muscle only, it seemed. But in his business it took luck or brains or both to survive into a fourth decade. His eyes were searching the doorways and dark alleys, but he lowered them as I approached, feigning disinterest. He might be more than he appeared.

I looked in the backseat. There was a round-faced boy of about fourteen holding a black pistol in his hand, with an attitude of sullen nonchalance. Next to him was a man whose head was shrouded in a dingy pillowcase. His arms were pulled behind him and bound with plastic strip ties.

I wanted to take the boy by the arm and tell him to go home. That he hadn't lived enough to risk his life for these men. He should be out playing soccer, or trying to get laid, or studying math. He should be anywhere but where he was.

"Where do you guys do your recruiting?" I said to Castillo. "Elementary school graduation?"

Whether he understood English or not, the boy knew he was being talked about—and patronized. He turned flat killer's eyes on me and I saw the rest of their plan. He would be the one to kill me. He was expendable. The *viejo* in the front seat was there to see it happen.

"These people grow up young," Castillo said.

"Take off his hood," I said to the young killer.

Castillo rattled off a quick order. The baby face pulled the pillowcase away. It was the man who had threatened me on the street. The man who had ordered the hit on my son. The driver of the van.

"Eh! Hector Sanchez?" He did not respond. *"Maricón! Mira. Mira esto."* I held up the hammer. "Hey! Say hello to my little friend," I said in an atrocious Scarface imitation. If I hadn't been scared shitless, I might have enjoyed myself.

He looked at me and glared with supreme confidence. He wasn't bothering to play his assigned role—the sacrifice. He was impatient, uncomfortable, and he wanted to see me dead.

"Let's see the product," I said.

Castillo led me around to the trunk and opened the rear door. There were two dark gray, oversized, hard suitcases in the cargo area. Castillo gave a sweep of his arm.

"All yours."

I hefted the big one on the left. Very heavy. The money. I grabbed the other, swung it around and opened it. The bag was packed with ten clear plastic bags of white powder. It could have been heroin. It could have been talcum powder. I wouldn't have known the difference. Sometimes you just have to go on faith.

I stepped back. "Looks good. Have them bring it over."

Castillo hesitated. He knew that the moment for avoiding more spilled blood had passed, had possibly never truly existed, but still his natural inclination was to find an alternative. Money had always been able to set things aright—it was his credo—and there was plenty to go round. But he had already sold his soul and my body to the ghouls of the drug trade, and they were not selling. When he spoke, it was much too fast for me to catch much more than *"rápido."*

The driver got out, came around to the back, and took both suitcases while the beardless Latino with the gun pulled his charge out of the backseat. Sanchez staggered for a moment as his feet hit the ground, his hands still bound behind him. The young gunman, briefly shaken out of his assigned role, reached out and steadied him with the kind of concern reserved for a despotic superior. It didn't matter. Events had their own momentum.

Black-uniformed men, wearing helmets and carrying clear shields and shotguns, appeared from those doorways and alleyways and began running toward us. The gate on the abandoned paint shop swung open, and a handful of black windbreaker-clad men came out bearing automatic rifles. Two large black SUVs pulled across the intersection at 126th Street, a long yellow bus and another pair of SUVs blocked the other corner. No helicopter. It was a low-key operation.

A voice blared from a bullhorn ordering us all to drop to our knees and place our hands on our heads. I did what I was told.

Castillo whirled and glared accusingly at me. I glared back.

The driver proved to have more brains than I had given him credit for. He dropped the two suitcases, sank to his knees, and placed both hands on top of his head. Youngblood didn't take it so calmly. He pushed Sanchez to the ground and stood in front of him, protecting him to the last.

"You!" a shield-bearing officer with three stripes on his sleeve yelled. "Drop the weapon! Drop the weapon. On your knees. Down!"

Castillo was still looking around. He was the only other one standing, making him as good a target as the boy. He fell to his knees and assumed the position. But the boy wasn't getting it. I couldn't make myself stop watching. He swung the gun up toward the shielded officer, like he must have seen some actor do it on-screen once upon a time. His face was blank. He wasn't angry or afraid. If he knew it was hopeless, he gave no sign. Five hundred years of exploitation had brought him here. He was bred for dying. And there were lots more at home waiting for their chance. He was just making room for the next one.

They didn't let him fire the gun. Three or four rifles cracked as one and he was dead standing up.

It was over.

FBI Agent Marcus Brady came striding across the street toward us, leading a phalanx of black-uniformed men. They rushed us, handcuffing the driver, Sanchez, and me. The whole operation had taken seconds. A ring of uniforms, weapons at the ready, formed around the body of the boy. The man with the bullhorn arrived, still bellowing out instructions. No one was paying attention. We were all caught already.

Brady walked directly over to Castillo, helped him to his feet, and brushed imaginary dirt off the knees of his trousers.

"Muchas gracias, Señor Castillo. Bueno. Bueno." Brady's Spanish accent was worse than mine, but it made for grand theater. "Nice work. Now, let's get you out of here, shall we?"

Castillo was both horrified and too confused to protest. Brady walked him away, an arm around his shoulder as though they were old friends, and helped him into the backseat of one of the waiting cars. Two agents in suits joined him. The driver and Sanchez saw it all and I could see the gears working behind their eyes.

Then the cops wrestled the three of us into waiting vehicles. I stumbled along, two cops holding me up by the arms, my feet barely touching the ground. They tossed me into the backseat of a black car and forced my head down. The doors slammed and the car bounced away over the broken pavement.

We lurched along for about two blocks, took a sharp left onto a smoother road and raced down another block or two. I was staring at the floor, my head was reeling.

The car slammed to a stop and the rear door opened. Brady reached in and pulled me up onto the seat.

"You okay?"

"Damn! One of those guys almost broke my nose throwing me in here."

Brady turned me around and removed the handcuffs. I flopped onto the seat and pulled myself up.

"Did that boy have to die?"

"You know the answer to that."

"You said there'd be no shooting," I said.

"No. I said that you didn't have to worry about shooting. And you didn't."

"He was a kid."

"The cop he was going to shoot is a father. Just like you."

"Castillo knows he was played."

Brady was chuckling. "Doesn't matter. He's already a dead man if he doesn't cooperate with us, and he knows it. Possession of ten kilos of heroin, one million dollars in cash that is probably covered in cocaine dust, and one hundred million in bearer bonds that we have a good chance of proving are part of a money-laundering conspiracy. He deals or he goes down. And after what the two cholos just saw, he won't last a long weekend in detention. I'm happy. Are you happy?"

I leaned back. "You think they bought into it? If they didn't, I'm prime for witness protection. And you know I don't want that."

"You didn't see the driver's face when I walked Castillo out of there? No? Beautiful. He looked like he would have bitten off Castillo's leg if we'd let him go."

"What about Sanchez?"

"I'd like to turn him, but it's not gonna happen. He'll do serious time, where he will be treated like visiting royalty, and when he's a lot older than he is now, he will be given a one-way ticket back to Honduras."

"Lean on the driver," I said. "He knows more than you'd think."

"I don't know. I think he will dummy up and take his chances. Unless Castillo gives us something else on the guy, his lawyer will plead him out. He'll do short time, get deported, and go home a minor celebrity."

"You owe me a million dollars, you know."

"I'm dying to hear how you make sense out of that."

"That was my finder's fee for their hundred mil. I'll put in a claim against it."

"And I wish you all the best with that, Jason. Really, I do."

"Sarcasm does not become you."

| 40 |

French toast. Sunday morning. The bells at Saint Fidelis had rung and rung again while I sat and answered questions for Brady and his team. They finally let me leave—we all had more pressing business that day.

I could smell breakfast cooking as I came up the stairs. Tom and Ivan were no longer waiting in the hall. The danger was past. My son was safe. So was I.

The Kid was up, sitting at the kitchen table with his bodyguards, all three huddled over a board game. Roger was at the stove.

"You're up early," I said.

Roger gave the Kid an evil glance. "His majesty ordered breakfast."

"Thanks. I owe you one."

"Ha!"

"Okay, I owe you another one. Put it on my tab."

None of the players had looked up.

"Pop still asleep?"

Roger nodded. "Any glitches?"

One dead juvenile. I didn't want to think about it. "No. No glitches." I was too exhausted and disgusted to explain.

Ivan suddenly leaned back and threw his hands in the air. He said one word. I didn't need a translation. The Kid glowered. He didn't need a translation, either. Playing a cooperative game was enough of an effort for him, playing with a sore loser was painful.

Tom harangued Ivan. Ivan pointed to the board, demonstrating his frustration. As near as I could understand, this was the third time he had landed on the broken window and slid twenty spaces back down the chute to empty his piggy bank. Tom slapped himself in the forehead, the universal gesture for "What? Are you stupid?" Ivan tried to repeat his complaint, but Tom wasn't having it.

"Has it been this exciting all along?" I asked.

"Ivan's the John McEnroe of Chutes and Ladders," Roger said. He flipped the French toast. Golden brown. Perfect.

"Where did you find the game?"

"Your pop's girlfriend brought it over last night. I went through the pile of stuff in your old closet. Two chess sets? Oh, and I thought we'd leave Risk and Scrabble for another time. What's Star Conqueror, by the way? I saw that in there, too."

Star Conqueror was a four-dimensional war game

that takes place across galaxies. It was in four dimensions because time travel was possible. Players needed to do trigonometric and geometric calculations in their head. Using a calculator was legal, but then you'd be giving away your strategy. I had been very good at it, but it hadn't always been easy finding someone to play with.

"I don't know. I forget."

"You were kind of a geek as a kid, weren't you?"

"You're just figuring this out?" I said.

It was Tom's turn. He spun the needle, got a five, and landed on the girl writing with crayon on the wall. He slid back down to 73—two spaces in back of Ivan. More hand gestures and unintelligible words. "See! You baby! Quit your crying. You're still ahead of me."

"How come the Kid is the little blue-haired girl?"

"Because he chose it. The FBI didn't ask about your buddy here? The gunslinger?"

"The subject never came up. I'm sure Brady knows he's here, but it's not his case and he's comfortable looking the other way on this. For the moment."

"So we can all go home now?"

The Kid spun a two. He wanted a one. He advanced past the ladder at 71. He was still in third place. He didn't throw up his hands and curse in Albanian. I was very proud of him.

"You can, if you want," I said. "This is Pop's day off, so he can take the Kid. I'll be back to pick him up tomorrow."

"And these two?"

"I want them to ride up to Newport with me today."

Rogers eyes popped wide. "You think you'll need them?"

"Not really. But I'd hate to get up there alone and discover I should have brought backup. At this point, the only person outside of this apartment that I really trust is Skeli."

Roger slid the French toast onto a plate.

"He likes it cut on the diagonal," I said. "Like they do it at the Greek coffee shop."

Roger nodded. "Got that. Butter? Or just syrup."

"Corn syrup," I said.

Roger gave me a skeptical stare. "Corn?"

"Pop keeps a bottle for the Kid." I found it at the front of the cabinet over the stove. "Pour it on the side. He dips."

"You're killing me."

"I find that life is so much less stressful when I just button it and do things his way."

Roger put the plate down next to the Kid. "You ever notice something? This game? The worst thing you can do is raid the cookie jar. Lookit. You ride your bike with no hands, you go back four. You pull the cat's tail, for the love of Mike, and you only go back twenty. But raid the damn cookie jar? It'll cost you sixty-something."

"Sixty-three. It teaches that life is neither fair nor logical."

"Yeah, I can see where little kids need to learn that early." He gestured with a jerk of his head. "Should I cut this?"

"I'll get it." I cut a piece of the French toast, dipped it in the clear syrup, and put the fork in my son's hand. The bread disappeared. I repeated the process.

Fortunes had shifted. Tom and Ivan were neck and neck at 89 and 90, preparing to make the clubhouse turn. The Kid was back at 79, seemingly out of the picture.

Chutes and Ladders is a simple game, with a limited probability tree—it's a Markov chain. The odds of the game running more than forty turns per player drop off dramatically. The formula was straightforward, and as the probability of spinning any given number was always constant and uniform, I could do the math in my head. Math soothed me, took away the tensions. Math was orderly, unencumbered with emotions, stress, or violence.

The Kid's turn. His only chance at a win—barring both Tom and Ivan sliding back down again on one of the three chutes in the top row—was to climb the ladder at 80 into the winner's box. He needed a one. We all needed for him to have a one. He spun the needle.

One. Roger whooped. I yelled, "Hey!" Tom slapped the table and grinned. Even Ivan looked happy. The Kid covered his ears and scowled. He did not like sudden loud noises. We all quieted down.

The Kid moved his piece up the ladder onto the 100 square.

"You won, son," I said quietly.

He was busy absorbing the moment. Then he burst into laughter, maniacal, ruler-of-the-world, B-movie laughter. He beat both fists onto the table and the board jumped, pieces flying.

"Whoa, there, half-pint," Roger said.

The Kid jumped up and began to dance in his usual way—lock-kneed, stiff-hipped, and as coordinated as a moose on ice skates—but he was dancing. And laughing.

| **41** |

Tom drove. I slept.

Ivan reached around from the front seat and shook my knee as we pulled off the Newport Bridge at the Jamestown exit.

"That was quick," I said, sitting up and wiping my eyes awake. In three hours I had almost caught up on three days of fractured, minimal, anxiety-ridden sleep. I felt ready to face the Von Beckers. Even the mother.

We passed through the town and saw that there were plenty of homes that had neither helipad nor deepwater dock. South of town, the houses just disappeared behind a curtain of old-growth forest.

"Take the next left," I said. "And watch for a break in the trees." Everett had given me directions the night before.

A few minutes later we saw the driveway. It wasn't

much bigger than a path. There were two small signs sticking out of the ground. One read CHILTON. The other read, RJC SECURITY PROTECTS THESE PREMISES. YOU ARE AL-READY ON CAMERA. A few car lengths into the woods, the path turned into a white-graveled drive and we passed through a stone-and-wrought-iron gate twenty feet high. The black iron filigree over the entrance formed the words CHILTON and beneath FAMILIA ANTE OMNES. Family before all others. Brush and trees had been cleared back from a massive stone wall that stretched away into the woods in both directions.

Through the gate, the vista opened up. The driveway led through a long green lawn, broken by stone benches, marble flower islands, small groves of birch. Towering over the scene was the house, a monstrous stone struc-ture that would not have looked out of place next door to the Ansonia. It had towers, crenellations, and a front en-trance that appeared to have been copied—or purchased—from an early Renaissance cathedral.

Ivan turned to Tom and mumbled something. Tom laughed shortly.

"What did he say?" I said.

Tom said, "He say, 'Down town Abbey.'"

"Exactly. Or Brideshead."

Tom gave me a quizzical look in the rearview mirror.

"Before your time."

Tom stopped the car in the turnaround in front of the towering black oak doors.

Blake and four of his gray-suited henchmen appeared from the side of the building and surrounded the car.

Blake was smiling, but the threat was there. He opened the back door and held it for me.

"Greetings, Mr. Stafford. Welcome back. May I take your bag?"

"No. I'll keep it." I looked around at the rest of the welcoming committee. There was one man in front, one in back, and a man at each of the two front doors, blocking Tom and Ivan from getting out. "We'd all like to go in and see Virgil now," I said.

"These two can wait here."

"No, they come with me."

"I'm afraid that after your experience on the street the other day, the family has decided to take stronger security measures."

"At your suggestion, I'm sure."

He smiled agreeably.

"Well, then. Give them my regards. Virgil knows how to reach me." I grabbed the door handle and pulled. There was a brief tug-of-war as he resisted, then the door closed with a sharp bang. "Home, James."

Tom didn't get the reference, but he didn't need to. He fired up the engine and waited for the bald-headed mountain in front to move out of the way. If being outnumbered two to one caused Tom or Ivan any concern, they did not show it. He put the car in drive and inched forward.

Blake rapped on the window. "Let's talk."

I opened the window a crack. "Rethinking your security measures yet?"

"I can't let you leave."

"It'll get ugly if you try to make me stay."

He thought for a moment. "Are either of these men wanted in connection with that shooting?"

Since the police had no idea who had done the shooting, the answer was an easy one. "No. Do we get to come in now?"

He tried humor. "It's not exactly friendly to bring hired gunmen to a meeting with your employer."

"It's been that kind of a week." If Blake could separate me from Tom, I would never see my son again.

He was still thinking it over when the front doors opened and Everett came down the steps, wading right in to the deep end.

"Jason! The family is waiting. What's going on?"

Blake gave him a quick synopsis of our conversation—remarkably balanced, I thought.

"Well, of course they can't come in," Everett said.

I pulled out my cell phone and dialed Virgil's number. I heard the click as the office phone automatically forwarded the call, and two rings later he answered.

"Virgil," he said.

"I'm out front. I brought two friends. There seems to be a problem."

He hung up without responding. Less than a minute later, he came storming out the front door. "What in hell is this about, Everett?"

Everett gave his version of events—one-sided and argumentative.

Virgil looked into the car and his eyes widened slightly at the sight of my two companions. But he recovered quickly.

"Mr. Blake, please have your men step back. Everett, escort Mr. Stafford and his friends to the library." And without another look at any of us, he turned and strode back into the house.

I gripped the tote bag as though it were worth a billion dollars and followed Everett—Tom and Ivan just behind me. Blake and two of his men brought up the rear.

We marched, maintaining parade order, through an entry hall that could have held a basketball court—if anyone had ever thought of covering the walls of a basketball court in pink-veined white marble. The next two rooms seemed to have been designed for the purpose of holding uncomfortable-looking antique furniture and displaying dark landscape paintings by some of the lesser members of the Hudson River School. The rugs were deeply worn where we walked, and faded three or four shades lighter by the windows. It appeared that someone in the last two or three years must have decided to save the rugs by not washing the windows. There was an aroma of dust and age mixed with a touch of mildew. The place wasn't about to fall down, but no one was spending much on routine maintenance.

The library, therefore, was a surprise. The bookshelves and writing table were well over a hundred years old, but everything else in the room was considerably more modern—and comfortable. There were plenty of leather-bound tomes, but also shelves of bestsellers—both fiction and nonfiction—two desktop computers with large flat-screen monitors, and mounted on a pedestal in the middle of the room, a well-thumbed single-volume *OED*. There was also a glass and chrome drinks cart—no modern library should be without one. The couches and chairs were all covered in an eye-soothing neutral gray fabric that matched the drapes around a great bay window that looked out on the west lawn and a boxwood maze garden shaped in a series of interlocking chevrons. The whole effect was of a working living room devoted to knowledge and literature, rather than a museum or repository for books that no one would ever read. The room encouraged putting your feet up and settling in under one of the score of reading lamps. Some other day.

Virgil was standing to one side, back to the window. I did a quick check around the room—there was no seat that did not leave him framed in light—and elected to stand. Morgan was seated on a short couch, still dressed in mourning—as was Virgil—but she had applied a few touches of makeup. It made a vast difference. Her pale gray eyes now had a hint of mystery—her lips appeared to be fuller, making her mouth softer. Blake went over and sat with her. Whether or not it was a conscious statement, it was blatant. Everett sat on the opposing couch. The guards—both mine and theirs—spread out along the walls.

The tote bag felt very heavy. I was more than ready to pass it on, but there was one more act to play out.

"Mission accomplished," I said.

"Shall I have Everett inspect the documents?" Virgil said. He was being polite, but it was an order. Virgil was changing. When I'd met him a month earlier, he was still reeling from his father's betrayal and the skiing-through-an-avalanche feeling of trying to run a firm that was supposedly in its death throes. A second son thrown unwilling into the spotlight. Now he was a CEO, chairman of the board. Win or lose, he was in charge.

I looked to Everett. "Have you ever seen a bearer bond before?" I was betting that he had not.

"I know what to look for," he said almost petulantly, but not answering the question.

I shrugged the bag off my shoulder and dropped it on the floor in front of him.

Only Tom and Ivan managed not to stare as Everett unzipped the bag and began removing stacks of heavy parchment.

"I went through them," I said. "They're sorted by denomination to make it easier to add."

Everett nodded absently as he broke the stacks into manageable sizes on the floor and began to count.

"Virgil. While he's busy, could we have a private word?"

Morgan frowned up at him. She didn't like it. Virgil opted not to notice.

He looked at the array of hired muscle in the room. "I imagine it would be safe to step out for a minute. This way."

I followed him through a doorway on the far side of the room leading into a well-used office.

"My mother's seat of power," he said, gesturing around the room. It was not a feminine space. It was Spartan, unadorned, utilitarian, and like the library, it did not fit with the rest of the house. It did, however, reflect the owner.

"She's not here?"

Virgil gave a flick of his wrist, which could have meant anything.

"Do I detect a shift in the power structure?" I said with a smile.

He gave me a half-smile back. It could have meant anything, too.

There was a desk with a multi-line phone and a sleeping laptop, two comfortable chairs facing it, cut low enough so that the average-height sitter would feel like a penitent to whoever was behind the desk. Beyond it was a bay window with a view of Newport Harbor.

"Please. Take a seat," he said.

We sat in the two low chairs. The shift in the power structure was still incomplete.

"Where do we begin?" he asked.

"Virgil, I need to throw you a curve. Don't take this the wrong way, but have you been having me followed?"

He took it the wrong way. For a moment, he looked stormy. "To what end? I gave you an assignment. Was I supposed to be watching over your shoulder?"

I held up both hands in surrender. "My apologies. I had to ask. Do you mind if I ask you another question?"

"If you are worried about the money, please don't. Your bonus is secure. One million a year, for as long as I can keep the firm running."

"Thank you, but that's not what I was going to ask. Do you trust Blake?"

That stopped him. He thought for a minute and replied cautiously. "Morgan brought him in. They've worked together for years."

"Hmm," I said. "How long have they been . . ." I stopped and searched for the word or phrase that would not piss off an older brother, yet still make my point. "An item?"

He hadn't known. The guy was floored. His sister had been boffing the help. But he was the product of umpteen generations of New England blue bloods—on his mother's side. He was polite. Correct. "My sister does not discuss her romances with me. Nor I with her. Is there some reason for your question? I assume that you are not looking to provide the *Post* with another headline about the family."

"No. I really am on your side. But the family is coming apart at the seams, Virgil. Where's Binks?"

"He had a call and left early this morning."

"You remember me asking about a man named Castillo?"

"And I told you that I had never met the man."

"He was arrested this morning. Right now he is with the FBI, naming names. One of the names he will certainly give up is one James Von Becker, your big brother and the main conduit between your father's money-laundering business and Castillo and the Central American drug cartels. Sorry." I was rocking the guy's world. He was a good man, and I felt bad about it. Besides, he was paying me a fortune.

Virgil was sinking into the chair—melting. I couldn't let him. I needed him fighting.

"Do you have his cell? Call him. Tell him to check himself into rehab. Between the doctors and your lawyers, the Feds won't be able to get to him for a while.

Do you need some recommendations about where he should go?"

"No," Virgil sighed. "Thank you for the offer. It will not be Binks' first time in rehab. He may be there already. He has a survivor's nose for this kind of thing."

"I see." You meet plenty of junkies in prison. They are the world's preeminent whiners and manipulators. They all die before their time, but they all see it coming a thousand times over.

"Yes." He knew what I was thinking. Enough said. "I'll make the call." He picked up a phone and hit a button on the speed dialer.

The conversation was brief and in shorthand. Both brothers had spoken similar words before.

"What about your sister?" I said when Virgil was done.

"Eh?"

"What happens when I take my two gunslingers and leave? Any thoughts?"

"What happens?"

"Before I'm out the driveway Blake and his crew will take the bonds, kill you and Everett, and try to make it look like I did it. Or Tom and his sidekick. Then he and Morgan disappear. Or they wait and watch. Either way, you won't be here to see it."

"How can you be so sure?"

"Did you get my message when I was in Zurich?"

"Morgan said something about you needing another day."

"Did she say what flight I was going to be on? I told her."

"I don't remember."

"Someone knew. Someone knew what time I was getting in. They were waiting for me. I think they paid my limo driver to set me up. But all they got was my briefcase, which, by the way, you owe me for. I will expense it."

"And you think that was Blake?"

"What does his security force use for transportation?"

"I don't know. Some big thing. White. Chevy? Ford? I don't pay attention. They have three or four of them."

"There were only two people who knew what flight I was going to be on. My kid's babysitter and your sister. Which one do you think told Blake?"

"You're accusing Morgan of being part of this plot?"

"Why do you think someone tried to kidnap Morgan? Twice?"

"Blake said there was no trail. It could have been anyone. My father made a lot of enemies."

"So, why not go after you? Or Binks?"

He didn't answer.

"Because instead of telling that Swiss lawyer to pass on the bonds to Castillo's guy the way your old man asked, she sent Blake or a couple of his henchmen over to squeeze the bonds out of him. For herself. Or herself and Blake. Only they fucked it up. The lawyer died before they got anything out of him and the Hondurans sniffed it out and went after her."

"Prove it."

"Not my job."

"Your job," he straightened and glared, "is what I say it is."

"Remember the clerk? Rose-Marie Welk? She's dead. She and her husband. She was tortured and murdered and the house was torched."

"Morgan couldn't have known."

"She's desperate. She needs one hundred million to make the drug guys go away. The rest is for her and Blake and a new life. Far away from your mother and this mausoleum."

He was thinking about it. He didn't like it. He didn't want to believe it, but he was thinking.

"You're next, Virgil. I don't know that your sister is in charge anymore. If she ever was."

"I will not believe this." He was arguing with himself, not me.

"Fine. But don't bet your life on it, okay? What's the chances I'm right? Even if you figure it's only one in four, that's a big roll of the dice, Virgil."

"What do you suggest?"

I checked my watch. "We have fourteen minutes until our options shrink to zero. That's when the FBI and the Rhode Island State Police are due to arrive, unless I call to stop them. About now, they should have the main road closed and boats watching the beach. Let's hand them Blake and all of his crew and you get to wash your hands of it."

"How?"

"Tell Everett to take the bonds to your office back in

New York. Now. Blake will insist on going along to provide security. Don't let him. Tell him that he's needed here."

"He will insist. If he's guilty, he can't afford to let those bonds out of his sight at this point, and if he is innocent, he will argue that the safety of those bonds is in the family's best interest."

"Watch Morgan when he starts getting insistent," I said.

"What do you think they'll do?"

"I'm hoping he takes the damn paper and leaves."

"But suppose he gets away? Suppose he gets past the police out there?"

"They'll get him someday soon. He won't be able to run far."

"With a billion dollars? He could hide on the moon with that kind of money."

"Not to worry. The bonds are all fake. Copies. I spent all afternoon yesterday at the color copier at Staples. By the way, you owe me for the copying, too. Do you know what they get for full-color copies? It's outrageous."

"The bonds are fake? Why? What were you thinking?"

"An FBI guy I know is holding the originals. He's waiting to hear when you want to have him come with you to deliver them to the court. If he doesn't hear anything by tomorrow night, he will deliver them himself."

"You didn't trust me to turn them in?"

"Virgil. You are one of the only people involved in this that I do trust. I was worried that you might be dead. The guy's name is Brady. I trust him, too." I looked at my watch again.

Virgil got the message. "What do you need me to do?"

"You're the king. Stay in character. Move the action along and keep your eyes open. As long as Tom and Ivan are there, Blake won't want to let things get out of hand."

"I do hope you are wrong."

"It's been known to happen."

There was a knock at the door—more a series of loud thumps than a polite knock.

"Virgil! What is the meaning of all this? What's going on?"

"Mother has arrived," he said, rising. He opened the door and she swept in, eyes ablaze.

"Explain all this," she demanded, waving a hand in the general direction of the library. Then, in an instant, switching gears, "Hello, Mr. Stratford. Has anyone offered you a drink?"

"I'm good," I said, wishing that someone had offered me a drink.

She nodded politely and turned her sights back on her son. "I insist that you tell me. You must keep me informed."

Everett's head peeked around the door. "I'm sorry, Virgil. I tried to keep her out."

"Exactly! Out of my own office!" she yelled. Everett's head disappeared. "In my own house!" she continued, turning her full fury on Virgil. She was winding up for a knockdown battle. I thought I'd rather face Blake and his mercenaries.

Virgil stayed loose. Calm, kind, and definitely in control.

"Mother, I would love to explain all this to you, but I can't do it this minute." He touched her arm lightly, affectionately. "I realize that we have all rather taken over in here, but please bear with us for just a bit longer."

"I don't want those men in the house. I have told Mr. Blake that before." She had quieted slightly, but she was still in battle-ready mode.

"If you'll wait here, I'll see that everything is cleared up in just a few. Then I'll have time to sit and fill you in."

"I'll join you," she said. There was no arguing with that voice.

Virgil gave a polite shrug of acceptance. "So be it." It wasn't surrender or even retreat; he was granting permission.

We walked back into the library. Everett was back on his knees, replacing the documents in the bag. "Just over a billion dollars, Virgil." He looked a bit dazed and feverish, as though holding a billion dollars was scaring the crap out of him. "Again, I am sorry for the interruption."

If Everett was kissing up to Virgil while Livy was in the room, then the scepter had been passed. Virgil was in charge and the only one who didn't see it was his mother.

Virgil held up a hand. "Thank you, Everett. I have an assignment for you. I want you to leave immediately. Take the bonds to Rector Street and lock them in the safe in my office. You and I will surrender them to Judge O'Rourke first thing in the morning."

I watched Blake. His eyes flared. He rose off the couch. "I'll drive him down. You'll want security."

"An excellent suggestion, Blake," Livy said.

"Not necessary," Virgil said, not even acknowledging his mother's interjection. His attention was on his sister. "I want to be sure that Morgan is kept safe, not the damn bonds. Besides, no one will try to interfere with Everett. No one outside this room will know what he is carrying."

Morgan was not maintaining. Her head was snapping back and forth from Virgil to Blake. She was on a count-down to an explosion.

Blake's two mercenaries were nervous, also. They knew the stakes.

"Really, Virgil," Blake said. "Let me handle the security measures. This is what I do, after all. I will only take two of my men. The other six can continue to watch the grounds. You'll all be safe. Anything could happen between here and New York."

I was sure something would happen between here and New York—like Everett's body being tossed in the Connecticut River.

"Besides," Blake continued. "You'll have Stafford here and his two men as well. Morgan will be kept safe." He didn't look at her when he said this or he might have had the sense to shut up. Morgan didn't like the idea of being left behind.

"Maybe we should all drive down together," she piped up.

"Absurd!" Livy said. "You are to remain here."

Virgil ignored them both. So did Blake. Morgan suppressed a wince.

"Mr. Blake, I have already decided the issue." Virgil turned to me. "Mr. Stafford, I am going to have to prevail upon you, if I may. Will you take Everett and the bonds back to the city? I'm sorry to send you off the minute you've arrived, and I know it's a long drive. Can we get your friends something to eat before you leave? Sandwiches? Morgan, please have Cook put something together for these people. Better yet, get her to pack it up. They can eat on the way."

Virgil was stellar, playing the royal role impeccably. He was gracious, concerned for the comfort of the help, absolute in his decisions, and impatient only with delay.

Morgan jumped up off the couch. "Virgil, you are being impossible. You should listen to Blake instead of just dismissing him."

Morgan was not the actor her brother was. Her voice rose in pitch, almost squeaking with nerves. She was not convincing.

Livy saw a fight she thought that she had a chance of winning. "Morgan, you are interfering. Virgil and I have had quite enough. Please do not interrupt."

Virgil was paying no attention to them. "Everett. How early can we get in to see Judge O'Rourke tomorrow? I want to be back in the office for the opening bell."

Morgan lost it. "Virgil!" she shrieked. "What is the matter with you? Do what Kurt says!"

Even Livy could see that there were currents flowing she did not understand. She gave a half-gasp of exasperation and then turned to impassive stone.

Virgil turned to his sister with a toothless smile and gently touched her cheek. "I know, Morgie. I know everything."

She had no poker face. The Kid could have read her. One look at that face and he would have said, "Guilty." Her eyes were wide, her mouth a perfect O.

Everyone in the room knew something had just changed, whether they could see Morgan's face or not. Blake moved first. He grabbed the tote bag and stepped back. It was an act of desperation. All the bodyguards— Blake's crew and the Albanians—drew weapons. Events were sliding toward chaos.

"Can we all play nice?" I said. I was back against the far wall and out of the way, but Virgil, my winning lottery ticket, was right in the center of the room. "Take the bag, Blake, and go. Just everybody take a breath, all right?" This was said to Tom as much as to anyone. I had no doubt that, if needed, he could take out both of the gunmen and put a round through Blake's left eyeball in less than a heartbeat. I just didn't want him to. I wanted Blake and Morgan and the two stone-eyed killers gone. Out the damn door and into the waiting arms of the police. And nowhere near me or my future meal ticket.

And it almost happened that way.

Virgil took a step back, gesturing for his mother to follow. She had the good sense to obey—she was heavily outgunned. Blake handed the bag to Morgan. She slung it over her shoulder like stealing a billion dollars was an everyday event. Being the good daughter to the aging queen of Newport couldn't compare with true love—and a billion dollars. Slowly they edged toward the door. Tom and Ivan kept their weapons up and trained on them the whole way.

Then the door burst open. Shit! It couldn't be Brady and the police. Impossible. They weren't due for another five minutes. It wasn't.

Ex–SEC accountant Gibbons strode into the room holding up his ID like a priest with a crucifix at an Anne Rice festival. "Everyone stand down! I have the house surrounded. Lower your weapons and no one gets hurt."

It was a bravura performance. Nathan Lane as the Great Detective. Equal parts chutzpah and shtick. Did anyone else in the room know the guy was a fake? A has-been, a screwup? Prime dupe for that master of deceit, Billy Becker? At least he had ditched the funny hat.

The black swan had entered the room. The unpredictable uncertainty. Blake's men were flicking glances in his direction, looking for a sign, but Blake was poker-faced, his gun still pointed directly at Virgil's heart. Tom and Ivan didn't blink, but I could feel the world starting to tilt. The first shot would bring a fusillade and half the people in the room would be carried out in body bags.

"Gibbons," I called. "Look at me. You're not holding a winning hand. Fold. Now, before someone gets hurt."

He pointed a finger at me and yelled. "Not one more word out of you, Stafford!"

Morgan broke the standoff. In one smooth movement, she slid the heavy bag off her shoulders, grabbed the handles, and swung it in a perfect two-handed tennis power shot, directly into the back of Gibbons' head. Venus Williams couldn't have done better.

Gibbons' eyes, blazing at me, registered shock for a split second, before they shut down and went blank. He hit the floor and didn't bounce.

"Morgan! Stop this! You are being ridiculous." Livy advanced on her daughter, directly into the line of fire, masterfully ignoring both the guns and the gunmen. "Put that bag down and get some help for this man."

But Morgan wasn't having it. "Shut up, you crazy old bat. I am so sick of your crap. Help him yourself, bitch!"

The b-word did it. Livy lost her cool, hauled off and swung, laying an openhanded smack on Morgan's cheek that snapped her head around and knocked her back two steps.

No one gasped. No one breathed.

Morgan reached up as though to touch her cheek but stopped herself, refusing to allow her mother to see her hurting. She drew herself up and stepped back in range, daring Livy to hit her again. She waited a moment and then spoke firmly and without emotion. "Good-bye, Mother."

"Let's go," Blake said. His voice had gone quite hoarse, ragged. We were all a bit ragged.

Morgan backed toward the door, following Blake. The two heavies were the last out, watching us with angry, confused eyes. The door slammed and it was over.

Virgil spoke first. "Morgan must not be hurt."

Livy turned to him. "I want her trust fund to be revoked at once. Freeze her accounts!"

I checked my watch. Still three minutes to go. "I've

got to call Brady. If Blake shoots, the SWAT team will take no prisoners. Tom, you and Ivan follow me." I speed-dialed Brady as I ran out the door and down the hall.

He answered on the first ring.

"Problems?"

"They're on their way out. The sister is with them. She is not armed."

"How did it go?"

"We've got one down. He took a well-deserved blow to the head."

"Will you need an ambulance?"

"Sure. But no rush."

"Who's down?"

"The ex-SEC guy I asked you about. Gibbons. How did he get through?"

"He didn't."

"Then he must have been here all along—before I got here, I mean. I thought he might have followed me."

"Negative. We would have spotted him."

"All right. Good luck."

"Yeah."

He clicked off.

We got to the front door in time to see Blake, Morgan, and the two guards fly down the driveway in one of the big white SUVs.

Tom and Ivan were looking antsy. Their part was done and neither wanted to be around when Brady and his team showed up. We had talked about it on the drive there. They needed to spend some time visiting foreign lands—at least until the furor died down over the shoot-out on Amsterdam. "You guys go," I said, leading the way down the front steps. "Tom, take the car. The police will lift the roadblock as soon as they have Blake. You'll sail through. Maybe have Ivan duck down—two men in a car is always more suspicious than one. Get back on the highway and take Twenty-four North toward Boston. Stay on it until you hit New Hampshire and get on Ninety-three. You'll pick up Ninety-one. That will take you straight to Canada. Montreal. You can be there for dinner. They rarely check people going in that direction. Wait. Wait. Change. When you get to Concord, take Eighty-nine North and cut across Vermont. It's a little shorter, and after Burlington you'll be driving along Lake Champlain, which is beautiful. Got it?"

Tom was smiling. He was laughing at me.

I couldn't stop. "Or if you want, when you get to Boston, take the Turnpike to Albany and take the Thruway north. You go right through the Adirondacks. Beautiful country. Lots of prisons. That's the long way round, but you've got the time and you still get to see Lake Champlain, but from the other side. I won't report the car missing until tomorrow, so you'll be in the clear. Long gone. Any questions?"

Tom held up his iPhone. "I have app. Is good. Is okay. You are nice man, Jason Stafford."

"Yeah, yeah." I didn't think I could say the same about Tom, but he had put his life on the line for me and the Kid for a dollar a day. I pulled a manila envelope out of my jacket pocket. "Take this and go."

He shook his head. "You owe me nothing."

"Take it. There's two million dollars in bearer bonds that I stole from Castillo. I swapped them for copies. No one will ever know. His bonds will be sitting in an evidence vault for years while they clean up this mess. They're all small denom. Untraceable. Any major bank in Montreal will take these."

He thought about handing them back. If he had, I would have let him. But he'd earned it, and I had plenty.

He nodded. "Is good."

Ivan was waiting in the car with the engine running. I went over and put out my hand. "Thank you, Ivan. From me and the Kid. You're a hell of a Chutes and Ladders player."

He understood nothing of what I said, but he shook my hand anyway. They drove off and I went back inside. There was one more problem to take care of.

Everett was still sitting on the floor where he had been counting the bonds. His face was pasty white, sweaty and bloated, as though he were about to vomit or have a heart attack. Gibbons was sitting up, but not looking much better. I could hear Virgil and Livy talking in the office next door, but it took a moment for me to realize they were not talking to each other. Virgil was engaged in a telephone conversation, speaking quietly and calmly, very much in control. Livy was on another phone trying to bully the weekend skeleton staff at the governor's office into giving her his private cell-phone number.

"He *will* take my call, young lady. Arthur *always* takes my call!" she boomed.

I went to the little bar on wheels and fixed myself a short vodka on the rocks. I'd earned it.

"How could you let them get away?" Everett sounded both harsh and faint.

"Don't worry about it, Everett. The police will get them."

"But you let them get away with the bonds. You were hired to find them. Now they're gone again."

Gibbons groaned.

"Everett, make yourself useful. Get this guy some ice for his head."

Virgil walked back into the library, his mother trailing and still booming.

"She'll take a message. I practically bought that man his position and she has the nerve to tell me that she will take a message!" And without a pause, "I would like a short cocktail, please."

Virgil came over to the drinks cart and fixed her a vodka on the rocks—a tall one—and handed it to her. I raised my glass in a polite silent toast, but I wasn't quick enough. Livy's drink disappeared in one swallow. I set my still nearly full glass down on the cart. I couldn't compete in that kind of company.

"I called for an ambulance," Virgil said, "but it seems there was already one on the way."

"I spoke to my FBI friend."

"Very good."

"Your FBI friend?" Everett squawked. "What are you talking about?"

"The police are right down the road. It was a setup, Everett. By now Blake and party are in handcuffs and the cops will be coming down the drive any minute." I was disgusted with him. "What was the plan, Ev? Gibbons walks out with the bonds and you two meet up later. Fifty-fifty?"

"Wh-wh-wh-wh—?" he stuttered.

"What a pair of dopes. Trying to play both ends against the middle. And neither one of you had a clue. Gibbons at least has a set of balls."

"Elucidate," Virgil said, moving forward and taking up his initial position, back to the window. Livy fixed herself another. She went easier on the ice than Virgil had.

"Everett has been running his own little sideshow, trying to grab the bonds," I said. "He brought me in to find the damn money, but he never meant for you to get it. The plan was always to let me find it, then make a grab for it either when I got close or just before you turned it in. He's been passing every bit of information I gave him over to his partner here. They got nervous when it looked like I was working for Castillo. Gibbons tried to warn me off with the same phony badge. Gibbons is no longer employed by the SEC—they canned him months ago. These two met when Gibbons ran the two audits on your father's funds—clearing them both times, a feat of either criminal stupidity or stupidly criminal. But even the SEC knows when to say 'Enough.' He got the ax, but only after the funds blew up and your father was in jail. But Everett stayed in touch. He knew he had found a soul mate. Gibbons didn't just show up here and he didn't follow me. He was here in the house already. Everett must have called him after he spoke to me last night."

"Is this true?" Virgil directed the question down at Everett.

Everett didn't answer. Gibbons groaned again.

"I can't prove a thing, Virgil, but if I'm going to be your fraud consultant, my first piece of advice is to can this son of a bitch immediately. I don't know why someone as brilliant as your father kept him around, but it's time to cut him loose."

"Don't listen to him, Virgil. The man has been jealous of my career for years."

"Shut up, Everett," I said. "No one's buying." I heard a commotion at the front door. Brady had finally arrived.

"The fucked-up thing is that I don't think there's anything to charge him with. What did he actually do besides screw things up? In the end, all it did was get his buddy conked on the head."

"The ambulance is on its way," Brady said, entering the library with a rare smile on his face.

"Who is this?" Livy was even louder, if possible.

Brady showed his ID. "FBI, ma'am."

"Did Arthur send you?"

Brady looked to me for clarification.

I shook my head. "Any trouble?" I said.

"Nobody's hurt, if that's what you're asking. The only problem I see is which one wins the race to cut a deal and put the blame on the rest."

"My sister?" Virgil spoke quietly, but with both concern and authority.

"We'll give her a head start, Mr. Von Becker. Meanwhile, get her a good lawyer."

I found myself smiling. "If you'd like a good recommendation, this is a subject I know something about."

| 42 |

I had another manila envelope in my pocket.

Brady drove. He was full of energy. He'd had a big day for a lawman. I tried keeping him company, but found my eyes kept refusing to stay open. It was late and the sun long set when we came across the Triborough Bridge. Now the Robert F. Kennedy Bridge. Another bit of change that I would never get used to.

"Do you mind getting a cab? I'm on my way back to the office downtown, and a trip to the West Side . . ." He let the sentence dangle.

"No problem. I've got a stop to make anyway. Leave me off on Second Avenue and you can cut over and get right back on the FDR."

He pulled over to the curb and I reached for the door handle.

"Just one question," he said.

If he asked about Tom, I would just walk away. It was late, and I was not in the mood to start lying.

"Shoot," I said.

"The lawyer in Zurich. Who did him? It's not my case, but I'm curious. Who do you think did it?"

"Blake. Had to be. He was either there, or he sent two of those goons to handle it. Morgan was supposed to be the messenger—Virgil told me she was the only one who visited the old man—and when she saw her chance, she grabbed it. When the father figured out that she'd switched her allegiances, he took the easy way out. He hung himself."

Brady stared out at Second Avenue. "I don't see any way to prove it."

"Morgan will talk. One night in a cell at MCC and she'll give up her lover gift-wrapped. Hell, she gave up her father for money, she'll give up Blake for freedom. You'll see."

"And on that cheery note," he said, offering his hand.

I shook it. "Good night, Brady."

"Stay in touch."

Hours after sunset and the temperature on the sidewalk was still in the nineties, and so was the humidity. I wanted to climb into my own bed and let the hum of the AC blot out the world for just one night. Just one. I'd take up my life again in the morning, I promised.

No deal.

LaGuardia Airport shuts down at midnight, and starting around eleven or so, cabbies stop bothering to wait and come back into Manhattan looking for a late fare. They come in over the Triborough. I put my hand up and had a taxi in under a minute.

THE BODYGUARDS WERE GONE—Tom must have gotten the word to them. Mistletoe answered the door in a floor-length orange and yellow dashiki that made her look like an explosion. Her hair was wet and hanging straight, as though she had just come from the shower. She'd been crying.

"Come in," she said, turning and fading away from me, her body slumped in defeat. She whispered, "I didn't think you would be coming to visit anymore."

"I can't stay," I said, walking into the living room. "I've been up since four this morning and I'm dying on my feet. I just wanted to check on you. When did the men leave?"

The cats peeked out from various hiding places— beneath the couch, behind the draperies, from the top of the kitchen cabinets.

"I don't know. I slept late and when I woke up they were gone."

"I'm sorry. Were you frightened?"

"No."

She wasn't—but whether from courage or despair I couldn't say.

"I brought you something. Something from Willie." I opened the envelope. "I was going through some of

Willie's private papers and I came upon these." I pulled out the top document and handed it to her.

She looked at the official German writing. "I can't read this," she said.

"No, neither can I," I said. "But I know what it says. These are annuities. Swiss insurance company annuities. I know because I own some myself."

She blinked her eyes as though I had begun speaking in Urdu.

"How much did Willie take from you?"

She blushed. "I don't talk about that."

"Around forty million U.S., I would guess, judging by what's here."

She gave a short intake of breath—not quite a gasp, but a startled response. "It was my aunt's money, not mine."

"Oh, it's yours all right. You see, Willie didn't really take it. I mean he took it, but he didn't dump it in with other customers' money. He kept it separate and put it into Swiss-franc-denominated annuities. They don't pay much interest, but they are about the safest investment on the planet."

"I don't understand."

"He protected you, Mistletoe. These are untraceable tax-exempt securities. Contracts, really. And thanks to the dollar crapping out, they're worth about twelve percent more than they were when he bought them two years ago. You are a wealthy woman again."

She nodded slowly, but I still wasn't sure she got it.

"The interest accrues, but you can have it put in your bank account instead. My accountant can help you with it. You'll like him—he's a little older than I am. The next three years will be a little tight, living on the interest, but you can begin cashing them in any time after that."

She sank into the couch and the cats began to creep in and settle around her. I could see in her eyes that she was starting to understand.

"I think Willie cared for you, Mistletoe. He watched out for you—even against himself."

"Do you have any Kleenex?"

"No. Sorry."

"It's all right." She wiped her nose with the draping sleeve of the dashiki.

"One more thing. You were wrong about Mrs. Von Becker. She didn't have Willie killed. Willie killed himself."

"She hated him."

"Maybe. She married a man she considered beneath her, because he was the only one who asked her. Or was ever going to ask her. It wasn't a bargain she made happily. And he cheated on her and stole from all her friends and then he did the unforgivable. He got caught. But she didn't kill him."

"He wouldn't kill himself. I know my Willie."

Enough people had already lost their illusions—or delusions. I didn't want to add to her pain.

"I can't say he was a good man, but I do think he loved you."

The cats felt the change in her and all three snuggled into her lap. She stared down at them so long that I thought she might have forgotten I was there.

"I'm going to go now," I said.

"But you will come back?"

"Maybe. But I'm not going to be taking Willie's place. And you need to get out. Start making friends." It wasn't impossible. People can change. I had changed. "Best of luck."

She didn't look up.

I left her surrounded by the cats.

| 43 |

Monday—the Kid was dressed all in blue. We waded along, side by side, through security at Penn Station— an experience slightly less onerous than at the airport. I had the Kid plugged into my iPod—he was obsessing his way through the early Beatles years. The music tuned out the unintelligible overhead announcements and allowed him to focus on placing one foot in front of the other through the line and onto the escalator.

We made it to the platform level without incident, but the gap between platform and train loomed just ahead. I steeled myself for the tantrum and played my wild card.

"Whoa!" I said looking up. "Did you see that?"

The Kid looked up but refused to acknowledge me. I could hear "Love Me Do" leaking from out of the earbuds.

"You missed it?" I said.

We stepped over the gap and into the train. The Kid scowled at me and removed the little white speakers.

"What?"

"The dweebus? I can't believe you missed it. They're very rare, you know."

He turned away and walked down the aisle ahead of me.

I found two empty seats, stopped him, and let him take the window. He took a book out of his backpack, flipped down the tray like an experienced rail commuter, and dropped the book on it. It was one of his old ones. *Ten Automobiles That Challenged Detroit.* He scowled again.

"What's a"—he paused as though wary of the word—"a dweebus?"

"A bird. It's rainbow-colored. Very easy to identify. They live in train stations, but like I said, they're rare."

He knew I was making it up, but he couldn't figure out why, so he merely scowled some more. I could handle scowls. Scowls were cake compared with screams.

"When we get out in Washington, you keep your eyes peeled."

He gave a look of great distaste.

"Sorry. Don't peel your eyes. Watch for dweebuses. Actually, dweebi. One dweebus. Two dweebi. Look for them when we get out in Washington. There are always more dweebi in Washington."

He began flipping pages, losing interest. "Why?"

"That's a very good question for Skeli. You may ask her when we get there."

He plugged back into the music. "P.S. I Love You." The train pulled out.

LATE THE NIGHT BEFORE, Tino had finally returned my calls. He was flying up Thursday to pick up the body. I offered him a bed for the night, but he wasn't staying over. There was to be a wake Friday night at the Benoit Funeral Home in Beauville and a Mass the next morning. I was not invited.

"Mamma has taken this hard and I'm afraid she needs someone to blame," Tino said.

Life is neither fair nor logical.

"I understand. I'll send flowers."

"You will be vilified for doing so, but of course, you would be vilified if you did not. On balance, I believe sending an impressive display is the wiser course. Victor's here in Lafayette do a nice job and they know me."

"I'd like to bring the Kid down for a visit sometime. He lost a mother; I'd hate for him to lose a grandmother, too."

"Give her time. She'll come around. Loving is the one thing she has always been good at."

"I'll keep that in mind."

THE KID AND I would have two days in D.C. with Skeli. Not a lot of time, but I was ready to make every minute count.

I reminded myself to call Heather, wondering how the Kid and I could possibly survive if she would not come back.

I closed my eyes and tried to remember everything else

that I was sure I had forgotten. Clothes for the next few days. In all appropriate colors. Cars? Plenty. Toothbrush? Yes. It was always a problem, breaking in a new toothbrush. The Kid had to see me take it out of the plastic wrapper and immediately douse it with mouthwash—a substance, I had managed to convince him, which would kill any germ. He often requested a splash on his cuts and scrapes. Had I forgotten lunch? I bent over and checked my bag. Lunch was there. Two sandwiches. American cheese on white bread, and smoked turkey, roasted pepper, and mustard on seeded rye. We would each think the other was devouring an abomination.

The Kid was reading out loud, this time in my father's voice. He was reading loud enough to hear himself over John Lennon screaming "Twist and Shout." A tie-less, blue-suited Washington corridor commuter, obviously trying to read something on his e-reader, gave me an annoyed look over his wire spectacles. I smiled back. Let him complain. I had intentionally chosen a train car that was not a "quiet car" on the likely chance that the Kid would not make the three-hour trip in monk-like silence.

The Kid turned the page and his voice changed.

"The Tucker 48 Sedan, initially called the Torpedo, was a car well ahead of its time. Many of the automotive safety innovations of the second half of the twentieth century were designed into the Torpedo."

It was Angie's voice.

ACKNOWLEDGMENTS

An author is often like a single parent, trying to raise and nurture a creation inspired in a moment of great passion. A creation that sometimes behaves in a most ungrateful, nearly spiteful manner, causing endless headaches and feelings of anger, remorse, helplessness, and depression. And sometimes joy.

And like a parent, the author depends upon a network of helpers—mentors, doctors, comforters, and commiserators—to remain relatively sane while completing the task of seeing this child out into the world. I wish to thank all those in my network: Jennifer Belle and the Muses, who make my Wednesdays heaven or hell; my lovely wife, Barbara Segal, aka Ruby, and the Pawley's readers, whose feedback and support are essential; Richard Fiske, Chris Gaun, Jesse Leo, Effie-Marie Smith, Tim O'Rourke, Melissa Mourges, and Robert LaRussa, all of whom gave invaluable advice and corrected so many of my mistakes (any remaining ones are entirely my own); my incomparable agents, Judith Weber and Nat Sobel, who inspire me to be "even better," and their team who magically solve all of my problems; Neil Nyren and the whole Putnam crew, without whose guidance I would be floundering in an industry that so rarely makes any sense to me; and to all of my readers, for this act of creation is not complete until the reader has shared in the experience.

Keep the Kid in your hearts.

TURN THE PAGE FOR AN EXCERPT FROM
MICHAEL SEARS'S NEW THRILLER

LONG WAY DOWN

*AVAILABLE FROM G. P. PUTNAM'S SONS
IN FEBRUARY 2015!*

The banker was not so much a traditionalist as he was simply a man who, somewhat lacking in creativity or imagination, greatly enjoyed the comforts of consistency in his habits. When he drank scotch, he took no water, soda or ice, never pouring more than two fingers into a wide-mouthed, heavy-bottomed glass tumbler. When he snorted cocaine, he always rolled a crisp one-hundred-dollar bill into a tube and used the same pearl-handled miniature pocket-knife to form the unvarying inch-long lines of the drug.

That night he had many crisp one-hundred-dollar bills to choose from. Five hundred of them. Five packets of a hundred each. Though they would easily have fit in a large envelope, or even the pockets of his suit jacket, they had been delivered in a small plastic attaché case. He removed them and stacked them on the glass coffee table. The briefcase went by the door so that he would remember to put it out with the garbage when he left for the office in the morning.

The Glenlivet 18 was running low. He thought he would finish the bottle that night. He wrote a note to remind himself to have a case delivered the next day. He was not an alcoholic—he rarely had more than two or three drinks in an evening—but he had a dread of running out and not being able to sleep. It was difficult to fall asleep alone. Ever since Agathe had taken the children and escaped back to his mother's house in Cornwall, he had begun to have problems sleeping. The big apartment, taking up the top two floors of the building, with views of Hamilton Harbour, the islands, and Great Sound beyond, felt both much too large and uncomfortably small. The humming of the electric clock in the kitchen could be heard in every room on the first floor. The electronic click of the American refrigerator—the one thing that Agathe probably regretted leaving behind—when the circulating motor turned on could be deafening in the vast lonely emptiness of three a.m.

The suspicion that fifty thousand dollars was too much—too big a bribe for the favor he had performed— nagged at him again. He sipped the whiskey, surprised as he always was by the strength of the peat in the long finish. There was so little in the nose, on the lip, but so much remained long after the swallow.

He had facilitated opening an account without checking the man's identification. The man's name was unknown to him, though the name on the account was not. He had seen that name on the pages of the *Financial Times* often enough. Questions as to why such a man would want to open an account at such a small private bank had been quashed by the first utterance of the man with the cold gray eyes across the desk. He was being paid not to ask.

Tomorrow he would write down all of the particulars—everything he remembered about the man, the words he spoke, the details of the transaction—and send the document to his uncle, a London barrister, to hold "in the event of my early demise." Then he would forget about it all and enjoy the thought of fifty thousand dollars—invisible to the tax authority, to Agathe and her solicitor, and even to his grabbing bitch of a mother, whom he had been supporting ever since his father's death a decade ago and who repaid his kindness, generosity, and filial duty by siding with Agathe in this latest episode of the guerrilla warfare that passed for their marriage, now halfway through its second decade of insult, degradation, and remorse.

He took the little polythene baggie from his pocket and shook it, admiring the mound of white powder. The American had offered a gram or two along with the cash, but the banker had insisted upon a full ounce. His business was negotiation; he never took the first offer. An almost iridescent light reflected off the rocks and shards of the coke. It appeared to be quite pure. Even at his current rate of consumption, an ounce of uncut cocaine would last him a month or more. Weeks of not having to speak to the acned social misfit in client accounting, who regularly supplied the banker and his colleagues with the crystalline spice that made life in the stultifying environment of Bermuda banking bearable.

The little knife made a grating sound as he chopped

the larger crystals into a fine powder. The consistency of the cocaine was slightly different than he was used to—flakier, he thought—a factor that he attributed to the described purity of the drug.

The banker broke the wrapper on a packet of hundreds, removed the top bill, and rolled it into a short tube. He preferred using American currency; it seemed appropriate, as the price of cocaine was, like petroleum or gold, universally quoted in U.S. dollars. The conversion factor for British pounds was something he knew much about, as the most updated number flashed on his Bloomberg Terminal all day long. Every transaction he engaged in for his clients—from purchasing German stocks priced in euros to South African real estate trusts offered in rands—he thought of in terms of pounds, making the conversion automatically and effortlessly. It was what his clients wanted. But whenever he thought of cocaine, and he thought of it often, he thought in terms of dollars. And with only a modest bit of self-discipline, he now had enough dollars to keep himself supplied for years.

He snorted the first line. The freeze hit immediately and he felt the left side of his face begin to numb. The cocaine was very good, possibly the best he had ever had. The big American with the odd request had outdone himself. The second line went up his right nostril, producing a similar glow and restoring his symmetry. He moistened the tip of his index finger and wiped up the remaining dust where the two lines had lain. He gently rubbed it across his gums and felt the cold numbness penetrate. Very good cocaine.

He put his head back and waited for the rush. A moment

later, his eyes closed. He sat up abruptly. That was the strangest reaction he had ever had to the drug. He felt good, warm and safe, languid, and at the same time sexually aroused. His whole body had become a single erogenous zone. A momentary flash of paranoia tripped through his numbed consciousness. This was very unusual. But the thought was gone before it had fully taken shape. The soaring euphoria erased all fears. He may have been a very small god, even a lonely one, the ruler of a small bit of couch in an empty apartment, but he was still a god. He took a breath. He was suddenly very aware of his breathing—not that it took effort exactly, because he was all-powerful on this couch and effort had become a meaningless concept, as though the very air had become irrelevant.

The cocaine dripped from his sinuses down to the back of his throat, coating, soothing, numbing. He lost all sense of taste; his sense of smell was already gone. His fingers seemed to be a long distance away. They were clumsy and thick and wooden. He forced them to pick up the paper tube and they answered slowly and reluctantly. He leaned over and snorted up the two remaining lines and felt the top of his head lift off. His eyes bulged, and he exhaled in a hoarse rasp, unable anymore to control even his vocal cords.

The hundred-dollar bill dropped from his fingers and slowly unraveled on the glass table. He stared at it, trying to think of why such a small piece of paper had any importance in his life, but his eyes closed and he forgot about it. He kept sinking. It was a long way down. Already half-dreaming, he took one last gasping breath. His heart continued to beat for a short while before it too gave up and surrendered.

| 2 |

We hadn't walked to school since Angie, my ex-wife and the mother of my unusual child, had been murdered on Amsterdam Avenue, shot by members of a South American drug cartel. She had been protecting the boy, throwing her own body between a hail of bullets and her son. I should have been the target, not the Kid, not my ex-wife. Angie and I had our history and our baggage, and her death had not released me from all the anger, resentment, hurt, and betrayal. I carried all of those, plus the guilt that if I had done things differently, or been a different man, she would still be alive.

My second career—the first as a Wall Street trader and manager having ended with a two-year stint in a federal prison—often put me in dangerous spots. I investigated fraud, sometimes acting as a fixer or a finder in situations where street smarts met up with prison-yard ethics. I straddled both worlds in ways that often surprised me. The work had changed me—was still changing me. I had become both more tolerant and more skeptical, stronger and less fearful, yet more thoughtful and forgiving. What was legal was sometimes just not right, and those who broke the law were more often merely weak rather than evil.

The Kid had changed me, too. My son. Now six years and eight months. I had barely known him when I was sent away. I certainly had not known of his autism. Seeing life through his eyes had opened mine. If you graphed the spectrum with Asperger's on the far left, the Kid was definitely right of center, but he was verbal and a bright and curious learner. He was also a handful. And though I would not have wanted my ex back in my life in any capacity, my son deserved a mother.

The school was just a mile up Amsterdam and a half block over. The Kid used to run ahead each block, dancing impatiently at the cross streets, waiting for me to catch up and burning off a small percentage of his post-breakfast energy spurt. Not *spurt*. Explosion.

I had changed our route these past six months.

When we left early enough, we would take the bus, the M104, up Broadway and get off at Ninety-sixth Street. The Kid liked the bus. It was rarely crowded at that hour, as we were heading in the opposite direction of the morning commute. The Kid would take one of the handicapped seats up front—though he was not physically challenged, his autism gave him squatter's rights to those seats—and I would stand over him. The Kid watched the driver, and I watched him.

Most mornings, though, we were in a hurry and took the subway. The Kid was not an easy, nor an early, riser, but there were other issues that slowed us down. Getting his shoes on was near the top of the list. I had bought him more shoes than worn by the whole cast of *Sex and the City* in a futile attempt to find ones that did not "hurt." It took the two of us a year to accept the fact that, though shoes are generally less comfortable than going barefoot, you can't go barefoot in New York City—especially in December. That morning we took the subway.

We were a few minutes behind schedule as we came out of the subway at Ninety-sixth Street and quick-walked toward Amsterdam. The Kid ran. I watched him as he bobbed, weaved, ducked, and sprinted, avoiding the many obstructions in his path—some of which were imaginary. I loved watching him run. When he walked, he tended to lock up his knees and hips, as though in constant fear of falling, so that he looked like a mechanical man, made up of nonmatching spare parts. But when he ran, he looked like a child. If not happy, at least untroubled. Free.

A blast of chill wind blew dust in my eye and I put my head down, taking the irritating assault on my nascent bald spot. For that one moment I was not watching my son.

The sidewalk was narrow just there, and broken, a nondescript and barren tree having driven its roots laterally in an attempt to seek nutriments in a concrete waste-land. On the other side was a short, spiked, black iron fence guarding the basement entrance and empty garbage cans of a six-story apartment building.

I looked up, my eyes watered and blurred in the wind, but I could tell that the Kid was not ahead, waiting at the corner. A momentary flare of anxiety caught in my chest and I whirled around in a panic. The Kid was a half block behind me, squatting at the curb and trying to engage the attention of a piebald pigeon.

Almost shaking with relief, I walked back to him, not trusting my voice to call, nor trusting him to come without an argument—and cursing myself for my inattention. I squatted down next to him. The pigeon ignored both of us.

"Come on, Kid. Time for school. Ms. Wegant will be worried about us if we're late." I had never seen his teacher worried, nor flustered, nor impatient, nor happy, for that matter. Mr. Spock had a wider range of emotion. "Come on," I tried again. "Mrs. Carter will be mad at me." This was much closer to the truth. Mrs. Carter held the desk in the entryway at the school, checking in all students and keeping out anyone who did not have a well-documented reason for being on school grounds. She was a large woman, but with both the strength and agility to carry it off. I was sure that I could take her in a fair fight, and I was just as sure that she wouldn't fight fair.

I took his hand. I was impatient. I knew better. He screamed.

I let go and stood up. The screaming stopped. A childish and unworthy thought of just walking away flashed through my head. I forgave myself. If I beat myself up every time I succumbed to despair, I would have been permanently covered with black-and-blue marks. I thought about just kicking the pigeon, but held back. I would wait. Patience was the best medicine I could offer my son. It also did wonders for me.

A sudden flash of déjà vu hit me. Not really déjà vu, more a distorted memory. When my ex-wife was killed, one of the assassins had escaped by running down a side street. Could it have been that block? Or was it a few blocks farther uptown? The Kid and I would have had to move out of Manhattan altogether to avoid any reminders of his mother, or her death. I had a touch of dizziness. Possibly, I had stood up too quickly. I was disoriented, the wind blew, and my eyes blurred again.

Two men turned the corner, coming down from Amsterdam. They were short, squat, and brown-skinned. Latinos. One had a black brush of a mustache; the other, slightly taller, had a badly broken nose. Despite the cold, they both wore nothing warmer than dark hooded sweatshirts, their hands tucked into the pouches in front. They looked just like the men who had killed my ex-wife—who had attempted to kill my son, and who had threatened to kill me. And I had wondered ever since if they were going to come back and finish the job. Or when. And here they were. Moving quickly. Stone-faced. Not angry, but determined. I imagined their hands coming out, holding small guns that grew in size every time I blinked.

The white van jumped the red light, accelerated across three lanes, and suddenly slowed. The sliding panel door opened and a long-barreled weapon emerged and began spitting red flashes. Phwat. Phwat. Phwat. Like the sound of slapping a rolled-up newspaper against your thigh. Only, it wasn't a rolled-up newspaper, and people were falling.

"Kid, get up. We go. Now." I took his hand and walked back toward Broadway. The Kid must have heard the fear in my voice because for once he did not scream or fight. He stumbled along with me, his feet barely touching the ground.

Just as we approached the entrance to the next building, a woman emerged with a small dog on a leash. I rushed forward and grabbed the door before it closed, pushed the Kid inside and followed him. The lock clicked as the door shut. We were inside and the two Latinos were outside. For the moment, we were safe. But only for the moment.

The Kid stood behind me, whimpering. He had caught my fear and absorbed it. His teeth were chattering and he was shaking. There was a mail alcove to our right. I pushed him toward it and backed him against the wall. I could see the street, but it would be very difficult for anyone to see in at that angle.

"It's all right, Kid. We're safe. Those men won't find us here." I didn't believe it and neither did he. He was crying and beginning to gasp. The gasping sometimes prefaced one of his seizures.

"I pick you up," he whispered. He never wanted to be held or picked up. Never except for the few times when that was all he wanted. I took him in my arms and held him tight. Squeezing helped. It helped both of us.

The two men stopped at the front door and stared in

the window. The window was plastic—Lexan probably—with a wire mesh running through it. An older building, a holdover from a less safe era. The one with the mustache pressed a button on the intercom and spoke briefly. He looked familiar. Had I seen him before or did he look like a thousand other Latino men I had passed on the streets of New York City?

No one buzzed them in.

We were trapped. We couldn't move without them seeing us, but they knew we had entered the building and it would not take much heavy-duty guesswork for them to realize we must still be hiding in the lobby. They would figure out a way to get in soon.

The mustache put his face up against the window and yelled. The blood was pounding in my ears and the Kid was crying—I couldn't hear a thing. The man grabbed the door handle and shook it. The door suddenly looked a lot less formidable a barrier than it had a moment earlier.

I pulled out my cell phone. Who could I call? How fast could a squad car get there? Five minutes? It seemed much too long. There was no one else. I punched in the numbers.

"911. State the nature of your emergency."

"I'm being followed. By two men."

"Are you in immediate danger?"

Define the word *immediate*. "I think so."

"Name and location."

"Jason Stafford. I'm in the lobby of a building just east of Broadway."

A short, thin Latino man in overalls and a red plaid shirt walked through the lobby toward the door.

"What's the address, sir?" the voice on the phone asked.

"Please hurry." I stopped and called to the man. "Hey. Hey. Don't open that door!"

If he heard me, he gave no sign.

"Can you give me the address, sir?"

"I don't know. We just ducked in here." We were on the north side of the street, so it was an odd-numbered building. Broadway divided the block in two. "It's 249 West Ninety-fifth," I yelled into the phone. I thought it was Ninety-fifth. Could it be Ninety-fourth?

The man in the lobby stopped and looked at us suspiciously. "Can I help you?" he said, sounding like he had meant to say, "Who the f are you and what the f are you doing here?"

"Don't let those men in here. They followed us."

"Those men? I don't think so," he said with a sarcastic cough that could have been a laugh.

"No, really. I've got police on the way. Please wait."

"Hey! No cops. Shit! Look, I'm the super here. These guys work for me. They're my painters." He opened the door and spoke to the two men in rapid Spanish. The man with the mustache laughed. The other guy looked worried. Below their sweatshirts, both men wore paint-spattered baggy blue jeans and canvas sneakers. They no longer looked like hit men, they looked like painters. Mustache didn't even look familiar.

"Sir? Are you there? Can I use this number as a call-back in case we're disconnected?"

"What? No. Sorry. Please cancel the call. I'm fine. It was a mistake." The three men walked past. The one with the mustache was grinning. The other painter didn't think it was quite so funny.

"Are you all right, sir? Are you under duress?"

"No, really. I'm very embarrassed. Everything is okay here." I wanted to melt into a pool of slime and seep out under the door and into the gutter. "Thanks anyway." I hung up.

The super was leading the other two through a door down to the basement. I called after them. "Sorry about that. Really." The mustached man turned and gave a wave and a last grin.

The Kid began hitting me in the chest with the heel of his fist. "Down. Down. Down."

I put him down. He shook like a wet dog and gave me a look of deep distrust. His beautiful platinum-colored hair shimmered.

Angie lay on the pavement, partially hidden from view by two parked cars. I stepped up and saw the blood. She looked so small. The breeze from a passing car blew her hair off her face. She looked surprised. Death was something for which she should have planned ahead.

Nice work, I thought. I had panicked, managing to racially profile two innocent men, possibly causing them a hurricane of troubles if the police had arrived. And I had terrified my son. I was supposed to be his anchor, helping and supporting him against all of his usual terrors; instead I had created a new one. His father was nuts.

"Sorry, bud. I don't know what happened." Yes I did. I didn't like it but I knew what had happened. "Are you all right? Shall we get you to school now?"

He walked to the door and waited for me to open it. I followed, feeling stupid and useless—and drained. My hand shook as I pushed the door open. It wasn't the first time something similar had happened to me. I'd experienced those flashes of paranoia before. I needed to shake it off, get the Kid to school, do my morning run, and go to work. I didn't need to spend a lot of time thinking about it, analyzing it, or explaining it to a child who would not understand anyway. Hell, I wasn't sure that I understood it.

| 3 |

Virgil Becker—he had dropped the *Von* to differentiate himself and his investment bank from his father's criminal past—was looking twenty years older than his age. It made me wonder if he was sick. Probably not, I thought, just mightily stressed.

The new offices were nothing like the old shop. The bankruptcy trustee had forced the sale of all the artwork by a range of twentieth-century American regionalists from Benton and Wood to Wyeth and Rockwell; the collection of nineteenth-century American West memorabilia; the one-hundred-year-old Sultanabad carpets; and the flame mahogany open-horseshoe-shaped conference table with built-in videoconferencing, data support terminals, and rosewood inlay cup holders. Virgil's office, the only one at the firm with four walls, wasn't much bigger than my old prison cell up at Ray Brook. And like my cell, the walls were painted a flat gray, the only window looked out on an air shaft, and the shelving was metal with an industrial look. The sole remaining piece of Wild West flotsam was a framed hunk of fraying rope with a small brass plaque that read THE NOOSE USED TO HANG THE OUTLAW JESSE JAMES, JUNE 6, 1886.

Virgil caught me squinting at the inscription. "Notice anything odd about that? The courts let me keep it."

"I'm no expert on the Wild West, I never even watched *Deadwood*, but didn't Jesse James get killed by somebody he knew? He got shot, right?"

"Shot in the back," Virgil said. "And he was already four years in the ground when that hanging supposedly took place."

"Is this a weird joke?"

"Nope. My father paid almost twenty grand for that. Bought it from a dealer in Oklahoma. I keep it to remind myself that anyone can get conned—even my father."

Virgil's father had run a multibillion-dollar bank that was revealed, after decades of operation, to be a multibillion-dollar Ponzi scheme. Investors were still haggling over the remains, but the old man had chosen to avoid all the controversy. He had hanged himself in his cell while awaiting trial. Maybe that old noose had given him ideas.

I was there as a consultant, having been originally hired by the family to help clean up the father's mess. After tracking down some of the missing funds, and cleaning the stables, I had been rewarded with a near seven-figure job for life, helping to keep the troops honest and upstanding. I didn't answer to Compliance or

Legal, I dealt directly with Virgil. I liked it that way. I had a hard time getting along with compliance officers and Wall Street lawyers. I worked when I was needed, otherwise I was free to take other consulting work, read books while in a recumbent position, or take my son to watch the dogs play in the park.

"So, what did you think? What am I supposed to do?" Virgil asked.

We had just interviewed two of Virgil's employees, a mid-level trader in the bond department, and his manager, a man who had worked for Virgil and his father for almost ten years. One of them was lying.

"I know what you want to hear, Virgil. But I can't say the words. The trader came clean. He admitted he was mismarking his book. He's done it almost every year in December. I don't blame him. I'm not saying that it's right, but the deck is stacked against him."

Traders get paid based on their annual profits, but decisions about their bonuses are usually made the week after Thanksgiving. Therefore traders have zero incentive to post any excess profits in the final month of the year. But if a trader posts a big loss that month, he knows his bonus will get cut back. So traders sometimes fudge the books. Managers are supposed to know about this and keep it from getting out of hand. Zero tolerance is a nice goal, but it's not always the best option.

I knew more than a little bit about trader's tricks, having been one for years, and having managed others, until I had done some tricks of my own. The fraud that took me down was entirely of my own devising, and I had spent two years in federal prison regretting it.

Virgil got stuffy when he thought I wasn't seeing the big picture, as he called it. "I can't afford even the hint of impropriety. Half my life is dealing with regulators and auditors these days."

The trader had hidden almost a million dollars in profit by mismarking one of his more illiquid securities. I had found it fairly easily on a firm-wide scan—he hadn't made much of an effort to keep it hidden.

"So you want to fire the trader. The guy who has been making twenty mil or so for you every year for the last five years. That's a hundred million dollars, Virgil, and you're going to can him for putting one percent of that aside for a rainy day—or January, whichever comes first."

"It's not the money. He's mismarking a position. The SEC will have us restating earnings going back to the firm's inception."

I saw the big picture; I just thought there was a better way of keeping the crowd of pirates, hustlers, gunslingers, and cowboys that comprised the workforce at a Wall Street firm from degenerating into a gang of thieves.

"The SEC won't care if you don't tell them. They don't want to know about it. This is penny-ante stuff. You want to send a signal? You want to stop this kind of thing? Fire the manager. He sat here, looked you straight in the face, and lied his ass off, Virgil, and you know it. And he knew you knew it, and he didn't care."

"It's a matter of 'he said, he said.' I can't fire a senior manager over some finger-pointing mess. I'd cut the legs out from under every other manager I've got."

"You hired me to find the cheaters, Virgil, not to tell you how to run the firm. I found this guy. Give me another week and I'll find ten more. What they're doing is not that unusual. If you fire the trader, you will have a late-year boost to earnings as every other trader marks his book correctly. And next December everyone will have forgotten the lesson and it will be the same crap all over again. But if you can the manager and bring in the head guy on every other trading desk and tell them *why* you are canning him, you'll have a much better chance of never having to deal with this little problem ever again. And," I said, smiling for the first time, "you'll still get the pop in earnings, just as soon as they get back to their desks and lay down the law."

He saw the logic, but it didn't make him happy. "He stood by the firm when we were badly on the ropes."

I gave him a look of open skepticism. "He had no choice. Where was he going to go? The guy swears he had no idea his trader was mismarking the book. So he is either a liar or a total incompetent. Either way, he's a loser. Give him the boot."

"And the trader?"

"Tell him he's on probation. But pay him a bonus based on what he legitimately earned. My bet? You will never have to have another conversation with him about this. Case closed."

"I may lose some of my top managers this way."

"And you'll be left with guys who aren't afraid to tell you the truth."

He was sold, but it might take him a day or two to admit it. The manager was toast. If the guy had any brains at all, he was already sending out résumés.

"Anything else we need to discuss?" Virgil sounded more than tired.

"No," I said. "Just that if you upgrade your oversight systems, as I recommended, you won't have to bug me with this nonsense."

My whining amused him. "You are not being sufficiently entertained?"

"Challenged," I countered. My contract with Virgil was unbreakable. He owed me, and the paperwork confirmed it. This gave me a certain latitude when discussing my assignments.

"The new systems will be in place and ready for testing by mid-January."

"And by next year this time, your traders will all have figured out how to circumvent them—if their managers let them."

He shrugged, dismissing the subject. "Maybe you're right. Meanwhile, I may have something that will stretch your mental muscles a bit more. What do you know about insider trading?"

"It's illegal."

"True. But I may need you to develop a more nuanced view. Read up on the subject and watch the news over the weekend. One of the firm's clients may need us to bail him out by Monday morning."

Philip Haley, the CEO of Arinna Labs and an early wunderkind in the field of bioengineering, was being investigated and might soon be charged with a single count of insider trading. It appeared that Haley had sold short the company stock, using an offshore bank, just before the board voted to announce the damaging news that the strain of algae the company was working on had been wiped out in a laboratory crash die-off. While this had happened before, and was a constant risk in this area of research, the board members were concerned that regulators might view silence as akin to fraud this close to a final-product rollout. Haley had repurchased the shares after the expected sell-off, and, in fact, the stock price had since recovered to its earlier level.

"Virgil, this sounds pretty open-and-shut to me. Can they tie him to the trade?"

"Mr. Haley claims that he did not do it."

ACCUSED SUSPECT CLAIMS INNOCENCE!

It was a headline ready-made for the *Onion*.

"Why does the firm care? Or is Haley a special friend of yours?"

Virgil made a steeple of his hands and tapped his index fingers together. I knew him well enough to know that was how he expressed great agitation. "The firm owns a substantial position of special nonvoting shares. A scandal could prove to be dangerously expensive for us. And, yes, Philip is a valued client. We have worked together through his first IPO, the subsequent sale of that company, and the creation of Arinna. And he has stood by me through the disaster my father brought down and the subsequent restructuring of the firm. I would like to see him cleared."

"I'll make some calls."